QUATRE SŒURS à Londres

De la même auteure, dans cette série :

Quatre sœurs en vacances
Quatre sœurs à New York
Quatre sœurs dans la tempête
Quatre sœurs en scène
Quatre sœurs en colo
Quatre sœurs et un Noël inoubliable
Quatre sœurs en direct du collège

De la même auteure, en grand format :

Dix jours sans écrans
Quinze jours sans réseau

Sophie Rigal-Goulard

Quatre sœurs à Londres

Illustrations de Diglee

RAGEOT

To my so british son.
A special thought
to Margaux.

Cet ouvrage a été imprimé sur un papier
issu de forêts gérées durablement,
de sources contrôlées.

Couverture : Diglee.

ISBN 978-2-7002-5333-7

Fog, cloud… and sun !

– Laure Juin ? Tu me donneras ton carnet de liaison afin que j'y inscrive ton heure de colle.

Et voilà. Dans un feu d'artifice il y a toujours un bouquet final.

Il est 15 h 56 et quatre petites minutes avant la sonnerie… le couperet !

Tout ça parce que je raconte à Héloïse l'épisode de *Love in high school* qu'elle n'a pas pu voir hier soir. Franchement, la prof de maths abuse ! Et d'un, je ne parlais VRAIMENT PAS fort. Et de deux, elle devrait avoir un peu plus

de compréhension pour ses élèves et réaliser qu'on ne peut pas se concentrer sur le théorème de Pythagore (trop gore, comme dit Noah, le comique de la classe) si on ne sait pas que Harry, le héros de notre série préférée, s'est enfin déclaré à Lily, son amoureuse secrète ! C'est JUSTE l'info du jour !

Je me lève et je tends mon carnet avec une moue qui marque ma totale désapprobation.

Cette journée est à oublier.

De A à Z.

D'ailleurs, si je dois écrire mes *Mémoires* un jour, je sauterai allégrement ce jeudi 16 avril.

Depuis ce matin, les problèmes s'accumulent.

Tout a commencé à 7 h 06, heure à laquelle j'ai ouvert un œil (je dis bien « un » puisque le deuxième était entièrement collé et que la paupière du haut refusait de quitter celle du bas). Le diagnostic a été immédiat. Il faut dire que je suis la fille de Stéphane et Stéphanie Juin, médecin et infirmière en pédiatrie. Avec les Steph au carré comme on les surnomme, pas besoin de se déplacer jusqu'au cabinet médical, puisque nous en avons carrément un à domicile.

Mon « œil collé » a été traité dans la minute qui a suivi ! Je m'imaginais déjà traîner au lit toute la journée en plaquant, si besoin, un foulard sur l'œil pour le protéger. Ça m'aurait donné un petit côté pirate… Sauf que mes parents n'ont pas eu la même « vision ». Ce doit être générationnel.

– Avec ces gouttes miracle, dans dix minutes tu iras beaucoup mieux, a affirmé mon père en me faisant pencher la tête en arrière pour inonder mon œil.

– Je t'en remettrai juste avant que tu partes au collège, a renchéri ma mère qui n'avait pas du tout l'air inquiète.

– Mais… Je ne peux PAS aller en cours avec ce regard immonde, j'ai lâché, angoissée. On dirait un lapin albinos.

– Tu es plus proche du cochon d'Inde albinos, a alors affirmé Lou, ma sœur aînée, qui venait aux nouvelles. À cause de tes joues toutes rondes.

– Vas-y, traite-moi de hamster aussi tant que tu y es ! j'ai rétorqué, super énervée.

Évidemment Lisa et Luna, nos deux petites sœurs, sont entrées dans ma chambre sans frapper, comme d'habitude, et elles ont voulu donner leur avis.

– Fais voir ? m'a demandé Luna. Le cochon d'Inde d'Amina, il est super mimi avec ses yeux rouges. J'en voudrai un comme ça quand John[1] sera mort.

– Mais tu es horrible de parler de la mort prochaine de notre animal de compagnie, a protesté Lisa. C'est triste !

– Ce qui est triste, c'est que je me retrouve avec un œil en moins et trois sœurs en trop dans ma chambre ce matin ! j'ai crié pour faire sortir la troupe.

Chez moi, il est très difficile d'avoir de VRAIS moments de tranquillité ABSOLUE. Une famille de quatre filles, ça « déménage du fro-

1. Lire *4 sœurs à New York*.

mage ». En ce moment, c'est l'expression favorite de Luna, la petite dernière de la famille qui a six ans. Elle vient de découvrir les rimes et elle nous sort des expressions moisies à longueur de temps. La plupart parlent d'animaux puisqu'elle les adore TOUS, surtout ceux qui n'existent pas. Elle a d'ailleurs l'ambition de devenir princesse dans une ferme avec des licornes.

Lisa, la cadette, a neuf ans. On a souvent l'impression qu'elle a déjà fait le tour du monde parce qu'elle a un avis sur TOUT. C'est à se demander si la maîtresse ne la laisse pas faire classe à sa place. Quand, par hasard, Lisa ne maîtrise pas totalement un sujet, elle se dépêche de lire tout ce que la bibliothèque du quartier possède en documentation !

Lou, ma sœur aînée, a l'expérience et la sagesse de « celle qui a vécu plusieurs vies ». Avec elle, on oscille entre le moine bouddhiste et… l'ado de dix-sept ans qu'elle est. Elle nous dispense gracieusement ses conseils et énonce ses principes de vie pour « nous éviter les écueils qu'elle a déjà rencontrés » (je cite).

Moi, j'ai treize ans, et en tant que deuxième L de la famille, je tape parfois du poing sur la table pour me faire entendre.

Je suis passionnée par le dessin mais je m'exprime autrement que sur une feuille Canson. J'ai mon mot à dire dans cette famille de filles. C'est d'ailleurs ce que j'ai fait ce matin en faisant sortir cette horde sauvage de ma chambre.

La situation ne s'est pas améliorée pour moi puisque, en arrivant en cours (avec un œil encore rouge, horreur absolue), j'ai appris que mon meilleur copain, Ulysse, serait absent pour la semaine. On avait prévu de passer du temps ensemble sur la bande dessinée qu'on a créée et je vais me retrouver toute seule.

Ensuite, c'est Justine, ma best friend, qui a fait un caca nerveux.

– Je ne peux pas venir samedi à la soirée de Coraline, m'a-t-elle appris à l'intercours du matin.

– Et pourquoi ? j'ai demandé, surprise. On avait dit qu'on irait ensemble, toi et moi.

– Morgan ne sera pas là…

J'ai regardé Justine avec une légère envie de lui tirer la couette.

– Évidemment qu'il ne sera pas là. Tu le savais déjà ! C'est une soirée avec des élèves de cinquième. Je ne vois pas pourquoi un troisième viendrait.

– J’ai mentalisé la soirée et j’ai compris qu’elle n’aurait aucun sens s’il n’y est pas.

Ma copine se tordait les mains d’un air désespéré. Voilà six mois qu’elle est amoureuse de Morgan, le BG du collège qui fait craquer toutes les filles. Et depuis six mois, elle utilise tous les stratagèmes possibles pour se rapprocher de lui… sans succès.

– Tu fais comme tu veux, j’ai déclaré. Passe ta soirée de samedi à pleurer sur ton lit, tu as raison. Et quand ta chambre sera inondée de larmes, prends un selfie. Ça peut toujours servir, une image de ton désespoir sur Facebook !

Justine a secoué la tête comme si je ne comprenais rien à l’amour.

Ce n'est pas le cas puisque je suis in love depuis cet été[1]. Et même si Alex habite loin de Paris, il est venu me voir pour mon anniversaire[2]. On s'est d'ailleurs rendu compte qu'on s'aimait comme au premier jour. Bon… Depuis, trois mois ont passé et il y a quelques changements. Il me parle beaucoup de sa « meilleure copine » Elsa et ça m'énerve ! Moi aussi, j'ai un meilleur copain, mais avec Ulysse, c'est clair, on partage une passion, le dessin. Alors que cette Elsa…

C'est elle qui a totalement gâché ma pause déjeuner aujourd'hui. À midi, Alex m'a envoyé un Snap où on voit une main DE FILLE SUR SON ÉPAULE ! J'ai fait une capture d'écran…

J'en avais les cheveux dressés sur la tête ! J'ai agrandi la photo et OUI, il y a bien une main entière posée sur le pull d'Alex, sur sa clavicule très exactement. Ce qui signifie qu'il doit y avoir un bras entier au bout de cette main qui enlace le dos de MON amoureux. Et ça, c'est carrément inadmissible.

1. Lire *4 sœurs en colo.*
2. Lire *4 sœurs en direct du collège.*

En début d'après-midi, la prof de maths nous a rendu l'interro que je n'avais pas trop réussie. Vu ma note, j'ai réalisé que « complètement ratée » était un terme mieux adapté à ce devoir.

6 sur 20, c'est bien peu.

– Fais pas cette tête ! Tu aurais pu avoir 4, comme moi ! a déclaré Noah, mon voisin en maths.

C'est sûr. J'aurais même pu avoir 0.

Sauf que j'avais vraiment bien révisé pour ce devoir et que je trouve profondément injuste d'être ainsi sanctionnée.

Cette heure de colle que je viens de récolter est le point final d'une journée archi-ratée !

En montant dans le bus, j'allume mon téléphone resté en silencieux au collège. C'est le moment où Justine me bombarde de SMS.

Ma Lolo, sorry pour samedi. Tu m'en veux ?

G reçu un snap d'Alex avec une fille.

Non ? Trop hoooorrible.
Dis-moi qu'elle est moche.

On voit juste 4 doigts vernis sur son pull.

Des doigts i2 alors ?

Vernis rose bonbon.

Le top du mauvais goût. Je le boycotte désormais en signe de solidarité. Je v enlever celui que g sur les doigts de pied.

Justine m'envoie des tonnes de ❤ pour me soutenir… J'en ai besoin !

En arrivant à la maison, je subis les assauts de ma mère qui veut absolument vérifier mon œil.

– Vous m'avez laissée affronter la pollution du collège et des milliers de microparticules se sont collées à ma paupière. Il va sûrement falloir m'opérer demain, je lance d'une voix sinistre.

Ma mère rit avant de me mettre à nouveau des gouttes en déclarant que « tout est OK ». Ben non justement, tout va mal ! En plus, je dois lui annoncer l'heure de colle que j'ai gagnée en cadeau surprise. Je retarde un peu ce moment en rangeant mes cours. Luna apparaît devant la porte de ma chambre.

– Laure... Je t'adore beaucoup, tu sais. Beaucoup, comme un camion énorme.

Je ne me retourne pas et je ne réponds RIEN. Quand ma petite sœur commence ses phrases comme ça, c'est qu'elle vient de faire une bêtise qui ME concerne, vu l'amour qui envahit soudain son petit cœur.

– Même plus qu'un camion, insiste-t-elle lourdement. En vrai, je t'aime comme une fusée ou...

– Vas-y, je lance, légèrement énervée. Qu'est-ce que tu m'as cassé ? Perdu ? Emprunté et donné aux copines ?

– Non. Mais je vais les retrouver, les feutres tout neufs que maman t'a achetés. C'est juste que je ne me rappelle plus où...

– T'as intérêt ! je rugis, tandis que Luna rebrousse chemin vers sa chambre à toute vitesse. Je les adooore, moi, ces feutres. Je t'avais INTERDIT d'y toucher.

Je suis prête à exploser pour de bon !

Quand mon téléphone sonne, mon « allô » est carrément agressif.

– Allô Laure, c'est Vic ! Ça va ?

Mon cœur fait un bond dans ma poitrine. C'est le bonheur d'entendre la voix de ma coloc préférée. Victoire et moi, on a partagé dix jours dans la même chambre en colo[1] et on est devenues des Best Friends Forever. Elle a déménagé à Londres en octobre dernier car son père, un DJ connu en Europe, et sa mère, une choriste de talent, travaillent là-bas sur un projet musical dans un grand studio d'enregistrement. Elle et moi, on se suit sur les réseaux et on s'envoie de très nombreux messages.

– Viiiic ! Ça me fait trooop plaisiiiiir de t'entendre ! je crie en sautillant sur place.

– Tu as l'air super énervée. Je te dérange ? me demande mon amie.

– Toi, me déranger ? Impossible ! C'est juste ma journée qui a été… Comment te dire ? Une JDM… Je te laisse décoder.

– Ça tombe bien parce que je me sens un peu magicienne en ce moment. Laure, sous tes yeux ébahis, grâce à moi ta JDM va se transformer en JDBA !

– Euh… Une Journée Des… Bonnes… Amies ?

1. Lire *4 sœurs en colo.*

– Non ! Une Journée De Bonheur Absolu ! hurle Vic. Je t'invite à Londres pendant tes prochaines vacances. Dépêche-toi de préparer tes valises.

Il faut environ une seconde pour que l'information atteigne mon cerveau, puis je pousse le cri de la mort qui tue qui démolit le tympan de Vic. Je l'entends rire comme une folle tandis que je commence une danse de la joie avec sauts multiples et variés.

Quelle journée merveilleuse, ce jeudi 16 avril !

London, here I am !

Voyager en solo dans un train, c'est le bonheur total. Dans moins de deux heures, Vic et moi, nous serons réunies. Vive l'Eurostar et le tunnel sous la Manche !

Je n'ai même pas besoin de consulter mon portable. Il est rangé dans mon sac à dos, à mes pieds. Ma valise, elle, attend sagement dans le compartiment bagages. Je me sens tellement détendue que RIEN ne me préoccupe. Même pas le dernier message d'Alex qui parlait encore d'Elsa…

J'ai déjà établi la liste des tortures que j'infligerai à cette fille si, un jour, elle a le malheur de croiser mon chemin. Je ne peux rien faire de plus.

Il ne me reste qu'à apprécier mon voyage. Je ferme les yeux pour me laisser bercer par le ronron régulier du train. J'approche de la zénitude absolue avec les doigts de pied qui s'écartent tout seuls.

– On parle du « tunnel sous la Manche » mais en vrai, ce sont trois tunnels qui ont été creusés. Vous le saviez ?

– Maman, tu as pensé à prendre du scotch épais ? Quelque chose me dit qu'elle va nous saouler tout le voyage.

– Eh ben, quand on sera sous le tunnel de la mer de la Manche, moi je vais avoir trop peur des requins.

Je continue à fermer les yeux. Si je le fais très fort, mon rêve de voyage en solo va peut-être se réaliser.

Parce que, évidemment, tous les Juin m'ont suivie jusqu'à Londres. Il manque mes grands-parents et on est au complet !

Il y a trois semaines, en annonçant aux Steph au carré que j'étais invitée à Londres, je pensais naïvement qu'ils se réjouiraient pour moi et qu'ils se chargeraient juste de m'acheter un billet aller-retour pour Londres. J'avais oublié que chez nous, les vacances en solo sont… une utopie !

– Londres ? What ? a crié Lou qui passait par là. Trop claaasse ! On rêve d'y aller, Maxou et moi. Enfin, surtout moi.

– Oh là là ! Si tu vas à Londres… Mais… tu vas voir LA FAMILLE ROYALE ! a ajouté Lisa dont les yeux sortaient presque de la tête. Tu te rends compte de ta CHANCE ?

Je m'attendais à une remarque de Luna pour compléter la chorale mais on n'en a pas eu besoin. À la place, c'est ma mère qui a lancé :

– Tu sais, Laure ? Je crois qu'on va t'accompagner à Londres parce que je vois que toute la famille a envie d'y aller ! N'est-ce pas Steph ? On n'a jamais eu le temps d'y aller quand ta sœur y habitait.

– Non mais attendez, j'ai protesté. On ne va pas débarquer à six chez les parents de Vic. Ça ne se fait pas.

Les parents ont ri et Lou les a imités, pour bien nous montrer qu'elle fait presque partie du monde des adultes puisqu'elle a le même humour qu'eux.

– Ne t'inquiète pas, a ajouté mon père. Voilà des années que James Brighton, mon ancien prof de médecine, un Anglais francophone, insiste pour que je vienne lui présenter ma petite famille, chez lui, à Londres. J'ai toujours remis ce séjour… Je vais lui téléphoner pour savoir s'il peut nous recevoir un long week-end.

Cette déclaration a été suivie par des cris de joie de mes sœurs. Luna, qui arrivait juste et n'était donc au courant de RIEN, s'est mise elle aussi à sauter partout en criant « Lone Done Lone Done » comme Lisa. Ça m'a passablement énervée. Mais, pour me rassurer, je me suis dit que James Brighton aurait sûrement plein de trucs à faire dans les semaines à venir. Sauf que ce monsieur était super libre, vu qu'il a l'âge de mon grand-père et qu'il est retraité.

La famille Juin m'accompagne donc… Ma seule consolation, c'est que je reste plus d'une semaine alors que mes parents et mes sœurs sont invités pour quatre jours seulement.

– On entre dans le tunnel, annonce soudain ma mère au cas où on n'aurait pas compris que lorsqu'on ne voit plus le jour, c'est qu'on passe sous terre.

Assise à côté de la fenêtre, Luna fait mine de trembler de peur.

– Fais-moi signe si tu aperçois un beau poisson, je lui chuchote à l'oreille en la serrant contre moi.

– Il a fallu six ans et 13000 personnes pour creuser les 50 km du tunnel dont 38 sous la mer ! annonce Lisa qui a dû apprendre ces chiffres par cœur puisqu'elle n'a pas de guide sous la main. Au plus profond, on atteindra soixante-quinze mètres sous le niveau de…

– Tu ne vas pas recommencer à nous balancer des nombres comme on lance des cacahuètes à des singes ? la coupe Lou exaspérée. Tu l'as suffisamment fait à New York[1] !

– Sois un peu sympa avec ta sœur, déclare mon père. Elle n'y est pour rien si Max a rejoint ses amis. Nous non plus d'ailleurs.

Notre père ne se mêle pas souvent de nos conversations, mais quand il le fait (en fronçant les sourcils), aucune de nous quatre n'ose lui tenir tête. C'est vrai que depuis que Max a refusé de venir avec nous à Londres (alors qu'il était invité !) pour participer à un séjour esca-

1. Lire *4 sœurs à New York*.

lade avec sa bande de potes, Lou est d'une humeur massacrante.

Quand le train accoste le long du quai de la gare de Saint-Pancras, ma sœur aînée n'a plus prononcé une seule parole. Par contre, grâce à Lisa, tous nos voisins sont désormais incollables sur « le tunnel sous la Manche, sa vie, son œuvre » !

Notre descente du wagon est laborieuse. Mes sœurs et moi, nous sommes hyper prévoyantes et nous envisageons toujours divers scénarios au niveau météo. Ce qui fait que nos sacs sont plutôt… nombreux et bien remplis !

– Mais pourquoi je n'ai eu que des filles, moi ? râle mon père en poussant un chariot chargé de bagages. Avec quatre garçons, une seule valise aurait suffi.

On ne relève même pas, on a tellement l'habitude… Par contre, on admire *toutes* le hall de la gare, immense sous son plafond en verre soutenu par de larges arceaux de fer.

– Ooooh ! crie soudain Luna, le nez en l'air. Regardez !

Au-dessus de nos têtes trône une énorme horloge dont les aiguilles peuvent se voir d'un bout à l'autre du quai.

– Je vais aller la décrocher, s'écrie mon père. On la rapporte pour notre salle de bains, comme ça, le matin, Lou n'oubliera plus jamais que c'est l'heure de céder sa place.

On se met *toutes* à rire, même Lou qui a retrouvé un semblant de sourire depuis qu'on a débarqué. Comme si l'air de Londres chassait sa morosité.

Après avoir passé la douane, un cri de guerrière me fait sursauter.

– Lauauaauauaauaure !

Vic est là, en face de moi ! Je cours vers elle et on tombe dans les bras l'une de l'autre en poussant des cris de joie.

– Bonjour la discrétion, commente Lisa en rigolant.

Vic finit par me lâcher pour embrasser le reste de ma famille. Elle n'a pas changé depuis l'été dernier. Elle porte son bonnet préféré vissé sur sa tête, comme les jours de pluie à la colo. Ses longs cheveux noirs tombent en cascade sur ses épaules et lui masquent à moitié le visage.

– Tes parents sont ici ? lui demande ma mère en observant les alentours.

– Ben… Non. En fait, ils… ils n'ont pas pu venir.

Ma mère regarde mon père qui me regarde.

– Comment ça ! s'exclame-t-elle. Vous allez faire des heures de voyage, seules, toutes les deux, dans le métro. Je sais à quel point cette capitale est grande !

– Des heures de voyage ! je répète, exaspérée. Il ne faut sûrement pas vingt-quatre heures pour rejoindre l'appartement de Victoire, maman. Et puis, Londres n'est pas une jungle sauvage non plus. Tu as vu, Vic est venue sans machette.

– Euh, comment vous dire ? chuchote alors l'intéressée. Il y a un petit problème.

Vu sa tête, on comprend très vite que le problème a l'air important. Les yeux humides, elle nous explique que ses parents ont juste oublié que j'arrivais aujourd'hui !

– Ils sont en plein enregistrement et aux studios, il y a eu du retard. Ma mère comptait m'envoyer chez sa copine jusqu'au week-end prochain et quand je lui ai rappelé que Laure venait...

Victoire s'interrompt car Luna lui tend un mouchoir.

– Serre fort les paupières aussi, lui chuchote ma petite sœur, bonne conseillère en tant que « championne des pleurs toutes catégories ».

– ... Elle est désolée, continue Vic en se mouchant. Mais elle a dit qu'elle n'était pas dispo, qu'on ne pouvait pas rester seules et...

– Ah ça non, vous n'allez pas vivre seules chez toi ! lui répond ma mère. Vous venez toutes les deux avec nous chez James.

Papa lève un sourcil, un peu inquiet.

– Mais oui Steph, insiste maman. Tu vas appeler ton ancien prof et lui expliquer la situation d'urgence. Il a bien dit qu'il avait une très grande maison, non ? Vic, sèche tes larmes, on est ravis de te garder avec nous en tant que « fille adoptive ».

Cette fois, mon père lève les deux sourcils... mais téléphone quand même à James Brighton.

Dans l'heure qui suit, nous arrivons donc à sept dans le quartier de Kensington devant la maison de notre hôte anglais. Elle est construite sur trois étages et se situe dans Lexham Gardens, une rue très calme où toutes les demeures se ressemblent.

Sa façade en brique est éclairée par une porte d'entrée et un porche en bois blanc, ainsi que par des encadrements de fenêtres de la même couleur.

Sur l'avant, une palissade en fer protège deux carrés de pelouse parfaitement symétriques de part et d'autre de l'entrée.

James Brighton nous accueille.

– Hello toute la jolie famille de mon ami Stéphane ! Vous êtes *la bienveniou* ici !

Notre hôte est super chic. Je ne sais pas si c'est pour nous accueillir ou s'il porte ce genre d'habit au quotidien mais il est en costume, avec un gilet assorti en dessous. Aux pieds, il arbore des pantoufles fourrées sur lesquelles on distingue le drapeau anglais. Vic, Lou et moi, on sourit devant ce détail qui tue tandis qu'il nous serre tous solennellement la main.

– J'ai mis *le* jeunesse en haut et *le* vieillesse en bas, nous explique-t-il en nous faisant visiter sa maison.

– Il ne sait même pas accorder le masculin et le féminin, me chuchote Lisa, choquée.

Vic lui explique que dans la langue anglaise, les déterminants du genre n'existent pas et que les Britanniques ont beaucoup de mal lorsqu'il faut les utiliser en français.

Mes sœurs, Vic et moi occupons trois chambres au dernier étage tandis que mes parents sont logés au rez-de-chaussée. Mes petites sœurs sont déjà surexcitées et n'arrêtent pas de pouffer en imitant l'accent so british de papy James.

À peine nos bagages sont-ils défaits que retentit un appel solennel.

– It's tea time ! nous crie-t-on depuis le bas de la maison.

– C'est un moment sacré ici, m'explique Vic alors qu'on descend les escaliers. Une journée sans thé, c'est une journée ratée pour les Anglais.

James a dressé la table et avec application et lenteur, il verse dans nos tasses le thé qu'il a laissé infuser au préalable. Une agréable odeur de caramel se fait sentir.

– Je vous ai préparé du thé « caramel toffee ». C'est celui que je préfère en fin de journée, nous détaille notre hôte alors que nous nous préparons à le boire.

Notre hôte pose ensuite un énorme amas gélatineux rouge grenadine devant nous et les deux petites L font une grimace épouvantable.

– C'est un jelly, nous annonce-t-il. Les Anglais l'aiment beaucoup.

Une fois sur la table, ce gâteau plutôt étrange bouge tout seul pendant au moins cinq secondes.

– Tu crois qu'il est vivant ? je chuchote à Lou.

– Il a peur qu'on le mange ? demande Luna. C'est pour ça qu'il tremble ?

On se met tous à rire, même James qui nous distribue des parts de jelly.

– James, we are so glad to be here with you ! You're so kind.

Toute la famille Juin se tourne vers moi. Je viens de faire mon petit effet. Je m'entraîne depuis la rentrée mais je dois dire que je deviens de plus en plus forte en anglais. Normal, j'adoore les pays anglo-saxons et leur langue !

Vic me fait un sourire de deux kilomètres de long.

Je sens qu'on va être bien ici…

A strange guy called Clark

Ce matin, il était 6 heures heure anglaise (donc 7 heures en France) quand on a ouvert les yeux, Vic et moi. C'est fou parce qu'on s'est réveillées pile ensemble. C'est bien la preuve qu'on est hyper connectées ! Allongées dans le noir, on a passé plus d'une heure à discuter des garçons avec en guest star Alex…

Je lui ai appris qu'une intruse était apparue dans la vie de MON « Apparition », puisque c'est ainsi qu'on surnommait Alex, elle et moi, à la colo l'été dernier.

– Tu sais, l'amour à distance c'est trop dur, commente Vic. Moi j'ai cassé avec mon amoureux en France quand je suis arrivée à Londres. Aujourd'hui, je suis libérééée, délivréééée !

– Alex et moi, c'est différent. Depuis notre rencontre, on ne s'est jamais perdus de vue. On s'appelle, on s'écrit. Tu vois, je pense que…

– *Hello Goud More nigue ! Ha dou you dou* ?

Une tornade vient de sauter sur mon lit et interrompre mon exposé sur « l'amour éternel et sans divorce » entre Alex et moi.

– Tu as vu, Laure, comme je parle bien anglais ? Presque comme toi ! C'est Lisa qui m'apprend, me hurle Luna dans les oreilles.

Vic rit avant de m'avouer :

– C'est ce qui manque dans ma vie. Des sœurs trop drôles comme les tiennes.

– Hum, je soupire. Je peux te les prêter si tu veux.

Notre premier English Breakfast est un véritable repas ! Notre hôte nous a préparé un petit-déjeuner typique, composé d'une assiette avec une saucisse, du bacon, un œuf, des tomates et des champignons, le tout ayant été très largement fried, c'est-à-dire frit à la poêle.

Je contemple longuement ma tasse de thé au lait pour ne pas rire. Les deux petites L viennent juste de s'asseoir à table et leurs grimaces respectives sont irrésistibles.

– Eh ben moi, j'ai pas très faim, chuchote Luna d'une toute petite voix.

– Moi non plus, ajoute Lisa qui est devenue un peu blanche.

– Eat breakfast like a king, lunch like a prince and dinner like a pauper, s'écrie James en surveillant sa casserole de haricots bouillis que l'on peut ajouter en option.

Lou s'empresse d'offrir des toasts beurrés à Lisa et Luna tout en précisant :

– En gros, ça signifie qu'on doit manger comme un roi le matin, comme un prince le midi…

– … Et manger comme un pauvre le soir, je continue à traduire. Plus la journée passe, plus nos repas doivent s'alléger si on veut être en forme.

– On ne pourrait pas plutôt manger AVEC le roi, la reine et les princes ? demande Lisa, les yeux brillants.

C'est surtout Stéphane Juin qui fait honneur au petit-déjeuner anglais puisqu'il dévore l'assiette de Lisa, puis celle de Luna après avoir englouti la sienne !

Au cours du breakfast, les Steph au carré questionnent Vic sur sa vie à Londres.

Elle nous explique qu'avec des parents artistes comme les siens, son quotidien est souvent compliqué.

– Mon petit-fils Clark est *une* artiste, lui aussi, déclare James. Il a arrêté les études pour peindre. Je suis inquiet pour lui. Ce n'est pas sérieux. Lui et moi, on se fâche souvent.

Notre hôte a soudain un air triste mais il secoue la tête et se reprend très vite.

– Maintenant si vous le voulez, je vous conduis à *le* London Eye pour admirer *la* panorama, lance-t-il alors que le petit-déjeuner s'achève. C'est *un* roue géante qui permet de découvrir tout London.

Les deux petites L manifestent bruyamment leur accord.

Vic et moi, on se regarde. On avait envisagé un autre programme puisque mon amie m'avait proposé de découvrir Camden Town. D'après elle, c'est juste « le quartier À VISITER si on veut comprendre Londres ! »

– Est-il possible de faire une visite en groupe ce matin et une autre en duo cet aprèm ? je demande alors.

– Et en trio, ce serait encore mieux, ajoute Lou qui lève les yeux au ciel en désignant les deux petites L qui sautillent.

Nos parents donnent leur accord, et du coup, je me dirige vers le van de James avec bonne humeur. C'est lui qui nous conduit jusqu'à la London Eye puisque son véhicule dispose de huit places assises. La conduite à gauche donne des sueurs froides à notre père qui s'est placé devant. Il n'arrête pas de sursauter et ça fait rire maman.

– La London Eye, qu'est-ce que je peux vous dire dessus ? lance Lisa en cherchant fébrilement des informations dans son guide pendant le parcours.

– Poids, taille, bonnet de soutien-gorge, habitudes alimentaires, allergies éventuelles ? ironise Lou.

– Moi, quand je serai tout en haut de la roue, je ferai un coucou à la reine d'Angleterre et à TOUTE sa famille ! crie Luna.

Lisa en oublie sa recherche sur la roue. Comme on parle de ses idoles, elle se met à rêver du moment où elle va les rencontrer. Quand on entre dans la capsule de la roue, elle est encore en train d'en discuter avec James.

Ma mère et Lou refusent catégoriquement de monter avec nous pour cause de vertige. Nous leur envoyons des tonnes de bises alors que nous nous élevons lentement dans le ciel londonien.

James nous montre les différents monuments. Je profite de ce moment de calme pour sortir mon portable de ma poche. Un SMS d'Alex m'attend !

> Laure g parlé de Londres à Elsa,
> elle te conseille de monter sur la London Eye !
> Lov

Ça y est, je suis de nouveau super énervée. Cette fille mérite des claques à jouer les guides touristiques depuis la France.

Je n'ai pas attendu Elsa pour y aller.

Je ne mets pas de ♥ ou de love à la fin de mon message.

Je mets juste un point. Ce qui veut tout dire.

– Tu as vu, Laure ? La Tamise fait un joli cordon bleu au milieu de Londres. Je te le fais à l'anglaise ? The Thames is like a snake in the city…

Vic a des antennes invisibles ! Elle vient de se rapprocher de moi et elle me prend par le cou.

– Range ce portable, va, me chuchote-t-elle. Dans quelques minutes, tu auras quitté le ciel anglais. C'est dommage de ne pas en profiter.

Je mets un bras autour de sa taille tout en glissant mon téléphone dans ma poche. Évidemment, les deux petites L nous rejoignent et mon père nous prend en photo toutes les quatre. Avant de sortir de la capsule, j'éteins mon portable pour de bon. Hors de question que cette Elsa pollue ma journée.

En descendant de la London Eye, Vic prend ma main, avec un grand sourire aux lèvres.

– À nous la liberté maintenant, me glisse-t-elle. Tu vas voir, Camden c'est énorme ! Tu vas adorer.

Avant qu'on les quitte, les Steph au carré nous font trois milliards de recommandations jusqu'à ce que Lou, exaspérée, lance :

– Je vous signale qu'à nous trois, on a quarante-trois ans ! C'est un âge raisonnable pour affronter la jungle urbaine, non ?

– Mais pourquoi elles vont dans la jungle et pas nous ? Moi aussi j'aimerais bien voir les…

On s'éloigne, sans attendre que quelqu'un réponde à la question existentielle de Luna.

Histoire de jouer les touristes jusqu'au bout, on décide de rejoindre Camden en bus. Lou et moi, on a trop envie de monter à l'étage de ces énormes autobus rouges qui circulent un peu partout dans la ville. Une fois assises tout en haut, on a une vue imprenable sur les rues de Londres qui défilent.

Vic nous montre au passage la façade magnifique du British Museum ou celle de la prestigieuse University College London, tout en nous expliquant que c'est la plus ancienne université de Londres.

– C'est encore plus beau que ce que j'imaginais, je déclare, complètement sous le charme.

– So British ! commente Lou enthousiaste.

En arrivant enfin dans Camden Town, je mesure la portée des paroles de mon amie. Ce quartier est à voir absolument ! Il résume à lui seul l'originalité et l'excentricité de la capitale londonienne.

Je n'ai jamais croisé autant de gens bizarrement vêtus à la fois.

– Si je demandais à ma coiffeuse le même genre de chevelure teintée, elle hallucinerait, plaisante Lou en désignant une ado à la crinière verte.

Le mot-clé de Camden, c'est « couleurs » ! Même les cheveux ont suivi la consigne... À croire qu'ici les gens ont décidé de lutter de cette façon contre la grisaille du ciel.

– Je vous emmène au Lock market, lance Vic en nous faisant signe de la suivre. On y trouve des magasins en tout genre et des friperies que j'adooore.

Victoire circule avec une aisance incroyable à l'intérieur de ce marché à ciel ouvert. Il y a des dizaines d'échoppes et on y croise des curieux mélanges de vêtements gothiques, mais aussi ethniques, disco ou carrément destroy ! Lou est en transe devant chaque boutique de fripes et il faut la tirer au-dehors à chaque fois pour qu'elle ne prenne pas racine. Moi je reste fascinée par les fresques de street art qui s'étalent un peu partout sur les murs. Elles nous feraient presque oublier la pluie fine qui s'est mise à tomber.

Vers quinze heures, on s'arrête toutes les trois pour déguster notre premier déjeuner british, debout devant l'un des innombrables food trucks qui encombrent les rues. Ce sont des camions ambulants qui préparent toutes sortes d'en-cas pour le déjeuner. Je décide de donner moi-même la commande et je m'en sors comme une Anglaise… ou presque. En tout cas, mon « three fish and chips with curry, please » passe super bien sans que j'aie besoin de répéter.

Ensuite, Lou insiste pour retourner dans l'une des friperies aperçue en début de visite. Évidemment, il nous faut trois heures pour la retrouver ou presque.

Finalement, on s'achète toutes les deux une combinaison super stylée à un prix carrément dingue. Vic préfère choisir une veste de l'armée toute trouée et un bonnet marin couvert de broches colorées.

Vers dix-sept heures, on part, la tête emplie d'images et de bruits. Au moment où je sors mon portable pour immortaliser le quartier, je réalise que je ne l'ai pas consulté depuis ce matin.

Un SMS d'Alex m'attend. Impatiente, je l'ouvre pour découvrir… une photo prise depuis la London Eye que m'envoie TOUT SPÉCIALEMENT Elsa. Alex a écrit :

> Clin d'œil juste pour toi de ma copine ! Lov.

Comment dire ?

Je sens monter en moi une envie furieuse de jeter mon téléphone dans le Regent's canal à côté.

– Il faut VRAIMENT que tu mettes les points sur les i à Alex, lance Victoire après avoir lu le MMS maudit.

On imagine des plans diaboliques et on pouffe devant nos scénarios tordus. On rit encore en entrant chez James mais on s'arrête immédiatement car il y a dans le salon un inconnu qui détonne tout à fait avec le décor très chargé et fleuri tendance « bouquets délicats dans la campagne anglaise ».

– Vous êtes sûres qu'on n'a pas été suivies depuis Camden ? chuchote Lou en le désignant discrètement.

Le garçon qui discute avec nos parents semble en effet droit sorti du marché d'où nous venons.

Plutôt grand, il a une vingtaine d'années, des cheveux hérissés sur la tête mais surtout… teints en orange ! Ses avant-bras qui dépassent de sa veste militaire sont couverts de tatouages. Le piercing en forme d'anneau accroché à sa lèvre inférieure fait briller son sourire sous la lumière du salon.

– Hi ! lance-t-il en s'approchant. Je suis Clark, James est mon grand-père. Content de vous rencontrer.

Les deux petites L le contemplent dans un coin de la pièce. Pour une fois, elles ne font aucun commentaire, elles semblent fascinées par son look.

James Brighton tire une tête de six pieds de long. Le moins qu'on puisse dire, c'est qu'il ne respire pas la joie face à son petit-fils.

– James a oublié de me prévenir de votre venue alors que j'adooore parler le français. Ma mère me l'a enseigné il y a très longtemps. J'ai envie de vous inviter dans mon atelier si vous voulez ? continue-t-il avec gentillesse. How about tomorrow ?

– Oh yes ! Good idea ! je crie, enthousiaste.

Lou lui répond avec le même sourire que moi. Je me tourne vers Vic pour connaître son avis mais elle est passée en mode apnée. Les yeux fixés sur Clark, elle est plus rouge que la jelly à la fraise servie par James. Je commence à m'y connaître un peu en amour et j'ai bien l'impression d'assister en direct à un coup de foudre.

To be continued…

Art and music

– Wake up, girls ! The sun is shining.

Lou vient d'entrer dans notre chambre et elle ouvre en grand les volets. Le soleil s'engouffre dans la pièce, ce qui nous change du ciel bas et gris qu'on a depuis notre arrivée. Vic et moi, on bâille à s'en décrocher la mâchoire tout en contemplant le papier peint qui semble encore plus fleuri sous la lumière éclatante.

– *Hello maï neyme iz Luna end aïe ame faïïve !*

Luna persiste et signe. Elle vient nous montrer ses progrès en langue anglaise.

Je lui désigne du doigt la porte de ma chambre pour qu'elle fasse demi-tour.

– T'es dure avec ta petite sœur, murmure Vic d'une voix endormie. Elle est tellement choupinette.

– Je te signale que si on est aussi crevées ce matin, c'est à cause d'elle et de Lisa la fofolle.

Les deux petites L étaient déchaînées hier soir. Elles ont mis un temps incroyable à s'endormir, on les a entendues piquer des crises de fous rires jusqu'à une heure avancée de la nuit ! Il a fallu toute la force de persuasion de Lou (qui les a menacées d'écarter définitivement Buckingham Palace de nos visites si elles ne se taisaient pas) pour qu'elles finissent par se calmer. Ce qui les faisait mourir de rire, c'était d'imiter l'accent so british de James et Clark.

– Aujourd'hui est *un* belle journée, n'*est-il pas* ?

Lisa recommence ! Je lui lance un coussin pour qu'elle disparaisse de ma vue. On entend Luna hurler de rire dans le couloir.

Au petit-déjeuner, elle rit beaucoup moins puisque James nous propose à nouveau son bacon-saucisse-œufs qu'il agrémente cette fois d'un pudding. Maman demande prudemment si elle peut avoir des fruits et un yaourt pour la « très Frenchie Luna » et la « non moins Frenchie Lisa ». Finalement, je me régale avec quelques fines tranches de gâteau trempées dans mon thé. J'évite soigneusement le bacon. À la fin du breakfast, mes parents suggèrent une balade vers la Tour de Londres. Vic, Lou et moi, on a un autre projet.

– Euh, on aimerait bien aller visiter l'atelier de Clark, je déclare. Il nous a invitées hier.

Vic arrête de mâcher son bout de toast, suspendue à la décision des Steph au carré. Pour elle, revoir Clark, c'est encore mieux que marcher sur une plage quand il pleut (et pourtant, c'est une activité qu'elle ADORE !).

– Faisons le contraire d'hier, propose mon père. Ce matin, vous visitez en trio, et vous nous rejoignez en début d'après-midi.

Enthousiaste, je tape dans sa paume. Notre hôte fronce les sourcils avant de murmurer :

– C'est juste *une* garage, cet atelier. Clark n'a pas peint grand-chose, vous savez.

Un malaise flotte dans la pièce, comme à chaque fois que James Brighton parle de son petit-fils. Le sujet a l'air de le gêner.

– Ce doit être super beau, murmure Vic, les yeux dans le vide.

Lou et moi, on se regarde d'un air entendu.

L'atelier du jeune peintre se situe dans Cornwall gardens, une rue à quelques mètres de chez son grand-père, en face d'un petit square adorable. C'était un grand hangar qui a été cloisonné et permet à Clark de disposer de plusieurs espaces pour travailler. Il vit juste au-dessus, dans un petit studio aménagé.

– Welcome home, nous lance-t-il en nous accueillant, une bombe de peinture à la main. Do you want me to show you around ?

On le suit et on constate qu'il a déjà réalisé quatre grandes fresques impressionnantes. Très inspiré par le street art, Clark est un VRAI artiste.

– Waouh ! lâche Lou en fin de visite. Je kiffe trop. Je peux faire des photos ?

– C'est carrément génial, j'ajoute. Il y a une lumière incroyable dans tes peintures. I like it ! Really !

Clark me fait un sourire triste avant d'avouer :

– My family doesn't agree with you, surtout mon grand-père qui a du mal à accepter que je devienne peintre. Mes parents habitent assez loin et on se voit peu depuis que j'ai décidé de vivre ici.

– C'est juste un problème d'âge ! je m'exclame. Ton grand-père est super gentil, je suis certaine qu'il peut arriver à te comprendre mais il faut l'aider. Non ?

Je me tourne vers Vic pour qu'elle nous donne son avis. C'est peine perdue. Elle a quitté la Terre.

– Tu en penses quoi ? je finis par lui chuchoter tandis que Lou parle avec Clark.

– Trop trop trop beau, lâche Vic qui ne le quitte pas des yeux.

Celui-ci explique à ma sœur que sa situation n'est pas facile.

– I'd like to be an artist but it's not easy. Pour ma famille, je ne suis qu'un *« bonne à rien »*. C'est comme ça qu'on dit chez vous ?

Lou hausse les épaules avant de déclarer :

– Tu sais, ce n'est pas nouveau, le conflit des générations. Les artistes mal compris, tout ça… Van Gogh est mort en génie incompris, sans un sou. Et il n'est pas le seul.

– I don't want to be famous when I die ! lance Clark en riant.

– Ben oui, c'est clair, s'écrie soudain Vic qui a l'air de se réveiller de sa transe.

En sortant de l'atelier, Lou, Vic et moi, on partage le même sentiment. Clark nous a fait de la peine.

– Il faudrait qu'on dise à James qu'on a adoré le travail de son petit-fils, lance Vic en secouant la tête. Ce n'est pas normal qu'il y ait un tel fossé entre eux deux.

– Tu n'arriveras pas à le convaincre juste en affirmant que c'est bien ou que tu as aimé, explique Lou.

– Il faut qu'il arrive à s'en rendre compte de lui-même, je renchéris. Un peu comme le jour où notre grand-père a réussi à se servir tout seul de son ordi. Ce jour-là, il a compris que c'était un outil indispensable pour tout le monde.

– Le problème reste entier. Comment James peut-il réaliser que son petit-fils est un vrai artiste s'il est déjà convaincu du contraire ? rétorque Lou en grimaçant. En plus Clark a un look difficile à accepter pour quelqu'un de son âge.

– Moi, j'adooore ce look justement ! s'exclame Vic.

– Ça, on l'a compris, je lui lance en faisant le signe du cœur avec mes deux pouces et mes deux index.

Ma copine rougit un peu en se cachant derrière une longue mèche de cheveux.

On retrouve mes parents, Lisa, Luna et James pour le déjeuner. Après le repas, on essaie de communiquer à notre hôte notre enthousiasme face aux peintures de son petit-fils.

– On a a-do-ré, j'explique en y mettant toute l'énergie dont je suis capable. C'est passionnant de découvrir le travail de Clark dans son atelier.

James hoche la tête d'un air sceptique.

– Clark is such a great painter, j'ajoute en pensant bêtement que des phrases en anglais seront plus convaincantes.

Mes paroles n'atteignent pas leur cible.

Vic regarde James, les sourcils froncés.

– Dans la vie, on a parfois besoin de se sentir soutenu pour être meilleur, lâche-t-elle d'un air décidé. Mon père a ramé longtemps mais ma mère a toujours cru en lui, et elle a eu raison.

Le téléphone de ma copine vibre et elle s'en empare en souriant.

– Tiens, mon père a un sixième sens. C'est lui !

Vic sort de la pièce quelques instants pour pouvoir discuter tranquillement et en revenant, elle m'annonce avec un grand sourire :

– Mes parents viennent de se souvenir qu'ils ont une fille. Et que cette fille a une amie. Du coup ils nous proposent de les rejoindre dans les studios d'Abbey road cet aprèm.

– QUOI ?

Mon père pousse un cri qui nous fait tous sursauter. Même le placide James !

– Attends, tu as bien dit « les studios d'ABBEY ROAD »?

Il a exactement la tête de Lisa lorsqu'elle parle de la famille royale.

– Ben oui, répond Vic, étonnée. C'est là que mes parents enregistr….

– Je viens avec vous ! s'exclame mon père en s'étranglant à moitié. Vous vous rendez compte que ce sont les studios mythiques qui ont vu passer les Beatles, Pink Floyd, U2 ou Oasis ?

– Énorme ! déclare Lou tout excitée à son tour. Je suis du voyage.

– Ah oui, trop bien, moi aussi je viens, commente Lisa, enthousiaste. Il y aura peut-être le prince ou la princesse ?

– Mais papa, on ne va pas pouvoir débarquer à cinquante dans les studios d'enregistrement, je proteste, agacée.

– Oh que si ! Et s'il faut commander un bus, no problemo, lance Vic d'un air buté. Je squatte chez James avec vous depuis deux nuits, mes parents vont vous recevoir. Il ne faut pas abuser.

Nous sommes finalement sept à découvrir les mythiques studios d'enregistrement d'Abbey Road (James hates pop music).

Avant d'entrer dans le bâtiment, mon père nous demande de traverser la rue sur le passage piétons juste devant et il nous prend cinquante fois en photo. Ensuite, il nous montre sur son portable la couverture de l'album *Abbey Road* des Beatles.

– Ils ont fait exactement comme nous, les copieurs, commente Luna en regardant l'image.

– Mais non, c'est nous qui les imitons ! Ils étaient déjà là avant.

Mes deux petites sœurs échangent des commentaires surréalistes tandis que Vic nous escorte jusqu'aux studios où ses parents nous attendent.

– Bonjour à tous, lance Yan, le père de Vic.

C'est un géant qui a des cheveux longs retenus par un serre-tête. Il porte un jean plus déchiré que celui de sa fille et une veste couverte d'inscriptions taguées.

– Quel plaisir de vous rencontrer ! ajoute Bridget.

La mère de Victoire a des yeux sombres et de longs cheveux noirs qui lui cachent une partie du visage.

Mère et fille sont deux copies conformes mais Bridget porte une tenue aux couleurs très vives, à l'opposé de celle de Vic.

La conversation s'engage tout naturellement entre les Steph au carré et les DJ Bryan, le nom d'artistes du duo. On apprend ainsi que le père de Vic est aussi musicien compositeur. La voix de Bridget apparaît souvent dans ses créations originales qu'il mixe ensuite sur des consoles lors de ses DJ sets.

Papa ressemble à un petit garçon et il est super attentif pendant toutes les explications. Maman, elle, écoute les essais de voix que fait Bridget avec mes deux petites sœurs pour les amuser.

Lou prend des tonnes de selfies et elle les envoie TOUS à Maxime.

– Je veux qu'il soit vert de jalousie, déclare-t-elle. Je pose avec un DJ super connu dans THE studios de Londres et lui, il se ruine les mains à escalader des montagnes. Bien fait !

Vic me fait tout visiter. Elle n'arrête pas de rire. Je sens bien qu'elle est heureuse que ses parents nous reçoivent ainsi et nous fassent découvrir l'envers du décor.

On entre dans plusieurs salles d'enregistrement dont celle où le célèbre disque des Beatles a été réalisé. Mon père la prend en photo sous tous les angles.

Vers dix-neuf heures, Yan et Bridget nous entraînent dans un pub à côté des studios pour qu'on dîne ensemble. Juste avant de m'asseoir, je jette un œil distrait sur mon portable. Un SMS d'Alex clignote. Je l'ouvre avec une légère appréhension.

J'ai raison…

Laure, je ne sais plus où j'en suis.
Mon cœur est partagé entre Elsa et toi.

C'est exactement comme si je venais de me prendre la porte du pub en pleine face.

Bonjour la douleur.

French girls' ideas

– Une réunion de crise, ça n'attend pas.

Ce matin, le ton péremptoire de Lou est sans appel derrière la porte des WC.

Lisa se dépêche d'en sortir en remontant son pantalon.

Je n'ai pas dit grand-chose quand nous étions au pub hier soir. J'ai essayé de paraître normale mais, une fois chez James, j'ai ouvert mon robinet à larmes. Il a coulé à flots.

Vic, catastrophée, ne savait pas quoi faire pour me consoler.

– Laure, voilà ce que je te propose, a déclaré Lou après avoir lu l'horrible SMS d'Alex. Dans l'immédiat tu dors parce que tu es crevée et demain matin, réunion de crise.

Curieuse, Vic a levé les sourcils. Il a fallu lui expliquer que ce type de rassemblement a lieu régulièrement à la maison. Dès que l'une des 4L a un gros souci ou un grand chagrin, les trois L restantes tentent toujours de trouver une solution, ou au moins de la consoler durablement. Sitôt le breakfast achevé, Lou a fait un signe discret au « club des filles du deuxième étage », puisque c'est ainsi que nous surnomme notre père.

Lisa boutonne son pantalon et elle se dépêche de grimper sur mon lit pour rejoindre Luna, super concentrée. Lou expose la situation en des termes très clairs.

– Laure a reçu un SMS ignoble de son chéri qui « hésite » entre elle et une autre. La question est : doit-elle casser sans en savoir plus ou le laisser s'expliquer mais le mettre au pied du mur ?

– Oui. Il est trop méchant. On va lui mettre les pieds au mur très longtemps et il aura mal !

Luna se jette dans mes bras pour me montrer son soutien.

– Je suis d'accord. Il faut même lui mettre un mur super lourd sur les pieds, ajoute Lisa très sérieusement.

– Bon, laissez tomber l'expression, les girls ! soupire Lou un peu énervée. Je voulais juste dire : Laure casse-t-elle direct ou lui accorde-t-elle une chance ?

– Alex était très amoureux d'elle, murmure Vic. Elle pourrait lui laisser une petite ouverture.

– Votons, déclare Lou.

Si j'obéis à la majorité des mains qui se sont levées en faveur d'une « rupture définitive », je vais casser avec Alex. Je regarde mon portable tristement. Je ne sais même pas ce qu'il faut écrire dans un SMS de rupture.

Pour essayer de me changer les idées, Vic nous branche sur Clark. Elle montre fièrement à Lisa les photos de ses toiles et un certain nombre de portraits du peintre pris à la dérobée.

– Il est drôle, Clark, déclare Luna en fronçant le nez. Il est un peu trop « décoré ».

La réflexion de la petite L nous fait sourire mais elle illustre bien ce que pense sa famille.

– C'est exactement ce qui lui est reproché, s'énerve soudain Vic. Son look excentrique et son métier d'artiste peintre, à l'opposé de l'image rêvée du « garçon présentable » !

– Ben justement. Moi, je pense qu'il devrait se servir de sa différence, je lance. Il faudrait qu'il expose son travail comme il le conçoit, dans son atelier. Il montrerait à sa famille qu'il a de vrais projets même en étant « trop décoré », comme dit Luna. En ouvrant sa porte à des visiteurs et pas seulement à nous ou à sa famille, il pourrait récolter des critiques positives qui l'aideraient. Je suis certaine qu'on ne sera pas les seules à Londres à aimer ses toiles et à les trouver belles !

Lou et Vic me regardent d'un drôle d'air.

– Ben quoi ? Qu'est-ce que j'ai dit ? Une expo, c'est faisable, non ?

– Mais c'est GÉNIAL ! hurle Vic.

– J'avoue, ajoute ma sœur en me faisant un check. C'est une idée top.

– Ce qui serait cool, c'est qu'il fasse son expo avant notre départ, je conclus, ravie. Pourquoi pas dimanche par exemple ?

On sourit en se regardant toutes les trois. Je viens de chasser tous les nuages qui avaient assombri mes pensées.

French girls ' ideas

Mon cerveau fourmille d'idées et il me tarde de les présenter au principal intéressé, Clark.

On décide de retourner le voir avant la fin de la journée mais, en attendant, Vic s'est engagée à jouer la London guide. Mes parents vont rendre visite à des collègues médecins anglais avec James.

Les deux petites L sont au taquet parce qu'il est prévu que nous allions faire un tour au palais de Buckingham. Lisa met deux heures à choisir sa tenue.

– Il est hors de question que la famille royale me voie mal habillée, explique-t-elle à Lou qui, pour une fois, est prête avant elle. On ne sait jamais. Si la princesse Kate arrose les fleurs dans son jardin et qu'elle nous aperçoit…

– Tu sais, lui précise Vic, ce sont plutôt des jardiniers qui s'occupent des fleurs royales. En plus, Kate n'habite pas à Buckingham.

– Peut-être, continue Lisa obstinée. Mais imagine que la princesse ait envie de se promener dans les allées du jardin avec ses enfants ? Et si, juste à ce moment-là, je passe à côté d'elle ?

Dans le métro, on a droit à un exposé sur la famille royale.

– Vous savez qu'en Angleterre les reines restent super longtemps au pouvoir ? nous précise Lisa. La reine Victoria l'a été plus de soixante ans, comme Élisabeth II. Et leur royaume est très étendu ! Il comprend aussi l'Écosse, l'Irlande du Nord, le Pays de Galles…

– Oui, avec l'Angleterre, ces quatre nations forment le Royaume-Uni, Lisa, ajoute Victoire patiemment.

– Sinon, il paraît que le prince Harry adore…

Je n'écoute plus les explications de ma sœur.

Je pense à Alex.

Je sais que je dois prendre une décision mais je me sens déchirée.

Lou est aussi peu concentrée que moi sur les paroles de Lisa. Elle échange une série de messages et vu sa tête alors qu'elle tape sur les touches, je parie qu'elle écrit à Max et qu'elle ne lui envoie pas des mots d'amour.

– Et bim, prends-toi ça dans les dents, lâche-t-elle en rangeant son portable, l'air satisfaite.

– Qu'est-ce qui se passe ? je lui demande, curieuse.

– Max m'annonce qu'il fait super chaud et qu'il a perdu sa casquette. Il va sûrement attraper des coups de soleil horribles.

– Le pauvre, lui qui a la peau super blanche…

– Justement, j'espère qu'il va virer au rouge homard, me répond Lou avec un sourire sadique.

Être en compagnie de mes sœurs et de Vic m'aide à oublier un peu mon chagrin. Devant le palais de Buckingham, on prend trois millions de photos ! Il faut dire que ce bâtiment tout blanc est impressionnant. Les Welsh guards qui le surveillent sont vêtus d'une tunique rouge vif et d'un pantalon noir mais ils sont surtout coiffés d'une longue coiffe en poil d'ours qui amuse beaucoup Luna.

– Il n’y a aucun membre de la famille royale au palais ce matin, déclare Lisa d’un ton doctoral.

– Pourquoi, l’un d’entre eux t’a envoyé un Snap de la campagne ? lui demande Lou, moqueuse.

– Non, c’est très simple. Il n’y a que deux gardes devant le palais. C’est donc qu’il n’accueille ni roi, ni reine, ni....

– Si la famille royale « serait » là, elle nous ferait coucou de toute façon, lance Luna.

– Non, rectifie Lisa, si elle « était » là, les gardes seraient quatre.

Vic siffle pour montrer son admiration devant tant de connaissances et Lisa sourit fièrement. Elle nous apprend aussi qu’il y a 775 pièces dans le palais mais seulement une douzaine de pièces au premier étage sont occupées.

– Moi si j’avais « soixante-quinze-cents » pièces, j’inviterais TOUTE mon école pour jouer à cache-cache ! crie une Luna enthousiaste.

Vic lui pince le nez avant d’ajouter :

– Et tu finirais par te perdre, ma puce.

– Ben non, parce que je prendrais la montre GPS de papa.

On félicite Luna pour sa prévoyance et on va acheter quelques souvenirs. Lisa tient à rapporter un livre de coloriages des différents palais de la famille royale, tandis que Luna préfère une poupée à l'effigie de la princesse Kate. Lou et moi choisissons deux bracelets aux couleurs de l'Union Jack.

À présent, nous sommes toutes devant un thé bien chaud et James se fait un plaisir de nous parler des diverses propriétés royales.

– Buckingham Palace est *just une* des palais de *le royal family* à Londres, nous explique-t-il. Il y en a bien d'autres. Comme *la* château de Windsor situé dans le Berkshire, à l'ouest de

Londres, *la* château de Balmoral ou *la Holyrood Palace,* tous les deux en Écosse.

– Waouh ! lâche Lisa, des étoiles plein les yeux. J'aimerais trop être invitée dans un palais.

– C'est *une* peu compliqué *la* protocole, tu sais. Il faut savoir quel couteau ou quelle fourchette prendre au bon moment, être bien habillé…

– Et si on faisait comme si on était invités chez la princesse et le prince ? lance Luna.

Les deux petites L quittent la table en riant et on les entend monter l'escalier quatre à quatre pour jouer à la poupée. Vic et moi, on finit par les rejoindre et on les coiffe comme pour un soir de fête. Lou s'installe avec nous. Elle veut fabriquer des tenues « pour rendre visite aux membres de la famille royale » à partir des deux combinaisons que nous avons rapportées de Camden.

Lisa a l'idée de nous prêter son guide pour avoir quelques photos sous les yeux et une séance customisation est lancée. Je dessine sur les combis des petits châteaux avec un feutre noir tandis que Lou s'amuse à les remplir avec des paillettes que Vic transporte dans son sac.

Mon amie nous donne l'idée d'y accrocher quelques broches.

Petit à petit, les combis commencent à avoir un « méchant look » !

Clark nous surprend en pleine séance.

– Hello girls, lance-t-il en apparaissant soudain à la porte de la chambre de Lou où nous sommes toutes réunies. Is it a fashion session ?

Ma copine se pétrifie sur place.

– Vic nous a montré des photos de toi, s'écrie Luna toute joyeuse. T'étais plein de peinture mais ça allait bien avec tes cheveux orange.

Mon amie pousse un cri de désespoir qu'elle étouffe en toussant bruyamment. Pour la sauver d'une mort imminente, je propose aux deux petites L d'aller dessiner avec mes nouveaux feutres dans ma chambre. Clark nous sourit gentiment. On sent bien qu'il aime notre compagnie.

– Clark, listen ! je lance alors. We've got an idea for you.

– Oooh, dit l'intéressé. I want to know !

– What about showing your paintings ? je continue, très fière d'avoir préparé ma phrase en anglais.

Clark ouvre de grands yeux en murmurant « showing my paintings ? ».

– Oui, ouvrir ton atelier et présenter ce que tu sais faire aux gens qui aiment l'art, insiste Vic.

– Nous, on adore ton travail, ajoute Lou avec conviction. Si tu veux te faire accepter en tant qu'artiste, tu dois te montrer comme tel. À tout le monde !

Clark nous regarde attentivement. Il semble hésitant.

– Right ! But… It's not easy…

– Easy easy, marmonne Vic. Nothing is easy ! La vie, c'est pas un kiwi, non plus !

– She's right, life isn't a kiwi, anyway ! je traduis très sérieusement.

On éclate de rire devant l'air ébahi de Clark qui ne comprend pas toutes nos expressions.

– N'empêche qu'une expo, c'est absolument ce qui peut te faire décoller, insiste mon amie. Ton atelier avec ses grands murs blancs se prête complètement au côté street art de ta peinture. C'est une évidence.

Vic parle comme si elle travaillait dans l'événementiel depuis toujours ! Clark hoche la tête.

Je ne suis pas sûre qu'il comprenne absolument tout.

– L'idéal, ce serait de faire cette expo rapidement, je suggère en parlant lentement. Enfin… Si tu veux qu'on te donne un coup de main. Et en plus, on est certaines que ça pourrait aider ton grand-père à mieux te comprendre. Et à te voir autrement !

Le jeune peintre sourit à nouveau. Il a un look d'enfer avec sa salopette trouée et ses cheveux qu'il a plaqués en arrière. Vic le dévore littéralement des yeux.

– Oh, murmure-t-il. I love French ideas ! No... I love French girls' ideas !

Ensuite, il tend la paume de sa main pour un check géant.

More time in London

Hier, notre soirée a ressemblé à un Luna Park géant. On était en mode « Montagnes russes » au niveau sensations ! Clark est resté un moment avec nous et on a parlé de son expo.

On était surexcités tous les quatre et on avait plein d'idées. Lou souhaitait s'occuper de la partie « com avant projet » grâce au réseau de Clark, Vic et moi de la mise en place des lieux, et notre artiste envisageait d'inviter deux amis, un artiste sculpteur et une jeune créatrice de mode habituée aux expos.

– L'idée, ce serait un mix « art and fashion », a déclaré Clark qui devenait de plus en plus enthousiaste au fil des minutes. On expose peintures, sculptures et vêtements.

– Great idea ! a approuvé Lou.

– Comme ça les visiteurs te découvrent, a ajouté Vic les yeux brillants.

– Et en plus, ils ont une vision de ce que font les jeunes créateurs. C'est important ! j'ai conclu.

On s'est mis d'accord pour réfléchir chacun de notre côté et se revoir dès le lendemain. Quand le jeune peintre est parti, on a annoncé la nouvelle aux Steph au carré. C'est là qu'on a pris une douche froide…

– C'est un projet sympa, les filles, a déclaré notre mère, mais impossible à réaliser pour la famille Juin. Nous ne serons plus là le week-end prochain.

– Mais… Laure est invitée huit jours. Elle peut rester avec moi. Et Lou aussi si elle en a envie, s'est empressée de proposer Vic.

– Bridget et Yan sont bien trop occupés par leur enregistrement, a ajouté maman. Les filles rentreront avec nous.

On était consternées.

More time in London

Ma nuit a été très agitée. J'ai rêvé que je revoyais Alex et qu'il s'était teint les cheveux en vert sur les conseils d'Elsa.

À mon réveil, j'ai su qu'il fallait que je prenne une décision définitive. Heureusement, parfois, un beau soleil se lève derrière les nuages ! En tout cas, à Londres c'est souvent le cas. James a illuminé notre breakfast puisqu'il nous a proposé de rester quelques jours supplémentaires.

– Je sais que vous adorez London et ma maison va être trop vide après votre départ, alors si vous le pouvez, je vous invite un peu plus *longue temps*…

Lou, Vic et moi, on a poussé un cri de joie en se jetant à son cou. On se voyait bien demeurer toutes les trois dans la capitale et naviguer entre les différents quartiers à visiter, la maison de James et l'atelier de Clark.

Sauf que mes parents ont eu la même idée que nous.

– C'est vraiment très gentil à vous, James, a déclaré ma mère, tout sourire. Je crois qu'on serait tous très contents de rester quelques jours de plus. En ce qui me concerne, il me reste des jours de congé. Qu'en penses-tu, Steph ?

– Absolutely ! a répondu l'intéressé, la bouche pleine de scones. I love London and I love English Breakfast ! Je dois m'assurer auparavant que mon remplaçant peut rester quelques jours de plus au cabinet.

Après avoir passé un petit moment au téléphone, notre père a confirmé l'information. Toute la famille Juin peut prolonger son séjour.

Notre « liberté londonienne » va être très encadrée jusqu'au bout.

Ce matin, James propose d'ailleurs ses services de guide pour faire découvrir à la famille Juin le British Museum.

Je regarde Vic en coin. Elle fait la même grimace que moi… Comme les parents sont de super bonne humeur à la perspective de rester quelques jours de plus en vacances, ils acceptent de nous laisser partir en duo.

Nous avons très envie de découvrir Madame Tussauds, le célèbre musée de statues en cire où sont exposées les reproductions grandeur nature de très nombreuses stars. Lou choisit de rester en famille ce matin.

Dans le métro, mon amie et moi sommes plus excitées que des puces jusqu'à ce qu'on se mette à parler garçons.

La perspective de choisir des mots pour ma future rupture casse un peu l'ambiance.

– C'est le moment, je déclare en sortant mon portable. Je dois signifier à Alex que je ne suis pas un produit de consommation devant lequel on hésite.

– Très bien dit ! approuve Vic en hochant la tête. Et, puisqu'on parle d'hésitation… Tu crois que Clark ?

Mon amie me regarde, rouge d'émotion.

– Il a presque huit ans de plus que toi, c'est énorme ! Je ne suis pas sûre que…

– L'amour n'a pas d'âge, m'interrompt Vic. Il abolit les distances, les frontières, les années.

Vic a vraiment l'air de croire au *power of love* et je n'ai pas envie de briser son rêve avec mes doutes. Je préfère donc me taire et je passe le trajet de métro à taper le message que je compte envoyer à Alex.

Juste avant d'entrer dans le musée de cire, je m'assois sur un banc et, une larme à l'œil, devant le regard ému de Vic, j'envoie :

L'amour ne se partage pas en deux parts égales et je ne fais pas partie d'un menu au choix. Dsl

Ensuite, je range mon portable dans ma poche en espérant sincèrement qu'Alex se dépêchera de m'avouer son erreur.

Grâce à Vic, je finis par me détendre et comme elle passe son temps à faire le clown devant les statues de cire, je ris comme une folle. Avec son portable, on fait environ un million de selfies. On pose en chanteuses à côté de Jennifer Lopez, Rihanna ou Beyoncé, elle fait des grimaces épouvantables devant Dark Vador ou Shrek, la révérence en face du prince Harry comme si elle allait l'inviter à danser.

– Prends-moi en photo ! hurle-t-elle devant le buste en cire de la princesse Kate. On va faire croire à Lisa qu'on l'a rencontrée dans la rue.

Je sors mon portable de ma poche. Trois SMS m'attendent. À mon plus grand désespoir, il n'y en a aucun d'Alex. Ils proviennent tous de Lou. Son premier message m'inquiète, mais les deux autres me font carrément flipper.

> British museum tellement géant qu'on vient
> de perdre… Lisa ! Pour une fois c pas Luna !

> H +15 mn Lisa tjs invisible.
> On se sépare en trois groupes

> T là ? Si tu as disparu toi aussi, préviens-moi !
> 20 km ds le musée j'étrangle Lisa
> dès que je la retrouve.

En voyant que Lou m'a écrit il y a quinze minutes, je me dépêche de taper une réponse.

> Elle est cap d'avoir suivi un groupe

Je décris la situation à Vic et on décide de stopper notre visite en attendant une réponse rassurante de Lou. Je suis très stressée jusqu'à ce que mon écran s'allume à nouveau.

Bien vu Laure !
Lisa a suivi la visite guidée en français
sur « Les tableaux préférés de la famille royale » !

J'envoie un SMS avec plein de smileys hilares tandis que Lou m'explique, dans un nouveau message, que James suit désormais Lisa comme son ombre dans le musée tant il a eu peur.

En sortant de chez Tussauds, on décide de marcher un peu dans le Regent's Park, qui se trouve à deux pas.

– Il va pleuvoir ! lance Vic enthousiaste en regardant le ciel se couvrir.

Je ris en repensant aux jours de pluie à la colo qui rendaient Vic si heureuse…

Le crachin se met à tomber et mon amie visse son bonnet sur sa tête avec un grand sourire. Elle me tire par la main et m'oblige à sautiller comme elle. Je finis par crier à tue-tête « It's raining in Lon-don, yes, yes, yes ! » Le crachin se transforme en déluge. On a très vite les cheveux qui dégoulinent et lorsque mon portable vibre, je ne peux même pas accéder au message car mes doigts sont trop mouillés.

On finit par trouver un abri et je lis le SMS que vient de m'envoyer ma copine Justine.

> Si tu parles encore français, tu peux me donner de tes nouvelles.
> Mais tu es peut-être au fond de la Tamise pour oublier les ongles vernis sur le pull de A ?

Je ne peux pas m'empêcher de sourire et je lui poste vite :

> I only speak English.
> Do you want a scoop ?
> Morgan is here with me, in London.

Il faut environ deux minutes avant que mon portable sonne.

– Lauauauare ! hurle Justine au bout du fil. Dis-moi que tu mens. Morgan n'est pas avec toi, là ?

– Hello Justine. How do you do ? je lui réponds en essayant de rester sérieuse.

– Laure, si tu ne dis pas la vérité dans la seconde qui suit, je lâche sur Facebook que tu as été amoureuse de Milan Fergeaud.

– J'étais en petite section de maternelle, il y a prescription.

– N'empêche, insiste Justine. Les gens retiendront que tu as aimé le plus gros boloss que la Terre ait porté !

Je ris tellement que Vic me fait signe de lui raconter la conversation.

– NON, Morgan n'est pas avec moi, il est peut-être devant ta porte, va voir !

– Si ce n'est pas le cas, je lâche l'affaire sur Facebook ! crie Justine avant de raccrocher.

En reprenant notre petite balade, je décris Justine et je montre quelques photos d'elle. J'en profite pour parler aussi d'Ulysse[1], un copain qui est passionné de dessin, comme moi. J'explique à Vic comme on est devenus proches et je lui présente quelques dessins qu'il poste régulièrement sur les réseaux sociaux. Je lui promets de l'inviter en France à mon tour pour qu'elle découvre en direct tous mes amis.

Lorsqu'on rentre chez James, on est trempées, elle et moi.

– Oh, mais vous avez nagé dans la Tamise ! s'écrie Lisa en nous ouvrant.

– Oui et vous ne savez pas que c'est interdit ? demande Luna, scandalisée.

1. Lire *4 sœurs en direct du collège.*

On monte à toute vitesse se changer. Vic a enlevé son bonnet et chante « I love la pluie » ! en secouant sa chevelure dans tous les sens.

– Hello girls ! lance Clark en nous voyant. I love la pluie aussi.

Vic est pétrifiée. Ses cheveux pendent sur sa tête, comme si une méduse avait élu domicile sur son crâne. Elle est au bord de l'évanouissement.

– Bonjour, je suis Margaux. Clark m'a proposé de venir voir vos créations.

Je comprends tout de suite que c'est l'amie française de Clark qui travaille dans la Central Saint Martins College, une école de mode prestigieuse à Londres. Je tends une serviette de toilette à Vic tandis qu'elle nous explique la situation.

– Clark m'a branchée sur votre idée d'expo et vos combis customisées, nous dit-elle. Je suis OK pour montrer quelques-unes de mes créations dans l'atelier, moi aussi.

– Oui, renchérit Clark. On prévoit une partie artiste et une partie fashion pour qu'il y ait plus de visiteurs.

– Vos combinaisons sont très cools, continue Margaux en hochant la tête. J'ai conseillé à Lou d'en customiser d'autres pour qu'elles puissent être exposées.

Ma sœur sourit à s'en décrocher la mâchoire.

– On est tous OK pour l'expo ! s'exclame Clark. Margaux s'occupe de la mode, moi des peintures et des sculptures, et vous de la présentation ? De la publicité ?

– Great, je lance enthousiaste.

Vic répète mécaniquement mon cri mais, une fois de plus, elle manque de conviction. Elle n'arrête pas de regarder Margaux. Je sais ce qu'elle est en train de se dire…

On passe une petite heure à discuter. Clark reçoit les sculptures de son ami le lendemain et il nous invite à le rejoindre dans son atelier en fin de journée. Lou veut lancer au plus vite l'événement sur les réseaux sociaux. Margaux déclare aussi qu'elle va faire passer l'information au sein de son école de mode.

Quand Clark et son amie française nous quittent, le projet commence à prendre vraiment forme.

– Je vais retourner à Camden Market pour racheter des combis, annonce Lou. Je crois que ma voie est toute tracée. Je me vois bien intégrer la Central Saint Martins College et devenir fashion designer. Je me sens à l'avant-garde des tendances, c'est clair. La mode a besoin de moi.

– Et Maxou, tu crois qu'il va apprécier de te parler uniquement par Skype ? je lui réponds, moqueuse.

– Toute carrière demande des sacrifices. Max devra comprendre que ma vie est en train de prendre un tournant. J'en discuterai avec lui demain matin.

Je hoche la tête en pensant au tournant que prend ma love-story. Mon message est toujours sans réponse.

– Laure ? me chuchote Vic alors qu'on est en train de se changer. Tu crois que Margaux et Clark… ?

– Bof, je lui réponds. Je ne les vois pas comme un couple, moi.

Mon amie soupire en regardant l'une des photos de Clark sur son portable.

Je soupire à mon tour en rangeant mon téléphone.

Une chose est sûre : elle et moi on peut, dès à présent, prendre la carte de membres du club des cœurs brisés !

Tim and Clark

Ce matin, quand on s'est levées, Vic et moi, Lou avait déjà disparu.

Elle est allée à la « cave de Dem » pour acheter des combis pas chères, nous explique Luna. Et elle n'a même pas voulu m'emmener. Pourtant, je parle bien anglais pour l'aider à faire les courses. Écoutez : *et lo… Cinq you… ouats ze priïsse ?*

– C'est super bien, commente Vic qui a un faible pour Luna. La prochaine fois que je vais à Camden, tu m'accompagnes.

Lou est de retour alors qu'on finit notre breakfast. Comme mes parents ont promis aux deux petites L une visite du London zoo et une croisière sur la Tamise, ils quittent la maison assez rapidement. Ils ont compris que nous avions d'autres projets et pour une fois, ils ne réclament pas notre présence auprès d'eux. Ma sœur aînée fait la tête de quelqu'un à qui on vient d'apprendre que la fin du monde est pour demain…

– Tu n'as rien trouvé ? je lui demande.

– Si. J'ai acheté quatre combis pour un prix défiant toute concurrence.

Elle sort ses achats de son sac. Vic et moi, on est super contentes. Il y a deux combis en coton, deux en jean et l'ensemble peut être largement customisé !

– Sympa, hein ? constate Lou d'un ton lugubre.

– Ta joie est trop intérieure pour être vue, ou tu la caches VRAIMENT ? je lui réponds, intriguée.

Ma sœur me regarde avec cet air qu'elle prend quand elle se sent obligée de m'expliquer « les choses de la vie ».

– J'ai eu des échanges musclés par SMS avec Max, figure-toi. Il ne comprend pas pourquoi je reste si longtemps à Londres. Énorme, non, pour quelqu'un qui n'a pas voulu venir avec moi !

Vic la regarde en coin.

– Je vais lui expliquer la life, moi, continue Lou en s'emparant des ciseaux de couture pour couper rageusement les étiquettes des combinaisons. Londres révèle ma vraie fibre artistique et il n'est pas content. Ce séjour marque le début de la fin de notre histoire.

Ensuite elle sort dignement de la pièce, les yeux humides.

– Waouh, ta grande sœur sait ce qu'elle veut ! commente Vic. Au moins, elle ne se laisse pas faire.

– Hum… C'est juste la « championne du monde et des environs » du changement d'avis sur Maxou. Leur histoire d'amour n'est qu'un éternel *revival* ! Tu as loupé le début de la série, alors que moi j'ai vu tous les épisodes.

Lou revient avec le matériel nécessaire pour travailler sur les combinaisons et on se lance sans plus attendre dans notre séance fashion.

Cette fois-ci, on a décidé de traiter les combis noires en mode flashy et celles en jean en mode vintage. Comme Clark nous a laissé un peu de peinture fluo, Vic et moi, on s'amuse à faire quelques taches éparses sur les combis noires. Lou, elle, s'occupe des combis en jean sur lesquelles elle transfère des fleurs en tissu très seventies qu'elle a récupérées sur des vieux coussins de James.

Celui-ci vient de s'installer à nos côtés, une tasse de thé à la main.

– Vous faites tout ça pour l'expo de Clark ? finit-il par demander. Vous savez qu'il n'y aura personne ? Clark is just an eccentric guy.

– Vous vous trompez ! s'exclame Vic toujours prête à défendre Clark. Votre petit-fils a un talent dingue et je parie qu'il y aura un monde fou à son expo.

– Vic a raison, j'insiste. Clark est un vrai peintre qui peut vivre de son art et vous allez en être convaincu. Laissez-le exposer, vous verrez…

– Les plus grands artistes ont souvent un côté excentrique, ajoute Lou. Ils expriment à leur manière leur sensibilité artistique.

James nous regarde toutes les trois. Il hoche la tête silencieusement. Je ne suis pas certaine qu'il adhère à nos paroles pour autant.

Nos combinaisons sont terminées en début d'après-midi et on envoie des photos de nos créations à Margaux qui échange des commentaires flatteurs avec nous.

Elles auront largement leur place dans l'expo avec mes Excentriques ! C'est le nom que je donne aux robes que je crée. Clark a prévu un corner dans son atelier pour la mode, ce sera cool.

Ensuite, on s'installe dans la chambre de Lou. Je jette un œil pour la centième fois à mon portable. Alex n'a toujours pas laissé UN SEUL message. Vic contemple les photos volées de Clark sur son téléphone. Ma sœur envoie son vingtième SMS de la matinée à Max en grimaçant.

– Bon, il faut faire quelque chose, je soupire. On fait peine à voir, franchement !

Vic lève un œil puis se replonge dans sa contemplation tandis que Lou tire la langue à son portable.

– Hurry up, girls ! We are so… stupid ! j'insiste en anglais pour nous motiver. London is one of the most beautiful cities in the world and we have to discover it.

Je me précipite sur un des guides que James laisse à notre disposition et je recherche une visite qui pourrait nous brancher.

– Il y a bien un truc qu'on pourrait aller voir, déclare soudain Vic en me voyant tourner les pages du guide. Mais il faut VRAIMENT ne pas être trouillardes…

Lou sourit crânement tandis que je hausse les épaules.

– Tu ne connais pas les sœurs Juin, lâche-t-on en chœur.

Une heure plus tard, on arrive toutes les trois devant l'un des ponts de Londres, bien décidées à vivre la London Bridge Experience !

– On se promène dans des souterrains et on vit presque deux-mille ans d'histoire de la capitale sous forme de scènes d'une réalité incroyable, nous explique Vic alors qu'on prend les tickets. Il paraît que côté effets spéciaux, c'est énooorme !

Lou ricane.

– Excuse-moi mais vu tous les films d'horreur que j'ai à mon actif, il n'y a plus grand-chose qui puisse me faire peur.

Elle nous fait signe de la suivre en entrant dans l'attraction, un grand sourire aux lèvres.

Ce qui saute aux yeux, c'est qu'en ressortant du London Bridge une heure plus tard, ma sœur a complètement changé d'avis. Comme elle n'a plus de voix à cause des hurlements qu'elle a poussés, elle chuchote :

– Je n'ai absolument pas pensé à Max et vous ?

– Moi je ne pense jamais à Max, je lui réponds en essayant de décrisper mes lèvres.

J'ai beaucoup de mal à soulever les deux coins de ma bouche tellement j'ai été tétanisée par la peur.

– Je ne vais pas réussir à dormir cette nuit, j'ajoute en roulant des yeux. Le passage sur Jack l'éventreur… ça m'a terrifiée !

– On m'avait prévenue que c'était *scary* mais je n'imaginais pas de telles sensations, avoue Vic qui est toute blanche. J'ai eu l'impression d'assister au grand incendie de Londres en direct !

– Et la pendaison de la fin ? Vous n'avez pas eu l'impression de la vivre RÉELLEMENT ? lâche Lou d'un air épouvanté.

On se dirige à petits pas vers le métro et quand le téléphone de Vic sonne, on sursaute toutes les trois en même temps !

Mon amie répond à son père visiblement. Elle fronce les sourcils pendant la conversation et finit par me demander le numéro de téléphone de mes parents.

– Mon père est complètement à l'ouest, nous explique-t-elle après avoir raccroché. Il se souvient de temps en temps que j'existe… Il voulait le 06 de vos parents. Si j'ai bien compris, les voix de vos deux sœurs qui ont été enregistrées avec celle de ma mère, l'autre soir aux studios, collent parfaitement avec un de ses projets et il veut en parler de vive voix.

Quand on arrive chez James, ma mère vient justement de terminer sa conversation téléphonique avec Yan.

Elle nous réunit tous dans le salon, James compris.

– Les parents de Vic souhaitent enregistrer un morceau qui s'appelle *Children forever*. L'argent récolté sera reversé à une association de défense des droits de l'enfant. Ils ont écouté les chœurs que Lisa et Luna ont enregistrés l'autre soir et…

– … Et quoi ? demande Lisa qui sent bien qu'il se passe quelque chose d'intéressant.

– Vos voix collent parfaitement avec la musique qu'ils ont créée et ils voudraient les mixer. Yan demande si nous pouvons revenir aux studios avec les deux petites L demain.

Ma mère n'a pas le temps de finir.

– On y va, on y va, on y va ! crie Lisa en sautant partout.

– Mais on va où ? demande Luna qui pleurniche. Moi je ne veux plus me promener, je suis trop fatiguée.

– C'est génial, on retourne aux studios d'Abbey Road ! lâche mon père qui redevient un enfant à chaque fois que ce mot magique est prononcé.

Luna retrouve son sourire dès qu'elle comprend qu'elle « chantera à nouveau dans le micro » et Lisa répète en boucle qu'elle sera sûrement « entendue par la famille royale » grâce à ce morceau des DJ Bryan.

– Peut-être que je vais VRAIMENT être invitée dans un de leurs châteaux ? lance-t-elle, les yeux brillants.

Pendant ce temps, Lou s'est installée à son ordi et elle fait un montage avec des photos des toiles de Clark et les « Excentriques » imaginées par Margaux. Elle y ajoute nos combis.

– Le visuel de l'expo prend forme. Dites à Clark qu'il me manque les statues de son copain et que je le mets en ligne dès demain. Tout son réseau FB sera notifié.

Vic et moi, on court littéralement à Cornwall Gardens rejoindre le jeune peintre.

Celui-ci attend toujours les trois sculptures que doit lui apporter son ami. Pendant que Vic lui explique (en bégayant à moitié) le travail de Lou sur l'ordi, je fais un tour rapide de l'atelier.

Je repère les endroits où il faudrait installer les toiles pour qu'elles bénéficient de la lumière des spots de l'atelier. J'ai aussi envie de réaliser une sorte de drapeau qui pourrait être accroché devant l'atelier. Il me manque un détail important.

– Clark, what's the name of your exhibition ? I'd like to make a flug for you !

– Oh ! Good, lâche Clark. What do you think about « London Art Eye » by Clark and Tim, with a special fashion session ?

Mon cerveau carbure déjà à deux-mille à l'heure. J'imagine un œil mais aussi la roue de Londres. Je pourrais écrire le nom des artistes en fluo à la bombe sur le drapeau et…

– Bon, il faut que je te dise quelque chose, Clark, lance soudain Vic dans l'atelier silencieux.

Un signal d'alarme retentit dans ma tête. Ma copine est rouge pivoine. Je prie mentalement pour qu'elle ne fasse pas une déclaration d'amour devant moi. Je retiens mon souffle.

– Tu as trop de talent, continue-t-elle d'une voix qui vibre. Et j'adooore aussi ton look d'artiste. Bref je te kiffe grave !

Clark sourit mais il fronce un peu les sourcils en répétant :

– Euh, what does it mean « Je te kiiife grââve » ?

Une voix nous interrompt.

– Claaark, I'm here ! Can you help me ?

– Oh ! It's Tim ! s'exclame Clark en se précipitant vers l'entrée de son atelier.

Le jeune qui vient à notre rencontre doit être son ami sculpteur. Il porte une salopette abîmée lui aussi mais, contrairement à Clark, ses cheveux sont coupés très court, ce qui fait ressortir ses yeux incroyables. Tim a en effet un regard couleur turquoise extraordinaire qu'on n'oublie plus une fois qu'on l'a croisé. Je suis tellement sous le charme que Clark doit me rappeler à l'ordre.

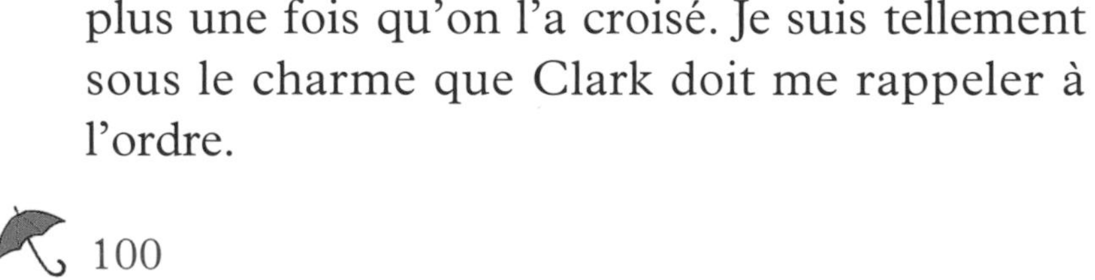

Tim and Clark

– *Lôôôre*… Here is Tim. He is my boyfriend and I'm very happy you meet him !

Une nouvelle alarme sonne dans mon cerveau mais je mets au moins trois secondes avant de comprendre ce qui l'a déclenchée.

Je vois d'abord la tête de Vic. Elle est plus blanche que les murs de l'atelier et semble terrassée par un poids énorme.

Ensuite, mon regard se pose sur la main de Clark. Il tient celle de Tim et il appuie même très légèrement sa joue contre son épaule.

Enfin, Clark vient de prononcer le mot boy juste avant le mot friend.

Ce qui signifie clairement que Vic n'a plus AUCUNE chance avec Clark.

This is the end.

Two young singers

Hier soir, on a frôlé le tsunami. Really.

D'abord, on a failli rentrer en barque chez James, Vic et moi. Ma copine pleurait tellement que j'ai cru qu'elle allait faire déborder la Tamise. Sur le chemin, j'ai essayé de la consoler mais une histoire d'amour ratée, ça reste une histoire d'amour ratée. Quels que soient les mots-pansements qu'on met dessus.

Après le dîner (pendant lequel Vic portait des lunettes de soleil), Lou a reçu quelques Snaps de Max. Il était clair qu'il s'amusait BEAUCOUP avec plusieurs AMIES.

D'habitude, face à ce genre d'affront, Lou réagit avec énergie et colère. Je ne sais pas si les yeux larmoyants de Vic ont eu un impact sur elle, mais ma sœur aînée s'est mise à pleurer elle aussi.

J'étais catastrophée ! J'allais me lancer dans un discours de consolation lorsque mon portable a sonné. Alex se souvenait que j'existais…

J'ai ouvert son message en tremblant.

> L'amour naît d'un regard, grandit d'un baiser et meurt dans une larme.

Ce proverbe est faux puisque je n'ai pas versé une larme en le lisant.

J'en ai versé… des litres.

Les deux petites L nous ont donc surprises en mode « torrent », Lou, Vic et moi : le bureau des pleurs était au complet dans ma chambre.

– C'est pa-thé-ti-que, a lancé Lisa qui adore ce mot depuis que Lou le met à toutes les sauces. Je suis sûre que vous pleurez à cause des garçons !

– Et si on faisait une réunion de crise ? a crié Luna qui a bien senti l'urgence. Moi je sais comment arrêter de pleurer et Lisa, elle…

– Pas besoin ! l'a coupée Lou en s'essuyant les joues. C'est juste un trop-plein émotionnel que j'ai eu besoin d'évacuer. Ce voyage à Londres, la future expo, mon engagement dans la mode...

On a hoché la tête, Vic et moi, comme si nous aussi on était submergées par la pression. Lisa nous a regardées toutes les trois en hochant la tête.

– Hum. C'est bon pour cette fois, a-t-elle conclu en prenant l'air sévère de ma mère quand on l'a poussée à bout.

– Oui, ça va que vous devez évacuer le « trop peint », a ajouté Luna en imitant la mine sérieuse de sa sœur.

On a fini par sourire. On peut être membres du club des cœurs brisés, on a aussi de l'humour !

Ce matin, alors qu'elle vient à peine d'ouvrir les yeux, Vic déclare d'une voix lugubre :

– Si Clark avait été amoureux de Margaux, j'aurais sûrement été moins triste.

– Et pourquoi ? je demande, étonnée.

– Parce que j'aurais pu imaginer un futur où éventuellement lui et moi... Tandis que là, je suis CERTAINE que JAMAIS je ne lui plairai.

Je hoche la tête et puis en voyant que ses yeux se remplissent de larmes à nouveau, je fais voler la couette de son lit en criant :

– Allez HURRY UP, miss ! Je ferme le bureau des pleurs.

Je la saisis par la main et je la pousse dans la salle de bains où elle subit un habillage-coiffage express et énergique.

En rejoignant le reste de la famille pour le breakfast, Vic oublie ses larmes. Il faut dire que mes petites sœurs nous font le grand show !

– Tea with milk ? leur demande James.

Luna désigne le lait et Lisa sourit bêtement en secouant la tête pour montrer qu'elle ne veut rien boire. Notre hôte continue à leur poser des questions mais elles lui répondent avec des signes.

– Vous vous sentez bien ? grogne notre père. Vous allez me faire le plaisir de répondre à James correctement !

– On préserve notre voix, chuchote Lisa.

– Il faut qu'on chante super bien ce soir, murmure Luna.

On réalise alors qu'elles portent toutes les deux un col roulé plus une écharpe, alors que le soleil est éclatant.

– C'est pour ça que vous êtes couvertes comme pour une visite au Pôle Nord ? constate Vic qui commence à rire.

Les deux petites L se tournent vers nos parents.

– Le moindre courant d'air peut nous être fatal, affirme Lisa d'une voix inaudible. Pas de visites pour nous aujourd'hui.

Les Steph au carré font une drôle de tête puis ils nous regardent en souriant, Lou et moi.

– Les filles, commence maman du ton tout doux qu'elle prend quand elle veut qu'on lui rende service. Vous avez des activités à faire « en intérieur » aujourd'hui ?

– Crochet et tricot, comme d'hab, je réponds en grimaçant. Tu sais bien qu'on adooore !

– Et accessoirement canevas, ajoute Lou. Quelqu'un veut se joindre à nous ?

– Oh ouiiiii, MOI ! crie Luna qui oublie, l'espace d'une seconde, qu'elle doit préserver sa voix tant la perspective de rester avec Lou la rend heureuse.

Finalement, ce sont quatre L (plus une) qui se réunissent pour organiser l'exposition. Nos parents ont profité de leur liberté TOTALE pour découvrir Londres en amoureux. James, que la perspective de rester seul en compagnie d'autant de filles paniquait un peu, s'est trouvé un rendez-vous au dernier moment.

– Et si tu envoyais un message d'invitation à la famille royale ? demande Lisa alors que Lou est en train de finaliser l'événement « expo » sur Facebook.

Lou soupire fortement avant de déclarer :

– Et d'un, tu peux parler plus fort parce que ça m'agace prodigieusement de tendre l'oreille pour t'entendre. Et de deux, si tu as le Facebook de Kate, de William ou du prince Harry, n'hésite pas à me les communiquer, que je puisse faire suivre l'info.

Lisa hausse les épaules et murmure encore plus doucement :

– Je les aurai bientôt, dès que j'aurai enregistré ce succès interplanétaire avec le père de Vic. C'est pour ça que ma voix vaut de l'or.

Vic éclate de rire, ce qui rend périlleuse ma création artistique. En effet, ma copine tient un drap tendu sur lequel je dessine les lettres de *London Art Eye*, le titre de l'exposition de Clark. Mais comme Vic n'arrête pas de glousser dès que les petites L chuchotent, ma création est mouvante.

Quand mon drapeau est prêt à être peint, je suis assez fière du résultat ! J'ai réussi à tracer une belle esquisse de la London Eye qui se détache devant un œil immense. Les lettres de Clark et Tim sont stylisées. Je compte les repasser en fluo. J'ai ajouté un encart : fashion

session. Il ne me reste plus qu'à rejoindre l'atelier de Clark pour la phase peinture.

– Vas-y sans moi, déclare Vic qui a repris un air triste dès que j'ai prononcé le prénom fatidique de son amour impossible.

– Et l'expo ? Tu vas aussi boycotter l'expo ? je lui demande, un peu énervée.

Ma copine joue nerveusement avec son bonnet.

– Tu sais que la fin d'une histoire d'amour qui n'a JAMAIS commencé, c'est tout de même moins HORRIBLE que la fin d'une VRAIE love story de dix mois ! je rétorque, les mains sur les hanches.

Je pense à nouveau à Alex et son message d'hier. Je sais qu'il va falloir que je trouve une réponse et j'en ai le ventre noué.

– C'est comme si j'avais VRAIMENT vécu cette histoire, insiste Vic qui décide de me suivre malgré tout. Ma douleur est réelle…

On passe le trajet à comparer nos niveaux de souffrance et on finit par en sourire… un peu !

Lorsque Clark nous ouvre, il est surexcité. Il a décroché ses toiles pour leur trouver des emplacements appropriés et a disposé les cinq statues de Tim de façon à ce qu'elles soient visibles de partout.

– J'ai reçu le visuel de l'expo de Lou, crie-t-il tout en s'activant. Amazing !

Je lui montre fièrement la bannière que je compte accrocher devant sa porte.

– You are so cute, Juin sisters ! lance-t-il en joignant les mains.

Comme Vic fait une drôle de tête, il ajoute :

– Oooh ! And YOU are so cute, beautiful Vic !

Mon amie rougit à nouveau et je la laisse reprendre une respiration normale tandis que Clark me montre le stock de peintures que je peux utiliser. Pendant que je mets le drapeau en couleurs, Vic et Clark déménagent les toiles et les accrochent face aux spots supplémentaires que Tim a apportés la veille au soir.

En milieu d'après-midi, « my flag is done » et l'atelier commence à ressembler à un lieu d'exposition. Lou et Margaux doivent se charger de la partie fashion session, donc Vic et moi on rentre vite chez James pour veiller sur les deux petites L et permettre à ma sœur aînée d'aller à l'atelier.

– Tu as entendu ?, me chuchote Vic alors qu'on s'installe avec James pour le tea time. Clark m'a appelée « beautiful Vic ». Tu crois qu'un garçon qui aime les garçons les aime toute sa vie ?

Je secoue la tête en regardant mon amie.

– Je ne suis pas dans la tête de Clark, Vic. Mais si j'étais toi, je laisserais tomber. Definitely.

C'est aussi ce que je m'apprête à faire avec Alex. Je prends mon portable et je tape la phrase que j'ai mis la journée à imaginer.

> Baudelaire a dit : L'amour est une rose,
> chaque pétale une illusion,
> chaque épine une réalité.
> Pour moi, la douleur reste vive mais il me
> restera la douceur des parfums de la rose....

Avant d'envoyer le SMS, je le fais valider par Vic. En lisant mon message, elle se remet à pleurer dans sa tasse de thé en affirmant que « mon message est tellement beau qu'il devrait être étudié dans toutes les classes pour le bac ».

Heureusement, le retour de mes parents empêche Vic de sombrer à nouveau dans la dépression.

Pour se changer les idées, on décide d'accompagner les deux petites L aux studios d'Abbey road avec mes parents.

Mon père commande un black cab. Ce taxi londonien, le plus souvent noir, est un véritable monument ambulant dans la capitale. Pendant que le chauffeur nous véhicule dans les rues, mes sœurs n'arrêtent pas de remonter leur col roulé pour protéger leurs gorges. Tandis que Luna chante en play back dans un micro invisible, Lisa s'évertue à garder la bouche fermée « pour empêcher l'air de polluer ses cordes vocales ».

– On a une paix royale, murmure mon père. Il faudra vraiment inscrire Lisa et Luna dans un cours de chant en rentrant à Paris. Tu imagines si c'est ainsi chaque soir ?

Ma mère hoche la tête d'un air rêveur.

Aux studios, les parents de Vic nous accueillent chaleureusement. Yan conduit mes deux petites sœurs dans l'une des cabines d'enregistrement où elles font quelques essais de micro. Les Steph au carré, Vic et moi, on les observe derrière la vitre.

Lisa n'arrête pas de remettre nerveusement ses lunettes en place. Luna, elle, continue à brandir un micro imaginaire, alors qu'elle en a un devant la bouche. Mes deux petites sœurs se conduisent VRAIMENT comme des chanteuses professionnelles. Elles mêlent leurs voix à celle de Bridget à chaque fois qu'il le faut et fredonnent en rythme l'air entêtant que DJ Bryan mixera en studio.

Enfin, Yan lance :

– C'est dans la boîte, les filles, vous avez été parfaites.

Lisa et Luna se précipitent dans la cabine avec nous pour entendre le résultat… qui est carrément génial !

Maman essuie une larme d'émotion quand le morceau s'achève.

Pour fêter l'événement, les Steph au carré nous invitent dans le fish and chips d'à côté.

Les deux petites L nous saoulent de paroles pendant toute la soirée comme pour rattraper le temps perdu dans le monde du silence.

Plus tard, dans le black cab qui nous ramène chez James, j'ai le cœur gros. Je repense à Alex. Je jette un œil à mon portable.

J'ai deux SMS.

Par solidarité avec toi, j'ai décidé de quitter Morgan. Notre love story n'aura jamais lieu. Tant pis pour lui

affirme Justine avec des tas de smileys qui pleurent.

Il me tarde que tu rentres, mes dessins sont tristes sans toi

m'envoie mon meilleur ami Ulysse en joignant par Snap une caricature de lui et moi séparés par la mer.

Vic me sourit puis elle pose sa tête contre mon épaule.

Une chose est sûre. Avec des amis comme les miens, je ne serai JAMAIS seule dans la vie.

Et ça, c'est le plus puissant des sèche-larmes !

A great idea

– Tu ne veux pas éteindre ? Ça me dérange !

J'ouvre un œil tout en fronçant les sourcils. Vic vient de me réveiller.

– LAURE, ÉTEINS LA MUSIQUE ! crie-t-elle en mettant cette fois-ci sa tête sous l'oreiller.

J'ouvre les deux yeux pour de bon. Effectivement, un son parvient jusqu'à nous. En tendant l'oreille, je reconnais tout de suite le morceau.

– Mes sœurs écoutent leur enregistrement, je marmonne d'une voix endormie. Je ne suis pas responsable de ce boucan…

– *HELLO ZE GUEURLES* ! hurle Luna qui vient d'entrer dans notre chambre. *Zaire iz oine surpraïïze for you.*

– Je t'ai toujours dit qu'il fallait arrêter d'encourager mes sœurs à parler anglais, je lâche en glissant à mon tour la tête sous l'oreiller.

– Et alors ma beauté des îles ? Tu dors encore ?

Notre chambre est un hall de gare, ce matin. Cette voix inconnue me fait m'asseoir d'un bond dans mon lit en déclarant :

– Les filles ! Vous avez fait de beaux rêves ?

Bridget est devant notre porte. Elle porte une tenue assez flashy pour quelqu'un qui vient juste d'ouvrir les yeux.

– Oh maman, ce rose bonbon ! C'est too much, vraiment !

Vic est assise elle aussi, à présent. Elle a l'air très surprise mais je me demande si c'est la tenue de sa mère qui l'étonne ou le fait qu'elle soit venue chez James.

– Je voulais les essayer avant le prochain DJ set ! s'exclame Bridget en montrant ses habits. J'ai besoin de m'imprégner des réactions.

– Ben, imprègne-toi bien de la mienne, commente Vic en faisant une grimace épouvantable.

– Au fait, vous êtes ici pour quelle raison ? Vous n'êtes pas venue m'enlever Vic, j'espère ? je demande, un peu inquiète.

– Non… Vous n'avez pas entendu Luna la chanteuse ? me répond la mère de Vic. J'ai une *surpriiise* ! Yan et moi, on vient vous kidnapper toutes les deux. On vous a trop négligées à cause de notre travail et on veut réparer ce comportement inqualifiable. Faites vos valises car on vous ramène à la maison pour vos trois derniers jours ensemble !

Ma copine pousse un cri de joie en sautant du lit et je l'accompagne.

On retrouve Yan au breakfast en compagnie de mes parents et James. Il fait écouter quelques

morceaux de sa composition à notre hôte qui hoche la tête en cadence, comme s'il assistait à des DJ sets tous les matins !

Nous quittons la maison de James après avoir subi les mille recommandations de ma mère. On a déjà fixé un rendez-vous avec Lou. Nous devons nous retrouver avec Margaux, Clark et Tim à l'atelier le lendemain pour nous consacrer aux ultimes préparatifs de l'exposition.

Yan a pris sa voiture. Il a relevé ses cheveux longs et les a cachés sous une casquette. Comme il porte une tenue classique en jean, il ressemble presque à un père normal, loin du musicien aperçu dans les studios d'Abbey Road.

– Direction Cyberdog, rugit-il dès qu'on monte derrière lui. Le magasin le plus branché et le plus crazy de Londres !

En arrivant devant la boutique, je comprends immédiatement pourquoi cette boutique est à voir. Elle est gardée par deux statues de robots gigantesques.

Une musique de folie et des flashs de lumière fluo s'en échappent. En y entrant, on plonge dans le noir… et dans le futur ! Seuls les néons et les cheveux fluorescents des vendeurs sont visibles.

– T'as vu, c'est dingue, non ? hurle Vic pour couvrir le bruit assourdissant martelé par les baffles de la boutique. Mon père est déjà venu y faire un set !

Effectivement, au premier sous-sol, un DJ est en pleine session sur ses platines et Yan nous abandonne pour le rejoindre. Vic, Bridget et moi on fait un tour au rayon des cosmétiques où sont vendues TOUTES les colorations possibles pour les cheveux déclinées dans TOUTES les teintes ! L'un des vendeurs a tellement de piercings et de trucs bizarres qui lui décorent le visage sous ses cheveux rouges que j'ose à peine le regarder…

On se promène dans la partie vêtements. On y croise des robes cosmiques, des leggings argentés, dorés ou en latex, ainsi que des tee-shirts avec affichage LED incorporé, qui véhiculent des messages.

Je ressors de là avec un magnifique vernis à ongles fluo pour Justine et un feutre noir phosphorescent pour Ulysse afin qu'il puisse dessiner dans le noir. Je prends le même pour moi, d'ailleurs.

En sortant de Cyberdog, mes yeux clignotent encore un long moment.

Yan et Bridget nous entraînent vers Hyde Park pour profiter du seul magnifique rayon de soleil de la semaine… ou presque ! C'est le printemps partout, mais à Londres les nuages font pas mal de résistance.

On loue deux voiturettes à pédales et on passe un long moment à parcourir les allées. Vic me fait beaucoup rire. Parfois, j'ai l'impression que c'est elle la plus âgée dans sa famille.

– Vous allez trooop vite ! hurle-t-elle à ses parents alors qu'ils s'éloignent un peu.

– Vous n'avez qu'à nous rattraper, lui répond Yan tandis que Bridget nous fait au revoir.

On pédale comme deux folles pour remonter à leur hauteur.

Vic ne peut s'empêcher de crier :

– Attention, vous n'avez pas de casque. Papa, ralentiiis !

– Même pas en rêve ! lui rétorque Bridget en riant. Hors de question de perdre.

Vic et moi, on finit le sprint cent fois plus crevées que Yan et Bridget. Pour se faire pardonner, ils nous emmènent déjeuner dans un pub où on ne mange que des desserts. Je savoure une part d'apple pie absolument délicieuse ainsi qu'un gros morceau de plum duff, une sorte de pudding aux prunes, à tomber par terre.

Vic, elle, préfère goûter à la cherry pie et à une énorme part de cake arrosée de lemon curd, une crème au citron.

En nous levant de table, ma copine et moi, on se sent… lourdes !

– Un peu d'exercice physique pour éliminer ? propose Bridget en quittant le restaurant.

On finit donc à la patinoire de Somerset House.

La dernière fois que j'ai chaussé des patins, j'étais dans le Sud-Ouest[1], j'explique à Vic en enlevant mes chaussures. Avec des pros ! J'ai dû prier le dieu Glaçon pour qu'il m'aide à rester debout… Tu patines bien, toi ?

– Bof, me répond Vic.

Une fois sur la glace, je comprends qu'on n'a pas la même définition du verbe patiner.

– Euh. Bof, ce sont des initiales pour toi ? je lui crie alors qu'elle fait sa deuxième pirouette. Ça signifie « Bien Ou Fabuleusement » ?

Vic sourit. Je jette un œil à sa mère. Elle est encore plus douée !

1. Lire *Quatre sœurs et un Noël inoubliable.*

Je ressemble à un oisillon tombé du nid avec mes petits glissés maladroits mais Vic saisit ma main et je retrouve un peu d'assurance. Quand le morceau de techno composé par Yan retentit sur la piste, je ne reconnais plus ma copine ! Elle se lance dans une choré endiablée et je découvre l'une de ses facettes qu'elle m'avait bien cachée !

– Bon, j'avoue, j'en fais quatre heures par semaine, lâche-t-elle avec un grand sourire. Et ma mère a été pro.

Bridget me fait un petit signe avant d'exécuter une double pirouette arrière… Quelle famille !

Mon amie habite Gilston Road, dans le quartier de Chelsea. Son immeuble recouvert de briques est le seul bâtiment un peu haut de cette rue.

La porte de l'appartement à peine franchie, le ton est donné. On a l'impression d'être dans un studio d'enregistrement.

Il y a deux claviers dans l'entrée, une console de mixage énorme dans le salon et au moins trois guitares posées contre le mur de la salle à manger. Des affiches de concerts et des photos encadrées sont accrochées un peu partout. La chambre de Vic est recouverte de posters divers et variés. La plupart font référence à la musique… et au patin à glace !

– Bienvenue dans mon univers, s'exclame mon amie en s'affalant sur son lit.

Je lui souris, heureuse de découvrir son monde perso. En installant nos affaires dans son armoire, on reparle de notre rendez-vous dans l'atelier de Clark, d'autant que Lou vient de m'envoyer des Snaps montrant l'espace mode. On y voit les Excentriques de Margaux et nos combis, suspendues devant les peintures et les sculptures.

– J'espère qu'il y aura du monde, murmure Vic en regardant les photos.

– Lou a lancé l'événement sur Facebook, Margaux a alerté tout son réseau à l'école. Les gens vont se déplacer, c'est sûr.

De la musique résonne depuis le salon. Yan s'est mis à la guitare. Il joue une mélodie tandis que Bridget chantonne. Vic s'assoit devant l'un des claviers et tout en interprétant le même air que son père, elle fait entendre sa voix.

Assise dans le canapé, j'en ai des frissons tant le résultat est harmonieux. J'avais presque oublié combien Vic m'avait fait vibrer avec ses chansons cet été[1]...

J'applaudis à tout rompre lorsque leur improvisation s'achève.

– J'adore *Children forever*, le morceau que j'ai composé avec tes sœurs, lance Yan. J'espère de tout cœur que l'association Enfants du monde à laquelle je cède tous mes droits va gagner beaucoup d'argent avec ce titre. Je veux le lancer officiellement ces prochains jours.

– Il faudrait trouver un endroit sympa pour le mixer, déclare Bridget.

1. Lire *Quatre sœurs en colo.*

Cette phrase allume mon ampoule à idées. Je regarde Vic.

– Oui ? « Qu'est-ce qu'il se passe-t-il » dans ta tête ? me lance-t-elle en riant. Tu as une révélation ?

– Le lieu sympa, Vic… Pense à Clark…, je murmure.

– Hum, continue mon amie qui n'a toujours pas saisi où je voulais en venir. Tu as subi un refroidissement du cerveau à la patinoire, avoue. Tu es tombée et on ne l'a pas vu ? Tu as une bosse sur le crâne ?

– Je te parle de l'endroit où ton père pourrait mixer son nouveau morceau, je chuchote à son oreille. L'atelier de Clark, ce week-end, ce serait trop cool ! DJ Bryan qui offre un concert improvisé, ça ferait un sacré buzz pour l'expo.

– Mais c'est GÉNIAL ! hurle Vic en me ruinant le tympan gauche.

Dans le quart d'heure qui suit, mon amie perd tout sourire. Elle a tenté de convaincre Yan et Bridget de réaliser « un méga DJ set dans un atelier branché le week-end prochain » mais ni l'un ni l'autre n'a l'air de trouver l'idée géniale.

– Évidemment, vous avez TOUJOURS autre chose à faire, grommelle-t-elle en mettant le couvert dans la cuisine. Pour une fois que je vous demande quelque chose…

– On ne va pas improviser un concert alors qu'on croule sous le travail, Vic ! s'exclame Yan, excédé. Sois réaliste.

Mon amie se réfugie dans un silence boudeur. Je la regarde tout en réfléchissant à une nouvelle stratégie. L'ampoule à idées se rallume dans ma tête. Franchement, patiner, même mal, m'aère grave lc cerveau et il devient super actif, du coup !

– Ce qui serait génial, c'est que votre nouveau mix soit lancé quand mes petites sœurs sont encore là, je déclare, mine de rien. Ce serait cool pour l'asso Enfants du monde que les deux chanteuses de *Children forever* en assurent la promo en direct !

Bridget approuve totalement mon idée.

– Laure a raison, Yan. Le buzz peut vraiment se faire comme ça. Un lieu, un set, mais surtout des voix d'enfants en live, mêlées à la mienne.

– Mais, vous partez bientôt, non ? me demande Yan en fronçant les sourcils.

– Ben, mardi matin. Il reste le week-end…

Vic a retrouvé son sourire, elle le cache derrière sa longue mèche de cheveux et en passant près de moi, elle me donne un coup de coude super discret.

– Oui, *Children forever* pourrait être mixé avec les voix des deux petites en live, réfléchit Yan. Ce serait bien pour l'asso, en effet.

Il sort de la cuisine tout en discutant avec Bridget. Ma copine me montre ses mains où elle a croisé tous les doigts en même temps.

– Vic, il est où cet atelier dont tu as parlé ? Il faudrait peut-être qu'on aille repérer les lieux, lance Yan depuis le salon. Je ne te promets rien mais on peut aller voir.

Vic sautille sur place en me prenant les mains.

– On a gagné grâce à toi, chuchote-t-elle, enthousiaste. C'est trop cool pour l'expo de Clark et Tim !

– Et sympa pour Enfants du monde, aussi ! j'ajoute. On fait coup double.

Coup triple, même, puisque je pense au bonheur de Lisa et Luna qui risquent de se produire devant un public. Quelle expérience inoubliable !

Je m'approche de mon amie et lui dépose une énorme bise sur la joue. Elle vient de parler de « Clark et Tim » à la fois, ce qui signifie qu'elle est passée à l'épisode suivant en ce qui concerne sa love story.

Je suis super fière d'elle.

Il me reste à suivre son exemple…

James and Clark

– Viiiic ? Hurry up, préparez-vous ! On a exactement douze minuuuutes trente.

J'ouvre les yeux. Je mets quelques secondes avant de me rappeler que je ne suis plus chez James et que c'est la raison pour laquelle le décor a changé autour de moi.

– Viiic ! Tu as entendu ? Il reste douze minutes vingt-deux.

Une tornade violette vient d'ouvrir les volets. Je comprends mieux pourquoi Vic passe son temps à porter du noir.

À force de voir les couleurs vives des tenues de sa mère, elle a dû faire une allergie…

Une musique retentit dans tout l'appartement et on entend Yan chanter d'une voix grave tandis que Bridget fait des vocalises super aiguës.

– Mes parents sont complètement barrés, j'avais oublié de te le préciser, soupire Vic en bâillant. Le matin, ils ne peuvent pas s'empêcher de faire du bruit.

– Il reste dix minutes quinze ! chantonne Bridget en passant en courant devant nous.

– C'est tous les matins comme ça ? je chuchote alors qu'on s'assoit à table. Ta mère fait un jogging dans l'appart et ton père commence à mixer ?

Vic agite la tête de haut en bas d'un air grave.

– Moi, je suis plutôt du genre escargot et ils me rendent dingue, m'explique-t-elle. J'ai droit à des annonces en mode « arrivée dans une gare », des comptes à rebours, des séances abdos fessiers ou même des mini concerts. Là, ils font un mix juste pour toi.

Yan circule devant nous dans le salon. Il a un serre-tête et porte une salopette noire qui colle parfaitement avec la partie fashion de l'exposition de Clark. Il a arrêté la musique mais sa bouche lui sert de beat box. Bridget, elle, vocalise (pour chauffer sa voix, m'explique Vic en levant les yeux au ciel) tout en faisant quelques mouvements de gym.

Je souris non-stop en prenant le petit-déjeuner. Je ne me sens pas trop dépaysée par rapport à chez moi, même si dans la famille Juin ce sont plutôt les 4 L qui produisent des sons !

Finalement, trente et une minutes chrono après notre réveil, Vic et moi sommes dans la voiture de ses parents.

Bridget a tenu à garder sa tenue flash « juste pour voir si elle s'accorde avec la lumière de l'atelier ».

Yan met la musique à fond avant de démarrer et pendant le trajet Bridget et lui se trémoussent comme deux ados sur leurs sièges. Vic leur demande de baisser le son pour qu'on puisse un peu parler, elle et moi.

– Tu ne trouves pas mes parents trop zarb ? me demande-t-elle d'un air inquiet.

– Arrête ! Je les adoore ! je lâche en riant. Il y a des tonnes d'ados qui rêveraient d'avoir un père et une mère aussi cools que les tiens.

Vic me sourit, rassurée, avant d'affirmer :

– J'ai une chance folle de t'avoir rencontrée à la colo. Dire que je ne voulais pas y aller…

On évoque nos souvenirs de cet été. Vic rit beaucoup mais alors que son père se gare devant l'atelier de Clark, elle retrouve sa mine triste de la veille. Je lui serre la main en murmurant :

– On laisse tomber la déprime, toi et moi. Le monde est plein de BG qui nous attendent !

J'arrive à lui arracher un sourire. Clark nous ouvre et les parents de Vic se présentent.

– Hello, lance Yan. Je suis le père de Vic. Elle nous a parlé de ton atelier et de ta volonté d'exposer tes œuvres. Puisque ma femme et moi sommes musiciens, nous avons pensé que si nous venions mixer notre dernier morceau pendant ton expo, on associerait nos performances artistiques.

– Tu nous laisses entrer pour qu'on t'explique ? demande Bridget.

Clark est planté devant sa porte et il ouvre de grands yeux.

Il a encore la bouche ouverte cinq minutes plus tard et il a du mal à dire autre chose que « It's amazing »… C'est un grand fan de leur musique et il connaît pratiquement TOUS les titres du duo.

En quelques minutes, les parents de Vic ont fait le tour de l'atelier.

– J'adooore tes peintures ! s'exclame Bridget. Tu as un sens inné de la couleur.

– J'étais sûre que ma mère allait dire ça, me chuchote Vic. C'était fichu si Clark était un peintre du noir et blanc.

Pendant que Yan repère l'endroit où placer sa table de mixage, Clark explique à Bridget ses techniques de peinture.

– Pour moi, c'est OK, annonce finalement le père de Vic. Si tu es d'accord, je lance l'événement sur ma page Facebook et mon manager s'occupe de la promo. À J moins 1, ça va faire un sacré buzz, je pense !

Clark est en apesanteur…

En repartant, les parents de Vic croisent Tim et Margaux qui viennent, eux aussi, prêter main-forte en cette veille d'expo. Lou débarque quelques minutes après.

Clark, encore surexcité par le passage des DJ Bryan, se lance dans de grandes explications.

– Il y aura un DJ set ici, explique-t-il, des trémolos dans la voix. Vic's DJ Bryan's daughter !

Il saisit Vic par les épaules et mon amie ne respire plus. Finalement, elle se love dans les bras du peintre, l'air de rien.

– Voilà, je me suis offert un petit kif perso, me raconte-t-elle un peu plus tard, j'ai goûté à la douceur des bras de Clark. Je peux tirer un trait sur mon histoire.

Je la regarde, surprise. Vic a cet air décidé que je lui connais. Je crois qu'elle vient DÉFINITIVEMENT de dire adieu à sa love story.

C'est ce que je dois faire moi aussi.

Je prends mon portable et je parcours les derniers SMS que j'ai échangés avec Alex. Je les sélectionne tous et je clique sur « supprimer ». Pour moi aussi, c'est fini.

Je n'ai pas le temps de m'apitoyer sur mon sort puisque tout le monde s'agite autour de moi. Clark dirige les opérations tout en plaçant ses toiles.

– Si James voyait son petit-fils, c'est évident qu'il arrêterait de le critiquer, me chuchote Vic. C'est un vrai pro de la peinture ET de l'organisation.

– Justement, c'est ce qu'il faut faire, je renchéris. Amener James ici et lui ouvrir les yeux. Il doit arrêter de voir Clark comme un « eccentric guy » !

En moins de dix minutes, on a rejoint la maison de James.

– Ooooh ! s'exclame-t-il en ouvrant sa porte. *Le* petite famille Juin est déjà partie. Tu voulais les voir ?

– Pas du tout, je déclare. C'est de vous dont on a besoin à l'atelier de Clark.

– Oui, ajoute Vic en hochant la tête. Il nous faut un avis extérieur sur l'agencement de l'expo et justement, vous êtes dispo.

James fronce les sourcils mais devant nos airs déterminés, il finit par nous suivre.

Clark est en train d'accrocher ma bannière à l'extérieur quand nous arrivons et il semble très surpris de voir son grand-père.

James l'est bien plus quand il pénètre dans l'atelier.

Lou et Margaux ont fini d'aménager le fashion corner et Tim place ses dernières petites sculptures dans l'espace expo. L'ensemble a pris sa forme définitive et les peintures de Clark sont éclatantes de couleurs au milieu de l'atelier.

– Oooh ! Ça ressemble à… *un* vraie expo, murmure James, admiratif.

– You know, Vic's parents are going to play live music here ! Just for the exhibition !

Clark s'adresse à son grand-père, un sourire éclatant aux lèvres.

– Oui, ce sera un grand événement, déclare Vic d'un ton professionnel. Quand mes parents font un set, ça déchire.

– Ah, « ça déchire », répète James en hochant la tête.

Vic et moi rejoignons Lou et Margaux pour préparer des étiquettes de prix tandis que Clark parcourt l'atelier avec James. Tim se joint à eux.

Après le départ de son grand-père, Clark a l'air super ému. Il nous explique combien il lui a été difficile d'avouer sa love story avec Tim à sa famille.

– Pour mon grand-père, c'est très compliqué. Je suis un artiste, et en plus je suis gay… Not easy to accept. Je suis très heureux qu'il vienne ici aujourd'hui.

Vic sourit autant que moi. Faire venir James était une bonne idée !

– Love is all we need ! chuchote Clark en conclusion.

Vic s'empare d'un micro imaginaire, se place sur l'une des marches de l'escalier et, de sa voix magnifique, elle se met à chanter :

– *Nothing you can make that can't be made.*
No one you can save that can't be saved.
Nothing you can do, but you can learn
How to be you in time
It's easy.
All you need is love

All you need is love, love.
Love is all you need[1].

1. *All You Need Is Love,* Lennon/McCartney, Sony ATV Music Publishing, 1967.

On reste tous scotchés sur place comme à chaque fois que Vic chante.

– En hommage aux Beatles, explique-t-elle en faisant une révérence face à nos applaudissements.

En fin de matinée, on déjeune tous ensemble dans l'atelier de Clark qui a tenu à aller nous chercher des Indian wraps, de délicieux sandwichs roulés au curry, au food truck du bout de la rue. Au cours du déjeuner, Margaux nous parle de son école de mode et Lou nous explique que Max envisage de venir vivre à Londres si elle s'installe ici définitivement.

– Mais, je croyais que vous étiez fâchés à ce sujet! je lance, étonnée.

– Ne cherche pas à comprendre, les mecs sont strange parfois, commente ma sœur. Max m'envoie des messages d'amour toutes les dix minutes depuis hier. Il ne peut pas vivre sans moi.

Vic soupire et me murmure :

– Tu crois qu'un jour, un garçon abandonnera tout pour nous ?

– Ne t'emballe pas, je lui réponds. Max n'est pas près de se faire hara-kiri pour ma sœur, non plus.

On se met à rire toutes les deux. Lou qui m'a entendue me tire la langue et finit par rire, elle aussi.

L'après-midi passe à la vitesse de l'éclair puisque les visiteurs se succèdent à l'atelier. James crée une deuxième belle surprise en revenant… les bras chargés !

– J'ai pensé qu'*un tea party* serait *la bienveniou* pendant *la* expo.

Il dispose des boîtes de thé sur la table de l'atelier et des sachets de scones et Clark le remercie chaleureusement. Ensuite, c'est le reste de la famille Juin qui vient visiter l'atelier.

– Coucou Clark ! crie Luna en entrant. On est venus t'aider.

– Surtout, tu ne touches à rien, lui ordonne Lou, déjà inquiète.

– No problemo, on est surtout là pour une « répète » avec Yan et Bridget, lâche Lisa qui se prend de plus en plus pour une vedette. Excuse-nous mais on a un DJ set, nous, demain.

En effet, les parents de Vic ne tardent pas à revenir et, tandis que les Steph au carré s'extasient devant les œuvres, les DJ Bryan installent leur matériel.

C'est très amusant d'entendre les deux petites L répéter. Leurs voix se mêlent tout naturellement à celle de Bridget. On dirait presque qu'elles ont fait ça toute leur vie !

Yan nous annonce que son mini concert est programmé sur tous les réseaux sociaux.

– Il y aura beaucoup de monde d'après notre manager, déclare Bridget.

– Est-ce que William et Kate seront là ? demande Lisa, les yeux brillants.

– Ils sont très occupés, tu sais, rétorque Yan en souriant.

Lisa secoue la tête d'un air désapprobateur. Si le couple princier ne se déplace pas demain, il va dégringoler dans son estime, c'est certain…

En fin de soirée, Yan décide de nous entraîner dans un pub à la mode où il a l'habitude de jouer. Les Steph au carré préfèrent ramener mes petites sœurs se reposer avant leur show du lendemain et pour une fois, elles ne protestent pas.

– On ne sait jamais, si le prince et la princesse sont là, il faut qu'on soit au top ! explique Lisa à Luna.

Lou, Clark, Tim et Margaux se joignent à Vic et moi, et on assiste au petit concert d'un DJ ami de Yan et Bridget. L'ambiance est électrique. Vic et moi, on est déchaînées !

Vers vingt-deux heures, Bridget sonne le rappel. J'ai envie de danser jusqu'au bout de la nuit mais une expo super importante nous attend.

– Il est presque déjà demain, bâille Vic alors qu'on se glisse dans nos lits un peu plus tard.

– Oui, demain moins quinze minutes, je murmure presque endormie.

Can't wait for tomorrow !

D-Day

Ce matin, nul besoin de tornade violette ou d'ouragan rose pour nous réveiller ! Malgré l'heure tardive de notre coucher, Vic et moi, on ouvre les yeux avant huit heures, tout naturellement.

– J'ai encore rêvé d'Alex, je déclare en m'étirant. Il se mariait avec Elsa.

– Tu étais invitée à leur mariage ? demande Vic intéressée. Tu étais leur témoin ? Et la mariée, elle avait une jolie robe ?

Je hausse les épaules.

– Il faut vraiment que j'arrête de penser à lui ! je m'exclame. Tu crois que dans dix ans, j'en rêverai encore ?

– Dans dix ans, c'est TOI qui te marieras avec un méga BG et on fera la fête jusqu'au bout de la nuit.

Je ris tout en me levant.

– Laisse-moi quelques années de plus pour le mariage… Par contre, c'est clair, dès que je suis décidée, je t'invite !

On se dépêche de s'habiller et de déjeuner pour rejoindre au plus vite l'atelier de Clark. On passe d'abord par la maison de James puisque nous sommes chargées de transporter de nouvelles boîtes de thé et de gâteaux secs. Mon père a l'air fatigué.

– Tes deux sœurs en sont au niveau 8 de l'échelle de Richter de l'excitation. Encore un palier et c'est l'explosion…

– Avec ou sans tsunami ? je demande en souriant.

On entend des rires qui s'échappent de l'étage et une cavalcade de pas retentit dans les escaliers.

– *Et l'eau* ! crie Luna qui a oublié toute prudence vocale. *A we dou you dou* ?

– Vous voulez des autographes ? demande Lisa, qui, elle, continue à préserver sa voix. On s'entraîne, Luna et moi, pour ce soir. On est super au point.

Elle nous tend un bout de papier sur lequel elle a écrit son prénom de la façon la plus artistique possible. C'est illisible…

– Waouh, commente Vic, sourire aux lèvres, c'est encore mieux que les autographes de mes parents. Je peux le garder pour l'encadrer ?

Lisa accepte (dans sa très grande générosité) et elle m'en prépare un « pour qu'il n'y ait aucune jalousie »…

Quand on arrive à l'atelier, Vic et moi, l'excitation est aussi à son comble. Tim tente de réparer un spot qui vient de lâcher tandis que Clark avale café sur café.

– Je vais ouvrir l'expo dans moins de cinq minutes, déclare-t-il, nerveux.

– Don't worry, lâche au bout de l'atelier une voix que l'on reconnaît sans peine. « Tout va bien se passer », as the French say !

James est déjà là. Il a préparé du thé.

– Vous pouvez m'aider au service, lance-t-il dès qu'il nous aperçoit, ma copine et moi.

Quand Clark ouvre la porte, Margaux et Lou sont prêtes, elles aussi, à accueillir les visiteurs. Il y a pas mal de personnes et on est tous super contents de les voir !

Vic et moi, on rejoint James au service du thé et des « *petites* gâteaux *sèches* ». J'observe attentivement les premières personnes qui découvrent l'expo. Elles s'attardent aussi bien sur les peintures que sur les sculptures ou dans le fashion corner.

– Ce ne sont pas de simples curieux, me chuchote Lou. Tu as vu ce monsieur là-bas ? Il a demandé à Clark s'il avait le droit de prendre des photos. C'est la preuve qu'il aime, non ?

J'acquiesce tout en observant ma sœur qui discute avec une jeune femme. Elles parlent mode parce que Lou lui montre nos combis. J'ai à peine le temps de servir deux thés. Ma sœur lève discrètement un pouce en ma direction. Visiblement, elle vient de faire sa première vente !

– May I have a cup of tea, please ?

– Would you like milk ?

– No thanks, I don't like it.

Je remplis la tasse du garçon qui me fait face. Il est à peine plus âgé que Vic et moi. Il a une

grande mèche bleue qui lui cache les yeux et un piercing dans le nez.

– I'm Tim's brother. My name is Abel. Are you Laure or Vic ?

Je tends une tasse à mon interlocuteur tandis que Vic se rapproche.

– I'm Vic and this is Laure, explique-t-elle en me désignant. What do you think about this exhibition ?

Abel engage la conversation et je lui souris avant de me décaler. Je laisse ma copine discuter tranquillement et je rejoins James qui circule avec des assiettes de scones. Au passage, il parle aux visiteurs et les entraîne dès qu'ils ont une question vers Clark ou Tim.

En fin de matinée, l'exposition a accueilli cinquante-huit visiteurs. Clark discute avec deux hommes depuis plus d'une heure. James n'arrête pas de regarder dans leur direction. Il finit par me murmurer :

– C'est peut-être pour acheter *un* toile ?

– Ce serait trop le bonheur ! je lâche, enthousiaste.

James fronce les sourcils et tandis que je cherche une traduction, Vic se dirige vers moi, radieuse.

– Tiens, mais tu étais là toi aussi ? je lance, ironique. Je ne savais pas que tu participais à l'expo.

– Arrête ! lance Vic en essayant de garder son sérieux. J'ai juste bavardé un moment avec Abel et…

– Un moment qui a duré a long long time…

Vic rougit un peu et je me mets à rire. Au moins, une chose est certaine, Clark est largement aux oubliettes ! D'ailleurs, celui-ci vient de serrer la main à ses deux interlocuteurs qui repartent et il rejoint son grand-père avec un grand sourire.

– Mes peintures les intéressent et ils veulent les exposer dans *un* galerie *in London center*. Ah, j'oubliais… J'ai aussi vendu une toile !

Je tends ma main et Clark me fait un check géant avant de retourner discuter avec d'autres visiteurs.

Quand les DJ Bryan arrivent en fin d'après-midi, l'atelier est plein à craquer. Le bilan de la journée est super positif. Tim et Clark ont eu un contact sérieux pour une galerie, Margaux est en grande discussion avec une styliste prête à la prendre en stage et Lou et moi, on a vendu trois combis !

Vic, quant à elle, connaît la vie d'Abel depuis sa naissance… et elle sourit non-stop. Elle ne voit même pas ses parents s'installer tant son interlocuteur la passionne. Par contre, elle remarque forcément mes deux sœurs qui font une entrée… fracassante !

Les deux petites L ont voulu s'habiller pour la circonstance et, vu la tête de ma mère, la lutte fut rude… Lisa est vêtue d'un ensemble en jean à la manière de Yan mais sa chemise est de taille XL vu le nombre de revers aux manches ! Elle porte d'énormes lunettes de soleil vert canard, qui lui donnent un look de star assez drôle. Luna a enfilé une combinaison qui appartient à Lisa. Elle a voulu imiter nos customisations puisqu'il y a des

paillettes de haut en bas ! Ses couettes sont complètement de travers sur sa tête et elle arbore des solaires rouges pétantes, assorties à la couleur de ses joues.

– Niveau 10 sur l'échelle de Richter, annonce calmement mon père en arrivant devant moi. On vient de créer un palier de plus, juste pour tes sœurs.

– Pour les tenues de scène, qui est responsable ? demande Lou en souriant.

– Pas moi ! s'écrie ma mère qui nous a rejoints. J'ai bien essayé de leur proposer deux jolis ensembles mais elles voulaient absolument être dans la « fashion vibe » dont tu parles tout le temps, Lou. En plus, elles ont trouvé de vieilles lunettes chez James.

Les deux petites L nous rejoignent. Il y a de plus en plus de monde dans l'atelier et le bruit monte en puissance tandis que les DJ Bryan font divers branchements.

– Je ressemble à une vraie chanteuse, non ? crie Luna qui sautille sur place comme si elle était parcourue par un courant électrique.

– William ou Kate sont là ? demande Lisa qui regarde partout fébrilement.

– Pour l'instant, zéro pointé au niveau famille royale, explique Lou en remettant les couettes de Luna en place. Par contre, côté visiteurs et donc spectateurs, on fait le plein.

Les deux petites L s'approchent de la console de mixage et en « professionnelles de la profession », elles s'imprègnent de l'atmosphère des lieux. Bridget a revêtu un ensemble bleu canard brillant qui s'accorde parfaitement avec les lunettes de Lisa !

– D'un point de vue couleurs, c'est désastreux, lâche Vic qui me rejoint. Si ma mère chantait comme elle s'habille, ce serait la cata.

Je me mets à rire et ma copine grimace. Très vite les premières notes du clavier de Yan se font entendre tandis que Bridget entraîne mes deux petites sœurs dans le studio de Clark, à l'étage, pour une ultime répétition. James continue inlassablement à servir du thé et des gâteaux, il paraît lui aussi chargé d'électricité !

Vers dix-sept heures, Luna, Lisa et Bridget font leur apparition sous les projecteurs. Le brouhaha qui régnait dans l'atelier laisse place au silence. Yan s'empare d'un micro. Son dis-

cours en français est traduit simultanément par un… James rayonnant !

– Amis visiteurs, fans d'art et de musique, vous êtes ici pour admirer les œuvres de créateurs. Que ce soit au niveau peinture, sculpture ou mode, les jeunes talents réunis dans cet atelier ont su vous captiver, vous convaincre, vous charmer. Je vous propose de les applaudir avec toute l'énergie qu'ils méritent !

Le bruit est assourdissant dans l'atelier. Tout le monde se met à taper des mains et à siffler en même temps. Luna se bouche les oreilles, patiemment. Quand le silence revient enfin, le père de Vic ajoute :

– Pour clôturer cette expo formidable, je vous propose de sampler le titre-phare de mon dernier disque. *Children forever* est un morceau qui me tient particulièrement à cœur. Tous ses droits seront reversés à une association humanitaire pour les enfants du monde. C'est pourquoi Bridget et moi tenons à l'interpréter avec deux voix prometteuses. Je vous présente Lisa et Luna, deux petites L françaises qui ont déjà des ailes, croyez-moi !

Nos parents sont carrément en apnée quand les premières notes du morceau retentissent. Bridget chante « Chidren we're always here for you » et mes deux petites sœurs lancent leur « you you… » l'une après l'autre, de façon quasi professionnelle. Pendant tout le refrain, elles alignent leurs voix sur celle de Bridget. C'est trop beau.

Je me sens si fière d'elles à la fin que j'en ai les larmes aux yeux ! Je ne suis pas la seule puisque maman s'essuie la joue et que Lou met ses lunettes de soleil…

Les DJ Bryan, Lisa et Luna sont ovationnés pendant de longues minutes. Mes sœurs agitent leurs mains un peu à la façon de deux princesses saluant la foule à leur fenêtre.

Ensuite, Yan mixe quelques morceaux de sa composition et l'atelier devient un dance floor. Lisa surveille régulièrement la porte d'entrée en espérant que Kate ou William finisse par la pousser.

– Tu sais, souvent le couple princier envoie un émissaire qui filme les événements à sa place et les lui projette plus tard, au palais, sur grand écran, je finis par lui chuchoter devant son air anxieux. Tu vois ce bonhomme là-bas, avec son portable ? Je suis sûre qu'il fait partie de l'équipe royale et qu'il était là pour ça.

Lisa observe l'inconnu en face de nous, qui semble apprécier la musique et filme les DJ Bryan.

– Oui, vu son costume il travaille à Buckingham, c'est sûr, admet-elle. Je suis rassurée de savoir que la famille princière va nous écouter, Luna et moi.

Je lui souris en la serrant contre moi. Elle prend ma main pour m'entraîner sur la piste. Luna saute sur place non-stop depuis le début du concert. Vic me rejoint.

– C'est carrément dingue ! me crie-t-elle au creux de l'oreille. Je ne suis pas près d'oublier cette journée.

– Parce que c'est la journée pendant laquelle a eu lieu l'exposition la plus réussie de tout Londres ? je lui demande en souriant.

– Parce que toi et moi, on est allées ensemble au bout d'un projet de ouf ! hurle Vic en m'attrapant les deux mains pour me faire danser. Et que du début à la fin, il n'y a pas eu un seul raté.

Toute la famille Juin est à présent sur la piste. C'est la première fois que je vois mon père bouger sur de la musique. Énorme !

Londres, tu nous as tous ensorcelés, c'est clair !

Souvenirs of London

Ce matin, alors que j'ouvre un œil, je réalise que je ne suis pas dans un lit et que quelqu'un tire sur la couette qui est censée me tenir chaud.

Une fois VRAIMENT réveillée, je constate que je suis allongée sur le canapé dans le studio de Clark.

Ma voleuse de couverture est Vic qui dort, tête bêche, par rapport à moi et s'agrippe à la couette comme si sa vie en dépendait!

– Vic, qu'est-ce qu'on fait là ? je murmure encore endormie alors que mes souvenirs se recalent petit à petit au bon endroit dans mon cerveau embrumé.

– Moi, je rêvais avant que tu décides de me jeter dans le froid matinal en t'appropriant la couette, me répond Vic en bâillant. Je ne dormirai PLUS JAMAIS dans le même lit que toi, tu es infernale !

Je me mets à rire en la poussant avec mes pieds.

– Je te signale qu'on n'est pas dans un lit, my dear.

– Ne change pas de sujet de conversation, Laure Juin. Tu es VRAIMENT INFERNALE !

Évidemment, on finit par une bataille d'oreillers monumentale.

– Tu sais que c'est la première fois que mes parents me laissent passer la nuit chez un garçon ? me chuchote Vic quand on se calme enfin.

– Moi aussi ! j'avoue en riant. Mais Clark est un peu comme un grand frère ou un cousin, non ? En plus, tout le monde a vu que son cœur était pris.

– Bouououh ! s'écrie Vic en faisant mine de pleurer. C'est bien ça le problème…

– Dis donc toi, je lui rétorque, la mine sévère. Il me semble bien que tu avais tourné la page, non ?

– Mais oui, me rassure ma copine, je plaisantais pour Clark. C'est juste…

L'intéressé qui dormait dans la pièce voisine apparaît à ce moment-là devant le canapé.

– Hello girls ! lance-t-il. Did you sleep well ?

Comme elle était en train de parler de lui, Vic rougit tellement qu'elle s'enfouit sous la couette. Pour la sauver d'une mort par étouffement, je change de sujet et j'évoque avec Clark la soirée d'hier.

– Pourquoi a-t-on passé la nuit ici, Vic et moi ? je lui demande. Je me souviens juste que je suis venue me reposer dans ton studio assez tard hier soir.

– Exactly ! explique Clark. Vic t'a suivie et quand je suis monté avec Bryan, vous dormiez trop bien. On n'a pas voulu vous réveiller…

On se retrouve tous les trois devant un breakfast qui ressemble à celui que je prends chaque matin en France. Clark nous sert un bol de lait et des céréales en continuant à commenter l'exposition de la veille. Son sourire est radieux dès qu'il évoque ses deux toiles vendues et la possibilité qu'il a d'exposer ses futures peintures dans une galerie du quartier super branché de Soho.

– This exhibition was a great idea ! I love you, girls ! s'exclame Clark avant de descendre dans son atelier.

– Il faudrait juste qu'il arrête de changer d'avis tous les matins, chuchote Vic. Does he love boys or girls ?

– Arrête de faire celle qui ne comprend pas, je lance en riant.

– Coucou les filles, c'est moi ! Vous êtes prêtes ?

Une tornade jaune fluo vient de débarquer.

– Maman, je t'ai déjà dit que trop de couleurs tuent la couleur ! proteste Vic. Mais qu'est-ce que tu fais en jogging d'abord ?

– Ce n'est pas un jogging, précise Bridget, horrifiée par la confusion. Je porte ma nouvelle tenue de fitness parce que j'ai fait une séance d'abdos avant de venir vous chercher. Et je vous signale qu'il vous reste dix-huit minutes vingt-et-une avant notre rendez-vous !

– Quel rendez-vous ? demande Vic qui bâille à s'en décrocher la mâchoire.

– On retrouve la famille de Laure devant chez Harrod's à dix heures, annonce Bridget. C'est la journée London souvenirs !

Vic et moi on a le même regard au même moment. « Souvenirs », qui se dit de la même façon en anglais et en français, signifie... départ !

– Allez ma bichette, il nous reste encore une journée, on oublie la déprime, me glisse ma copine au creux de l'oreille.

Moins d'une heure plus tard, Bridget, Vic et moi sommes devant le magasin Harrods, une véritable institution dans la capitale britannique. Le bâtiment est majestueux et il m'évoque un lointain cousin de notre Printemps parisien.

– Hello girls ! crie Lou en arrivant avec ma mère. « Awe dou you dou ? », comme dirait Luna.

– En parlant de Luna, où est-elle ? Et où sont Lisa et papa ? je demande en embrassant ma mère et ma sœur.

– Ton père a décrété qu'il était hors de question qu'il passe « l'après-midi dans cette pieuvre » qui va engloutir sa bonne humeur, s'exclame ma mère en montrant le grand magasin. Il a préféré rester avec tes sœurs qui dorment encore.

Bridget se met à rire en ajoutant que Harrods n'engloutit pas seulement la bonne humeur des visiteurs.

– Vos économies aussi risquent de subir le même traitement, remarque-t-elle en riant.

Finalement, Vic et moi, on décide d'aller ensemble vers Piccadilly Circus où Bridget nous assure qu'on trouvera des boutiques de souvenirs à des prix raisonnables. On se donne rendez-vous pour déjeuner « ensemble entre filles » un peu plus tard.

On entre dans une boutique assez géniale qui possède deux étages et un choix immense en matière de souvenirs ! Je rapporte un tee-shirt *I* ♥ *London* et un mug aux couleurs de l'Union Jack pour mes futurs breakfasts français. J'ajoute deux porte-clés pour Maëlle et Maureen[1], mes jumelles préférées. Vic et moi, on décide d'acheter un petit carnet pour James dans lequel je compte bien laisser un dessin souvenir et mon amie une spéciale dédicace.

En sortant du magasin, mon portable sonne. Je suis soulagée en voyant apparaître un Snap d'Ulysse. Alex a tourné la page comme moi.

> Laure where are you ? I'm so sad.

dit le message qui accompagne le dessin de mon meilleur ami. On y voit sa silhouette qui regarde au loin, au bord de la mer, tandis que le drapeau anglais flotte à l'horizon. Je me dépêche de lui répondre que je rentre sous peu

1. Lire *Quatre sœurs en scène*.

et qu'il me manque beaucoup en ajoutant des tonnes de bisous à mon message.

Vers quatorze heures, on retrouve ma mère, Bridget et Lou, qui ont fait quelques emplettes.

– Achats très raisonnables, précise ma sœur en roulant des yeux. Je peux à peine m'offrir un foulard avec mes économies.

– Tu vois ce qu'il te reste à faire, plaisante ma mère. Deviens une fashion designer reconnue et tu pourras toi-même te fabriquer les plus beaux vêtements de Londres.

C'est mon dernier fish and chips à Londres et j'avoue qu'il a un goût particulier, celui des bons souvenirs que l'on quitte à regret…

On rejoint la maison de James en fin d'après-midi. Bridget et Yan nous ont donné rendez-vous chez eux ce soir pour partager un dernier dîner. Je dois aussi récupérer ma valise puisque je dors chez James pour la dernière nuit : notre départ est matinal demain et nos parents souhaitent gérer TOUTE la famille en même temps.

– How was your last day in London ? nous demande notre hôte qui nous a préparé un thé comme à son habitude.

On n'a pas le temps de lui répondre. Lisa et Luna débarquent comme deux furies ! Elles ont de la peinture plein le visage et sont suivies de très près par Clark.

– Eh ben nous, on va devenir des vraies « peintresses » ! C'est Clark qui l'a dit, s'exclame Luna que ma mère entraîne directement dans la salle de bains.

– Moi, j'hésite encore, ajoute Lisa en fronçant les sourcils. Chanteuse professionnelle me tente beaucoup…

Clark, hilare, nous explique qu'il a gardé mes petites sœurs deux heures cet après-midi puisque mon père était invité à rejoindre Yan… aux studios d'Abbey Road !

– Encore ? Ne me dites pas qu'il est allé enregistrer un titre ! s'écrie Lou.

Je me mets à rire en imaginant mon père chantant des « you you » derrière un micro.

On savoure notre thé tout en montrant nos achats aux petites L. Maman leur a rapporté une trousse avec un drapeau anglais et un tee-shirt à chacune. Lou s'est acheté un *London Passport*, qui est une sorte de guide pour les fashion girls.

– Ce sera très utile quand je serai dans l'école de mode de Margaux, déclare-t-elle.

– Moi, je te dis qu'elle n'y est pas encore à Londres, je chuchote à Vic en regardant Lou pianoter sur son portable. Max, c'est une ancre qui la retient au port… en France!

– To be continued, comme on dit ici, me répond mon amie. Peut-être que l'amour de la mode sera plus important pour Lou.

Je lève les yeux au ciel avant d'entraîner Vic à l'étage.

Je prépare un dessin pour James dans le petit carnet qu'on lui a acheté pendant que Vic lui écrit une dédicace très sympa.

Vous qui avez accueilli une horde sauvage de filles, vous savez maintenant comment on gère « a lot of girls »!

En plus, vous avez renoué avec Clark.

We are very proud of you…

Thank you so much papy James!

Dans le carnet, je représente un bout de l'atelier avec Clark devant une toile et James juste à côté.

Sur les cinq pages suivantes, j'essaie de « croquer » les quatre L et Vic.

Mon père rentre dans la soirée et j'ai à peine fini ! En sortant dans le couloir, je remarque que mes sœurs ont déjà fait leurs valises. Leurs chambres ont pris l'aspect triste des pièces qui vont se vider de leur vie. Mais je préfère ne pas rester à contempler la fin des vacances. Je rejoins le salon où mon père est en train de crâner grave.

– J'étais en cabine avec l'ingénieur du son pendant l'enregistrement de deux titres de *Black Mouth*, nous explique-t-il. C'est dingue, non ?

Lou, Lisa, Luna, Vic et moi, on secoue la tête pour ne pas lui faire de peine mais en vrai, PERSONNE ne connaît ce groupe, à part leurs parents. Et encore…

– Ils sont juste un peu moins bons que Lisa et Luna, affirme Yan qui a raccompagné mon père.

Lisa approuve évidemment.

– Ce soir, j'ai invité James à dîner au studio avec Tim et moi, nous raconte Clark. I must cook so… I have to leave !

On se place toutes à la queue leu leu pour embrasser notre peintre préféré. Il nous serre très fort dans ses bras avant de murmurer :

– Je suis tellement heureux d'avoir croisé votre *cheminée*…

Comme on se met à rire en lui expliquant que nous, on est plutôt heureuses d'avoir croisé son « chemin », il dégaine son sourire qui fait briller son piercing et nous dit au revoir. Vic soupire un bon coup… avant de sortir son portable de sa poche car elle vient de recevoir un SMS d'Abel !

On distribue ensuite nos cadeaux à James. Mes sœurs ont eu le temps de mettre un petit mot dans le carnet.

– On t'offre *une* carnet, papy James, pour que tu aies *une* souvenir de *la* club des filles du deuxième étage, lui dit Lisa en lui tendant notre cadeau.

Notre hôte, très ému, enlève ses lunettes pour essuyer la poussière qu'il a dans l'œil. C'est une poussière qui insiste puisque James doit à nouveau frotter ses paupières quand mes parents lui annoncent « qu'il est attendu quand il veut chez les Juin, à Paris » en lui tendant une caisse de... bons vins français évidemment !

– Thank you so much, déclare-t-il. Je sais gérer *un* horde de filles et je sais aussi grâce à vous qu'il faut parfois enlever les caches qu'on a sur les yeux pour y voir plus clair sur les gens qu'on aime.

C'est une vraie séquence émotion, interrompue par Luna.

– Laure, ils étaient où les caches de papy James ? me demande-t-elle intriguée. Moi, j'ai rien vu et toi ?

Vers dix-neuf heures, on rejoint la maison de Yan et Bridget.

Pour une fois, la mère de Vic a une tenue presque normale.

– Elle n'a pas pu s'empêcher de mettre un tee-shirt vert fluo sous son pull, regarde, me chuchote Vic en levant les yeux au ciel.

Avant le repas, les DJ Bryan chantent pour nous et c'est carrément génial ! Les deux petites L crânent parce que dans le salon de Vic figure un Polaroid où elles posent dans l'atelier de Clark devant la table de mixage.

Notre tout dernier dîner anglais est délicieux, Bridget cuisine aussi bien qu'elle chante. Vic et moi, on n'arrête pas de reparler du séjour et de ceux qui suivront en France, ou ailleurs.

Au moment de partir, les larmes sont au rendez-vous. J'ai quand même passé dix jours fabuleux en sa compagnie.

– Don't cry, Laure, me console-t-elle alors qu'elle pleure encore plus que moi.

– Rendez-vous à Paris cet été ? je lui réponds en la serrant fort dans mes bras.

En entrant dans le black cab qui nous ramène chez James, j'ai encore les yeux très humides. En grande « technicienne », Luna m'explique patiemment comment arrêter de pleurer.

Sur la demande de nos parents, le taxi fait un détour par Buckingham Palace pour qu'on puisse le voir éclairé. Alors qu'il passe au ralenti devant le palais, Lisa s'écrie :

– Regardez ! J'ai vu un rideau s'ouvrir !

On penche la tête pour observer la fenêtre que Lisa nous désigne. Évidemment, on ne distingue rien parce qu'on est bien trop loin.

– Ah oui, affirme Luna d'un air convaincu. Il y a quelqu'un qui me faisait bonjour.

– C'est elle, c'est Kate ! Ou peut-être William ! s'exclame Lisa déchaînée. Ils savaient qu'on allait leur dire au revoir.

Je jette un œil par la vitre arrière du taxi. On n'y voit plus rien.

Le fog vient d'apparaître d'un coup, c'est incroyable !

Il nous signifie que le rideau est tombé sur notre séjour…

Good bye London !

London I miss you

– Lauauaure ! Lève-toi, c'est largement l'heure !

J'aimerais bien savoir pourquoi, le samedi matin, jour où je peux dormir longtemps, il y a TOUJOURS quelqu'un pour perturber mon sommeil.

Je m'assois dans mon lit pendant que ma mère ouvre mes volets. Il fait toujours aussi gris. Depuis que nous sommes rentrés de Londres, le temps est super moche. C'est comme si on avait rapporté la grisaille londonienne.

– Il est à peine onze heures et demie, je grommelle. C'est tôt pour une grasse mat !

Ma mère secoue la tête en riant.

– Il te reste juste un mois avant les GRANDES vacances. Là, tu en auras, des grasses mat !

– Mais... Qu'est-ce que tu fais dans cette tenue ? je lance en constatant que ma mère porte un jogging jaune fluo.

– J'ai décidé de faire des séances d'abdos-fessiers à la maison, comme Bridget, m'explique-t-elle en s'observant dans mon miroir. J'ai commandé la même tenue qu'elle. C'est joli, hein ?

Je fais à peu près la même grimace que Vic. C'est clair, on n'a pas rapporté que la grisaille de Londres finalement.

Voilà quinze jours que nous sommes revenus. Le retour au collège a été super dur, même si j'y ai retrouvé Justine ma best friend forever, Ulysse mon co-dessinateur de BD préféré ou Héloïse et Thomas, mes copains de classe. Vic me manque, parler anglais me manque, le tea time me manque, la folie de Londres me manque. Bref, je suis encore en mode *I* ♥ *London* et je n'arrive pas à penser à autre chose.

– Tu sais, on a une capitale génialissime en France, a déclaré Lou hier soir alors que je me plaignais.

– Tiens... Je croyais que toi aussi tu ADORAIS Londres et que tu souhaitais y vivre très rapidement ? je lui ai rétorqué. Tu ne parlais pas d'intégrer la Central Saint Martins College ?

– Tout à fait. Mais je n'oublie pas que Paris reste LA référence absolue pour l'élégance et la mode dans le monde entier.

– Tu n'oublies surtout pas que Max veut faire des études de kiné ici, dans notre capitale, je lui ai rappelé, moqueuse

Lou a froncé les sourcils, l'air profondément choquée.

– Mais pas du tout Laure. Je suis libre. Je suis une femme du XXIe siècle ! Et si je veux étudier à Osaka, New York ou New Delhi, je le ferai, avec ou sans Max. Qu'est-ce que tu crois ?

La discussion en est restée là. Ma sœur est une femme libre, OK.

Même si elle est scotchée à Max depuis qu'on est rentrés.

De la musique provient du salon où ma mère est bien en train de faire des exercices d'abdos-fessiers en rythme. Je n'ai pas besoin de tendre l'oreille, j'ai reconnu le morceau. C'est *Children forever.* Il tourne en boucle chez les Juin depuis quinze jours. Grâce à nous, les droits d'auteur versés à l'association Enfants du monde vont être conséquents ! On a fait télécharger le titre une bonne centaine de fois autour de nous. C'est simple, depuis qu'on est revenus en France, dès que mes parents croisent une de leurs connaissances, ils ne peuvent pas s'empêcher de dire :

– Vous avez déjà entendu le titre *Children forever* de DJ Bryan ? Non ? Il faut absolument le télécharger. Nos deux petites y ont leurs voix enregistrées et en toute modestie, elles chantent VRAIMENT BIEN. En plus, vous faites une bonne action !

Parfois, ils vont jusqu'à mettre des écouteurs sur les oreilles de leurs victimes pour les convaincre que ce morceau, c'est very very good (comme dit mon père) ! Le titre commence à passer sur les ondes françaises et mes deux petites sœurs n'en reviennent pas de s'entendre à la radio.

– La prochaine fois qu'on reviendra à Londres, Kate et William auront envie de nous inviter dans un de leurs châteaux, a affirmé Lisa qui n'abandonne JAMAIS une idée.

– Oui mais moi, je préfère retourner chez James, a rétorqué Luna. Il était rigolo parce qu'il ne savait même pas qu'on dit *une* fille et *un* garçon ! Vous vous souvenez quand il demandait « Voulez-vous *une* sucre dans *le* tasse » ?

– Et quand il nous a chanté *Sur le ponw d'Avignonw, on y danse*, en pensant que c'est LA chanson préférée des Français ? s'est écriée Lisa.

Les deux petites L ont évoqué leurs souvenirs en riant pendant un moment. Elles n'ont pas pris la grosse tête. C'est rassurant !

Justement, Lisa se précipite vers moi tandis que je baisse un peu le son des baffles.

– J'ai fini mon quizz sur Londres. Je l'apporte à l'école lundi mais je vais vous le proposer ce soir, m'explique-t-elle.

– Ah… Super ! je commente tout en priant mentalement pour qu'elle ne me suive pas dans la cuisine.

Mes prières sont vaines puisqu'elle continue tout en s'asseyant à table avec moi.

– Je vais faire un exposé sur Londres aux élèves de ma classe et ensuite, ils devront répondre à mes questions. Ce soir, je vous les poserai sans lire mes notes avant. Vous revenez juste de London, ce sera facile !

Je me dis qu'on a beaucoup de chance de ne pas avoir à subir les cinquante pages de l'exposé de Lisa et je lui souris.

– Tu veux connaître mes questions ? me demande Lisa qui n'attend pas ma réponse pour commencer. Alors, number one : comment s'appelle le palais où loge parfois la famille royale à Londres ?

– Facile. Buckingham Palace, je réponds en remplissant ma tasse.

– OK. Number two : comment s'appellent les enfants de Kate et William ?

– Euh… (Petite pause.) Tu as prévu combien de questions ? je demande prudemment.

– Juste quarante-cinq, explique Lisa.

– Je vais être la meilleure si je connais les réponses ! Tu me laisses déjeuner tranquillement et on revoit ça ce soir, OK ?

Lisa s'éloigne et je pousse un soupir de bonheur. Je peux boire mon lait.

Sauf que le calme est de très courte durée dans ma famille…

– Laure, je me souviens d'une phrase de plus en anglais ! crie Luna toute contente en entrant dans la cuisine. Écoute : *Dou you l'aïe que ti ouize milk* ? C'est ce que nous demandait James quand il nous servait du thé, tu te rappelles ?

Je souris à Luna en répétant quelques phrases en anglais pour elle. Je ne suis pas la seule à être nostalgique…

Quand je regagne ma chambre, j'allume mon portable pour avoir des « nouvelles du monde ». Justine m'a déjà envoyé deux SMS.

Scoop DLMQT : Morgan sort avec
la nouvelle de sa classe, suis deg

C mon frère qui m'a filé l'info. Je le hais.
Je m'en cherche un nouveau (de frère pas de chéri).

Justine avait promis d'oublier Morgan, elle a du mal. J'essaie de la lancer sur une autre piste depuis mon retour de Londres mais elle a la tête dure !

Laisse tomber Morgan !
Tu as vu que Paul te matait grave l'autre jour ?

Beurk. Paul = beurk.
I got Morgan under my skin.

Je me mets à rire. J'ai cru aussi avoir Alex « under my skin » et pourtant, j'ai réussi à le chasser de mes pensées. Depuis son SMS de rupture à Londres et ma réponse, on n'a plus échangé un seul mot. J'avais même envie d'effacer ses photos et puis, au dernier moment, j'ai renoncé. Il fait partie de mes beaux souvenirs et, à ce titre-là, je n'ai pas le droit de le faire totalement disparaître.

Vic, elle, commence une belle histoire d'amitié avec Abel. En tout cas, d'après son message d'hier, elle n'arrête pas de rire quand elle est avec lui. On s'écrit deux à trois fois par semaine, elle et moi, et on s'envoie des kilos de Snaps. Son dernier la montrait avec Abel à Camden devant une super fresque sur un mur. J'ai tellement eu envie de les rejoindre là-bas…

– Lauauauare !

Ma mère me tire de ma rêverie et j'en profite pour envoyer un SMS à Ulysse qui doit passer chez moi cet après-midi.

– Lauauaure, insiste ma mère. Un paquet pour toi. Le facteur vient de l'apporter.

Une cavalcade me précède dans le salon. L'information est arrivée jusqu'aux oreilles de mes petites sœurs qui débarquent toutes les deux en même temps.

– C'est quoi ? me demande Luna intriguée.

– Ben, j'en sais rien, je réponds en attrapant le colis.

– Il vient de Londres, précise ma mère qui est aussi curieuse que mes sœurs !

Mon sourire est immédiat. S'il est Anglais, il va forcément me plaire.

Je mets environ quatre secondes pour déchirer le papier et ouvrir la boîte volumineuse.

– Ooooh ! s'exclament mes deux sœurs de concert.

J'ai dans les mains une petite toile carrée qui doit mesurer trente centimètres de côté environ.

Je n'ai pas besoin de regarder la signature pour savoir qui me l'envoie…

Clark a dessiné un soleil central avec cinq branches sur lesquelles on devine cinq visages féminins. Derrière, sur le côté droit, on voit la maison de James, un peu floue, comme perdue dans le *fog* et sur le côté gauche, deux jeunes hommes ont les doigts enlacés, avec un troi-

sième, bien plus vieux, qui pose sa main sur une des épaules du couple.

– C'est très symbolique, tout ça, déclare ma mère en observant attentivement la peinture.

– Ça veut dire quoi « saint bolik » ? demande Luna.

Je laisse maman interpréter le tableau pour mes deux petites sœurs et y retrouver les visages des quatre L et de Vic qui y sont dessinés ainsi que ceux de James, Clark et Tim.

Je déplie la feuille qui accompagne ce merveilleux cadeau.

Laure, je sais que ce n'est pas ta fête, mais je voulais t'envoyer un souvenir que tu peux accrocher... ou ranger dans un placard, as you like ! Tu as eu une idée formidable avec the exhibition, et avec Lou et Vic, vous avez été so so great ! Je ne peux pas offrir un cadeau à Lou car son lover serait jaloux ! C'est toi que j'ai envie de remercier alors.

James m'a demandé de vous faire le bise. Lui et moi, on n'a plus the fog qui nous sépare et c'est un peu grâce à vous.

Thanks to you Laure
Kisses from Clark (and Tim !)

Mon cœur bat très fort.

Je replie soigneusement le mot de Clark que je lirai à Vic, bien sûr. Il me tarde que Lou rentre de sa leçon de conduite pour lui montrer message et peinture. Elle sera sûrement jalouse de voir cette magnifique toile dans ma chambre mais elle a trop de photos de Max sur les murs, il n'y a plus de place dans la sienne. Et puis, Clark l'a bien précisé, c'est moi qu'il a envie de remercier en premier.

Je pars déposer la toile dans ma chambre et juste au moment où je m'empare de mon téléphone pour envoyer un message à Clark, un selfie s'affiche.

Vic pose avec une petite sculpture magnifique dans la main. Elle représente des mains enlacées.

Tu as eu ton cadeau, toi aussi ?

me demande-t-elle en joignant un SMS.

Je poste tout de suite une photo de moi et de mon tableau avec un :

Je viens de le recevoir !

Dans la seconde, mon téléphone sonne.

– Aloooors ? me demande Vic à l'autre bout du fil. Tu la trouves comment, ta surprise ?

– Au top ! je réponds enthousiaste. Clark est juste un amour.

– Et Tim aussi ! En fait, ils sont adorables tous les deux. Je suis tellement contente d'avoir pu les rencontrer.

Un silence s'installe.

Je sais qu'on est en train de penser à la même chose toutes les deux. On aurait tellement envie de recommencer.

– C'était trop génial ce séjour, vraiment, je murmure.

– Et tu sais quoi ? Il peut y en avoir un autre… Perhaps ! chuchote à son tour Vic. Je te file un scoop, Laure. Mes parents ont un projet de ouf pour l'année prochaine. Ils ne veulent pas trop en parler tant que rien n'est signé, mais a priori, on déménage cet été.

– Tu veux dire que tu reviens habiter à Paris ? je crie toute contente.

– Euh, pas vraiment. En fait, ils m'ont demandé de ne rien dire mais comme tu es ma meilleure amie, on reste en famille, non ?

Alors… Roulements de tambours… Il y a de fortes chances que l'année prochaine, je t'invite à…

C'est pile le moment où mon portable s'éteint.

Plus de batterie. Je me précipite sur la prise que je ne trouve pas, évidemment. Mais je ne m'énerve absolument pas. Au contraire, je souris toute seule.

Je sens que je ne vais pas m'ennuyer cet été…

À suivre...

Table des matières

Comme Laure, **Sophie Rigal-Goulard** a toujours adoré parler anglais. Au collège, c'était le cours qu'elle préférait et elle était toujours la première à participer ! Elle s'imaginait marcher dans les rues de Londres, avec ses copines, tout en ayant de longues discussions… en anglais bien sûr !

Sophie Rigal-Goulard a toutefois mis un peu de temps avant de réaliser ce rêve. Il a fallu que son fils déménage à Londres… pour qu'elle s'y rende enfin. Elle a donc longuement arpenté les rues de la capitale britannique pour pouvoir écrire cet épisode de la série et restituer l'ambiance si particulière qui y règne.

Et comble de bonheur, c'est son fils qui a pu jouer au « London guide » !

Vous pouvez retrouver Sophie Rigal-Goulard sur les salons car elle aime les rencontres avec ses lecteurs et sur son site : sophie-rigal-goulard.fr

Diglee est une jeune illustratrice au sang anglais passionnée de littérature et des années folles, qui dessine depuis toujours.

Elle travaille beaucoup pour la jeunesse, notamment pour les préadolescents et adolescents, mais fait aussi de la BD et de la publicité. Née à Lyon, elle travaille chez elle sur son ordinateur, après avoir passé à dix-sept ans un bac Littéraire puis être sortie diplômée de l'école Émile-Cohl en 2009.

Elle tient un blog dessiné depuis 2007, dans lequel elle a d'abord raconté ses péripéties quotidiennes avec humour (qui ont été adaptées en deux BD : *Autobiographie d'une fille Gaga* et *Confessions d'une Glitter Addict*) et qui prend aujourd'hui une tournure plus engagée : elle y parle avec tendresse de ses interrogations de jeune militante féministe.

Elle rencontre beaucoup de ses lecteurs et lectrices étudiants, pour répondre à leurs questions et les découvrir au-delà d'Internet.

Vous pouvez la retrouver sur les salons (elle adore faire des dédicaces !) et sur son blog : diglee.com

Retrouve Lou, Laure, Lisa et Luna dans :

SOPHIE RIGAL-GOULARD
4 Soeurs
En scène
RAGEOT
SOPHIE RIGAL-GOULARD
4 Soeurs
En colo
RAGEOT
SOPHIE RIGAL-GOULARD
4 Soeurs
En direct du collège
RAGEOT
SOPHIE RIGAL-GOULARD
QUATRE SŒURS
et un Noël inoubliable
RAGEOT
gulli

De la même auteure, en grand format :

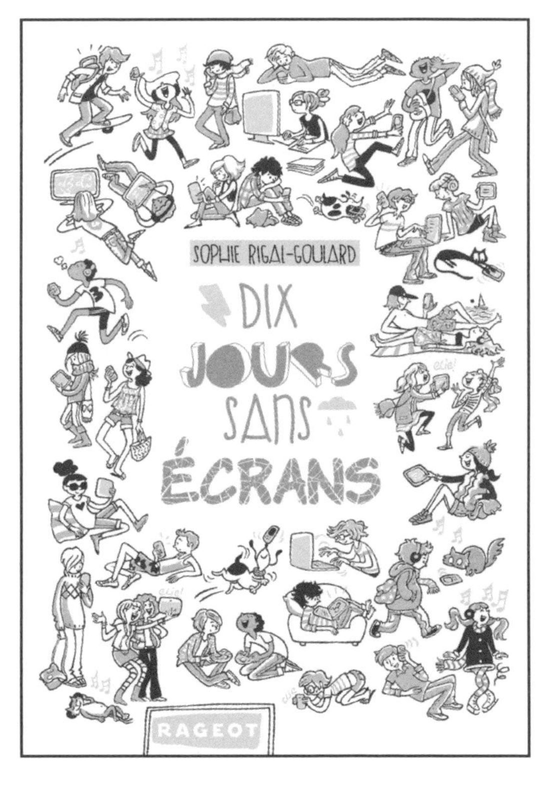

10 jours sans écrans

Dix jours sans le moindre écran ! C'est le challenge proposé à la classe de Louis et Paloma par leur maîtresse. Il faudra laisser éteints son ordinateur, sa télévision, sa console, et rester éloigné des téléphones portables et des tablettes… Qui, de Paloma ou Louis, va craquer le premier ?

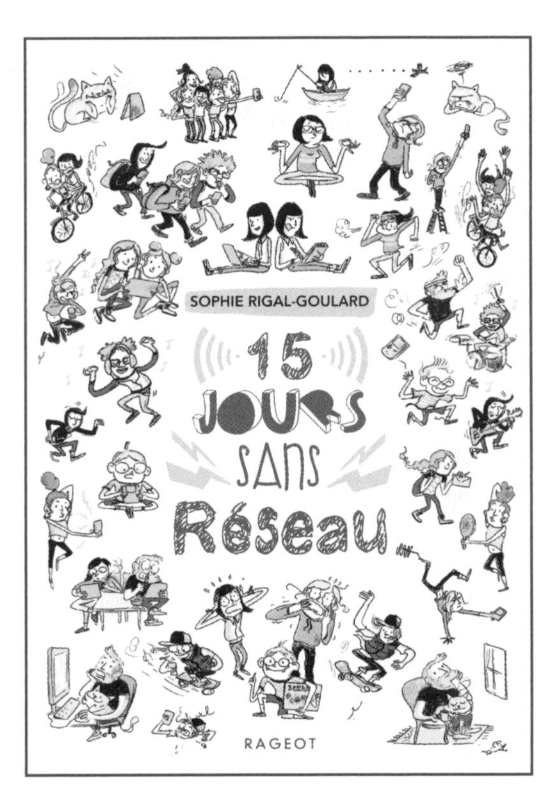
SOPHIE RIGAL-GOULARD
15 JOURS SANS Réseau
RAGEOT

15 jours sans réseau

Privés de réseau ! Pour Émilie, qui adore FB et Instagram, Ambroise, qui ne peut vivre sans être connecté à sa *team*, et leur petit frère Lucien, ces vacances de sevrage numérique à la campagne sont un cauchemar. Il faut cesser de tweeter, liker, poster, snaper, scorer… et laisser tous les appareils hors de portée. Supporteront-ils de vivre 15 jours sans Wifi ? Et passer un été inattendu avec eux-mêmes, leur famille et des vacanciers ?

Retrouvez toutes les nouveautés
sur le site :

www.rageot.fr

RAGEOT s'engage pour l'environnement en réduisant l'empreinte carbone de ses livres. Celle de cet exemplaire est de :
1 kg éq. CO_2
Rendez-vous sur www.rageot-durable.fr

Achevé d'imprimer en France en août 2017
par l'imprimerie Pollina (Luçon)
Dépot légal : juillet 2017
N° d'édition : 5333 – 02
N°d'impression : 81777

ALSO BY JOSH MA

Bird Box

BLACK MAD WHEEL

Josh Malerman

HARPER

HarperCollins*Publishers*
1 London Bridge Street
London SE1 9GF

www.harpercollins.co.uk

This paperback edition 2017
1

First published in Great Britain by
HarperCollins 2017

A catalogue record for this book is
available from the British Library

ISBN: 978 0 00 753009 0

This novel is entirely a work of fiction.
The names, characters and incidents portrayed in it are
the work of the author's imagination. Any resemblance to
actual persons, living or dead, events or localities is
entirely coincidental.

Printed and bound in Great Britain

IN MAY OF 2012 *the High Strung had just played the record release show for our album* ¿Posible ó Imposible?, *I'd just set the microphone back upon the stand, and Derek (drums) and I were stumbling out of the bar. From the bar's shadows, an imp came, a gorgeous pair of bright green eyes and legs so long she must have been standing in the cellar. She spoke, too. "Do you have any more of that face paint?" Before the show I'd used a Sharpie on myself. Easy designs. "Yes," I told her, reaching into the pocket of my jacket. But the imp had hands and she took hold of my face and rubbed it against her own.*

Voilà. A painted face. And the beginning of something, too.

This book is for Allison Laakko, who got Black Mad Wheel *piecemeal, spark by spark, as every night I relived for her the day's excited writing. For that, there will always be a path, tracks, made by a wheel, perhaps, leading from her to me, then to the book and back to us again.*

I like that.

We'll forever know which way the wheels rolled.

I love you, Allison.

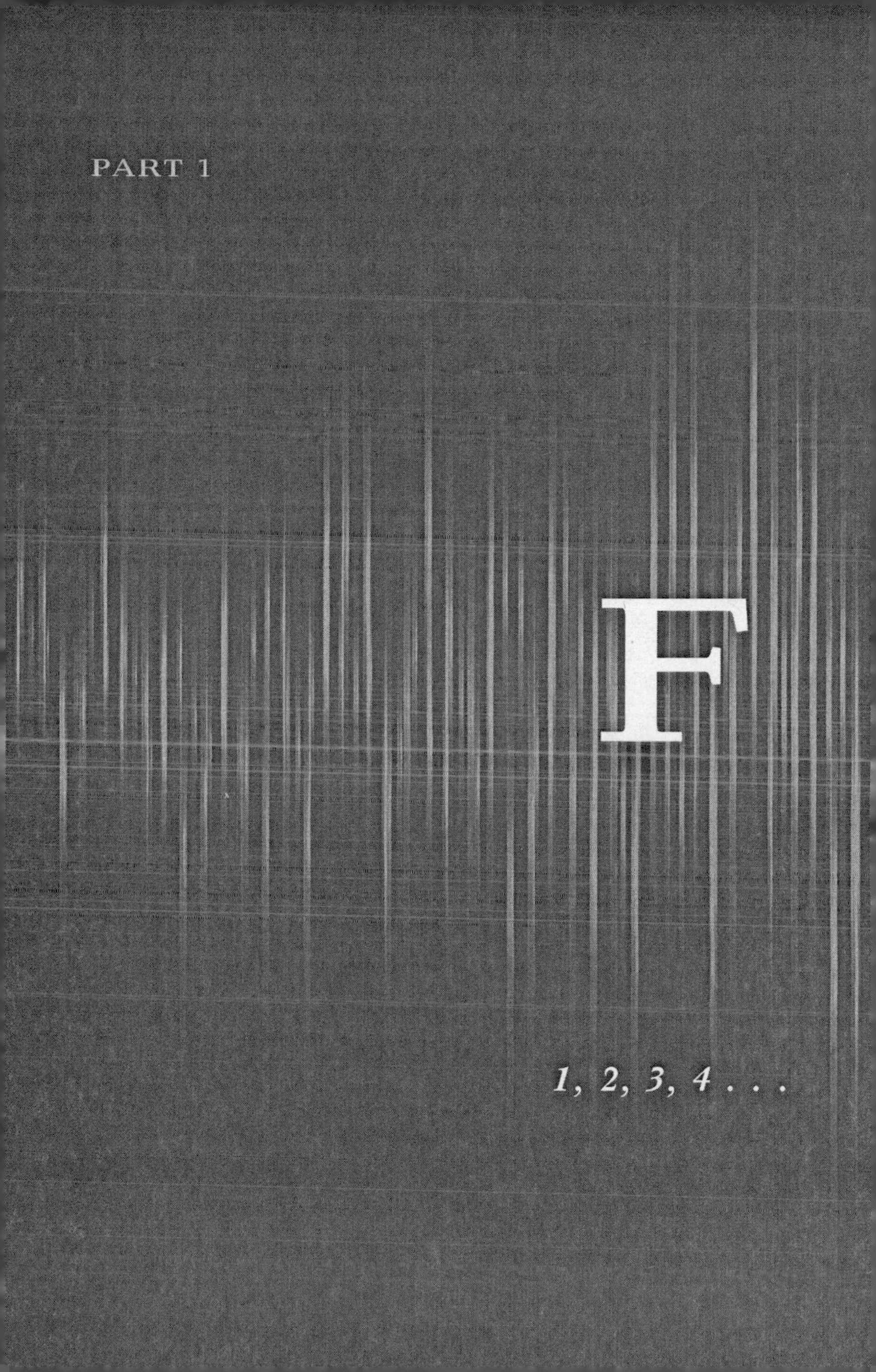

PART 1

F

1, 2, 3, 4 . . .

1

The patient is awake. A song he wrote is fading out, as if, as he slept, it played on a loop, the soundtrack of his unbelievable slumber.

He remembers every detail of the desert.

The first thing he sees is a person. That person is the doctor. Wearing khaki pants and a Hawaiian shirt, he doesn't dress like a doctor, but the bright science in his eyes gives him away.

"You've been hurt very badly." His voice is confidence. His voice is control. "It's an unparalleled injury, Private Tonka. To live through something so . . . " He makes fists about chest high, as though catching a falling word. ". . . *unfair.*"

Philip recognizes more than medicine in the man who stands a foot from the end of his cot. The strong, lean physique. The unnaturally perfect hair, the skin as unwrinkled as a desert dune.

This doctor is military.

"Now," the doctor says, "let me tell you why this is such an incredibly difficult thing to do." Philip hasn't fully processed the room he is in. The borders of his vision are blurred. How long has he been here? Where is here? But the doctor isn't answering unasked questions like these. "Had you broken only your wrists and your elbows, we might surmise that you fell, hit the ground in just such a way. But you've broken your humeri, radii, and ulnae, too; your radial tuberosities; coracoid processes, trochleas, and each of the twenty-seven bones in your hands." He smiles. His smile says Philip ought to share in the astonishment. "I don't expect you to know the names of every bone in the human body, Philip, but what I'm telling you is that you didn't just break your wrists and elbows. You broke almost everything."

Sudden whispers from somewhere Philip can't see. Maybe voices in a hall. Philip tries to turn his head to look.

He can't. He can't move his neck at all.

He opens his mouth to say something, to say he can't move, but his throat is dry as summer sand.

He closes his eyes. He sees hoofprints in that sand.

"Now, had you broken only both hands and arms, I might dream up an accident you were involved in; the victim of a press, say, a vise of some sort; possibly both your arms were on a table when a heavy weight fell upon them. But, of course, it was *not* only your hands and arms that were broken. The femurs, tibiae, and fibulae on both legs were cracked, too, as were the patellae, medial epicondyles, every transverse axis (which ought to have been enough to cause a coma itself), as well as most of the twenty-six bones in each of your feet." The doctor speaks with such freedom, moves with such *health* that Philip feels parodied by comparison. "I suppose one might reenact the scene, place you on a cliff's edge, arms and legs hanging *over* that chasm, as something so cruelly shaped, *just* wrong enough to connect with each of the aforementioned bones, fell from the sky, delivering you the most violent community of fractures I've ever observed. But no. Your woes do not stop there."

Behind the doctor, where the beige wall meets the powder-blue ceiling, Philip sees an African desert at midday.

He thinks of the Danes.

"Your pubis, ilium, sacrum . . . crushed. The pubic symphysis, anterior longitudinal . . . ruptured. Your ribs, Philip, each and every one . . . along with every intervertebral disc, the sternum, manubrium, clavicles, up through the neck, to the mandible, zygomatics, temporals, frontal, and . . . even some teeth." The doctor smiles, showing his own. "Now, one might hypothesize such a result befalling a man who had been lying down upon a stone slab, unaware that a second stone slab would drop from a height, crushing him entirely, all at once. Such a theory might be of interest had each of the fractures been close to the same distance from the surface of your body. But, of course, this isn't the case. The fracture in your anterior longitudinal is a full inch disparate from the one suffered by your mandible. In fact, there isn't a single uniform break in your body; no pattern to divine an object, a cause, a picture of what hurt you. In other words, Philip . . . this wasn't caused by a single solid object, and yet . . . it all occurred at the same time."

The doctor steps aside, revealing what looks to Philip like black canvases glowing with shining white paint. Unfinished shapes. Cracked patterns.

X-rays.

More than one of them look like hoofprints in the sand.

"I dare say," the doctor marvels, "it's the most breathtaking injury I've ever encountered. Some would call it . . . uncanny. Observe for yourself, Philip."

More whispers from somewhere Philip can't see.

"Now," the doctor says, turning from the X-rays to face Philip again. "You've just woken up . . . just *come to,* and I realize this must all be a considerable shock. You've been our charge, comatose, for six months." The number is impossible. The number is cruel. The number adds distance between himself and the Danes. "That's six months you couldn't possibly be aware of, and so now must begin the process of healing. Both physically and emotionally." He brings a forefinger and thumb to his chin. "But there *are* questions."

"Where are the Danes?" Philip croaks. And his voice is creaking wooden stairs. His voice is an old piano bench tested.

A whispered gasp from out of Philip's field of vision. A female voice.

He spoke! it said.

"The obvious initial question," the doctor continues, ignoring Philip's own, "is . . . how could a man survive such a thing?"

A breeze stirs his manicured brown hair.

Philip tries to raise an arm, can't.

The doctor easily extends an open, flat palm, as though showing Philip the difference, now, between them.

"But then . . . here you are . . . you've survived. And so the second, more urgent question is . . . what happened out there, Private Tonka?" He plants his hands on his knees, bends at the waist, and brings his blue eyes level with Philip's own. "What did you and the Danes find in the desert? Or, rather . . . " The doctor waves his hands in the air, playfully erasing this train of thought. The gesture is so out of place as to seem irreverent. "Let's forget your fellow musicians, your band, the Danes." The cold measure in his eyes suggests he already has. Again, Philip sees hoofprints, a trail of them extending.

He hears a sound, too, sickening and sentient, creating a trail of its own, curling up and over the horizon of his memory. He tries to fight it with his own song. His and the Danes'. The song that kept him company as he slept.

But the doctor's voice quiets it once again.

"The question is not what you found . . . but what found you?"

2

Philip is on the Path. That's what he's always called it. The Path. Not the Right Path or the Wrong Path. He's careful not to specify. So when any of his friends or family ask him if he's drinking too much, wonder aloud if he's hanging out in the bars too often, he always answers the same way.

Hey, broom off. I'm on the Path.

Philip's symbol for the Path is a single piano key, an F, worn on a necklace. The key itself was torn from the first piano Philip saw when he returned from the war, World War II: a trashed upright left on a curb not two hundred yards from the airport in Detroit, Michigan. Despite its missing leg, cracked wood, and flaked yellow paint, the piano was a portent to Philip; a welcoming committee couldn't have given him a warmer reception. After hugging his parents hello, after stowing his bags in their new 1945 Chrysler, Philip asked them to wait, so he could bring a little of the piano home with him.

Into the future with him. Postwar.

Onto the Path.

Choosing the key was easy. F. Because F was the only note in both mnemonics for beginner piano players:

EGBDF (Every Good Boy Does Fine)

FACE

One mnemonic ends, another begins.

As ends war, so begins life . . . at home.

Life on the Path.

Twelve years later, at thirty-one years old, Philip may not have the same army physique he had when he and the Danes performed for soldiers in England, but he has the same philosophy he had back then. Let his acquaintances in Detroit (and there are many of them; the Danes are bar owls) think the Path is religious, unreligious, unhealthy, delusional, or insane. It doesn't matter. After a world war and a hit song, living free is the only path to walk.

Today the Path has led him to a good place. A recording studio in downtown Detroit, at Elizabeth and Woodward, in this, the year 1957. The Danes ("the Darlings of Detroit," as the *Free Press* named them) own it. A four-way split. Larry, the fun-loving bassist of the Danes, the long-haired freak, found the place. An empty square made of cinder blocks, once used for plucking livestock, the acoustics were too perfect to let go.

This is it, Larry had said months ago, extending his hands out, palms up, like the goofy host of the game show *Who Do You Trust?* on television. *This is Wonderland.*

But not all the other Danes were convinced. A former chicken coop didn't quite feel like the place to make hit records.

You love everything, Duane said, *the first time you see it.*

And you, Larry said, pointing at the other half of the Danes' fabled rhythm section, *are way too conservative to play rock 'n' roll. Did you see the elevator?*

Duane frowned.

You mean the wooden box full of chicken feathers?

I like it, Philip said, already seeing the partition that would separate the control room from the live room.

Well, shit, Duane said. *Once you got Philip on board it's a done deal.* He looked around the cold space and saw Ross was smiling, too. *Shit again. We're doing this, aren't we?*

Larry put his arm around Duane's shoulder.

Can you see it?

Nope. I can't see it.

Right there . . . a sparkling set. Larry snapped his fingers, as if capable of manifesting Duane's Slingerland drums.

I don't see it, Larry.

Oh yes you do.

I see a cold place to record come December.

Larry laughed. His leather coat crinkled as he pulled Duane closer.

Come here.

Where?

To the window.

The window was just a small square cut unevenly into the white cinder-block wall. The four bandmates pressed close together and looked out at Detroit below.

Look at that girl. Ross whistled softly.

I know her, Philip said.

Know her? Ross asked. *How is it that you know every girl in Detroit, Philip?*

Philip shrugged.

Girls like the piano, Ross.

Well, shit, man. All my life I heard that it was girls and guitars, guitars and girls. I picked up the guitar for girls. And now you're telling me—

Look. Larry pointed. *There's another one. Just as fine.*

The Danes grew quiet. Their ears were almost touching.

You know her, too, Philip?

Philip paused for effect.

Naw. I don't know her.

But I bet she walks by every day, Duane said, his voice distant.

Oh man, Larry said, turning to face the drummer. *Oh MAN, Duane!*

Now, hang on, I didn't say—

We're doing this, Duane!

Now hang on, Larry—

We're buying our own fucking studio space!

Today, Wonderland is full. The Danes have been hired to produce an album, a rock and roll record, because they're good at what they do and the space they got is legendary around the city for its "room sound." Even jazz players have recorded with the Danes, despite the band's reputation as being crazy. *That room might be as professional as my uncle's liquor cabinet,* Clay Daniels once said, *but fuck me if it doesn't sound like gold.* The Danes recorded a hit song and two follow-ups in Wonderland. "Make Noise" reached number seventeen on the regional charts and "Killer Crawl" spiked at number six. But it was "Be Here," at number one, that propelled them. And still, the fact that they served in World War II is the bigger draw. It doesn't matter that they weren't on the front lines. To most Americans, being in the army band was just as good as being in the army. And the tag *veteran* is the reason locals who have no interest in music at all stop in to see what happens at Wonderland.

Some of these people have become drinking buddies. Others have walked away worried about Philip Tonka, the piano player who took more shots than he played notes.

Broom off. I'm on the Path.

What Path?

Look down. You don't see it? You're standing right on it, too.

Some think the Danes are damaged. They drink more than the veterans of World War I. They never miss a party. And they're spontaneously writing the postwar soundtrack that's equal parts angry, joyful, confused, and intentionally ignorant. As in, let's move on. As in, that was yesterday. The name of their number-one hit song unintentionally sums up their collective worldview.

Be here.

Breathe it.

Be it.

"Put a blanket in it," Larry says into the control room microphone. Today they have a job to do. But will they do it?

"Really?" the kid drummer of the Sparklers asks. Through the glass he looks like a lost child. "A blanket in a bass drum?"

Duane gets up from the control room couch and speaks into the microphone. His deep voice has always been the most authoritative of the Danes'.

"Makes it less plastic, son. More of a thud. Trust Larry. Put a blanket in the bass drum."

The Sparklers' drummer, a suburban kid, clean curly blond hair, looks for a blanket.

"On the cots," Philip says, pointing through the glass. He sips from a bottle of Ronrico rum. The Sparklers' guitar player is helping his drummer look. He accidentally knocks the tuning pegs of his Fender Stratocaster against the wall. Because he's already amped, the sound blasts through the control room speakers.

"You see those four cots in the back?" Duane tells them.

The Danes often sleep in the studio; wild nights, wee hours, right where they need to be come morning. The floor is littered with empty fifths.

The drummer picks up a sleeping bag.

"No," Larry says into the mic. "Too thick. Something lighter."

Now the drummer is blushing. Thinks he's being put on. The band's manager, Arthur, a rich kid from Birmingham, looks bothered. He's standing by the leather couch in the control room.

"Fellas, we hired you to make a record, not decorate Fred's drum kit!"

"You see that yellow-and-black blanket there, Art?" Larry asks him, pointing with a pencil through the glass to an unmade cot against the far wall.

"Yes. Of course I see it."

"That's the same one we used on 'Be Here.'"

The manager crosses the control room quickly. He takes the microphone from Larry.

"Freddie," he says. "How about the yellow-and-black blanket on the mattress by your knees?"

The drummer's pants slide down his butt as he bends to get it.

Philip plants a hand on the manager's shoulder.

"You know what your boys need?" he asks.

"What?" Art checks his watch. He keeps checking his watch. He's worried about time. Time and money.

"Your boys need an afternoon out of the house."

"No way," Art says, holding out both palms toward Philip. Philip sees a flash of what Art will look like when he's older, when managing bands is a novelty item on the shelf of his past. "We've been here for two hours and still haven't done a lick of work."

"What do you mean?" Duane asks. "We picked out the blanket, didn't we?"

Philip takes the manager by the wrist.

"Take your watch off," he says.

Art covers his watch with his other hand. As if he's being mugged. By Philip. The Danes have that quality about them.

"What is it with you, Tonka?"

"I mean it. Take your watch off."

Hesitantly, the manager does. He hands the watch to Philip.

"What are you going to do with it?"

"I'm gonna smash it."

"Wait!"

Philip smiles.

"I'm gonna wear it is what."

Philip puts it on his wrist, adjusts the clasp.

"Hey, Tonka! We agreed on a price, fair and square!"

"We did," Philip says. "But that's half the problem."

"You want to renegotiate? Dammit, I knew I couldn't trust you guys!"

"Who said anything about renegotiating? Relax. We agreed. Fair and square. The 'square' is the problem."

"What do you mean?"

Philip leans over the control room microphone.

"Gentlemen," he says. "Set your instruments down. We're going out."

Behind the glass the band looks scared.

"There's a hole in your soul," Duane tells the manager. "Big enough to swim through."

"And you're going to fill it?"

"Not all in one afternoon," Larry says, already putting on his leather jacket. He runs his callused fingertips through his long hair. "But we're gonna try."

Art is shaking his head, pleading, whining, as Duane slips into his black leather coat and Philip checks his jean jacket for money. The Sparklers enter the control room, slumped, confused.

"Come on, guys," Philip says.

"Where?" the guitarist asks.

"We're going to get inspired."

On the way out, as they're leaving the studio, the phone rings. Philip pauses at the door and looks.

Some rings, Philip thinks, are more loaded than others. As if a man might be able to hear an important call . . . before answering.

He locks the studio up and follows the others outside.

3

Philip can move more today than he could yesterday, but that little is frighteningly small. He remembers all of it: The Danes. Africa. The desert. The sound. But right now these memories must wait; the current state of his body is all that matters.

And the hospital. The motives behind this place. Philip has been around enough military to know that almost none of it is on the level. And the stuff that is is uneven at that.

He wants a drink. So badly he wants a drink.

He's alone, looking to where the beige wallpaper meets the powder-blue ceiling, the colors of the Namib at noon. To his right, where he can't see, a fan whirs. A radio plays, a quiet drama that does battle with the sound of classical music coming from another room farther down the hall.

Philip's room is big. He knows this because he's speaking out loud, gauging its size by the length of the echo on his voice.

"Mom," he says. "I'm alive."

Philip has been scared before. Many times, in many ways. From the basement in the house on Wyoming Street, the cellar where he learned the piano, to the flight to England in '44, when he and the Danes and the rest of the army band were set to entertain a thousand young men who knew they were too young to die.

"Dad. I'm alive. I'm okay."

But he's not okay. And saying it doesn't make it so.

There's a musical instrument in the room. Philip isn't sure what kind yet, but the sympathetic vibration tells him it has strings.

A guitar, then? Maybe.

A flapping to his left. He thinks it's drapes, moved by a breeze. A window, then. So the light upon the ceiling could be sunlight.

He listens for a ticking. A clock. He finds one. Far off. So quiet that it could be coming from outside.

He counts along with it, desperate for something to relax the nerves he can't stabilize. Meditation.

The Danes followed hoofprints in the desert. Only two. As if the beast walked upright . . .

Philip has to focus on something else. He closes his eyes. Imagines himself at that piano in the cellar. His sneaker tapping an intro on the dirt by the pedals.

"One, two, three, four . . ."

But counting one two three four reminds him of Duane on the drums, of a Danes song just beginning, of the fact that Philip can't move a finger, will probably never play piano again.

"Duane," he says. "Larry. Ross. I'm alive."

Then a voice, so close to his ear, Philip would jump if he could move.

"That's a good thing."

"Hey!" Philip yells.

Some gentle laughter. It's a woman.

"I haven't scared someone like that since Halloween 1949," the voice says. And the voice is the same he heard whispering when he woke. "Hid under my daughter's bed. Wore a rubber dish glove. Grabbed her ankle."

"Who are you?! Show yourself!"

"Relax," she says. "I'm Nurse Ellen. I'm the one who's been taking care of you for six months."

A creaking chair beside him. A face emerging from his right.

She looks young. Fresh-faced. Bright. Freckles across her nose. Granite-gray eyes. Black hair. White uniform.

"Are you hungry?" she asks.

Philip doesn't respond. He stares. When she speaks, her head tilts to the side. Does she realize how easily she moves?

"Let me get you something to eat."

She rises and vanishes somewhere to Philip's right again. Her heels against the unit tiles give him a better sense of space than his own voice echoing did. At what could be the door, she speaks.

"I can't tell you how glad I am you're awake."

Then she exits and Philip listens to her footfalls in the hall.

He imagines other people, silent in the unit with him. Other faces, other eyes. And the faces he sees are military. And the eyes in those faces want to know more than if he's hungry.

"Hello?" he asks, trembling, unable to abate the anxiety that's consumed him since waking. The Danes. The Danes. Where are the rest of the Danes? "Is anybody else in here with me?"

The nurse, Ellen, taught him something very important in the half minute they shared: not only can Philip barely move . . . but he can't know who watches him try.

And the faces he imagines open their mouths. And questions pour forth like grains of bodily sand.

The questions will come. Philip knows this. Questions about Africa and the source of the sound. Questions about the rest of the platoon, the Danes, what Philip heard and what he recorded out there. Crazier questions, too. Like who took Ross? Who took the others? And where did he take them? And why do you look so scared, Private Tonka, when we ask these simple things?

The questions will come.

And when they do, how much will Philip tell them?

How much will he sing?

4

Hey, Philip," Misty says. "Looks like you've already been drinking."

It's always *looks like* with Misty.

"I'm all right." Philip smiles.

"Looks like you're recording a band of stiffs." Misty nods to the Sparklers, who stand awkwardly farther down the bar. "What do they call themselves? The Bland?"

"The Sparklers."

"Jesus H."

Larry winks at Misty from over Philip's shoulder.

"It's our job to loosen them up," he says.

"You can't make a record with no grooves," Misty puns.

"They'll groove," Larry says. Then he shrugs. "I don't know. Maybe they won't."

"Help us out," Philip says.

"Sure. What do you want me to give them?"

"Something terrible. Something strong."

Misty considers this. But not for long. It's not the first time the Danes have brought a band into Doug's Den on Beaubien Street. She arranges five shot glasses.

"And we'll have the same," Philip adds.

Misty smiles something maternal. Philip likes Misty. With her short dark hair and strong eyes she looks like she could be his sister. And she's always been good to the Danes.

"You planning on getting any recording done today?" she asks, already pouring the shots.

"We haven't made it past the drum kit yet."

Thurston Harris's "Little Bitty Pretty One" comes on the jukebox.

Duane, dancing as he moves, takes half the shots from Misty. Philip grabs the others. They carry them to the Sparklers, now congregated on the dance floor. But still not dancing.

"You guys like this song?" Philip asks.

"Yeah," the Sparklers' bassist says. Philip catches himself reflected in the kid's glasses. He looks drunk. "It's fun."

"Good," Duane says. "So let's have fun."

As he and Philip distribute the shots, the door to Doug's Den swings open and Ross enters. His hands are stuffed into the pockets of his coat and he's hunched, as he always is, even when playing the guitar.

The young Sparklers stare at Ross with reverence. After all, it's his guitar line on "Be Here" that gave the Danes their instrumental hit.

"Sorry I'm late," he tells Philip. "Long night."

Philip understands. This isn't the first time a Dane has pleaded hungover.

"Ross, meet the Sparklers."

Ross checks them out. He knows Philip well enough to know why he's brought them to Doug's.

"You're Ross Robinson," the Sparklers' guitarist says, eyeing Ross's uncombed curly hair. "I curled my hair so it looks like yours."

"You look like a clown," Ross says. Then he takes one of the shot glasses, downs the whiskey within.

"Better?" Larry asks.

Ross wipes his mouth with the sleeve of his corduroy coat.

"Might be worse."

Philip raises his glass, inspiring the Sparklers to timidly do the same.

Art, the band's manager, rushes to stop this. His hair is wet with sweat. His tie is loose.

"Now hang on a minute! We've got a session to finish! My boys can't be whooping it up like this!"

The music gets louder. Philip looks over his shoulder. Misty is smiling behind the bar.

"This is all part of the session," Philip says. "This is tracking."

Philip downs his shot, grabs the lead singer of the Sparklers, and dances with him. He places the kid's hand on his back, asking him to lead.

The Path has taken Philip to amazing places, but sometimes, like when he looks into the naïve eyes of a younger musician, he wonders how far it can go.

These kids, Philip knows, haven't left home yet.

Ross squeezes himself between Philip and the singer with another round of shots.

"No more of this," Art says, stepping in. "I mean it. No more!"

"Little Bitty Pretty One" ends and Sonny James's "Young Love" begins. It's not yet noon and the regulars are watching the Danes. These men, veterans of the First World War, have been here since eight.

Larry starts dancing with the manager of the Sparklers. Art looks like a child in his arms. The drummer of the Sparklers unbuttons his shirt.

"There he goes," Ross says to Philip. "He'll be a drunk in no time."

The Sparklers are getting loose. Strange dance moves. The guitarist is kissing a poster featuring an actress from a new monster movie, *From Hell It Came.*

The front door opens and daylight cuts a fresh silhouette of a man in the door.

Philip doesn't see him.

"Think we're ready to record?" the Sparkler asks Larry.

Larry smiles but shakes his head no.

"In about another twenty years."

He twirls the kid.

Philip feels a tap on his shoulder. He turns.

The face he sees, the pale blue eyes, the set jaw, the manicured hair, is more familiar than it is friendly.

Military, Philip thinks. He hasn't seen a face like this one in a long time. Veterans are one thing, and they change through the years. But the men who give orders do not.

The Path, it seems, is unsteady now. Different footing.

"Philip Tonka?" the man asks.

"Yeah?"

A serious expression grips the lower half of the man's face, but his eyes still sparkle. Nothing shines, Philip thinks, exactly like military.

Could it be? Here?

"You a fan of the Danes?" Philip asks, hopeful, yet staring at a ghost, an era he thought was over.

The man nods.

"Yes. I am."

Philip notices the man's pressed suit. The lint-free overcoat.

"You looking to record a song?" Philip asks. But he's only stalling.

"My name is Jonathan Mull. Join me for a drink?"

"We're in the middle of a session."

Mull surveys the bar. Takes it in.

"This will only take a moment."

But Philip knows it's going to be longer than that.

He leads the man to a booth. On the way, Duane watches. Philip meets his drummer's eyes and they share a silent worry.

Military? Here?

"You're an army man?"

Mull slides into one side of the booth, Philip the other.

"Good eye. Military intelligence. Most of my colleagues know me as Secretary Mull. This is about an opportunity for you and the rest of the Danes."

"A gig?"

"Of sorts."

"Where?"

"Well, that's what I'd like to talk to you about."

"Let's talk, then."

"Africa."

Philip has a hard time believing this. Maybe it's the shots. Maybe it's the military.

"That's gonna cost a lot of money."

"We're certainly going to pay you. A considerable amount. A lot. But this gig is a little different from what you're used to."

"How different is different?" Hope in Philip's voice. What already feels like a memory, the last vestige of levity.

Mull tents his fingers on the tabletop.

"You won't be playing any music with this gig. You won't be making any noise at all. In fact, you'll be *listening* for a particular sound instead."

Philip looks to his bandmates. He feels a sudden longing, as if painfully watching the way the world used to be.

The Path.

Has he stepped off?

"What kind of sound?" Philip asks, turning back to face the military, to face the change.

"A sound you've never heard," the man says.

And Philip doesn't doubt it. Doesn't have any reason to believe that anything is familiar where this man wants to send them.

"Can I hear it?"

"Not here."

"Why not?"

Mull pauses.

"As you know, Private Tonka, the army's primary function is to protect the country's citizenry."

Philip smiles, but not because what the man has said is funny.

"What kind of sound could put people in danger?"

Mull places his elbows on the table and for a beat Philip sees the top of a reel jutting from the breast pocket of his suit coat. Mull's eyes travel to Philip's lips, as if asking him to remove the smile.

It isn't applicable here, he says without words.

"A malevolent one, Private Tonka."

Philip is still thinking about that reel.

"You make it sound like it's alive."

Mull leans back in the booth again.

"Let's go somewhere quieter to talk."

As if cued, the ruckus behind them rises. Larry is lifting one of the Sparklers by the waist.

"Wonderland," Mull suggests.

"To talk," Philip repeats.

He could stop this now. Whatever this is. He could say no. I like it here. I don't wanna go anywhere else. You can't make us.

"To listen," Mull says.

A malevolent sound, Private Tonka.

"Give me a minute," Philip says. "I'll gather the Danes."

But even as he slides from the booth, as he crosses the bar to retrieve his friends, Philip is telling himself no, no amount of money, no amount of curiosity is enough to leave all this behind.

And yet, the image of that tape in the military man's pocket . . .

Maybe it's because you can't see where it'll lead, Philip thinks, as he plants a hand on the shoulder of Ross's corduroy jacket. *Maybe it's because people can't see the end that they agree to begin.*

"What's up?" Ross asks. But Ross saw the man, too.

"This fella wants us to go up to the studio. He's got a reel he wants us to hear."

Ross hesitates.

"He's army."

"Yeah."

"Is there any money in it?"

"He said it's 'considerable.'"

"Is that for them to consider or for us?"

"He said it's a lot."

Ross looks to Larry, dancing down the bar.

"Then we'll come right back down?" he asks Philip.

"Yep," Philip says.

But the two friends stare into each other's eyes for a beat, and in that brief rhythm is the truth that they both know they won't be right back down.

"What is it?"

"A sound."

Ross smiles. But it's not a nice one.

"Well, shit, Philip," he says, sweating now. "How much trouble can one sound be?"

5

I wouldn't do that if I were you . . .

Fissures, cracks, clefts, canyons.

And it's not just in his bones.

Philip is trying to make connections.

It's midday and sunlight penetrates the unit's one window. A blond nurse, Delores, administers a shot and even this contact, needle to skin, is something.

Philip feels frighteningly alone.

There was Secretary Mull walking into the bar, Doug's Den. There was the sound. There was . . .

But in a way, there was nothing after the sound. As if, once Philip got out of the booth and gathered the Danes, reality eroded, the daily ticks and tacks, the hum of existence, the unheard sound of the planet spinning, all of it was replaced . . . with the *sound.*

"Radio?"

Delores is asking him if he wants to listen to an afternoon drama. The concept is so far from what Philip is thinking about that it almost feels like she doesn't mean what she asks.

He doesn't respond.

Instead, he's sensing a change.

Was it the shot? It must be. The sensation of being stuck, paralyzed, unable to bend a finger, is lessening. Pieces are being put back together, the picture the puzzle makes . . .

There was Mull. There was agreeing to go listen to the sound . . . there was Africa . . .

Yes, Philip almost feels able to turn his head, to lift his hands, to speak easily. But when he tries, he discovers he still can't.

And yet, things *are* changing.

Connections.

I wouldn't do that if I were you . . .

That's a big one. The "who" in "who said that?" Philip remembers the words, even remembers the voice, but can't place where he heard the warning.

Was it in the desert? Was it in Detroit?

And "wouldn't do" what?

"I'll put it on," Delores says, out of Philip's field of view. "And you tell me if it's too loud."

Philip isn't listening to her. He's making connections. His bones, his body, his brain . . .

For the first time in his life, Philip's identity is at stake. Maybe he'd acted too cool for his own good, before the Namib Desert, before the hoofprints in the sand. Maybe all the things that he thought meant something don't mean anything after all. Maybe Detroit was a fantasy land, Wonderland, where he was a hero, where he was a star, where he walked the streets and nodded to some people and ignored others, too cool, the man in the band, the man in the army, the soldier musician who flirted without words, who awed the younger piano players, the young men weighing the options of war.

How many locals joined the army because of the Danes?

The radio is playing, two voices, back and forth. A husband and a wife? A husband and a mistress? Even this, the roles of the voices he hears, even these are suffering from some sort of identity breakdown, an erosion, who is who, who did what, who took the Danes and where did they take them?

Who said what?

I wouldn't do that if I were you . . .

He must have groaned, must have made a sound, because Delores is suddenly beside him, placing a hand on his forehead.

"Are you okay?"

But what kind of question is this?

The unnecessary answer is no.

He thinks of the nurse from the night before. Ellen. Was that her name? She seemed to emerge from the shadows of the unit, the shadows of his injury, his thoughts, the space between his connections.

What else might rise from those regions?

Has he ever been this scared before?

Identity.

And yet, the shot, the medicine is doing something profound. Philip knows enough about drugs to know that this isn't like getting high. This isn't a pill to relax you or a joint to set your thoughts aflame. This is the gradual easing of bones, muscle, and skin into preformed foam, a return . . .

To what?

To normal.

Or a better normal. Yes, Philip thinks, seeing a window, a sliver of hope for a calmer day, a reality in which he might move again.

Might make connections.

"Is it always this cold in the summer?"

Philip said that. And his voice was splintered wood.

Because she hesitates to respond, Philip knows Delores is surprised to hear him speak.

"Would you like me to close the window?"

"No," Philip says, still staring to where the wall meets the ceiling. "Just . . . strange weather."

"Well," Delores says. And before she says what she's about to say, Philip knows he's fooled her. "Nobody said Iowa was reasonable."

Iowa.

"Iowa," he repeats.

And he can see her now, her features in his field of vision. She's brought a hand to her lips, as if questioning herself, debating quickly whether or not she was supposed to tell him where he was.

"I'll close the window partway."

She crosses by the foot of the cot. As Philip hears the window sliding half shut, he's making connections. Bodily. And in mind.

Iowa.

It isn't just that he's fooled Delores into telling him their location; he's gotten her to show him that whether or not Iowa was a secret, there *are* secrets in here.

Things kept from him. The look on her face tells him so.

As his body mends, stitching itself together, temporarily or not, Philip wonders at his new identity, his new scared self, how the hospital has secrets, and how he must keep secrets of his own. And he thinks of his former self, too, an aloof drunk in Detroit, a musician soldier who once believed that a man was defined by how much awe he struck in others.

But exactly when did that mind-set change? Was it when Secretary Mull opened the door to the bar? Was it when Sergeant Lovejoy pointed to the prints in the desert and said "this way"?

Was it when someone warned him, in a voice he still can't place, the only detail he can't remember from the desert?

I wouldn't do that if I were you . . .

As Delores passes by the foot of the cot again, Philip is almost able to shake his head no.

No. Not those times. Not those places.

It happened when he was with his best friends. In a place he felt more comfortable than any other in the city. At a time when he felt on top of the world.

Philip changed forever, got unconnected, the first time he listened to the sound.

6

Will I be court-marshaled if I record this?" Ross asks.

Secretary Mull smiles. But shakes his head yes.

"That's against the rules, Private Robinson."

"A recording studio probably isn't the best place for a clandestine meeting," Larry says. Like Duane, Larry hasn't sat down. As if the pair won't commit even that much yet.

Mull nods. Papers he's brought rest upon the mixing console.

"But we do what we can," he says.

He's likable. Philip doesn't like that. Mull's full black hair brings out the blue shine in his eyes. If not for the sadness in those eyes, and the wrinkles on his strong face, he might look something like Superman.

Mull removes the quarter-inch reel from the breast pocket of his suit jacket.

"Mind playing this?" he asks Ross.

"That's the mystery sound?" Philip asks.

"It is," Mull says. Still seated in the engineer's chair, he hands the reel to Ross. "Thank you."

The Danes are suspicious. With good reason. Secretary Mull has proposed they fly to a desert in Africa to "identify the source of a dangerous sound."

A new weapon? The United States Army thinks so.

Mull leans forward, places his elbows on his knees, rubs his hands together.

"You can roll the tape," he tells Ross. "There's quite a bit of headway and discussion before the sound begins."

Ross threads the reel and presses play. He looks at Philip.

What's going on? his expression asks.

"We first heard the sound in '48," Mull begins. "Came through a routine radio check conducted in Tallahassee, Florida. We understood it was a disturbance but we didn't consider it a threat. We asked our radio men to isolate the frequency. The problems started to surface immediately. We weren't able to determine what it was. And of course we're not in the business of ignoring unknown signals. Rather quickly it became a priority in our offices. Then the Pentagon got involved. Audio experts removed the static, isolated the tone, got it as clear as they could get it. But at some point it became clear that if we wanted to know what was making this noise, we'd have to go find it. We've already sent two platoons. All soldiers. No musicians. That's why we're interested in you."

Voices on the tape. Muffled. Military men. Philip can almost see the dimensions of the conference room in which the tape was recorded. The echo is tight, suggesting low ceilings, long walls.

"The only positive ground we made was determining its relative location. Partially. The Namib Desert. Africa. But that still doesn't tell us what's making it."

"Hang on," Larry says, putting his hands on his hips. "You're telling us there's a sound coming from somewhere in all that desert and you want us to find it?"

"Yes. That's it exactly. We think sending in experts, live, to experience the sound live—"

"Did either of the first two platoons have any luck?" Philip asks.

Mull nods slowly.

"Some."

"What's some?" Duane asks.

"It's buried," Larry says. "Beneath the sand. That's obvious, right? If soldiers go looking for a sound in the desert, and they can't find it, that thing's gotta be buried. Right?"

"The Pentagon doesn't get involved unless they have to," Duane says.

"Right," Ross says, his elbow just inches from the revolving reels. "Until it's a matter of national security—"

"The sound," Mull says without looking any of the Danes in the eye, "inoculated one of our nuclear warheads."

A moment of static on the tape. No voices.

"What does that mean?" Philip asks.

"That means that we believe the frequency somehow . . . robbed our most powerful defense weapon of its . . . power."

"How do you know—" Philip begins.

"And there's more," Mull says.

"Oh, I bet there's more," Duane says.

Mull breathes deep.

"Once the alarm was sounded, the notification that the warhead had been sterilized, an MP drew his gun and quickly discovered it, too, had been rendered useless."

Philip imagines an entire army with impotent weapons. How different they would look.

"So," Mull continues, an ear on the muffled voices from the speakers, "a matter of national security indeed. A weapon like that could make us all . . . the whole country . . . vulnerable."

"Listen," Larry says. "We may have served, but we were only in the band."

"That's what makes you gentlemen ideal."

Some silence. Big thinking.

"And it's up to us to find out where it is?" Duane asks, but still far from committing. Philip is surprised his drummer hasn't walked out the door. All this feels like the top of a slide. A return to the army, the life they've left behind, is waiting for them at the bottom.

"Yes," Mull says. "But, of course, there's a bigger question than where."

"What?" Ross asks.

"Who."

"Hey," Duane says, having finally heard enough.

Mull removes earplugs from his jacket pocket. He places them firmly in his ears.

"I'm sorry, gentlemen. The sound is about to begin and I can't stomach hearing it another time. Please forgive me in advance."

"What?" Philip asks.

Mull adjusts his earplugs.

"Hang on a minute," Duane says, holding out a black palm toward Mull. "How bad can it be?"

Philip looks to Ross as Ross falls to his knees by the playback speaker.

"Ross?"

He looks back to Mull, sees the military man has adopted a new expression, one of study.

Philip throws up.

He hardly felt it coming and he looks to his lap, sees the bronze sheen of booze. He grips the soft arms of the control room chair.

The sound, Philip understands, has begun.

But does he hear it?

He feels sick. Drunk sick. Worse. Stronger. Like his skin is now made of leather. He's sweating. Colors, gray and black, snake in his belly. He's bringing a hand to his forehead.

The others are covering their ears. Larry looks like he's been hurt.

Philip opens his mouth to say something and saliva pours from his lips. Feels like he's going to vomit again. Larry gets up to leave the control room but can't bring his hands from his ears long enough to open the door. He wobbles, falls against the wall for support. Vertigo.

Duane is on his side on the ground.

Mull leans back in the engineer's chair, patient, with folded hands. His eyes reveal that he knows exactly what the Danes are experiencing. He's experienced it himself.

The inimitable sensation of fingertips in Philip's ears. He turns fast. Nobody there.

Mull smiles without mirth. Nods.

What do you think it is? he seems to ask. *What is it, Philip?*

Philip is shaking his head no.

I don't know. I don't understand. It's not a sound. It's a feeling.

But it is a sound. Listen.

Philip strains for it . . . an ear to the speakers . . .

. . . there *is* a sound.

It's more than one note, Philip thinks, staring Mull in the eye. *A chord.*

He's trying to raise his fingers to play the chord on an unseen piano before him. But he can barely move, barely lift his arm.

The sound is more of a flood than a reverberation. More like something coming toward him than a song. As if the air it travels upon is scorched, rendered black, leaving a trail as wide as the studio, and maybe the entire city beyond the studio walls.

Larry falls to his knees by the front door. Ross rolls to his side on the carpeted floor of Wonderland.

Are they speaking? The other Danes? Are they telling Mull to turn it off?

From the ground, Ross reaches for the control panel.

Mull watches all of this. Silent. Patient.

Philip throws up again.

Duane rolls onto his belly. Ross's fingers are contorted, arthritic bones testing the flesh of his hands . . .

Philip hears a chord, three successive half steps played at once, as if someone has flattened their hand upon a piano. He's done it himself, drunk, playing for girls, trying to make them laugh; a flat hand was funnier than a melody; but it's a mean sound, the three notes no superstitious musician will play at once.

Philip tries to say that, tries to open his mouth. Then—

The sound stops.

And for a beat there is only the silence of men trying to process what they've endured.

The vertigo has passed. The sickness is gone.

"Jesus *Christ,*" Larry says, getting again to his feet. "No way. I'm out."

Mull nods. He's expected this response.

Ross brings the wastebasket close like he's going to puke. He gags instead.

Duane is standing unsteadily in the center of the room.

"What was *that?*" he asks, out of breath.

Mull looks to Philip.

"Private Tonka said it's a chord. Did you all hear it that way?"

Philip is shaking his head no.

"I didn't say that."

Mull smiles coldly.

"Sure you did."

"No, Secretary. I didn't." Philip is sitting up. "I didn't say that at all. I thought it."

Mull shakes his head no.

"You made a sound, Private Tonka. And I heard it. Am I wrong? Did you not think it was a chord?"

Philip looks from bandmate to bandmate, finally back to Mull.

"I did," he says. "I heard a chord."

As the other Danes debate what they heard, Philip stares Mull in the eye.

You made a sound, Private Tonka. And I heard it. Am I wrong?

Philip breathes deep and thinks of Africa. Thinks of two platoons, unable to find a sound that changes how a man feels, changes how he listens, changes how he speaks, too.

"Three hours," Mull says, rising, handing each a small pile of documents. The military man's number is written in pen on the papers. "Three hours to tell me whether or not you're going to Africa." He removes the reel from the machine and tucks it into the inside pocket of his suit coat. "I've already told Private Tonka that we plan to pay you for this mission. But perhaps I failed to say how much."

The Danes, still recovering, wait.

"One hundred thousand apiece," Mull says. "Four hundred thousand for the band." He adjusts his suit coat. "I'm not one for theatrical exits, but the stakes here are rather high. If it is a weapon, maybe the four of you can stop it from being used." He steps to the door. "Three hours, gentlemen. We expect a decision by then."

7

Ellen watches Philip from behind the glass of the nurses' station. She's observed him every day for six months, and it's still shocking to see him this way. Awake. Blinking. The subtle movement of his lips. The sweat at his black hairline. When the orderlies Carl and Jerry wheeled him into the Observation Room, Carl mentioned that Philip was in a rock 'n' roll band. The Danes. Jerry said he never heard of them.

But maybe Ellen has. The name rings a bell, sparks something, but she can't think of what it is. Maybe it's just because Presley has a hound dog.

The Danes.

Ellen thought he was going to die. It's how the nurses view most of the patients who're brought to Macy Mercy. Comatose. Or near. And near death, too. So close you can feel it when you walk the halls, day or night; a black fog, formless fingers reaching for the doors of each unit, capable of opening them, prepared to pull the life from the still, barely, living. Why, just the day before Philip woke, the patient in Unit 9 died. His vital signs had looked promising; the chances of a recovery were being considered. The nurses agreed he was looking much better than Philip himself, and yet . . . those fingers. Some days

Ellen felt the full hands of Death in the halls of Macy Mercy Hospital. Impatient, greedy, perverted.

When Philip was first brought in, the nurses ogled the X-rays that showed fractures in so many bones of his body, as if someone had intentionally set out to hurt him, premeditating the unbelievable construct of jagged lines, the chaos of fissures, a lack of logic, of plausibility, of survival.

And yet, Ellen is no stranger to the weird. Almost every patient who arrives at Macy Mercy is in an anomalous condition. And as long as Ellen's been employed here she's had to juggle the sensibility of a modern woman of 1957 with the understanding that those who run the military hospital know more than she does. It's part of her occupation, keeping questions to herself. And like most employees the country over, Ellen wouldn't be here were it not for the money. Living alone in an apartment on Carter Street, she needs this job. And she likes the work. And sometimes, but not always, she even finds herself trying to solve these mysteries that come through the front door of the hospital.

Like this man. Philip Tonka. The one she watches now through the glass of the nurses' station. The sight of Philip's X-rays will never be removed from her memory, and it's difficult, even now, to observe him without thinking of those broken lines, some small, most not, knowing that they exist in some form beneath the incredibly bruised and discolored flesh.

Christ, it's like watching an episode of that television show *Science Fiction Theatre.*

Philip blinks.

The skin around his eyes is especially badly bruised, but not too much more so than the rest of his body. Barring a quantum leap in cosmetic surgery, his features are forever distorted. His face is dented, his chest asymmetrical, and yet . . . there is a kind of cohesiveness to him. Ellen wonders if it's because there's no one else in the world quite this . . . color.

As she takes notes, minor scribbles marking the blinks, his tongue across his lips, she can't help but wonder what he once looked like.

Which side of his crooked face is the real him? Is either?

Ellen uses lined paper; a white that rivals her uniform, gives her a sense of illumination here in this nurses' station furnished with gray filing cabinets, brown drawers, and black desks. Behind her, Nurse Francine is preparing medicine for Philip. She'll administer it, as she and Delores always do, twice a day. It's Ellen's job to mark the physical progress of the freshly woken patient. After an injury such as his, even a blink counts.

But aside from his eyelids and his lips, he hasn't moved yet. He hardly speaks at all, and when he does it sounds like his throat is sandpaper dry, whether or not she's just given him water to help.

"Amazing," Francine says, looking through the glass with Ellen.

"Yes," Ellen says. "Didn't think we'd be tracking movement with this one, did we?"

"No, ma'am," Francine says, her nose less than inch from the window. Ellen sees the older nurse reflected, her black-rimmed glasses superimposed over the heavy wrinkles of her wide face. "Not a chance in hell."

Then they're silent. No jokes from Ellen. No hypotheses from Francine. They don't guess as to what happened to Philip because they've already done that, six months of it, leading up to yesterday's surprise awakening. Some of those speculations were too incredible to fathom, and yet something incredible must have occurred. Delores wondered if it was the work of one man; the patient's injuries, it seemed, had to be intentional, designed. Francine thought a fall from a cliff could've done it. The orderlies, Carl and Jerry, talked about bomb blasts. But Philip's body is devoid of shrapnel. And there isn't a surface abrasion on him.

The bruises, the endless spread of purple and orange, mud brown and yellow, are from the injuries within.

Philip lies on his back, stares to the ceiling, his chest, arms, and hands exposed.

For Ellen, the answer lies somewhere in that skin. Sometimes, when forced to touch it, removing or applying the IV, she's felt a certain falseness there, a rubbery replacement. As though Philip's skin had been exposed to something powerful enough to change it. Ellen didn't think it would ever fit right again. The word she didn't want to use was the same one all the nurses had avoided for six months running.

Nuclear.

In this day and age? Who knew. It was on the cover of every newspaper and magazine, on the mind of every man and woman in America.

Just last week, Ellen woke from a nightmare, an image of Philip removing his skin, a costume, allowing it to fall in folds to the floor.

I'm radioactive, he'd said. *Touch me,* he'd said.

Now, in the light of the observation room overheads, Philip's skin looks phonier than ever.

"But life goes on," Francine says. "For this one."

The soft click of the door opening and closing behind her lets Ellen know she's alone in the station. Francine will administer Philip's shot, then leave to tell Dr. Szands in the office.

Ellen tries not to think about the mysteries here. The host of *Science Fiction Theatre* was Truman Bradley, a former war correspondent long before he started introducing the pseudoscientific episodes. He was an actor, too. A good-looking one, if Ellen remembers him right.

Did Philip once look like Truman Bradley?

Maybe it's the way he looks at the ceiling, as though questioning something himself.

Maybe it's because he's the first to answer her silent nonreligious prayers.

Philip blinks.

Ellen notes.

As a girl, Ellen saw herself one day walking the streets of New York City, shopping with friends, meeting at ethnic restaurants with complicated names, eating lunch on the benches in the parks.

But then, love . . . a brief, tragic motherhood . . . and here her life has led up to this moment . . .

. . . nursing.

It's not lost on her that her profession could be seen as a way of atoning for the loss of her daughter, a need to heal, a need to ward off those black fingers in the halls of Macy Mercy, arriving herself at the doors before they do, perhaps this time with the right dosage of medicine, or a miracle joke to make.

Even here, forty miles outside of Des Moines, Ellen has friends who act as armchair psychiatrists.

You should get away from the hospital, some say. *You should get away from sadness,* others.

Ellen thinks they're right, of course, all of them. And yet she can't bring herself to go. Can't bring herself to walk away from men like Philip Tonka, who was most certainly left in a basket at death's door, and now blinks in rhythm with a beating heart.

As Francine gives him his shot, Ellen spins in the seat of the office chair and rolls to the small cooler kept in the corner. She takes a can of soda, wheels back.

She likes her job. She does. She takes pride in the fact that she's helping others, even if most of those others aren't conscious of her help. She'd rather be here, marking the progress of a man who has life yet inside him, than spilling cocktails with friends in the big city.

Yes? Isn't this true?

Ellen shouldn't ask herself questions like these.

She looks to the clock on the wall.

She notes the time on the paper.

When she looks up, Philip is looking back at her.

Ellen, middrink, gasps, spills some of the grape soda onto the front of her white uniform.

Philip is looking at her out of the corner of his eye.

And he's moving the tips of his fingers.

"Oh my God," Ellen says, standing up, then sitting down. She wipes the soda from her uniform, starts to make a note, writes messily, looks through the glass again. Francine has already left. "Oh my God, he's moving."

She's too excited to write. She gets up instead, turns to leave the station, then rushes back to the glass.

Through it, their eyes meet, momentarily.

The bent fingers of his right hand, all five, are moving. It may be slight, but it's movement.

From a man who broke almost every bone in his body.

Ellen smiles. She can't help but smile. But Philip only stares. And there is fear in his eyes. A fear Ellen doesn't believe she's ever felt herself.

She rushes from the station with the news.

8

For his three hours to think, Ross heads home. Mom is home. And as far as Ross can remember, Mom knows best.

He's got the data, his copy of the papers, folded and stuffed into his coat pocket. It's an important feeling, walking the streets of Detroit with a secret in his coat. On a different day, he might find it thrilling, like espionage on television. But right now his enthusiasm is tempered by the crystal memory of the sound he listened to in the control room.

Ross brings a hand to his belly as he crosses the grass on Indiana Street and takes the steel stairs that lead to the back door of the duplex he shares with Mom.

Mom.

And how's he going to ask Mom about this one?

If there's one person Ross knows who is unimpressed by the United States Army, it's Mom. Hell, back during World War II, when the other Danes were getting praise and encouragement from home, Mom would send Ross letters beseeching him to go AWOL. *War is embarrassing,* Mom would say. *And none of this fighting will mean anything in ten years.*

Of course she was both right and wrong about that. Twelve years removed from the war, it did feel a lot less important. And yet . . . the world had changed. In many ways for the better. And if Ross were given the chance to contribute like that again . . .

. . . shouldn't he?

He finds his keys in his pants pocket and unlocks the back door.

"Ross?"

Right away. Ross doesn't even get the chance to take a deep breath. It's like Ruth Robinson can hear it when her son's got a big decision to make.

Can hear it. Like a sickening sound, eh, Ross?

"Hey, Ma. Home."

"Why?"

Mom doesn't miss a beat. She may be fifty-eight years old and walk around the house in her pajamas all day, but Ruth is as sharp as she's ever been. Ross knows this better than anybody else.

"Session was canceled."

He reaches into his jacket pocket and fingers the document that he's already read.

"Why?"

Ross looks up and sees Mom is already standing in the kitchen doorway. Glasses on a band around her neck. No hiding from her now, she's already seen his face. She already knows something is on his mind. Still . . . he'll try.

"Oh, you know . . . kids. We got any chicken?"

Mom pauses an unnatural beat before answering him.

"Sure. In the fridge."

Ross is trying to act cool, but at thirty-one years old, it's harder to deceive Mom than it used to be.

And isn't he going to have to tell her? Isn't he planning on saying yes?

For a hundred thousand dollars each, aren't all the Danes planning on saying yes?

"Thanks, Ma," Ross says, pulling a plate of chicken from the fridge and placing it on the kitchen table. Mom is wearing a blue bathrobe, her hair as curly as her son's. She's leaning against the doorframe. Studying him.

Ross sits down at the table and looks at the chicken and suddenly feels ill. As if the sound from the control room was made of chicken, too.

"Take your jacket off," Mom says.

His jacket. Ross hasn't taken it off. Why not? He knows why not. Because there's something to hide in one of the pockets. A piece of paper explaining why he should fly to an African desert and put his life on the line. For America.

Again.

"What is it, Ross?" She doesn't mince words. She doesn't wait on things long.

Ross shakes his head.

"Nothing, Ma. Just . . . nothing."

He jams some chicken in his mouth and for a second he thinks he's going to vomit it right back up. The initial taste is stunning to his system. He looks to the plate again, half expecting to see gray meat there; something bloated, something bad.

"Nothing," Mom repeats. And the way she says it, Ross has no choice but to look at her.

So he does. And the two hold each other's gaze for a full thirty seconds before Ruth shakes her head.

"The army," she says.

"Yes."

"What do they want?"

Ross reaches into his coat pocket and pulls out the folded paper. He holds it for her to take. Ruth looks at it like it's a spider, like something she isn't sure she wants to put her fingers on. But she crosses the small kitchen and takes it from her son. She slides out the second chair at the table, sits, unfolds the paper, and places her glasses on the bridge of her nose.

Ross, feeling better for having eaten after all, eats the rest of the chicken as Mom reads. When she's done, she doesn't turn the paper over, doesn't crumple it up, doesn't toss it away.

"Don't do it," she says. Flat. Three syllables.

"I'm going to, Ma."

"Don't."

"Why not?"

Ross feels a rush. He's decided to do it after all.

Ruth places her elbows on the table and leans closer to him.

"Mystery," she says, "is bad enough on its own. But mystery with the army?" She shakes her head. "Means they're hiding something."

"They don't know where it is. Somebody's hiding it from them."

"Uh-huh."

Dismissive. But even now, with Mom saying no, Ross feels the swell of yes.

It all comes down to a single word, doesn't it, Ross? he thinks. *A single word that propels you and your bandmates, your best friends. One word that got you guys in the army in the first place, got you into a band, gets you into trouble three or four times a week. One word that weighs more than one hundred thousand dollars apiece.*

"Adventure," Mom says, shaking her head. "You can screw your adventure."

Ross nods. Of course, she's right. And yet . . . that *is* the word. Always has been.

Philip calls it the Path.

"They need us," Ross says.

"Who's they?"

"America."

Mom scoffs and slams both hands down on the table. Hard enough to rattle the chicken bones on Ross's plate.

"America doesn't *need* you, son. America needs a psychiatrist."

"We know sound. We can find it for them."

"And then? Then what? You just point to it and . . . presto . . . you're back home?"

Ross hasn't thought this far ahead. It scares him, briefly, that he hasn't thought this far ahead.

"Well . . . yeah. Something like that."

Mom shakes her head again.

"That's not even mystery, Ross. That's ignorance. Don't go."

"Ma."

"I don't like it. Don't go."

"Ma."

Ross is smiling. Peacefully. Any red rush has left his cheeks and he looks the part of the grown man he is.

Adventure.

The Danes.

And the popularity and esteem he and his friends have received from being both veterans and musicians. How can they say no when they get so much out of saying yes?

"Did you read what happened to the other two platoons?" Mom asks.

Ross nods.

"Of course I did."

"*Did* you?"

"I did. They all came back home safely."

"No," Mom says. She slides the paper in front of her son and points to the part she's talking about. "Read."

"Ma, I read it."

"Read again."

Ross sighs and looks down. He feels a pang of fear, embarrassment, like he's about to see a whole new paragraph that states clearly the first two platoons were sentenced to death by hanging.

But that's not what Mom is pointing at.

"All members of the previous platoons returned home safely. Empty-handed and flummoxed, but safe."

"That's it," Mom says.

"They couldn't find it," Ross says.

Mom shakes her head for the last time.

"Flummoxed, Ross. You know what that means?"

"Of course."

"No you don't. Flummoxed doesn't just mean they couldn't solve the mystery. That would be 'unsatisfied.' Flummoxed stays with you the rest of your life."

"Ma."

"These men, they're gonna wonder about that sound . . . forever."

"Ma."

"They're gonna hear it in their sleep. They're gonna hear it awake . . . on the streets."

"Ma."

"Don't do it, Ross."

Ross places his hands over hers.

"A hundred thousand dollars," he says. "Each."

Mom gets up from the table. She takes the plate from in front of him, holds it sideways over the small silver garbage can so that the bones slide into the bag. Then she places the plate in the sink.

"Flummoxed," Mom repeats, leaving the kitchen. Then she appears again in the doorway. "Two weeks?"

"Two weeks," Ross says. "In and out."

Mom nods.

"Bring me back some sand."

DUANE AND LARRY hit the bar. Where else are they going to go to make a decision like this? Duane takes the stool facing the door. He always faces the door, wherever they go. World War II did that to him. Larry doesn't mind. Duane faces the crowd, too, sitting at the drums.

Together they've got this corner of the bar covered. An old bluesman, Swoon Matthews, sits alone at the other.

"You know Philip is gonna want to do it," Larry says. "He doesn't say no to anything."

"Doesn't mean we have to."

"No, it doesn't mean we have to."

They order White Russians, the drink they drink when they're trying to mellow out. Both of them can easily recall the sound of the air in the studio splitting apart . . . the sound of scorched space, and the image of a black mad trail behind it.

"What do you think?" Larry asks, already knowing what Duane thinks.

Duane shrugs.

"Sounds dicey is what I think."

"How so?"

"The other two platoons. I don't like it."

"Don't like that they didn't find anything?"

Duane shrugs again, but it's not dismissive.

"Yeah, maybe."

Larry weighs out how to say what he wants to say.

"I bet we can do it."

"Of course we'll find it."

The drinks come. Larry pauses. Sips. Then says,

"You just said that like we're going to go."

"So I did."

"So you think we're going?"

Duane points discreetly to the end of the bar. He whispers now.

"Check out Swoon," he says. "You checking him out?"

Larry is.

"Yeah, sure."

"What do you think Swoon would do? You think he'd fly to Africa for the army?"

Larry thinks about it.

"No. I don't think he would."

"And why wouldn't he?"

"I don't know, Duane. Because he's a hundred years old?"

Duane shakes his head no. Sips from his Russian.

"Because he's content with doing the same thing every day."

"And you're not?"

"Have we ever been?"

Larry nods along. Entering the bar, he thought he was going to be the one doing the convincing. But Duane has turned the tables. Feels wrong. Like one of them ought to be saying this is crazy.

"We're thrillers," Duane says. "If you haven't figured that out by now, go hang out with Swoon for the rest of the day."

Larry eyes the old bluesman. His curly white hair sleeps uneven upon his black wrinkled forehead. He wears sunglasses indoors. Maybe he's looking back at Larry. It doesn't matter. Right now Larry needs to look at this man. Needs a reminder of how easy it is to slip into the rest of your life.

"Some people settle before they should," Larry says. He doesn't have to explain what he means. Duane gets it. He speaks this language.

"No doubt."

The two former soldiers and current bandmates sip their drinks. White Russians are to be enjoyed, endured. And decisions like this one are meant to go slowly, even if the decision is already made.

"So what's holding us back from telling the others?" Larry asks.

Duane shrugs.

"Nothing. We got three hours is all."

"Something's bothering you."

"Yeah, something's bothering me."

"In the report."

"Yeah, in the report."

"What is it?"

Duane pauses before reaching into his pocket. Larry thinks his drummer, his friend, is going to pull forth the folded papers. Instead he pulls out a packet of cigarettes, taps one out, and lights it.

Duane breathes deeply. Exhales.

"Why didn't he stay?"

"Who?"

"Mull."

"What do you mean?"

"You didn't read the papers."

"Yeah, I did."

"Well, you didn't read them close enough. Mull flew with both platoons to the desert, but he didn't stay for the mission. Why not?"

Larry opens his mouth to speak. He raises his glass, drinks, instead.

"He's got different work to do," he finally says.

"Mm-hmm. You see Swoon there?"

"Yeah, I see him, Duane."

"Yeah. You know why he's content just being Swoon in Detroit?"

Larry thinks about it. Sometimes Duane gets like this. Cryptic. Usually it leads to something profound. But right now Larry doesn't want profound. He wants easy. He wants Duane to say they're going to make a lot of money doing a good thing.

"It's because he's scared," Duane finally says.

"Sure. But what does that have to do with—"

Duane grabs Larry by the wrist.

"Mull is scared of that sound. Scared him whiter than the white he is."

Duane slowly releases Larry's wrist and settles back onto the stool.

"Naw," Larry says without confidence. What he thinks is, *So am I.*

"Uh-huh," Duane says. He sips from his drink, allows an ice cube into his mouth, crushes it. "Here's an officer in the United States Army, brave enough to step into the lives of four strangers with a pocketful of sound, but he's too chicken to sit out there and listen to it himself."

"It's the army, Duane You know how it works."

"This is different. I saw it in his eyes in the studio. When the tape started rolling. Saw him looking at those wheels like they were delivering the worst of his nightmares. He knows that tape inside out, every beat of it. Slipped on those earplugs just before the sound started. He's scared, Larry. Scared of something more than a new weapon."

Larry laughs. "Now you're just talking crazy."

But Duane doesn't smile. Smoke rises around his eyes and for a ghastly second he looks mummified to Larry. Like he's never gonna move again.

"There are things worse than a new weapon," Duane says, finishing his drink.

"Like what?"

"Like the kind of person that would build it."

"THE FIRST PLATOON was deployed a year ago. Almost to the day. I wonder what I was doing that day."

"You might've been in this exact same bedroom."

Philip smiles. Not without concern. He's lying down beside a girl named Marla. He's dressed. She's not. They don't love each other, but Christ they have fun. Philip met Marla on the Path.

"But get this," Philip says, sitting up so that he's resting on his elbow. "The second platoon was deployed six days after the first returned. So that would make it . . . about . . . about ten months now since the second platoon returned."

"So?"

"So why the long wait? That's what's got me worried."

"They were looking for guys like you," Marla says. Her red hair half hides her face. The bedsheet only mostly covers her.

"Maybe," Philip says. "And another thing." Now he sits up, cross-legged on the mattress. "Why hasn't the sound gotten any more intense?"

"How do you know it hasn't?"

"The report has wave files. There's absolutely no difference between the first time it sounded and the last."

"So?"

"So that means that . . . if we're talking about a weapon or something being built . . . it was already built by the time they first heard it."

Marla nods her head.

"So don't go."

Philip's face scrunches up in a way that makes him look ten years younger.

"Don't go? No, no. That's not what I mean. Look, I don't expect the army to tell us . . . *everything*. They never do. It's the army."

"Okay," Marla says. Her smeared dark eyeliner gives her face a Day of the Dead feel in the waning sunlight. "Then go."

Philip agrees. Mostly.

"Yeah. Go. *Go.* But don't go . . . naïve." He gets up out of bed. "The reason for the wait is . . . " He looks up to the ceiling, thinking. "Is because they decided to forget about it. But then . . . then . . . the sound kept showing up. So they decided to go looking for it again. Maybe that's what happened."

Marla smiles.

"Either way. Two weeks in the desert. A lot of money and you're a hero all over again."

She's only half kidding, but the look that crosses his face worries her. He doesn't smile. He only nods, and Marla understands that she's accidentally spoken the exact reason and motivation for Philip wanting to go.

"And the reason the sound hasn't changed . . ."

Philip stops speaking halfway through the sentence and looks out Marla's apartment window. Below is Detroit, its streets bustling with teenagers in cars, homeless men and women folded against building foundations, stray dogs and men in suits who avoid them.

"Just be careful," Marla says. She gets up, too, but doesn't bother getting dressed. She leaves the bedroom.

"I gotta split," Philip calls to her. He looks through the glass, not quite realizing that he's hoping to see Larry, Duane, and Ross down there in the streets. Is he hoping to see them confident, their bags packed?

Philip feels a solitary slash of fear course from his neck to his legs. Then it settles somewhere inside him, but does not leave.

Marla reenters the bedroom with a glass of water. When she hands it to Philip he sees he's still wearing the watch he took from the manager of the Sparklers.

He thinks he should find the guy, return it.

Can't go to Africa. Gotta return a watch.

A silly thought, of course; further proof that Philip is scared.

"Don't get killed," Marla says.

"I won't."

"Oh yeah?"

"That's not my story. Not how my story is gonna end."

"That's just about the most naïve thing I've ever heard you say. You think anybody thinks their story is gonna end the way it does?"

Philip drinks the water.

"Don't get killed," she repeats.

"And don't get dressed," he tells her.

Marla smiles.

"I figured you're gonna be gone two weeks without a woman. May as well give you a two-week memory on your way out." She touches the piano key hanging at his chest. F.

Philip only half laughs. He looks so serious to her. Too much so.

"Hey," Marla says, folding her arms under her breasts. "What's wrong with you?"

"This is a big deal," he says. And even now there's a different look in his eyes. Something childish.

"I know," she says. "I've just never seen you this way before."

"It's nothing," Philip says. "I mean, it is, but . . . it's just . . . the sound staying the same . . . never changing . . . worries me. Nothing is like that, you know? Everything . . . changes."

Marla opens her mouth to say don't go, but Philip places a finger over her lips.

"I'll see you in two weeks," he says.

Marla salutes him. And Philip leaves her apartment.

Below, on the street, Philip tries to shake the feeling, the fear. Everywhere he looks, Detroit seems an exaggeration of itself. The man sweeping the sidewalk outside Bankman's Diner is dressed so right for the part that he almost looks staged. The awning for Adele's Hair and Beauty practically shines. In fact, looking around, it's as if the whole city is a set, a movie being filmed, everything in its place.

Even the orange-painted bricks that make up the front wall of Perry Drugs, the place the Danes shot the cover for their 45 "Be Here," look perfectly, symmetrically stacked.

Philip feels like he's seeing it all for the first time. Through other eyes. Eyes watching that movie, maybe. And the effect the filmmakers are going for is . . .

This is a great city. Don't leave.

Christ, even the sky looks painted.

He makes a right on Elizabeth and sees his three bandmates standing outside the studio door.

Their bags rest at their feet.

For a moment, Philip wonders if they've seen him, too. And if they haven't, could he duck around the corner, slink into a shadow, think about it a little longer?

Ross waves.

Philip waves back.

He's stepping off the Path. He can feel the tug of someone else's rope, mystery dirt beneath his boots.

"Fellas," Philip says, arriving. "Looks like we're going to Africa."

Ross smiles.

"I've already got a theory on what's making the sound. I think it could be a combination of—"

Philip raises a finger.

"Hang on. Let's call Mull first. Tell him we're in."

Philip opens the studio door and takes the carpeted stairs two at a time. Passing through the lounge, he spots the same books that have been lying on the coffee table for months. The kitchen smells like coffee and booze. He experiences an alien combination of feelings: nostalgia for a place he hasn't left yet, and claustrophobia, too . . . as if the walls of the studio get narrower the deeper he goes into it.

By the time he reaches the control room, he feels a little dizzy with it. As if the sound he is agreeing to go hunting for remains, lingers in the room.

He picks up the phone, planning to call Secretary Mull.

But Philip calls home first.

When his mom answers, he feels that fear again. That movie set feeling, too. As if the phone is a piece of plastic and the woman speaking is an actress. The alternative, Philip thinks, explaining to her what he's about to do, is too unreal to accept.

This is a great city. Don't leave.

"Well, if you think it's the right thing to, Philip, then nobody's going to stop you. You always do what you feel you should."

"Mom," he says, looking through the control room glass, into the live room, where he imagines he heard a sound, the furthest phantom wisp of a chord. "Thank you."

9

Are you afraid of flying, Philip?"

"No."

"Heights?"

"No."

"Spiders?"

"No."

"Spiders?"

"You asked me that."

"Spiders?"

"No."

"Snakes?"

"No."

"You would handle a snake if I asked you to?"

Philip pauses. One of the twin tape recorders is rolling behind Dr. Szands. The identical machines, Revere T-700Ds, were the first thing that caught his eye when he was wheeled into this room. Dr. Szands, sitting, cross-legged, like a disappointed father, was second.

"Not in the condition I'm in right now I wouldn't."

Szands rings a bell on the table beside him. Philip knows that the sound of the bell will show up as a spike on the VU meter. It's the doctor's way of telling the tape that something of note was said.

"Cats?"

"No."

"Small spaces?"

Philip thinks of a red piano. But doesn't mention it.

"No."

"Death?"

Philip pauses again. The Revere T-700D wasn't made for recording music. But it's ideal for interrogations.

"Yes."

Szands rings the bell.

The meters spike.

"Women?"

"No."

"Speeding in a car?"

"Sometimes."

One word answers. Just as Szands asked for.

"Do you believe in ghosts, Philip?"

Philip closes his eyes. The reels are rolling and he thinks of Private Greer's theories in the desert. Greer's Wheel, they came to call it.

The sound of history spinning.

"Yes."

The bell.

"Have you seen a ghost, Philip?"

"Yes."

The bell.

"Where was the sound located, Philip?"

"I don't know." No hesitation. But he does know. And he could direct Dr. Szands to it himself. Almost.

"Are you afraid of needles, Philip?"

"No."

"Large crowds?"

"No."

"Loud sounds?"

"No."

"How about this sound?"

Szands reaches to the second T-700D and presses play. Before he even hears it, Philip starts to feel sick.

"Turn it off."

The bell.

"Does this sound scare you?"

"Turn it off, doctor."

The bell.

"Where was the sound located, Philip?"

"I don't know."

"Why do you believe in ghosts?"

"Turn it off!"

Szands turns it off. Philip looks to see if the doctor got sick from it. But Szands, his upper half in shadows, his arms and legs emerging from what looks like solid tar, isn't giving anything away.

"Why do you believe in ghosts, Philip?"

"Because I saw one, dammit."

The bell.

"Where?"

Philip doesn't answer.

"Where, Philip?"

"In the desert."

The bell.

"You saw a ghost in the desert?"

"I saw a hundred ghosts in the desert."

The bell.

Philip is crying now. The questions, the list of fears, the sound . . .

The bell.

"Where was the sound located, Philip?"

"I don't know."

"You do know."

"I don't know, doctor!"

But he does.

"Philip, this test isn't designed to elicit true or false answers from the subject. The test is supposed to give us a clear understanding of whether or not a man has any secrets. And whether or not he's keeping them."

"I'm not keeping any secrets."

"But you are."

But he is.

"Now, Philip, you have a choice to make. You can either play dumb or play smart. And the longer you play dumb, the longer I'll have to simmer. And you don't know me well enough to know where that might lead. Do you understand? I may be a doctor, but that doesn't mean my only concern is *your* well-being. There are many other people on this planet, Philip Tonka. So play dumb or play smart. Get to it or suffer my simmering. Now. Tell me about the ghosts. Tell me about every one you saw. And when you're done . . . tell me where the sound is located. Every turn you took. Every door you opened. Every nightmare you encountered on the way."

10

You won't be alone, of course. That wouldn't be any good for anybody."

A silent soldier is driving the brown express van. Mull is sitting in the passenger seat, but he's turned almost entirely toward the Danes, who occupy the two benches in back.

"Three others will join you. A photographer named Jonathan Stein. He's a spectacular photographer, especially at close range. Uses a mobile dark room. You've also got a soldier who knows the history of the area. Private Gordon Greer. And of course, a platoon leader, a veteran of World War II as well. Sergeant Billy Lovejoy."

"Lovejoy?" Larry asks.

"Yes. You've heard of him." This is not a question.

"Who hasn't? Lovejoy was a legend in basic training."

"The bogeyman," Ross says. "The Mad Blond."

Mull smiles.

"He's deserving of every nickname you can give him. Bogeyman certainly works. He's also a brilliant and patient tactician."

"What do we need that for?" Philip asks. "We're not going to war, Secretary."

Mull tents his fingertips.

"No, you're not. But that doesn't exclude danger. It never does."

Philip can feel Duane's uneasiness beside him.

"I saw Lovejoy in action once," Ross says. "He was wearing clown makeup while he punished his platoon. That's a true story."

Mull smiles again.

"He's an interesting man, no doubt. And absolutely the right one for the job."

"Did he lead the first two teams out?" Philip asks.

"No." Mull shakes his head. "Nobody has returned to Africa. Nobody who went there for this reason."

The driver carefully takes a sharp turn and the tarmac and plane come into view. A second brown van is approaching from the other side of the concrete.

Mull is removing documents from a briefcase. He hands them to Philip.

"Please, take one of these and pass them along."

Philip does. He's looking at a photo, an aerial view of the Namib Desert. Behind the Danes, packed into a small trailer hitched to the van, is all their gear, supplies, clothing, bedding, etc. Ninety percent of the space is occupied by recording gear, top-line stuff that the Danes have dreamed of owning for their studio. Two Ampex model 350 quarter-inch two-tracks. Five Behringer ECM8000 condenser mics. Three RCA 88-As. An Electro-Voice EV C100. Four GPP 73 preamps. A rare signature Glasgow eight-channel mixing console. A Koz Copicat echo chamber. A Boris 5 compressor. Two 678 Michael governors. The other 10 percent is for living out there; the Namib's western end is bordered by the Atlantic Ocean, and temperatures drop mightily at night.

"It says here it's uninhabited by humans," Ross says.

"The area you'll be going to, yes."

Larry smiles. "*Someone's* making that sound."

"Likely," Mull says, and the sadness remains in his blue Superman eyes.

Ahead, through the glass, the second brown van with a second trailer is parking near the plane. Philip watches as the driver's-side door opens and the driver steps down to the tarmac. He walks to the back of the van.

Back to the photo. The Namib. He reads the notes:

Sand seas. White gravel plains. Mountains. A perpetual layer of mist where the Benguela Current and the Hadley Cell meet.

"A lot of fog," Philip says.

Mull agrees.

"Good thing your mission is to listen."

They've reached the plane. The driver parks the van. Through the glass, Philip sees a second soldier emerging from the open side door of the second van. Mull points.

"There's Lovejoy now."

A dark silhouette with patches of wiry blond hair partially protecting a balding head emerges through the open sliding door. Slumped shoulders. Heavy feet. He looks something like a musician himself, Philip thinks. An old and tired bluesman.

"Is he gonna be okay out there?" Larry says. "Could be a lot of walking."

Mull watches Lovejoy, too. It's hard not to. Philip recognizes that there's something immediately magnetic about the man. The physical makings of an army rogue, a legend. Perhaps it's the fact that he looks nothing like a legend at all.

"He'll be fine," Mull says.

The Danes and Secretary Mull exit the van. The drivers of both vehicles and the pilots of the small plane assist in transferring the gear from the trailers. It's a long process. And despite the warm air, Lovejoy rests on a brown suitcase, crouched upon it, a scarf wrapped over his shoulders.

"Jesus," Ross says, thumbing toward Lovejoy. "We're going to have vultures circling us out there."

"He looks like a vulture himself," Larry says.

A third van appears, speeding. The Danes watch its arrival silently. As the last of the gear is loaded onto the plane, the third van parks and two soldiers emerge from the sliding side door.

One, small and squat, with glasses and short black curly hair, struts with confidence toward the others. The second, tall, thin, smiling, his brown hair blown back by the wind, pulls a camera from a case slung over his shoulder.

He snaps a photo of the Danes on the tarmac.

"A rock and roll band," the photographer says, "about to deploy." He extends his hand. Philip shakes it. "I'm Private Stein. Jonathan Stein. And I'm excited as hell to meet you guys. Mind if I get a close-up?"

The Danes are used to photo requests. It's common in Detroit.

"Could be our next album cover," Ross says.

"Oh, hey," Stein says. "Don't even joke about that. I would be *thrilled.*"

"Photos are bad luck," Private Greer says, wiping his glasses clean.

"Oh yeah?" Stein says, smiling, bringing the camera to his eye. "Says who?"

The Danes look into the lens.

"Some cultures believe that when you take a photo, you're saying this period, this phase, is over with," Greer explains. "So if you enjoy your life as it is, mourn. Because now it will be as it *was.*"

Stein snaps the group photo.

Lovejoy rises from the suitcase.

"Gentlemen," Mull says, clasping his hands together. "All aboard."

11

Ellen watches from the doorway. She's carrying a tray of food: vegetables, bread, tomato soup, water; lunch. She'd planned on entering with a joke, something spirited to liven Philip's day, but when she sees him, she pauses.

It's the classical music, she thinks. The phonograph in the main office, just down the hall from Unit 1. The music is soothing, of course, but Philip, who is healing from so many broken bones, doesn't need soothing.

He needs a push.

Ellen steps from the door just as Philip's eyes seem to be straining to see who is in the hall. She carries the lunch tray to the office, enters, and places it upon the closest desk.

The phonograph is set up in the corner, on a short-legged white table. Beside it is a filing cabinet, fake flowers in a plastic vase.

Dr. Szands is not here. The office is empty.

Ellen eyes the box of records on the floor.

Beethoven.

Brahms.

Liszt.

Mozart.

At present, Debussy is playing, and Ellen finds three more records of his music.

But in the back, the very back, she finds what she's looking for.

Rock 'n' roll.

The pickings are slim, six or seven albums, but she allows herself to hope that some of her favorite stuff might be tucked back there.

A quick search shows her it's not. But she finds one that will do.

On the Road with Rock 'n Roll.

She rises and removes the Debussy without a fade. She replaces it with Mando and the Chili Peppers, fetches the lunch tray, and exits the office.

Even the walk to Philip's unit feels different when the first chords of the first song roar out behind her.

It's not the best song she's ever heard, but it's got spirit. And if you ask Ellen Jones, what Philip Tonka needs more than medicine right now is spirit.

When she reenters his unit, his head is facing her.

"Holy shit," she says, and because her hands are occupied she has no free one to bring up to her mouth, to retrieve the swear word.

Philip is nodding his head.

"Did you play this?" he asks.

"You moved your head."

She crosses the unit and places the lunch tray on the foldout table beside the cot.

It's astonishing. Yesterday his fingertips, today his head. Is it even possible? *Should* he be healing this fast?

She sits down beside his cot.

"Do it again," she says. Like she needs proof. Needs to verify that Philip is able to move his head.

But Philip doesn't do it again.

"Am I the only patient in here?" Philip asks. Terse. His voice is different. Clearer. But something else.

Angry.

Why is he asking about other patients? He's *moving.*

"No," she says. "There are others."

Philip nods.

He nods!

"And what's wrong with them?"

What's wrong? she thinks. *What's wrong with you? Can't you see you shouldn't be alive and yet . . . here you are . . . asking questions?*

"A wide variety of things. Many things. But—"

"Are you hiding something from me?"

"What?"

"Are you lying to me?"

"No . . . what . . . about what?"

"Are there other patients?"

"Yes, Philip. I said there were."

"What's wrong with them?"

"Philip, we're not allowed to disclose a patient's—"

"Bullshit."

"Philip." Ellen wasn't expecting this.

"You can't even tell a man like me? A man who can't get out of his own bed?! Are you crazy?"

Ellen has encountered hostile patients before. Of course she has.

She searches her head for her professional voice. Barely finds it.

"Yes," Ellen says. "Even a man like you. Because the injuries the other people in this—"

"Has anyone told my parents that I'm here?"

Ellen doesn't know this answer.

"I don't know."

"You don't know?"

"Philip . . ."

"Does *somebody* know?"

She can see him sitting in a bar, four or five beers deep, the same frustration on his brow, the same foulness rising from within. He's justified in his anger, she understands. But there's something else here, a particular type of rage, like when her alcoholic brother-in-law quit drinking.

"I will find out, Philip. And that's going to have to do."

"For who?"

"For you."

"That's not going to do."

Ellen is getting angry, too. She doesn't want to. Knows better. But the way he's talking to her, after all she's done. Six months of caring for him. Six months of driving to and from Macy Mercy. Nights at home alone, wondering if the patient in Unit 1 was going to die tomorrow, praying that he did not.

"I'm not allowed to—"

"I heard you. Not allowed. And would it be so hard for you to break one fucking rule?"

Ellen stands up.

"Where are you going?"

"I'm leaving you alone for a while, I'm—"

"Sit down!"

Now Ellen doesn't have any difficulty finding her professional voice. The tone of his command, the way he's taking his frustration out on her, it's enough to steel her.

One song ends on the record, another begins. The discrepancy between the music and the mood in the unit is big.

"Philip Tonka. You have every right to be angry. But my job is to help you, not to endure you."

Philip turns his head so that he's facing the ceiling again.

Even now, the movement thrills Ellen.

The two stay silent this way for sixty clicks of the clock.

"You moved your head," Ellen finally repeats.

Philip nods.

"You're getting stronger. Already."

When he speaks, she hears tears in his voice.

"Those X-rays . . ."

"Yes. Scary."

Philip breathes deep. Ellen can see him trying, trying to calm down, trying to be patient, trying to accept what's happened to him.

"Is there an instrument in this room?" he asks.

"Yes, there is. How did you know that?"

"I can hear it. Is it a guitar?"

"It's a piano."

"What color is it?" he asks. Memory in his eyes. Fear.

"What?"

"What color is the piano?" He's yelling again.

"Christ, Philip. It's *wood.*"

"They're all wood. What *color* is it?"

Ellen looks left, to the back of the unit, to where Philip can't see.

"Brown wood. It's not painted."

"Show me," he says. Then, gentle, forced, "Please."

He's whiter than Ellen's uniform.

"All right," she says.

She vanishes out of his field of vision. Philip hears shuffling behind him. Like hands through a purse. When she returns, she's holding a small square mirror.

"There," she says, placing the mirror by Philip's chin, her arms across his badly bruised shoulders.

She shivers at the contact with his skin. Skin she has touched so many times. But now . . . awake.

In the glass, at first, Philip only sees Ellen. Her freckled nose. Her smart, gray eyes. Her raven-black hair. But as she tilts the glass, he sees the piano against the beige back wall of the unit.

He remembers a red piano. Paint flaking. An instrument in a room it had no business being in.

But this piano is not that one. And for first time all day, Philip exhales with relief.

"Why is it in here?"

"What do you mean?"

"Why is there a piano in a hospital room?"

"The doctors used to talk about musical therapy. But they haven't done any more than put pianos in some of the units. Either way, it's nice to have it. To play for the patients. To calm them down."

"Hang on," Philip says, as Ellen makes to move the mirror. "Hang on."

She knows what he wants to see.

The song playing in the office ends. Before the next one begins, in the silence of the unit, Ellen can hear both of their breathing.

Both are nervous for this.

She angles the glass toward his face.

Philip sees it for the first time. The disfigurement. The asymmetry.

"Jesus," he says. He closes his eyes.

Ellen takes the mirror away.

She wants to say something, anything to make him feel less . . . broken.

"Philip . . ."

He looks up at her, but his eyes are distant. She knows he still sees himself.

"I'm gonna flip the record," she says. "Or maybe I ought to put something else on."

She crosses the unit, frazzled with warring emotions. The argument, the fear, the sadness. And the almost forgotten triumph of him moving again.

"Thank you," Philip says.

Ellen pauses at the unit door.

"For what?"

"For the music."

It's the spaces between words, the downbeats in a conversation in which two people feel bad for having fought.

Thank you.

"One day I'll bring in my own records from home. Then you'll hear the good stuff."

"The good stuff," he repeats, nodding. And the movement of his head already looks stronger, more fluid, than it did when she walked in.

12

The soldiers are allowed to smoke on the plane. At twenty hours, the flight is trying, claustrophobic, and the Danes can still hear the echo of Mull's sound in their memories.

The sound inoculated one of our nuclear warheads, Philip recalls. He's alternately studying the info packet on the Namib Desert and eyeing the faces of the others on the plane who are doing the same.

At 250,000 square kilometers, the chance of finding the source appears remote. Mull has already said twice that the plane will be returning in fourteen days to the hour, and Philip can't help but think it doesn't matter if they find it or not. The part of him that is supposed to be assisting America and the United States Army has gone quiet. Maybe it's because the part of him that is leaving Detroit is loud. For a hundred thousand dollars, they'll try their hardest. But if they don't find it?

So be it.

The map of the Namib is intimidating. The two thousand kilometers of desert coastline is the lone comfort, as the rest is without landmark. The gradations from yellow to orange speak of how hot it can get in the Namib during the day, and the fact that it's the world's oldest desert adds a heat that can't be quantified.

The information packet lets Philip know that the word *Namib* means *empty*. But there's more: "Nobody knows this for sure. The languages used in the region are so old as to have undoubtedly gone through many changes." The desert itself has gone through big changes. It was here, during the Jurassic Age, that the continental split occurred. Tracing his fingertips across the paper, Philip can almost feel the violence of that moment in time.

He looks up to see Duane is reading as well. The drummer's black face is mostly hidden in the shadows of the overhead compartment, and his white eyes travel back and forth across the page like the nocturnal desert bugs described in great detail.

There *is* life in the Namib. Animals and insects that have become so adept at bearing the great heat that some of them don't even drink water.

Philip reads on.

In 1908 German miners traveled to Namibia intent on robbing the region of its diamonds. By the 1930s, the diamonds they knew of were gone, but some of the edifices the foreigners erected remain. Philip studies a photograph of what looks like a ranch house overflowing with sand; the color beige pours from the windows, creating solid buttresses that connect with the desert floor.

Larry flips the pages of his packet and the crinkling of the paper brings to Philip's attention how quiet all the passengers are as they study.

Philip looks over his shoulder to the back of the plane.

Lovejoy sits alone, asleep. He's no less interesting, no less strange to look at, with his eyes closed. The blondish thinning hair is arranged unlike anybody else's Philip has ever seen. As if it has fallen from the ceiling to the former general's head.

Former general, Philip thinks. *Demoted.*

This is common knowledge to anybody who has heard of Bill Lovejoy. In training camp, soldiers mocked him out of earshot. Called him crazy. What sort of army man, once demoted, remains in the army? Once the ladder has been folded up and there's no higher to climb?

Arms folded across his chest, half leaning into the empty seat beside his, Lovejoy's body rocks with the plane and, to Philip, he looks like a judge, deep in thought, considering the final arguments of both sides. A red armband around his left bicep reads:

EVERY GOOD BOY DOES FINE

Philip touches the F key hanging around his neck.

Being the piano player in the band doesn't mean Philip's the only member of the Danes to know what that phrase means. It's the singsongy nursery mnemonic by which kids learn the lines on the music staff, EGBDF, the locations of the notes, the piano and how to play it. Seeing it reminds him of his first recital in Detroit, Mom and Dad in the audience. He recalls how his fingers trembled above the keys.

"He's not as chaotic as he looks."

Private Greer is peering over his seat back, his head like a sweaty pumpkin, grinning.

"I don't know him at all," Philip says.

"You will," Greer laughs.

"I don't know you at all."

Greer shrugs. Or maybe the slight turbulence made him do it.

"I'm proof that the army has gotten smarter."

"Yeah?"

"First they sent in soldiers. Now they're sending a historian."

"And why is that any smarter?"

"Because history isn't inactive, Private Tonka. I know your name because I know all your names. I study. I research. And if there's one thing that stands out above all others in my research, it's that history doesn't sit still. Doesn't sit silent. It makes noise." He wipes his nose with the back of his hand.

"Sounds chaotic after all," Philip says.

"I'll tell you what I believe, Tonka. It's not a weapon."

Larry, who has been playing an imaginary bass while studying, his fingers running the scales, leans across the aisle. His long hair hides half his face.

"Bullshit."

"Can't be," Greer says. "It's been sounding off for close to fifteen months. If it was a weapon, they would've disabled it by now. You can't be smart enough to design a weapon we can't find and not smart enough to know the sound would draw us in."

"Maybe they're confident they hid it well," Duane, seated ahead of Larry, says. "Maybe they don't care that it's loud."

"Maybe. But consider this." Greer raises a single finger. "If that sound you heard is the sound of a weapon, we're certainly too late to put a stop to it."

"Why?" Philip asks.

"Because that's not the sound of progress," Greer says. "Whatever that noise is, it's a desired endpoint."

"Bullshit twice," Larry says, half-confidently. "We don't know a thing about it."

Greer smiles.

"Sure we do. We know a thing about it because we know our history. We know what sounds things make. It's not a horn, buried in the sand, Private Walker. And if it's a weapon? And they don't *care* that it makes noise? Well, then we're in some trouble. Imagine that." Greer snaps his fingers. "A weapon so destructive, so deadly, you don't even mind showing it off to your enemies first."

"It makes music," a voice from the back of the plane says. Deep and dulcet, but clipped and quick. "So they're sending musicians."

Philip turns, expecting to see Lovejoy staring ahead. But the mysterious sergeant's eyes are still closed.

Former general. Demoted.

Why?

Greer shrugs.

"So says the sergeant. And so I partially agree. Whatever it is, it's not afraid to be heard."

Ross gets out of his seat and crouches in the aisle between Greer and Larry.

"You guys ever hear of the precedence effect?"

Nobody has.

"It's an auditory trick." Ross is using his hands to express it. "Wherein the echo is louder than the source."

"How is that possible?" Duane asks.

"It's a matter of where you're standing and what's obscuring the sound. Imagine you're in the control room, Duane. Philip sits down at the piano in the live room. There's a divider, blocking Philip and the piano. And the microphone is set across the room, pointed at the ceiling. Far away. Wouldn't it be possible for the echo to be louder to you than what Philip played?"

Philip understands immediately.

"A decoy," he says.

Secretary Mull rises and moves back a row, stumbling with the lilting of the plane.

"That's exactly why we're not sending you to the same location the first two platoons explored."

His face looks different to Philip now. Mull is no longer the man selling the idea; he's now a superior to the soldiers who've already bought it.

"What do you mean?" Larry asks.

Philip looks over his shoulder. Lovejoy's eyes are still closed. But is he awake?

"You'll begin your search along the ocean."

"In the fog," Duane says, examining the photo in his dark hands.

"Yes. In the fog. You're certainly equipped with the necessary lighting, the requisite gear."

"A decoy," Ross repeats.

"In any case," Greer says, "source sound or echo or second echo, whatever. We will find it."

"Why are you so sure of that?" Philip asks.

"Have you considered the point of view of the sound itself yet, Private Tonka? Have you considered that it's been making a sound for over a year for a reason?"

Philip remembers his conversation with Marla before leaving. Recalls his thoughts by her apartment window. He was trying to find an answer to the very same question.

"Yes. I have."

"It knows," Greer says, confidently, with sweaty swagger. "It knows we can hear it. And it's doing it on purpose. Think of yourself, standing in the fog where the ocean meets the desert. You're making the same sound for fifteen months. Why?"

"'Cause I've gone mad," Duane says.

Greer laughs.

"Maybe," he says. "But mad or not, you're making that sound because you want to be heard." Greer nods in the silence he's created. Relishes it. Then, "Where we're heading, there's something that wants us to come." He has their full attention. He pauses dramatically and the plane whimpers against the wind. "I'd go so far as to say we've been invited."

13

It's the day after Ellen showed Philip his reflection. The day after their brief argument. And most important, the day after he moved his head freely.

Dr. Szands is going over notes in the office. Ellen enters.

"Afternoon, doctor."

Szands doesn't respond. Ellen looks at him and sees he's wearing headphones; a tape recorder is rolling on the table in front of him.

Ellen removes her coat and hangs it on the rack.

She can't help but notice her own handwriting on the papers the doctor is reviewing. But what is he listening to?

Nurse Delores enters the office. Delores usually works the morning shift, Ellen the afternoon. It's not hard to see the symbolism there: Delores with her morning-sun blond hair, her conservative, company-line demeanor, and Ellen with dark hair, pale, joking the patients into the night.

Szands presses stop. Rewinds. Plays again.

"What's he up to?" Ellen asks Delores. It's a futile question and Ellen knows it. Even if Dr. Szands explained to Delores in great detail what he was listening to, she wouldn't be the one to repeat it.

Delores shrugs. Removes her coat from the rack. Slips it on.

As she leaves, Ellen tries to sneak another look at the papers the doctor is studying. The page on top no longer has her handwriting.

She sees the words GHOST: WORLD WAR II. Circled. Szands is tapping a pencil against the paper.

Whistling one of her favorite tunes, a song she had played on the piano in Philip's unit often during his six months under, Ellen wants to know what Dr. Szands is listening to. It's a foreign urge, silly really. Never before has Ellen felt a desire to pry, certainly not with Dr. Szands.

But maybe it's the speed with which Philip is healing. Ellen Jones would be the first to tell someone that Macy Mercy has its mysteries, carries its own kind of uncanny energy, but the fact that Philip is already moving his fingers, his head, is too curious to ignore.

Is the solution to this mystery somewhere on the reels that are rolling? An easily explained and just as easily overlooked concept?

Ellen sees sweat marks on the doctor's flower-patterned shirt. She's not moving, she realizes, she's simply staring at his back, as he's seated facing the machine.

Then Szands spins in the chair to face her. It's clear he didn't know she was in the office with him.

His eyes, distant, listening, are fixed on hers.

Ellen nods, takes a clipboard from the stack on the wooden table beside her and leaves the office.

In the hall, she still hears the whirring of the reel-to-reel machine.

GHOST: WORLD WAR II

She enters Unit 1 and sees Philip is asleep. Quietly, Ellen checks to make sure it's not too cool in here, places a palm delicately on Philip's forehead, looking for a fever.

Still whistling, again she studies the uneven features of his face. The right cheek is a full half inch higher than the left. His nose is so crooked it looks as if it's made of clay. And although both eyes are closed, one eyelid looks wider than the other.

Again she wonders, *What did he look like before?*

Carl, the orderly, told her he was in a band called the Danes.

Where are they now? The other band members? And why does that name ring a bell?

She should move on, of course, to the second unit, work her way through the permitted rooms. That's how she begins every shift, every day. But today she doesn't feel like following the rules, the pattern, the protocol. She crosses the unit and stands close to the door with an ear to the hall. She listens until the whirring of the reels in the office ceases, hears the chair slide from the desk, hears Szands's shoes on the office floor, then in the hall, coming her way.

Ellen backs up and holds her breath. As if, by exhaling, she might reveal her thoughts.

Szands passes Unit 1 without looking inside.

What is she thinking of doing exactly?

She looks to Philip.

Once the doctor's footfalls grow distant, she peers into the otherwise empty hall.

She waits.

She waits a little longer.

Then, incredibly, instead of moving on to Unit 2, Ellen crosses the hall, back to the office, and slips inside.

The tape recorder is empty. Szands took whatever reel he was listening to.

Ellen exhales and laughs at herself. What *is* she doing? Did she think Szands was listening to some sort of *evidence* of what is happening to Philip, why he's healing so well, so uniformly, so fast?

She flattens her uniform at her waist and makes to leave. Out of the corner of her eye she sees that the papers Szands was studying are still piled upon the table in front of the machine. On the top page he's scrawled a question.

She leans closer and reads it.

Why does he care what color the piano is?

Did Philip ask Dr. Szands what color the piano was also? He

must have. Yes. He must have. And yet, leaving the office, taking the hall toward Unit 2, Ellen feels the beating of her own frightened heart. It beats that way because, for a moment—silly of her, really—yes, for a moment in the office she believed that Szands had been listening to her and Philip's conversation, prerecorded, from the day before.

14

Turbulence. The worst Philip has ever known. Feels like the walls of the plane are billowing in, then out, creaking heavy metal, making it hard to sleep.

Philip tries.

It's all broken up, pieces, fractured images. A huge desert. Diamond mines. Turn-of-the-century Germans. Impenetrable buildings filled with sand. Desert wasps and spiders. The wasp paralyzing the spider. The wasp egg surviving off the paralyzed spider. Shimmering diamonds underground. The banks of the Kuiseb River; incredible vegetation splitting the picture of so much sand. The Namib's lifevein. The life the river attracts. Miners. Snakes' patterns, but no visible snake. All underground. All either avoiding the heat or averting other eyes.

Men obsessed with diamonds, with digging.

Wasps digging, too, burying paralyzed spiders three times their size.

Holes in the desert.

There is no sound in the desert, the packet said, *except wind.*

All life in the desert, the packet said, *hides.*

Other images, too, here, between the groaning walls of the aircraft, as Philip undulates between sleep and wakefulness.

One image is of Lovejoy standing at the head of the plane, ducking his head beneath the low ceiling. Another sees Lovejoy crouched in the aisle, eyeing Larry, then Ross, as they sleep.

Philip blinks and the former general is staring at him.

A pocket of smooth air and Philip sleeps again, dreaming unsettling pictures of a poorly quilted desert, as though it is barely held together by twine.

15

Philip wakes to find Dr. Szands sitting in a chair beside the cot. His smile looks new, and Philip wonders what face the doctor was making before he woke.

"Philip," Szands begins, "there's a man here to see you. He's with the United States government. I've informed him that you're available for a brief interview."

"Interview?" Philip is hardly sharp, not yet fully awake.

"He wants to talk to you about Africa."

Szands says "Africa" as if he wouldn't go there in a thousand years.

"Interview?" Philip repeats.

"He's going to see you now."

United States government.

"We'll just be a moment," a voice says. It comes from the area of the room Philip can't quite turn to see.

Szands rises and exits the unit. Philip hears the door lock for the first time.

United States government.

Silence. The man is not speaking, not showing himself, not yet. Philip tries to roll over, to see back by the piano.

The man is coming toward him.

"Hello, Philip. Mind if I sit down?"

Philip smells cologne. Soap. He isn't surprised by this. Military men, high ranking, take their cleanliness seriously.

"I'm sorry we have to meet under these circumstances, Philip. I'm sure we'd both rather it weren't happening."

Philip doesn't respond. Not yet.

"My name is Scott Malone. I have a particular interest in the events that brought you here."

"Are you an army man?"

A pause.

"Well, no. I'm not an army man in the way you're asking. I never served. I directly represent the government."

"Are you with the CIA?"

"No. Not that either. Mind if I ask you some questions?" An inhale. "Do you remember what happened to you?"

"I have an idea."

"I've read the account you gave Dr. Szands. Has your opinion changed on the matter?"

"My opinion?"

"Your memory."

"No. What I told Dr. Szands is all I remember. A room."

"Indeed. And do you remember the events leading up to you entering that room?"

"Yes."

"Very good." Hesitation. Then, "Tell me about that first encounter with the first dead body you found."

"I told Dr. Szands all about that, too."

"Yes. But I'd like to hear it from you. Sometimes, when you hear it in person, you unearth new information."

Unearth. As if Scott Malone is digging. Digging in the sand.

"Lovejoy spotted it. Greer dragged it wherever we went."

Philip blinks. In the moment his eyes are closed he sees the body again. Clearly.

Malone continues. "Let's try a different course here, okay? I'd like you to meet someone, Philip. An artist. Len?" Philip hears movement behind him. Back by the piano. Papers shuffling. The squeaking of leather soles.

A bearded man with thinning black hair leans into Philip's field of vision. His argyle sweater and significant belly do not look army. He slides a chair beside Scott Malone's.

"Why don't you describe the body for Len, Philip," Malone says. "Tell him what you found. What *Lovejoy* found."

The artist clears his throat.

"I'm ready when you are," he says.

Philip closes his eyes. Sees the body again.

"Have you ever seen a flounder out of water?" he asks.

"No. I have not," Len politely answers.

"Flounders are a flatfish. They're born with eyes on either side of their head but by the time they're adults, one of those eyes migrates to the other side. So they can lay flat on the ocean floor and keep both eyes looking up."

Len looks to Malone. Back to Philip.

"And?"

"Can you draw a man like that?"

"Excuse me?" He looks to Malone again. But Malone is not smiling. He's already heard this description. He nods to the paper.

Len begins drawing. Philip tells him more. And as he speaks, the artist's expression changes from friendly to confused until he's actually looking at Philip with suspicion in his eyes. Len turns once more, possibly expecting Malone to put a stop to this absurdity.

"Is this him?" Len asks, holding up the paper, the finished drawing.

Philip opens his eyes and stares for a long time.

"Yes," he says. "But older."

"Older . . . wrinkled? White hair?"

"No. Not that kind of old."

Malone leans forward, closer to Philip.

"What kind of older, Philip?" he asks.

Philip breathes deep.

"The desert wasn't linear," he says. "The desert wasn't in chronological order."

16

"As we come in," Mull says, half in his seat, facing the platoon, gripping the seat back for support, "I'd like to tell you what happened the first time we came out here."

Rough winds. Heavy clouds outside the small oval windows. If not for the heat, it might feel like they were flying through packed snow.

"This is before the first platoon was deployed," Mull begins. "A foundations check, as we call it, to map the logistics before sending soldiers in. Planning stages for a mission." He has to speak up; the airplane walls continue to creak. "We didn't hope to find what was making the sound. Rather, we were looking for locals, anybody who might know more about it than we did."

Mull has taken this flight before. Same plane, he says. Made the mistake of listening to the sound, airborne, causing the small crew to get sick, a severe illness they couldn't shake for the duration of the flight. They threw up in the barf bags and when the barf bags were full they threw up in the hoods of their unpacked sweatshirts, into the feet of their socks, into their sleeves. There was a very scary moment when the pilot appeared too vertiginous to continue. When they landed, they had to postpone their directive for two days; two days they spent camped close to the plane, hoping the sound wouldn't arrive, live, in person, as they tried to get better. To protect themselves, they slept with headphones, the silencer type, the kind the men wore on the tarmac to save their ears from the perpetual roar of engines. But no sound came. Not the bad one. And on the third day they felt stable enough to proceed. Mull says there was some concern when they set out; nobody could say for certain that they'd "come back" from the illness. He explained this to mean it was difficult to determine whether or not the sickness had fully left them, or if they were all perhaps a little changed by the experience and would never again know the former, good way they felt.

"You gentlemen have heard of LSD," Mull says. The Danes have. They've all tried it. Larry was pulled over on Woodward Avenue for driving only seven miles an hour. "We were concerned with a similar residual effect. Taking a trip without proof of returning."

Philip sees something foggy pass over Mull's eyes. Memory.

Mull and the radio crew bivouacked beneath the wings, then left camp. Intelligence had already located a settlement, three huts made of cow dung, eleven miles east of the Atlantic Ocean. The crew wore sand masks and carried sparse gear: a tape recorder, flashlights, extra pairs of boots, handguns, and a change of clothes for the night. They weren't planning on staying long. The group's translator, Doran, a native Namibian, expressed concern as to whether or not he would understand the exact language used there.

"I sensed fear in him," Mull says. "Which of course frightened me in turn." Mull himself spotted the huts first. Two were in bad shape, their roofs half caved in. But the third appeared lived in. American shoes lay outside the hut's front door. The smell of the settlement caused more vomiting.

"His name was Nadoul. By our way of thinking, he was the poorest human being I've ever encountered. And what I mean by that is, the man had never heard of money. Not in the way we know it. He was the son of a larger family, the former occupants of the other huts, and the cattle they raised were their currency. But by the time we met him, there were no cows, and Nadoul trekked five miles every day to a natural spring, where he gathered fresh water and the edible plants that grew there. He'd had a wife once. They'd taken turns making the trek; Nadoul would go in the mornings, Ka in the afternoons. They were worried, Nadoul told us, about leaving their hut unwatched. When we asked him why he'd be worried about other people in a landscape where nobody lived for dozens of miles, Nadoul told us that he and Ka were never alone. That's how he put it, though Doran said it was more of a colloquial phrase that meant, *nobody is ever truly alone.*"

Philip hears movement behind him and he turns to see that Lovejoy's eyes are open. He's staring at Philip without expression. Arms crossed. Armband clearly visible. Philip turns away and looks out the window. Absently he fingers the ivory F key hanging around his neck. Through the glass he sees clouds as thick as the pillows on his parents' bed that he'd crawl into after a particularly bad dream.

"We asked Nadoul about the sound and he nodded like he'd expected as much, like he knew somebody was bound to come asking about the sound. Later, Markus, one of the radio operators, commented on Nadoul's change in pallor when we brought it up. Like he'd blanched, causing his dark skin to lighten a shade. 'Can't you hear it now?' he asked us. We were justifiably surprised by his question. Markus and the others hurriedly readied their gear. We recorded, we listened, but we heard nothing."

Philip watches Mull's lips move, remembering the moment in the control room, the words he didn't think he spoke, the words Mull heard anyway.

Did you say you hear a chord, Private Tonka? Did everybody hear the same?

"Nadoul looked at the tape recorder and shook his head, laughing at us. We couldn't be sure he even knew what a tape recorder was, but the spinning reels must have reminded him of something, because he understood it well enough to mock it. He spat a word in the direction of the recorder and Doran told us he thought it meant *slippery.* But more like . . . a fictional creature or idea that a man can't hold. Can't cage. I took it to mean Nadoul was saying the sound was uncatchable. Some of the others thought he was simply scared of the device and was asking for it to be removed from his home."

Outside the window, the clouds have doubled, tripled, and to Philip it looks like they're traveling, impossibly, through solid alabaster.

"We asked him where his wife Ka was, what happened to Ka. She'd either died or left him, and either way, we were talking to a man with no possessions who probably felt a loneliness we couldn't possibly imagine. But he was surprisingly spry as he began telling us her story, as much as he knew, as if the subject of his former wife was more pleasant to talk about than the sound he claimed was still playing, then, as we stood before him. Ka, he told us, started complaining about a bad back. She told Nadoul that her walks to the spring were becoming more trying, more difficult. She called it her 'burden' and told Nadoul it was causing her 'great pain.' Neither Nadoul nor Ka thought it was a matter of sore muscles or aging. As wild as it sounds to us, they immediately assumed Ka had someone unseen attached to her back, someone who'd been watching them and had finally decided to close in. I assumed he meant a spirit of some kind. Surely Nadoul didn't see a physical man sitting on his wife's back. Through Doran, we told him that the sound made us feel sick, and maybe Ka had been experiencing a similar sickness, but Nadoul shook his head no and told us Ka found the sound pleasant, sometimes even sang along with it. We asked him if he'd seen any military in the area, anybody who might have built something to make such a sound. He laughed again. Briefly. Clipped. But he didn't answer that question directly, just went on to talk about the increasing difficulty of Ka's daily treks to the spring and how finally, one day, Nadoul decided he would have to make the treks himself. Ka would have to rest until the thing . . . left her back."

A pocket of rough turbulence and Mull grips the seat back harder; for a moment he loses his professional visage and instead looks like a frightened civilian. A shrill howl erupts outside the plane and for two heartbeats Philip thinks it's the sound.

He reaches absently for a drink that isn't there.

"Nadoul was afraid to leave Ka alone but more afraid of what would become of her if she didn't get proper nourishment. At one point she'd told him the sound was playing inside her ear. She asked him to look for it. By now, Ka's feelings for the sound had changed. It was no longer a thing to sing along to. She believed it was the voice of the thing attached to her. She thought it possible the thing had left her, but its voice remained, lodged in her ear. Nadoul found nothing, of course. But Ka insisted. *It's in there,* she told him. *And it's not coming out.* By this point, Ka wasn't looking good. Nadoul had to act quick. He decided she needed more than what was available by their daily treks. Rather, he'd visit the nearest settlement, though it was a day and a half away. There he might speak to a medicine man, return with a cure. So with only his baboon-hide canteen, he bid her farewell and left her alone in the hut."

Outside, the clouds part, only for the duration of a single intake of breath, and Philip thinks he sees beige, blue . . . the colors of a desert beside an ocean.

Then the sky swallows his view once more.

"The Himba medicine man offered Nadoul nothing. He actually advised him to move. Told him it was the fault of the sound and that it made men sick, made them see things. Nadoul, stubborn, left the settlement empty-handed."

"And when he got back?" Larry asks suddenly. "She was dead?"

Mull breathes deep. Smiles sadly.

"We don't know," he says. "Only her ears remained. Cut off, there on her pillow."

"Hold on a second," Duane says. "Are you telling us she was murdered?"

"Murdered?" Mull asks. "Not according to Nadoul. He believed she'd cut them off herself."

The door to the cockpit opens and one of the young pilots informs Mull that they've begun their descent. The secretary thanks him and turns to face the platoon.

“We’re landing,” he says, then secures his seat belt.

Each of the Danes, the photographer Stein, and Private Greer stare out the small windows as the clouds part, leaving a trace, the fog, barely obscuring the shore below. Even from this height, the ridged sand appears endless, too big to harbor success, and Philip searches for a hut.

“We’re coming in hard,” Larry says, a tremor in his voice.

Is it turbulence? Is it fear?

Philip closes his eyes and pictures one hundred thousand dollars; imagines what he’s going to do with it when he gets back to Detroit.

The equipment the Danes will buy. The nights out they’ll have.

Again his fingers travel to the piano key around his neck.

When he opens his eyes he sees the desert in greater detail.

Even now, anxious, uncertain, impatient, Philip is able to comprehend that what he sees is like nothing else on earth.

The Namib Desert looks as primal as Mull’s papers described it.

And beyond the boundaries of an impenetrable band of fog, below the surface of the crystal water, he sees shipwrecks, too.

Dozens.

“Jesus Christ.”

Philip thinks maybe he’ll buy just a single drink with all that money. Just one. Sitting on a stool at Doug’s Den, shooting news with Misty.

Yeah, Philip thinks, as the plane lowers, as the sand rises to meet it and the waves roll like unsteady earth, a one-hundred-thousand-dollar drink sounds good right now, if only because it would mean he was back home, where he belongs.

17

In her apartment on Bettman Street, Ellen usually finds some degree of solace, a break from the sadness, injuries, and death of Macy Mercy. Nursing is not an easy job, and often she fantasizes about leaving the hospital altogether. Though jobs are hard to come by, and she knows she should be grateful for what she has, there isn't a store she enters, a diner she eats at, where she doesn't imagine herself working instead.

There are loftier scenarios, too. Getting in her green New Yorker and driving west to California is one.

It's Jean, she thinks, tonight, removing her coat and tossing it on one end of the brown couch she sometimes sleeps on, as the static of the television plays like the equivalent of the recordings of ocean waves her friend Lucille uses to help her sleep.

Jean is the name of her daughter, who died at only three years old.

It's Jean, and it's always been Jean. You're trying to make up for it, Ellen. And good luck with that.

Ellen understands how potentially detrimental it is to her own mental health, constantly playing catch-up, rewind, attempting to heal someone, anybody, to fill the frighteningly limitless void left by Jean.

And yet, there's Philip.

"Stop it," she says out loud, as she crosses the small carpeted living room and enters the half kitchen with a mind to fix dinner for herself. She flattens the front of her beige slacks out of habit, the way she flattens the front of her nurse's uniform all afternoon and evening at the hospital. It bothers her, the way she can't leave work at work.

Philip.

If she's honest with herself, she's got to admit that nursing Philip, both during the silent six months and now that he's awake, is the first time she's felt differently about that void. As if, through Philip, she's heard the first reverberation in there, the first echo, suggesting there's a bottom to that pit after all.

She takes a pan from the hanging rack (it saves room in this tiny apartment, hanging pans and lids, utensils, and mugs with handles, too) and places it on the stove. She lights the next burner, brings the temperature to medium, and places the pan upon it. Actions like these are supposed to do some good for her. The motions of a simple, everyday life. But when she drops some butter onto the pan and it begins to sizzle, she immediately thinks of the sound of the reel machine in the main office rolling, as Dr. Szands sat listening, taking notes that reflected a particular conversation, a private moment, she'd had with Philip.

Philip was scared when she told him there was a piano in the unit. For Christ's sake, he asked for a mirror to see the thing before he asked to see himself. And he absolutely asked her what color it was.

Unless he was listening in, how could Szands have known?

She realizes the butter is browning.

"Shit."

She flattens the front of her slacks again, then carries the pan to the sink. She dumps the burnt butter and begins the process again. For a place that's supposed to be a safe haven from the perilous moods of work, home has never been good to her.

But tonight it's especially taunting.

She'd planned on frying leftover rice, vegetables, and lemon, but this time, once the butter is melted, she simply cracks an egg. One egg will do. Ellen can't seem to focus beyond that.

"Why?"

She's talking to herself at home. Not for the first time. The one-word, one-syllable question comes as if attached to the single egg, but Ellen knows better. She can't crack the question away. And she can't help but go on.

"Why is he healing so fast?"

Today Philip didn't only move his head, he was gesturing with it and his shoulders, as he spoke to her.

As the translucent white of the egg turns opaque, she places both hands on the oven handle and closes her eyes. She sees him again, dented and deformed, discolored and fearful, flat upon the same cot that's held him for over half a year.

Shouldn't Ellen be glad that he's healing? Isn't that the ideal scenario? And for crying out loud, why does she care as much as she does? Why does she feel like *she* has to be the one to point this out?

Ellen opens her eyes.

She sees the egg is brown, burnt. She grips the pan handle hard and tosses it, egg and all, into the sink. She jams the burner knob to off and flees the kitchen.

It's one thing to say she took the job to fill the impossible void left by not having been home when Jean died, but it's another to think she should feel responsible for a patient's welfare to the point of suspecting the hospital of misconduct.

Is she? Is she suspecting the hospital?

She breathes deeply. An old standby, still the best way to calm herself down. She thinks of how that battered body once played music.

And yet, he was scared of the piano.

When Philip first came to Macy Mercy he was in worse shape than any patient she'd ever seen. The limited information Dr. Szands had given the staff didn't do much to shed any light on the person Philip was beneath the bruises. It took Carl, the doughy-faced manchild orderly, to tell her Philip used to play in a rock 'n' roll band.

The Danes.

Ellen looks at her record player, situated on a flat brown table by the living room's one window. She's had the 1954 Admiral AM Radio/Record Player for three years now, and it is her prized possession. If she can't distract herself with dinner, she's going to have to do it with 45s.

The records are in a neat carrier she also bought three years ago. Not much taller than the discs themselves, the aqua-and-white box holds forty-five 45s. Ellen hasn't quite filled it, but she's more than two-thirds of the way there. As she gets to her knees beside the couch, pulls the box from under the table, and starts thumbing through the records, she compares the percentage of the box that's filled with Philip's recovery.

Is he also two-thirds of the way to being back to normal?

In only a few days after waking?

As she riffles through the various paper sleeves, she clears her throat, like she's telling someone else in the room to stop bringing up Philip Tonka, the obviously (and justifiably) troubled patient at Macy Mercy who really plays no bigger part in her life than any other patient in there does. No, for Christ's sake, he's not two-thirds healed. Just because the guy can move his head and wiggle his finger doesn't mean he's about to drive a car, run a race, win a boxing match. And if she's really going to harp on it, Ellen must factor in the six months, inert or not, as being half a year the man has had for getting better.

"Aha," she says, stopping at a record. "Here you are."

Like a lot of music lovers, Ellen doesn't really know the names of all the songs she likes or the musicians who made them. There's the well-known ones like Jerry Lee Lewis, Buddy Holly, and Little Richard, and they're on the radio all the time. But Ellen likes the deeper stuff, the music you hear in the car late at night, driving home from a diner. The music you hear playing in a bar. A lot of the time, the names of these artists don't stick. Don't stay with a person. Don't stay with Ellen. It's the music that moves her, after all, not the names.

But there's more: some of these deeper cuts are packaged in a more creative way. Without the major record label money determining which song makes it to the radio, the smaller ones need to be smart. Some of them, like the one she's chosen, use "cover art" for the front of the sleeve. A fancy way of writing the song title. Bright colors for the name of the band. Ellen understands that it's marketing, that there's something carnival-barker to it, maybe even cheap, but she likes it, too. And though she's not looking at it now, she's also a fan of the photo of the band on the back of the sleeve. Four guys standing in front of the orange bricks of a city drugstore.

Ellen slides the record from the sleeve and places it on the Admiral. She sets the needle. Only one song per side, she's gonna have to flip the disc in a couple minutes, but still she goes to the couch and falls flat on her back, the sleeve between her fingers.

Ah, how Ellen Jones loves an instrumental.

The song begins. Big, rolling drums. A steady bass. Sprinkles of a piano. And that guitar line . . .

Ellen closes her eyes.

There's no job in this song.

No sadness, either.

No healing or not healing, secrets or mysteries.

Ellen smiles.

Outside her apartment window a tire squeals and she looks up. The guitar is soaring by now, but it's the piano that's caught her ear.

What color is it?!

There's no room in her mind and heart for hospital memories now. She looks to the back sleeve of the 45.

"'Be Here,'" she reads. "By the Danes."

Ellen sits up fast. Despite the fact that she doesn't entirely believe it yet, that she's still piecing it together while looking at the whole, she feels like a teenager again, back when a photo of a matinee idol was enough to make her scream.

She speed-reads the back of the sleeve. Reads the names of the band members.

Duane Noles—Drums

Larry Walker—Bass

Ross Robinson—Guitar

Philip Tonka—Piano.

"No *shit!*" she yells. "Philip!"

She's up now. She sits again. She can't believe it. "Be Here" by the Danes.

She's got the 45.

And it's well worn.

"Holy shit!"

The song comes to its signature uneven end and Ellen starts it over again.

She feels like she's gotta call someone, tell someone that this happened.

So, I've got a patient who was under for six months, and he comes to, and I'm worried sick about him and I need to calm down and I play a record, a favorite record, and holy shit holy shit—

"Holy shit!"

She laughs because there's nothing else to do. She laughs and crosses the living room to the kitchen, grabs a second pan from the rack, and puts it on the stove.

She's gotta keep moving.

She goes back to the couch, sits, watches the record spin, reads the name as it's spinning.

The Danes, The Danes, The Danes, The Danes . . .

"Philip Tonka," she says. "Wait until I tell you this."

As the song comes to its end for the second time, as the apartment goes silent, as even the street outside seems to hold its breath, Ellen realizes that on the other side of the sleeve is a photo. And in that photo are the four men who made the music.

She's seen it before. She knows it's there.

Ellen flips it over.

She can't read the name on the blue and white sign, but behind them, through the open front door, an old man, the proprietor, is looking toward the camera. Of the four band members, the black man is featured most prominently. He stands out against the orange brick. He looks confident, soldier strong, his arms folded across the chest of a powder-blue T-shirt. To his right, a long-haired guy is laughing hard enough that his eyes are closed. To his left is a shorter guy, curly hair, sporting a smirk. And to the left of the guy with curly hair is . . .

"Philip," Ellen says, bringing a hand to her mouth.

To say he looks different now is to say a white house looks different from the White House.

"Oh my God."

Dark hair. Dark eyes. A half smile as powerful as the black man's physique.

"Oh my God."

Philip is leaning against the orange wall. One shoulder is raised a little, and the wind tousles his hair.

It occurs to Ellen that Philip was as good-looking as any of the matinee idols she loved as a teenager.

Without getting up, without taking her eyes off the photo, Ellen reaches out and starts the song over again.

When the needle connects, she brings the same hand to the album sleeve and touches Philip's symmetrical, unbruised face with her fingertip.

"Oh my God."

And by the time the guitar line begins, she feels like she's there with them (*be here*), the Danes, the band whose name spins over her shoulder, in rhythm with the song, spinning as if on wheels, rolling from the past to the future or perhaps the other way around.

It's impossible not to compare what Philip looks like now to what he looked like then. Impossible not to note the carefree swagger in his expression, the almost bullish confidence of all four men.

But their name continues to spin, as if trying to generate enough momentum, enough torque, to bring back this great moment in their past, to resurrect the ghosts the four of them have become.

"Philip," Ellen says, her elation giving way to tears. "I'm so sorry, Philip . . ."

18

Because Philip isn't expecting a storm, because he's expecting only the desert flat, not rising, the columns of sand in the distance at first don't register.

As he steps from the airplane stairs, as his boot actually touches the sand of the Namib Desert for the first time, he hears Stein calling out, sees Duane hurrying to unload the larger cases.

But despite the chaotic activity and the sense that he should get moving, Philip has to pause, for a single breath, and acknowledge the panoramic beauty of the Namib.

It's the most gorgeous thing he's ever seen in person.

A high wind flattens against his body, presses against every bone, it seems, strong enough to push Philip back against Sergeant Lovejoy, still descending the stairs.

The airplane has landed in the fog, where the ocean meets the desert. Belts of mist curl up around Philip's boots, the green short sleeves of his shirt.

And in the distance, columns of sand.

The pilots are moving quick, moving gear, unloading, hollering about the need to leave, the lack of time.

Before, they say. Before this storm hits.

Philip listens. Despite the beauty, he's anxious.

It's as if he wants to locate the sound immediately, before the plane takes off again without them. So that Mull and the pilots have to stay, long enough for them to get it on tape, long enough for Philip or Larry, Duane or Ross to say it must be here, it must be there, we found it, our mission is complete, and we'll be going home with you after all.

He looks to the active sand in the distance. Has it gotten closer?

"Right here," Lovejoy says, ten feet to Philip's left, pointing to the sand at his boots, directing the pilots and soldiers.

It makes music, so they're sending musicians. Lovejoy had said that.

Think music, Philip tells himself. *You're here because you're good at what you do. You're here because your country needs a musician, needs you.*

"Private Tonka."

Philip looks up to see that the photographer, Stein, is handing him a sand mask.

"Do I need this?" It's so sudden, so present.

The photographer is already wearing his. He lifts the camera from around his neck and turns to take a photo.

The façade of sand is barreling toward them. As if ten thousand Africans are behind it, delivering it, walling the soldiers in, telling them *now you stay HERE you don't leave HERE you stay HERE.*

Philip puts on his sand mask.

Stein snaps a photograph.

"Sandstorm," Stein says. "Fucking *huge.*"

The pilots are rushing behind them.

The compartment with the gear is closed. The Danes have everything they've brought with them, whether they need more or not. Secretary Mull is holding a hand in front of his eyes, blocking the already rising dust, talking to Lovejoy, patting him on the shoulder, then making for the airplane stairs.

Two steps up he turns. Sees Philip. Salutes him.

Philip salutes back.

Stein snaps another photo. Holds an already grainy thumbs-up to Mull.

The airplane stairs are vanishing into the wall of the plane, a ladder nightmarishly receding from a burning building.

We've saved everyone we can. You're on your own now.

The propellers begin spinning.

The plane is lifting. Rising.

So much sand. The voices of his platoon. The voice of Lovejoy.

And . . .

. . . water.

Philip turns to see he's less than forty feet from white rolling surf. The ocean exposed by the propellers. Parting curtains of fog.

Secretary Mull's info packet called it "the Skeleton Coast."

Philip imagines an audience behind that curtain, his parents at his first piano recital.

"Philip!"

It's Stein. He's got one hand on Philip's right shoulder. The other still holds the camera.

He says something, gestures toward the others. Philip turns to see a bivouac erected.

And the coming bulwark of sand.

The airplane is already out of sight.

With Stein, Philip rushes to the others. He finds them crouched behind the makeshift cover, shoulder to shoulder, masked. He squeezes in beside Larry, his back to the hard plastic.

Already . . . here in the Namib . . . a storm.

Philip braces himself. Duane begins to say something but his words are drowned in the rumble.

Then the sand hits, and the words, whatever they were meant to be, are as unreachable as the airplane in the sky.

19

Ellen knows how to play the piano, too. Well enough. And she's been thinking about it all day. Since waking on Bettman Street, while getting a coffee and reading the *Des Moines Register* at Uncle Danny's Diner, she's been visualizing herself playing the piano in Unit 1 of Macy Mercy.

As a nurse, she's always looking for a joke, a story, something she can bring into the hospital, a window of light for an otherwise dark home.

She's gonna surprise Philip with his own song.

By the time she enters the hospital, hangs her coat in the office, and changes into her uniform, Ellen is nervous. She wants to make sure she gets it right. The E minor intro. The lift to the F sharp minor. Then landing on the E major, where the song really begins.

Philip should recognize it by then.

She takes the hall to Unit 1, practicing the chords at her hips, careful not to whistle the tune like she did for six months as he slept.

She stops.

Is it possible Philip heard his own song during those long six months? Is it possible she was helping him in a bigger way than she could've possibly known?

How many times did she play it on the very same piano as he worked his way through a darkness she can't fathom?

The thought is exciting. And it propels her to the unit door, across the threshold, where she stops again, this time as though in a very bad dream.

"Philip!"

It's the worst she's seen him since he woke from his coma. The angles of his face look sharper, the shadows darker, so that the blue bruises look purple, and the purple ones black. Sweat pools on his pillow, his breathing is labored, and there's an almost audible sound of creaking, as if Philip's bones are finally declaring their true condition.

"Dr. Szands!" Ellen calls, hoping he's within earshot.

"Ellen," Philip manages to say. "It hurts."

"Okay. Okay. Hang on."

It strikes her that Philip didn't turn his head toward her when he spoke. That his fingers look like pieces of petrified driftwood on the bedsheet.

Ellen checks for a fever. It's scorching.

"Don't worry," she says. But she's very worried herself. "You're running a little fever. I'll be right back."

Philip doesn't nod, doesn't say a word. Instead, as Ellen leaves the unit, she hears a slow, guttural hissing. As if whatever pain he's experiencing has only a small window from which to be expressed.

In the hall, Ellen calls again for the doctor. Instead, Nurse Francine, huge and wrinkled in her white uniform, peers out of the office door.

"What is it?" she says. Her glasses magnify the concern in her eyes.

Ellen points to Unit 1.

"It's Philip Tonka, he—"

"Oh no," Francine says. Then she's out the office door and thumping away from Ellen, toward the hospital's front doors. She turns left and Ellen knows she's heading for the Medicine Unit.

There are simple medications in the nurses' station: aspirin, cough syrup, antihistamines. But in the hall that Francine thunders down is one of the rooms Ellen Jones isn't allowed to enter.

Ellen can't think about that right now.

She hurries back into Unit 1. Inside, Philip looks even worse.

His fingers are curved unnaturally, like the arthritic claws of an elderly man. His Adam's apple is pointed to the ceiling, his back arched.

Ellen goes to him, kneels beside the cot.

"Francine is getting your medicine. Hold on, Philip. It's going to be okay."

Francine storms through the unit door.

"Move," she says.

She's carrying a tray with two syringes. Ellen has never seen her this way before.

"Do you need help? What can I do?"

It's hard to look at Philip. The way he's stuck, frozen, as if every bone inside him has turned to wood.

Francine waves a dismissive hand.

"Nothing," she says. "Or . . . play for him. Like you used to."

Like she used to. Yes. During Philip's six-month sleep, Ellen played for him often.

She crosses the unit quickly, feels helpless, like she's no use as a nurse if she can't help Philip, can't help him right now.

Then, without consciously deciding to, operating with severely frayed nerves, she plays the same song she played for him over those six months.

"Be Here."

She almost stops when she realizes what she's doing. Hearing his own song might be too much excitement, too crazy to comprehend. But she's already begun.

The E minor. The F sharp minor. E.

In the silver metronome, reflected, she sees Francine inject Philip's shoulder.

By the time she reaches the end of the first round of the song, she's sweating.

Francine administers the second shot.

Ellen doesn't watch. She's gotta watch her fingers. Wants to play this right. Play this man's song for him here, now, as he experiences a pain she can't know.

She worries, irrationally, that she's ruining it, speeding up, playing it without feeling it. This isn't how she imagined this going. This isn't how she saw herself, this morning, surprising Philip, lessening the loneliness, the pain, the horror.

When she reaches the end, she lets the notes dissolve, then hangs her head so that her black hair is touching the keys.

Silence. Almost. The far distant cry of those final notes.

Ellen looks up to the metronome. Sees Francine is gone.

Sees Philip's head is angled toward the back of the unit, watching her.

She spins quickly.

"Jesus Christ," she says. "You scared the hell out of me."

"You . . . you played our song . . ."

"Yes," Ellen nods. But she's struggling to reconcile the sight of him now with what she saw only a minute ago.

"You played that for me when I was under, didn't you?"

"Yes. Many times."

Philip smiles. It's the first time she's seen it.

The satisfaction Ellen feels is foreign to her.

"It's one of my favorite songs."

"And you knew that I—"

"No!" Ellen says, getting up at last and taking the chair beside his cot. "No. I figured it out last night. I have your record."

They look into each other's eyes for a long time.

"Ellen," Philip says. "Will you draw something for me?"

It's the last thing she expects him to say. And she can't help but notice that the angles of his face look rounder again, the shadows shallower.

"Draw?"

"I can't grip a pencil yet. But I wanna see . . . something. Something I saw in the desert."

Ellen looks to the bookshelf behind her. To the filing cabinet against the wall by the door.

Are they listening? And, if so, can they hear a drawing?

"Color or pencil?"

"Color."

Philip raises his arms. He slowly extends his fingers, slowly curls them back into a fist.

Ellen gets up and leaves the unit. When she returns with colored pencils and a paper pad, Philip is relaxed again. His eyes are bright with memory.

"All right," she says, sitting down. "A drawing."

Philip doesn't hesitate.

"A goat."

"A goat?" Ellen begins to sketch a goat, then pauses. "You saw a goat in the desert?"

Philip nods. He remembers hoofprints.

Arms up, arms down.

"A long-haired white goat," he says. "Facing right. Side view."

"And you're sure you saw this in the desert?"

Philip is looking at her directly. Ellen can't help but think of the X-rays, the cracks in Philip's bones, the photo of him on the cover of the 45.

"Large horns," he says. "And between them, a piece of steel."

"What do you mean?"

"I'm not sure exactly."

"A piece of steel where the horns meet."

"Yes. Like . . . like an emblem."

Ellen is drawing. This is another first for her. First time a patient woke after a six-month coma. First time she feared the hospital was listening in on their conversations. First time she's drawn for a patient.

First time she's ever seen a man go from paralyzed to moving in less than the length of a three-minute song.

"Like this?"

She holds the paper for Philip to see.

"The hair should be longer. Knee length. The hooves barely visible beneath it. Long white hair. And the steel between the horns, bigger."

Ellen makes the changes. She notes the change in Philip, too. As though his spirit is recovering at the same rate as his body. He's talkative, mobile, and his eyes are only getting brighter.

"Here," Ellen says. And she recalls the reflection of Francine in the metronome, administering the medicine.

"Good," he says. "Now could you color the entire background red?"

"Red," Ellen repeats, already reaching for the pencil.

"The whole thing."

Beginning at the top, Ellen shades the page red.

"Yes," Philip says. He raises an arm, reaching unsteadily for the paper.

His expression changes with such immediacy, Ellen almost pulls the drawing away from him. He looks suddenly ill, she thinks, completely blanched, as though the image she's given him, the simple child's drawing of a white goat on a red canvas, has set him back.

His arm falls to the cot.

There are tears in his eyes.

"Philip, I'm sorry. Here, let's put this away for now." She tries to think of a joke. Tries to be funny. "How about a boring radio drama instead?"

She expects him to say *no, no, it's fine, no, it's not your fault, it's me, I was only remembering.*

Instead, with wet eyes, he only stares to where the wall meets the ceiling.

"Philip . . ."

But he's not talking anymore.

Ellen rises. She flattens the front of her uniform with one hand and carries the drawing in the other.

"You should have some water," she says. "I'll get a glass."

He's crying. Silently. Staring to where the wall meets the ceiling.

As she crosses the threshold, he speaks.

"You played our song as well as we did."

And his voice is wet with tears.

Ellen wants to tell him that he's helping her as much as she's helping him. Instead, she watches him. Then quietly leaves him to cry, to remember, alone.

20

Larry and Ross are setting up the Ampex machines, using shovels to dig holes in the sand, deep enough to keep the recorders stable. The sandstorm was brief, gone as quickly as it came, but served as an immediate notice of how far they are from home.

Foreign topography.

Foreign continent.

Foreign threats.

Camp has been set up between two distinct gravel plains, large dry pools of brittle rock that look more like scorched land than beach. Mountain outcrops can be seen in the distance and the dunes between here and there look as kinetic as the ocean Philip stands in. Despite the fog, the sun is high, though Lovejoy warns that, come nightfall, it'll be as cold as Minnesota out here. They're using canvas tarps and metal poles as tents; they'll be sleeping like cowboys from America's Old West. A different kind of soldier.

Greer is a bottomless pit of information. Now, as he assists with setting up camp, he extrapolates on the information from Mull's packets. Greer, it seems, knows more than the military that sent him here.

"The desert is somewhere between fifty-five and eighty million years old. The site of our absolute earliest ancestors. The first known people. This is a fact. You think they frolicked in the waves, Private Tonka? I bet they did. And I bet we lost many of them to storms like the one that greeted us."

The bivouac stood up to it, though, and they have Lovejoy to thank for that. Greer says Lovejoy is an expert in creativity.

"It's why he was a general. His mind doesn't stop. And he's always got a bigger plan than you do."

Duane, who has never been to a beach that doesn't border the Detroit River, is marveling at the white surf rolling less than a hundred feet from where he kneels. He taps a drumbeat on his thighs. Playing along to the rhythm of the waves.

"Two weeks," he says, reminding whoever is in earshot that their stay here is finite.

Lovejoy is securing short wooden legs to a plastic board that will act as a table to support the radio, a Korean War field radio phone, model 71 B; the platoon's only line of communication with the United States. Each of the Danes has inspected the unit, and they agree that it's much more sophisticated than what was being used twelve years ago, near the end of World War II. And yet, nobody has gotten it to work, not yet.

"It's a long way for a signal to travel," Ross says. "And the sound, our sound, might obstruct it."

Our sound, Philip thinks. The phrase doesn't sit well with him.

Philip and Larry are assembling the microphone stands. They use rope and rocks to secure them against potential wind and sand. The rocks are found in the knee-deep lip of the ocean. Philip stands in the water, his green pants rolled up to his thighs, his bare feet on moss-covered rocks. He reaches his hands into the water, feeling for the heaviest ones, then hands them to Larry.

Behind him, probably no more than a hundred yards, must lie one of the sunken ships he spotted from the plane.

He thinks, back and forth, of two things:

First, he's wearing military clothing again. When the war ended, and long before Philip landed back home in Detroit, he accepted that his days in the service were over. Not partially over. And not the sort of over that a man might return to. Like an ex-girlfriend. Or a drug habit. This over was true; he had served his country.

And yet . . .

Philip is wearing dark green army pants and a dark green T-shirt. His helmet rests on the beach. In his pack are the same variety of socks, underwear, gloves, and boots that he once wore, back when he packed for the United States Army.

It's a strange reality to swallow. As if he's a soldier from the past, dead then, living again, rejuvenated on a desert-beach in Africa.

The second subject he thinks about is a single word. Three syllables that have come to frighten America more than any enemy army ever has. A word that appears in his mind, then quickly disappears, over and over, as if looped through the two Ampex machines in the sand.

Nuclear.

Because nuclear is scary as hell. Nuclear is new, and nuclear means whole countries can disappear with the pressing of a button. *It isn't war,* Duane said. *It's a decision.* Stein may morbidly imagine himself photographing the mushroom apex of ultimate destruction, and Greer may find fascination in the chain of events that could lead to such a decision, but the Danes are dreaming of Detroit. A Detroit that will always be there.

Home.

Mull's mention of the word in the studio, the inoculation of the nuclear warhead, was unsettling enough. But to be out here, closer to whatever did that, takes a bravery Philip isn't sure he possesses.

Two weeks.

Larry rams the shovel into the sand, then wipes sweat from his forehead. His long hair is already damp from the heat. He's shirtless.

"Better be careful I don't set something off."

But he does not say *nuclear.* Not yet.

And Philip, searching the water for rocks, wonders if the source of the sound might not be submerged.

Toxic waste.

Dark syllables under a bleating sun. A frightening new-world phrase, new-world fear. Images of deformities, fish swimming sideways, nature forced inside out.

Philip's stomach turns.

He absently brings a handful of water to his forehead, trying to cool off what feels like a sudden fever. He rises to his full height and breathes deep, slow, believing he's panicking a little. If he's going to be out here for two weeks, he needs to learn how to be here.

"Be Here."

The hidden wilderness of dark ocean ahead, Philip looks over his shoulder to Larry, expecting to find his friend waiting for another rock.

But Larry is on his knees, a pained expression on his face.

Beyond him, Duane and Ross are stumbling.

Stein and Greer.

Feeling sick now himself, Philip scans the sand for Lovejoy, finds him sitting, lotus position, eyes closed.

"Larry, hey," Philip starts to say, but the words are too sticky, glued together; the individual letters feel bulky, keep his lips from fully parting.

He looks, too fast, dizzying, to his feet beneath the rippling water. He sees thick yellow liquid floating above them, pooling about his ankles.

He backs up on the slimy rocks, and falls, back first, into the water.

The yellow liquid has clusters of food in it. Philip understands that he's thrown up.

He throws up again.

He looks out to the horizon, rippling with waves. Throws up again.

The sound, he knows, is here.

But he doesn't hear it, not exactly. A rippling of something thinner than sound, perhaps the space the sound has to travel to reach his ears. Philip retains a vivid image of this as he rolls onto his side and dunks his head beneath the surface.

Down here . . . the sound is different than it is above.

Not louder . . .

. . . but clearer.

Down here he can hear individual notes, a chord again, momentarily, before the notes retract, back into the fold, back into the waves.

Philip opens his eyes.

Ten feet from him, the water is dark. And in the water is another person.

Red pants.

Black boots.

But are they boots? Shaken, disoriented, Philip thinks he sees . . .

Hooves.

Clomping toward him in the mud.

Philip rises and gasps for breath. There is nobody standing in the water, nobody breaking the undulating horizon, nobody in the ocean but himself.

He dunks back under. Looks. Sees Nothing. The sound is a chord, the sound is not.

He turns toward shore.

Shadows. Boots. Movement.

Red.

Philip emerges again.

He clutches his stomach with one hand and points to shore with the other, points where the figure should be, where a body *must be* because he saw it, saw it exiting the water.

But no.

No red pants. No black

(hooves)

boots.

The sound is fatter, wider, heavy, like it's physically capable of squeezing Philip's ribs.

He thinks he hears the chord again, a triad of unnatural, unmusical notes. Played by a hand with only three fingers, each with only one purpose; to play, to press, *that* note, *these three* notes, three half-steps, the sickening sound of a musician gone daft; a child angrily pressing his fingers upon the exact three keys that he knows will force his mother to her knees, reaching out for him, pleading . . . *Stop playing! Stop playing!*

STOP MAKING THAT FUCKING SOUND!

On his knees, the F key loose around his neck, Philip cuts his hand on a rock. He wipes blood from his palm. More appears. He wipes. More. He cleans. More. He dunks his hand into the water.

(what's in the water, Philip? nuclear?)

When he pulls his hand out it looks like his palm is split in two. In his deliriousness, in his crazed state of what can only be called hallucination, Philip imagines the sound is coming from the wound in his hand.

"Help!" he yells.

But the syllable is thick honey, a spoonful of glue.

He dunks his hand again. Looks to shore.

Sees him.

Standing above the others as they writhe in the sand. Stout as an officer.

Red pants. Red coat. No shirt beneath the coat. A white beard, long enough to touch Larry's shoulder as Larry attempts to get to his knees.

The space between Philip and what he sees is rippling, as if the sound itself were visible.

Can't see the features. Can't trust what he sees.

Sees hooves.

Sees horns, too.

A shimmering reflection of the sun between the horns. Metal there . . . diamond there . . .

Philip feels pressure at his temples. He blinks sticky eyelids, looks up to see the man (he can't call it a man, can't name it) crouching by Lovejoy. The sergeant's eyes are closed.

The thing in red brings a rippling hand to the former general's lips.

Philip can't see details, can't see a face . . .

He has to say something, he *tries* to say something, tries to warn Lovejoy.

The thing looks to Philip.

Like it heard him. Heard him like Mull heard him in the studio.

Philip has to close his eyes. The pain is too much; unseen fingers pressing against his pupils. When he opens them again his vision is as distorted as his balance, his stability, his stomach.

He sees a silhouette, rising. He sees hooves. He sees horns.

He dunks his head under. Brings it back out. Gasps for air.

It's something in red. It's a shadow. It's something in red. It's a silhouette. It's stepping toward Ross. It's a shadow. It's a silhouette. A thaumatrope. Two pictures. One disc. String. Rotate. Back and forth. Flip it. Like a wheel.

It's something.

It's a shadow.

It's something in red.

It's a bleeding shadow.

It's kneeling beside Ross in the sand. Ross who is helpless on his back. It's sliding indecipherable hands under Ross's shoulders, under his knees. It's opening its mouth. The white beard hides Ross's rippling face. Philip screams but can't scream. Instead what comes out is spittle, vomit, toxic—

STOP!

And the thing

(man shadow thaumatrope)

does stop.

Like he heard him. Heard him thinking, heard him unable to speak.

Then he's moving, carrying Ross, rippling, a pulsating ribbon of red. Philip gets up and stumbles, runs, barefoot on the slimy rocks, runs toward the thing, to Ross, to put a *STOP!* to all of this before it begins because if this is how it begins how will it end?

Philip makes it two steps, feeling vertigo, running sideways; slips, falls, smashes his head against a rock.

Philip blacks out. Instantly.

Out.

On the way, he half dreams of the sound traveling over black hills, through black woods, on black paths, the Path, Philip's own, charred black, with no boundaries, no demarcation, no signs either, telling people to stay out, stay away, you had it good in Detroit, the Darlings of Detroit, the Danes, you had it good, and this, this won't end well, this won't end.

Black quicksand on the Path.

Everything sinks.

Into nothingness. Into tranquil, brainless silence.

When Philip wakes again, when he comes to, sweating from a sun hotter than all American suns, he will bring a hand to his bandaged head and look into the horrified eyes of his fellow soldiers, all of them on edge, all of them panicked, all of them needing to know if he knows any more than they do about the whereabouts of Ross.

When Philip emerges from the black, Ross will be gone.

And only hoofprints, traveling into the desert, will remain.

21

To Philip, in the dark of his unit, the footsteps in the hall sound wet. The suction sloshing of damp, bare soles on administrative tiles. He can almost see the shape of the naked feet, the sound is so clear, can hear the contact between the heel and the tile, the toes like a quiet roll on the snare. The lifting again, the next step. The coming down.

Coming down the hall.

Philip is able to turn his head entirely to the closed unit door.

Footsteps. Bare skin in the hall.

How far off? Philip can guess. Forty feet off. Is it another patient? Up to use the bathroom? Maybe someone else in this hospital is healing too quickly, too.

Thirty feet. Twenty feet. Less than that now.

Philip stares at the door, looks to the thin rectangle of light at its base.

Thinks of Africa.

Thinks of a sight just like this. A different door. Same rectangle. Same evidence of somebody being home.

Silence from the hall.

Philip waits.

Silence.

He looks to the ceiling. Closes his eyes.

Begins to drift. But does not dream.

Instead, he experiences the lack of pain without asking what it is that's helping him. What's in the syringes he receives, the two shots twice daily, and the dosage that was no doubt upped this afternoon, as Ellen played him his own song on the piano.

Now, floating painlessly, so long as he remains this way, arms at his side, head straight, on his back, Philip feels capable, or like he's on his way to being so, almost there, closer, healing, soon able to rise, to go to them, to find them, to rescue the rest of—

The Danes.

A creaking of a door, but Philip is at peace, so close to sleep, balancing on the spire of a dream, delicate, still, momentarily uncluttered, and that moment is long enough to show him it's possible, it's true, there is hope, there is a new Path being forged, or perhaps it's the old one all along, there is a light at the end of this, all of this, Iowa, Macy Mercy, himself, the Danes.

But the light he senses, the light he sees, is not imagined. And Philip opens his eyes.

The door to his unit is open, allowing a slat of hall light to illuminate the tiles to his right. He attempts to raise his hand to his face, to wipe the near-sleep from his eyes, but it's too much effort, too painful, and he lets his palm fall to the bedsheet once again.

There is a figure in the room with him.

At first, not yet adjusted, Philip thinks it must be a shadow, but as the darkness recedes, as the details of the unit rise to the surface of the shapes they make, Philip sees a man.

Dr. Szands is standing naked beside the cot.

Philip does not speak.

Szands is staring at Philip's body and Philip understands, realizes, that his sheet has been lowered, exposing the injuries, the bruises, the brokenness.

He tries not to move. Doesn't want the doctor to know that he's awake.

Dr. Szands is touching his own body; mobile, fluid fingers across a symmetrical chest; smooth white wrists against his neck and chin.

He's comparing, Philip believes. Reiterating his authority.

Philip does not speak.

But the doctor does.

"This is a healthy body," he says, running his palms up the sides of his torso, the muscles of his belly. "Not battered with breaks. Uncluttered by drugs. Do you see, Philip? Do you see the difference?"

The voice is frightening in the half shadows. The slow drawl. The lesson he's trying to teach.

Philip does not speak.

"I want you to remember this, Philip," Szands says, running his hands from his neck to his waist. "I want you to remember who holds the power in this place."

He stares into Philip's eyes for a long time. Because no part of Philip is visible in the scant light, he hopes the doctor can't see his fear.

Szands sighs. He remains still a minute longer, then leaves the unit as slowly as he approached down the hall.

The door closes quietly behind him.

Philip is left alone, but the image of the doctor remains.

You gotta leave this place, Philip thinks. And the words waver, the words are weak. *Something bad is going to happen to you if you don't.*

He tries to recall the visions of rescuing the Danes, but the picture is flat. And in every scenario he imagines, he must return to this place.

For the drugs.

He does not turn his head to the ceiling. Despite the pain just blossoming in his neck, he stares to where the door is closed, unseen in the dark, thinking of the drugs, his own capabilities, his own knowledge, secrets, yes, and the fact that one of two things must happen, one of two things must give:

Either Philip heals enough to escape, or the doctor will retain that power until the end.

22

Ellen sits alone at a bar. The Corn Maze is less than thirty miles from Macy Mercy, but it's not on the way home. She hadn't planned on coming, didn't make the decision outright, but now that she's here, she understands that she wasn't going anywhere else.

A drink.

Space.

To think.

About Philip and the hospital and, yes, the drawing she did for him today, too.

How badly was Philip hurt? Of course she knows that his bones were broken, and she's noting the daily progress of his body healing . . . but how much does she or anybody else really know about head injuries? How much of what Philip tells her can be trusted? There's endless literature on the subject, journals, essays, articles, books; but an injury to the skull must be different from an injury to the unseen mind within.

And not only is Ellen very worried about Philip, she worries that she's too obvious in her caring for him.

But why?

"Whiskey on the rocks," she tells the bartender. The woman,

older, false blond, shows surprise, as if Ellen has ordered the one drink she hadn't already imagined serving her.

The bar Ellen sits at is shaped like a big wooden L, and at the other end sits another woman, dark hair, pale, like Ellen. But not like Ellen. This woman is a regular. Ellen spins on her stool and faces the room at large. Sees two men in overalls sharing a pitcher at a round low-top. Sees a man in a suit, tie undone, slumped in the corner of a booth, as if crumpled and left there.

When her whiskey comes, Ellen sips; she does not take big gulps, though she feels like she should. These thoughts about Philip are confusing her. She's never been one to shy away from how she feels, but she's never felt exactly like this before.

She sips.

She thinks.

Philip is an extremely unsettling case, equal parts light and dark. A piano player, but momentarily disturbed by the piano in the unit. Devastatingly wounded, yet healing so fast.

Dammit, she thinks, what happened to him out there?

Ellen wants to know. But nurses aren't supposed to ask.

And yet . . . there *are* places she could look.

"Another?" the bartender asks.

It's dark in here. Bar dark. Ellen hadn't noticed she was finished with the first drink. She's chewing a piece of ice. Hadn't noticed that, either.

"Yes. Thank you."

This is a standard Iowa bar: wood-paneled walls, signs for Budweiser, Pabst, and Knickerbocker beer. A jukebox in the corner. Posters of famous Iowans: Marilyn Maxwell, Jean Seberg, and of course John Wayne, born in Winterset, thirty-seven miles southwest of Des Moines. These same faces decorate most dive bars within a hundred-mile radius, but there are others on these walls, too. Drawings, caricatures, men and women with big noses and ears, huge smiles and cleft chins.

"Regulars," the blond bartender says, noting Ellen looking at the walls. "You've gotta drink at the Maze for ten years 'fore you get a drawing done."

A drawing.

A goat.

Ellen sips her drink.

"Maybe I'll stay for ten years, then," she says. This makes the blonde smile, but there's a sadness there; the bartender knows all the people who have done just that.

Realizing she's still wearing it, Ellen removes her coat and places it on the stool beside hers. It's a good coat, black like her hair. She's wearing a tan blouse and black slacks. A far cry from her white uniform, the uniform Philip sees her wearing every day. He knows her only as a nurse, nothing more. Is it strange that she should want him to see her as something more?

The front door opens and yellow light from the parking lot lamps gets in. Ellen squints at the form, the big form, of a man entering. She turns her attention to the bottles lined up behind the bar and the rectangle of dressing room lights framing them.

From her purse, Ellen removes the sketch she drew for Philip today.

She smiles because it looks like a child's drawing. And yet, whatever it is, it made Philip cry, it rattled something buried inside him. She wonders if it has something directly to do with his injury, or maybe with his band. Or both.

Or maybe, she thinks, despite what he said about seeing it in the desert, it's even older. A memory from childhood. Philip is missing home, wants to talk to his parents, wants to talk to his friends, his bandmates, tell them he's alive, he's in Iowa, he's healing.

Where are they? Where are the rest of the Danes?

Ellen doesn't know.

Her partial smile falls from her face. It wasn't the funny kind to begin with.

"Another?" the bartender asks.

Ellen looks up from the drawing. She wonders what this woman might think of it.

What does it mean?

"Yes. Thank you."

A crinkling beside her and at first Ellen thinks it's the paper, thinks she's mussed it up, then sees the big man take the stool two down from her own. When he looks at her, Ellen averts her eyes. The last thing she wants right now is the sloppy advance of a stranger, drinking.

"You got a kid?"

Ellen, staring ahead, thinks of Jean, her daughter. Thinks of her small body at the bottom of a fire escape. Broken in the alley below.

"No."

She doesn't look at the man, but recognizes the tone of voice: playful now, but angry, soon, when he doesn't get his way. She begins to wonder if a bar, alone, was a bad idea.

"Looks like a kid's drawing," the man says.

"Yes."

The bartender eyes the interaction. *How many variations of this has she seen,* Ellen wonders.

"May I?"

His fingers are already on the paper and Ellen pulls it away.

"Hey," she says, facing him now. "Who told you it's okay to grab something that isn't yours?"

The man laughs. A black mustache frames his smiling upper lip. He's bigger than he looked coming through the door. Wears a beige overcoat. Suit beneath. Brown hair, blue eyes. By the time he's finished laughing, Ellen thinks maybe she recognizes his type.

"You sure sound like a mom," he says. He snaps his fingers at the bartender. "Heidel-Brau."

One elbow on the smooth dark bar, the man is facing Ellen completely.

"If you don't want people asking after your artwork, you shouldn't flash it around."

"Okay, you know what?" Ellen says, anger rising. "You can—"

"And you should most certainly not flash any artwork you did at the hospital."

Ellen's mouth is still open, but no more words escape. She does recognize the type; this man is military.

"Who are you?" she asks, already sensing a loss of leverage. More surprisingly, she's afraid.

The man smiles and knocks back the first third of his beer. He wipes the foam from his mustache with his coat sleeve.

"I'm me," he says, shrugging. There's a vitality to him, and a violence below the innocuous gesture.

"How do you know where I work?"

Now the blond bartender is watching the man, too. Small consolation, Ellen knows. No cavalry in here.

The man smiles.

"What matters now," the man says, "is that he likes you."

"What?"

But Ellen knows what.

And the man knows she knows.

"He talks to you more . . . freely than he does the others. He's . . ." the man waves his plump hands above the bar, as if searching for the word. "He's *inspired* by you."

Ellen feels hot. Cornered.

"You followed me here."

The man shrugs again.

"Followed, knew, needed to talk . . . however you wanna put it."

He sips his beer.

"I'm not working right now," Ellen says.

"But you are. You're working out in a very big way. He talks to you. And we need you to"—more hand gestures—"keep that up."

"I don't understand."

But she does. She understands what the man is asking her to do.

"May I?"

He reaches politely for the drawing now. Ellen lets him take it.

The man places the drawing on the bar and shakes his head, whistles through wet lips.

"You think this one is weird, you should've seen the last one."

Ellen breathes deep. She knows that asking the question she wants to ask will be like giving in to this man. But she can't stop it from coming out. Maybe it's the whiskeys. Maybe it's the new feelings.

"How did he get hurt?"

For the first time since taking his stool, the man genuinely smiles.

"Now we're talking," he says. "Now we're friends?" He holds out a hand. Ellen doesn't shake it. He wipes his palms together. "I'll answer your question because I think it'll help you get him talking. Your patient was sent to Africa to find out what's been driving the army radios crazy. He was asked to locate the source of a disturbing sound. He found it. That's about all you need to know. What we'd like you to do . . . is get him to tell us where it is."

"Why wouldn't he tell you if he knew where it was? Philip's a good—"

"Nuh-uh." The man raises an open palm. "No names. Not here. Not anywhere outside. Do you understand?"

Ellen looks to the bartender, but the woman is at the other end of the long L, elbows on the bar, rags in hands, talking with the other lone brunette.

"He's a good man," Ellen finishes, sipping her third drink.

The man laughs.

"Just make sure you do your part in healing him back up. The faster the better for all of us. And get him to talk. Get him to do more . . ." He gestures, dramatically, at the drawing. "Get him to do more of these."

Soft country music plays on the bar's speakers and Ellen doesn't know when it began. There is no humor, no kindness in the man's eyes.

But she asks it again.

"What happened to him?" Thinking somehow that she does have leverage, that this man wants something from her. And she wants something in return.

A long, expressionless hesitation before the lower half of the man's face erupts into a smile, exposing bad teeth.

"He broke every bone in his body. Remember?"

Ellen wants to leave this bar. Leave this state. Suddenly, very badly, she wants to get to her apartment, pack her things, leave Macy Mercy and Iowa far behind.

But Philip.

"Do your job," the man says. "But do it even . . . more so. Get him to talk. Keep inspiring him."

He snaps his fat fingers; they make a soft sandy sound.

"How do I know who you're with?" Ellen asks, frightened by her own question.

The man nods.

From his pocket he removes a photo. He hands it to Ellen. In it, the man, wearing a T-shirt and jeans, is crouched beside a wounded body. There are other people, but none of their faces are visible. None except the one on the body on the floor of what must be a helicopter. Below the helicopter, through its open door, she sees sand.

"Philip," she whispers.

The man swipes the photo back.

"No names."

Ellen saw the bruises, the broken body, what should've been a corpse, but lives.

"I was one of the men who picked him up," he says, getting up off the stool. He nods to the bartender and she comes. "I'll get hers, too," he tells her, then lays a bill on the counter. To Ellen he says, "Keep drinking if you wanna. Drink the night through. But do as I've said. And oh," he raises the drawing. "May I?"

Ellen doesn't speak. Doesn't stop the man as he folds the drawing and slips it into his long coat.

He tips an imaginary hat Ellen's way and leaves the bar.

"Was he bothering you?" the bartender asks as soon as he's gone.

Ellen looks her in the eye, but she's not seeing this place right now. She's hardly here. Rather, she's in the hospital, Macy Mercy, tending to those same bruises, those same broken bones.

You inspire him. Do your job . . . only more so. Get him to talk.

Ellen knows she should leave Iowa. Either that or drive directly to Macy Mercy now, right now, tell Philip he's in trouble; people are watching him, people believe he's hiding something from them.

She gets up to go.

"You sure you don't want one more?"

Ellen places her hands on the bar.

Just make sure you do your part in healing him back up. The faster the better for all of us.

She takes her seat again.

"Yes," she says. "One more."

23

I'm telling you I saw something, dammit. Not a man . . . I don't know what it was. I saw it in the water and then I saw it on the beach." Philip is yelling because he's just as scared, just as worried as they are. "It was wearing red. It had . . . horns."

"No man with horns," Duane repeats. He can't stop pacing.

Lovejoy is looking through binoculars, far out into the desert. Stein is doing the same with the zoom lens of his camera.

"Duane," Philip stresses. "I'm telling you what I saw."

"Nadoul," Larry says. He's searching the water. He searched the water for the hour Philip was knocked out, too.

"Who?" Duane half asks. He's breathing hard.

"The local from the hut. The one Mull talked to," Larry says. And his voice is tremor, his voice is fear.

"No," Philip says. "This wasn't a local . . . this was . . ."

"A white *ram,*" Duane chides.

Bandaged head and all, Philip rushes his friend, grips him by the sleeves of his shirt.

"I saw him!" he yells, his lips inches from Duane's. *"What did YOU see?!"*

"Hey, whoa." Larry steps between them, pries them apart. They've already talked about this. Nobody saw a horned figure. Nobody saw anything at all.

Larry looks out to the ocean, as if Ross might wash up now that he's turned his back on him.

"We're not leaving this spot until we find him," Duane says, straightening his sleeves, wiping sweat from his forehead. "And we're not looking for any sound anymore."

Lovejoy doesn't acknowledge this remark. Greer does.

"Hallucination," he says, as if casting a final judgment. His glasses are fogged and hide his eyes. "Just like when you thought your hand was responsible for the sound. One hallucination . . . then another."

But Philip can see in the historian's eyes that he hasn't cast final judgment quite yet. He's still studying.

"Doesn't matter," Larry says. "Doesn't matter *what* Philip saw. Duane's right. We're not moving until we know what happened to Ross, and once we do . . . we're not moving until the plane gets back."

Lovejoy lowers the binoculars.

"He took him," he says.

"That's what I've been saying," Philip says. "Jesus Christ, guys. I saw—"

Lovejoy raises the binoculars for any of the platoon to take.

"Look."

Larry takes them. As he squints into the eyeholes, Lovejoy guides the lenses.

"Those aren't bootprints, Sergeant. They're . . ."

"They're what?" Duane asks, reaching for the binoculars.

As he sees for himself, Larry says, "Hooves."

"Really?" Philip says, reaching for the binoculars. "I told you I fucking saw it!"

Duane doesn't put up a fight. But he's not convinced.

"Hey. Man, just because there are some goat prints in the sand doesn't mean Ross rode off on the thing."

"He carried him," Lovejoy says.

They all imagine the same thing at once. An impossibility lifting Ross from the sand, carrying him into the desert.

Stein snaps a photo.

"No way," Duane says. "We are *not* tracking Philip's hallucination through the desert. We are *not* leaving this spot until we *know* what happened to Ross."

Only the wind now, as if Ross were turned to air.

Lovejoy breaks the silence.

"Pack up, soldier."

"We're not soldiers."

"Pack up."

"We didn't agree to this. We agreed—"

"You can stay behind, Private Noles. But night *will* come. And that sound may come with it. And I don't think you want to be alone with either."

It's the first they've seen of Lovejoy as leader, Lovejoy as military man.

Duane looks to Larry for help. Looks to Philip. But the other Danes are decided.

"Check the shore again," Duane says, uncertainly, to nobody. "Check the fog."

His fear of leaving this spot, of trekking farther out from where the plane will pick them up, is palpable.

"Pack up!" Lovejoy roars.

It's the voice of a commanding officer in the United States Army.

Then he's off to pack his own gear.

Duane goes to Philip.

"We retired a long time ago," he says.

"I saw someone," Philip repeats, and maybe it's because it's just the two of them, but Duane seems to listen, really listen, this time. "And those prints—"

"Philip, we don't know what's out there, we don't know—"

Philip plants a hand on Duane's shoulder. Looks him level in the eyes.

"It's Ross we're talking about, man. *Ross.*"

Duane breathes deep, looks once to the water, then gets to his knees by his own gear.

When Philip is packed, he joins Greer at the edge of camp. The others are still working behind them.

"Do you guys know why Lovejoy was demoted?" Greer suddenly asks.

"No," Philip says. "And right now I don't care."

Greer squints into the sun, into the body of the desert.

"Maybe it's important for you to know."

Philip looks back to see that Duane and Larry are packing the second Ampex. Philip has the first.

"Go ahead."

"Sergeant Lovejoy, once *General* Lovejoy"—Greer is affecting a proper but condescending accent—"was relieved of his higher rank for . . . *fixation on the deceased.* The Mad Blond was caught trying to pump the blood of the recently dead into the bodies of the recently wounded."

"What does that mean?"

"It means he borrowed blood pumps from the medical stations without authority to do so. It means he knelt beside bodies in the middle of battle and tried to deliver still-usable blood to those who were losing theirs too quickly to survive."

Larry emerges from the fog. Then returns to it.

"And it wasn't just because they caught him doing it, either; it was because he'd *proposed* the idea to the army first, and they'd said no."

"How do you know all this?" Philip asks, looking alternately back to the remaining Danes and out to the desert, where he hopes, prays, to see a flash, a shape, a sign of his missing friend.

"My brother was one of the soldiers he saved."

Philip looks to Greer.

"What happened?"

Far behind Greer, Lovejoy is slipping his arms through the straps of his pack.

"My brother Jeff was badly wounded," Greer continues. "Gunshot to the right thigh. Dead leg. He said he'd seen a fella's chin blown off. Another shot through the gut. He said the earth was red with blood. 'Crayon red,' he said. Said it smelled like a garage, like he was getting his car fixed. He was bleeding out fast. He started to cry out for help but help was already on its way, in the form of the then–General Lovejoy. When our sergeant emerged from the war-fog, Jeff said he just about shit himself, couldn't believe a general in the United States Army was out there in the field. Jeff thought he must've been death-dreaming. He watched from on his back as Lovejoy signaled blindly over his shoulder and two soldiers showed, dragging a corpse through the mud."

Behind Greer, Lovejoy is approaching. The sun reveals his reddening scalp, the tufts of blond hair.

"Jeff thought they were gonna bury him and the other guy together. Then he saw the pump. Lovejoy brought his face close to Jeff's. He said, 'I'd ask you what blood type you are, but I don't think I'd get an answer outta *him.*' The soldiers jammed the pump into the eviscerated guts of the corpse and Jeff threw up. The tube filled quickly. Lovejoy pointed to Jeff's wound and the soldiers stuck the other end of the pump into my brother's exploded thigh." Greer is rubbing his own thighs anxiously. Philip sees Lovejoy has crossed half the distance to them. He walks slow. He looks to the sun. "But what really scared Jeff was the look in Lovejoy's eyes, the way he perched on his bootheels, without a helmet, as bullets swarmed his head. Said his hair was waving as if the thoughts inside his skull were made of electricity."

"Sounds like he saved his life," Philip says. He's thinking of saving Ross's life.

"Lovejoy doesn't give up," Greer says. "Ever."

The sergeant reaches them, then passes. Ten feet farther, he stops and stares out.

Duane and Larry emerge from the fog. They're dragging the second Ampex the same way Philip has the first, on its plastic lid.

Sleds.

"Philip," Duane says, the gravity of death in his eyes, "we can't go home without him."

"I know."

Stein joins Lovejoy ahead. He takes a photo of the desert. Then he takes one of Lovejoy, as the Mad Blond calls for the hunt to begin.

They head out.

Philip looks back to the water once and feels a chill. Not because the air is cooler here than it will be where they're going, but because the sea feels somewhat like a tether, and in the name of finding Ross, they've untied it.

24

Philip hasn't slept. Instead, he weighed.

It's not only that Szands is mad, it's that last night Philip recognized the brand of crazy in the doctor's eyes.

Philip's seen it before in other musicians in Detroit. Flavors of the moment, beats of the week, bands that get drunk on the little fame they savor.

Dr. Szands is drunk, too. And Philip doesn't have to look far to determine what it is that he's drinking.

It's the way Philip is healing. And the sense of godliness that must come to a doctor capable of making such a recovery happen.

Without rest and restless, Philip has been weighing who to tell. *Dr. Szands is crazy. He came to my room last night.*

Help me.

But Nurse Delores is as straight as the unit door. The orderlies Carl and Jerry are as loyal and dim as dogs. And Francine is almost as frightening as the doctor.

Who to trust in here?

Of course, there is only one. But the distance between a healthy patient–nurse relationship and that patient defaming the doctor to that same nurse is a big one.

Will she think Philip is the mad one?

If Philip is honest with himself he'll admit that Nurse Ellen is exactly the kind of girl who would have made him nervous back in Detroit. Pretty, sure, but it's Ellen's mind that frightens him. She's smarter than he is. Probably more honest than he's been. Probably knows how to have a drink without the night becoming a lawbreaker. Yes, Ellen is the kind of woman Philip would have walked away from at the bar, sure that if he were to talk to her, any words at all, he would be in danger of losing himself.

Is she the right one to tell? Will she believe him? Or will she convince him otherwise?

Now, watching the soup tremble in the spoon, aware that she's shaking, Philip wonders what she's afraid of.

"I'm sorry," she says.

"It's okay."

All afternoon she's been this way. When she came in, her eyes traveled to each corner of the unit and she spent some time staring at the filing cabinet, too.

Philip knows paranoid when he sees it.

But does she have a right to be?

"It's war," she says. "And what it's done to me and what it's done to you."

She gets up and walks to the bookshelf. Philip is able to turn his head far enough to see her. She's looking between the books, under the radio.

Like she's looking for bugs.

"A daughter," Ellen says, flipping through the pages of the books, no humor in her voice. "Very young. She was three. People say that means she'll always be three, but that makes it worse. I like to imagine her aging." She looks up at Philip. Back to the pages. "Sometimes even faster than I have. I like to think of her as a very old woman, sitting across the kitchen table from me. She's got stringy gray hair and an angry look on her face and she's saying, *Will you please hurry up and join me so we can finally have our time together? The time we never got?*"

Ellen lost a daughter. Philip understands. But watching her put her hand up the lampshade and feel around is making him edgier than he already is.

So much sound. Everywhere. In Detroit. In the Namib. In here.

"Her father was a clerk. His name was Al. I liked Al because he was funny, he was straight, and he didn't believe in war." Her eyes shine, wet, but her voice doesn't waver. "I met Al in '44. We dated for a year before we got married. He was a good man. He'd take me to quiet, dark restaurants. He laughed at my jokes. We danced." She's behind him now. He hears the lid of the piano bench lifted. "It wasn't passionate love, but it was kind. And the kindness between us led to a pregnancy. We had a little girl. Jean. I love that name. One syllable. Done. Clean. Jean. But by then, Al was falling apart."

She's across the room, in front of him now, kneeling by the filing cabinet. Tugging open the drawers.

"There was World War I and then World War II and oh, we may as well include all the wars before then. Al sure did. He felt like something bad was building. A bad feeling was growing. A pattern. He pointed it out to me. 'Keeps happening,' he'd say. 'And why?' He was obsessed with the whys. Why do we do this? Why do we *continue* to do this? Al was in Germany with his brother Jimmy. They fought together. Jimmy was hurt bad. And when Jimmy died over there"—slower now—"Al lost faith in everything. Everything except the pattern."

Philip remembers Greer huddled around a fire, talking about wheels. Drawing circles in the dirt.

He thinks of the horns and hooves he found in a room buried beneath the sand.

"He'd lock the bathroom door and stay in there for hours. Jean would ask where Daddy was and I'd tell her he was bathing. I'd make her laugh. Because when she wasn't laughing we could hear Al crying. Jean would look over across the apartment to the bathroom and I'd make another joke. Another face. Just to cover up the crying. But no matter how loud we were, we could always hear Al when he started hollering. He'd say, 'Jimmy, you've already been shot! You just don't know it yet!'" Ellen pauses, for effect, looks at Philip wide eyed. Then she's up and searching the window drapes. "He was doing the same thing the day Jean fell from the fire escape. Must have been locked in the bathroom when she fell, because that's where he was when I got home and I was the first person to tell him she wasn't in the apartment, me, who had been at work for the past six hours. Me, who didn't have to go to war to understand it." She's on her knees by the cot now. Sweeping her arm beneath it. "I knocked on the bathroom door. I said, 'Al, where's Jean? Is Jean in there with you?' He opened the door, his eyes red, and he said, 'He was already shot, Ellen. He was telling the rest of us how afraid he was, afraid of getting shot. But he didn't understand . . . it'd already happened. He'd already been shot.'"

She pops up, facing Philip. She looks like a mother to him now.

"I'm sorry," she says. "I suppose we're all a bit wounded."

They stare at one another, connected by the hospital and more.

"I'll be right back," she says.

She gets up and leaves the unit.

Philip thinks of Al's pattern. Of what the platoon started to call Greer's Wheel.

If there's one thing that stands out above all others in my research, it's that history doesn't sit still. Doesn't sit silent. It makes noise.

Philip hadn't noticed the classical music coming from the office until it stops. After a momentary pause new music begins. Philip has this record at home.

Ellen returns.

"It's not the Danes," she says. "But it'll do."

"What's it going to do?"

She crosses the unit. Looks down into his eyes. For Ellen it's the man in the bar who took her drawing. For Philip it's the fluctuating features of a thief in red.

For now, though, their monsters are put away.

But not forgotten.

"Let's dance," Ellen says.

She takes Philip's hand. She drags her fingertip across his palm.

She steps to the center of the room.

Philip watches from the cot. Imagines he's standing beside her. No . . . *sees* himself there.

Ellen is dancing.

And for an incredible, impossible moment, Philip believes he's dancing with her.

It's something Philip has needed. Something he didn't know he needed.

Touch.

Ellen dances, slow, in and out of the increasing shadows, across the unit, her heels echoing in step with the drums, her eyes closed.

Philip is holding her in a bar in Detroit. Gets into a cab with her, takes her home, runs his fingers through her black hair. In the morning he'll show her his favorite diner, order his favorite breakfast. They'll spend the day together, see Detroit, visit Philip's parents, his friends, the Danes. They'll search for another thrill that night, dancing again, another dance, and create their own wheel, their own pattern, their own sound.

When the song ends, Ellen opens her eyes.

"That was . . . really very good."

Then she laughs and it's the laughter of the grieving, but it is not mad.

She needed it, too.

A beat, a break.

A dance.

She turns off the lamp. At the cot again she brings the blanket up to Philip's chin. Moonlight illuminates her features and the wall beyond her.

"Plans?" Philip asks. And his voice is less wooden than it was when he woke in this place.

Ellen does not wipe her eyes dry. She leaves the tears alone.

"Yes. Big plans tonight. I am going to eat ice cream alone on my couch. And if I spill any I'll clean it up with a paper towel."

Philip smiles, but the heaviness remains in this room. Ellen's daughter. The Danes. Al's pattern. Greer's drawings in the desert sand.

"Date?"

"Didn't we just have one? And don't we have another one tomorrow?"

Something has happened in here tonight. Something has passed between them.

"Don't dream of anything too horrible," she says. "And if you do, just add a naked woman on roller skates. That always puts an end to a bad dream."

They stare at each other in the half darkness.

"Good night, Philip."

"Don't leave."

"You're braver than you realize."

"Don't leave."

"I'll be back tomorrow."

"Ellen . . ."

"Yes?"

"Come here."

She lowers her head close to his.

"Closer."

She does.

He whispers in her ear.

"Dr. Szands is mad."

She leans back, looks long into his eyes. She opens her mouth, as if to say something she's thought herself.

Then she leaves.

The fan is whirring on the bookshelf.

Philip stares at the shadows on the ceiling. In them he sees the Danes. Onstage in Detroit. On an airplane to Africa.

Then, one missing, as the others cross the desert to find him.

Night at the hospital is upon him.

"Evening, Philip."

It's Nurse Francine in the doorway. She's carrying a tray. His medicine.

And the ghosts that haunt Philip's mind rise again.

25

The sun is going down, but it's not down yet. And the water is far enough behind them that the waves sound more like whispers.

He's not dead yet, Philip tells himself, dragging one of the sixty-pound Ampex machines on its plastic lid. *He's missing.*

This is more manageable. This keeps Philip's sanity safe.

Until they see Ross's body, unmoving, there is no dead.

They've reached a row of dunes they're not going to be able to avoid.

Philip pauses at the base of the one they stand at, sees his shadow on the sand.

Once upon a time that shadow carried a gun . . . then a microphone.

Now it's both.

Lovejoy plants a boot into the dune and looks up.

"Prints," he says.

Maybe it's the combination of the sun and fatigue, but Philip hadn't seen the prints until Lovejoy pointed them out. He sees them now. Faint hooves. As if they step lighter than the Americans do. Know the desert better.

Know where to hide.

Lovejoy begins the climb up.

Stein snaps a photo of him and Philip can see the picture as if it's already developed: black and white, the sweating former general leading the platoon on this dark day, the day Ross Robinson went missing.

The rest follow.

When Philip reaches the top, Lovejoy is already there, already looking through the binoculars. He points to a distant dot.

"Is it him?" Philip asks, breathless.

Stein snaps a photo.

From the peak of the dune it's the size of a black crab.

"A dead body," Lovejoy says.

Philip takes the binoculars from the sergeant's hands.

He looks. He sees.

"What is it?" Larry asks. "Is it him?!"

Lovejoy begins the descent.

"Philip?" Larry repeats, because his friend's verification trumps the sergeant's.

Stein snaps another photo. Greer is descending now, finding balance where he can.

"I'm not sure," Philip says. "It looks more like . . . a uniform."

"A what?"

Magnified, Philip sees what could be a long-sleeved shirt and pants. The arms are raised, as if in self-defense.

"What kind of uniform?"

Philip studies it longer, stares until the distant details begin to make sense.

"It looks like a textbook," Philip says.

"What does that mean?"

Philip lowers the binoculars.

"It's not Ross. But it's army."

"Oh, fuck," Duane says. "The other platoons."

“No.” Philip is shaking his head. “Old army.” He hands the binoculars to Duane.

“Old?” Larry asks.

“Like it crawled out of a textbook. That’s a dead body, all right. But it’s dressed in a Civil War uniform.”

26

I wouldn't do that if I were you . . .

This phrase, these words . . . again. As Philip sleeps, they're spoken. An old voice. A familiar voice. From where?

I wouldn't do that if I were you . . .

But who said that?

There's an accent. There's age. A warning. An admonition.

Philip knows the voice, and it's not just because he heard it repeated for the six months he was under.

He hears it now, in his dreams, coursing over the smooth arc of dunes, flying low through their slacks. It, too, tracks the thing that took Ross, follows the same prints, until it reaches the same end.

And there, at camp, that voice is used, that accent is hidden, on purpose, like the spiders that dig holes beneath the sand, like the miners who once looked for diamonds down there.

It's night at Macy Mercy.

A sleeping body healing itself breeds nightmares.

So Philip wakes.

Or maybe it's the sound that wakes him.

Philip opens his eyes, sees moonlight where the ceiling meets the wall. The desert at night, too.

Creaking wood? Maybe boots on stairs. Or maybe someone sitting down to play an old, red piano.

Philip wants to sit up. He can't. Instead, he cranes his neck, tries to see behind the cot, to the back of the unit.

But the sound isn't coming from inside this room. It's coming from the hospital hall.

He's able to turn his head just far enough to see the beginning of the open door.

A voice from the hall says, "Lights out!"

"Duane?" Philip asks, as a cruel swirl of emotions accosts him.

Duane used to call "lights out" at the end of every set. It was the title of their closer.

"Lights Out."

Whispers in the hall? Something. A rhythm to it. Footsteps, creaking wood, a low hum.

Szands?

"Duane?"

Philip says "Duane" but he's thinking "the Danes."

"Guys! Are you out there?" His voice is shrill. Like someone he'd never thought he'd become.

Desperate.

The band is dead, Philip thinks.

YOU DON'T KNOW THAT FOR SURE!

More noise and it doesn't sound like a band out there after all. No. Why did he think it did?

It's Dr. Szands, he thinks. *And he's coming to play God.*

"Nurse."

But Philip only partially calls for a nurse. He wants to hear this sound through, wants to see for himself what's coming.

Because something *is* coming.

Less like music, more of a wave; a singular solid block of sound, unraveling from deep down the hall.

Philip imagines his bandmates, dead upon that wave.

Lights out!

Duane floating beside a broken drum kit, a wobbly stool, his black skin peeling off cracked, broken bones. A ripple travels across the drummer's body, a wave trapped inside the man, nowhere to go, nowhere to get out.

Lights out.

Larry. Larry's out there, too. His blond hair is white with desert dust from a desert grave.

"Nurse!" Philip calls again, and this time he means it.

Lights out!

Philip is sweating. Breathing too hard.

Lights out, lights out, we've got one more for you, and then it's lights out.

The sound is getting closer, the spool unfolding, a desert blanket unrolled, coming down the hall, revealing his friends, dead, all of them, the whispers out there, boots on wooden stairs, a piano bench sliding, the hum of the hospital at night.

"Ross!" Philip feels feverish, delirious. He's calling out for his dead friends.

NOT DEAD!

But they might be. They might be.

Philip hears a round of laughter . . . sounds like a television show, an audience:

PLAY FOR US! PLAY FOR US! PLAY FOR US, LIGHTS OUT!

"Nurse!"

Philip wants out. Off the cot, out of this room, out of this battered body. He grips the sides of the cot and pulls, tries to turn himself, all of him, at once. Closes his eyes, sees a dead Duane.

Lights out, Philip. I'm out of gas. Lights out. One more song. Then we can get out of here. One more song. Then it's over. Tell 'em it's over. Tell 'em we found the source of the sound. Tell 'em we found it and tell 'em it wasn't any good.

Philip grips the cot harder.

In the folds of the swelling sound, Philip hears heavy slippers in the hall.

Move.

He's trying. He's sweating. His bruised arms and legs are pushing back.

He rests.

He tries again.

He rests.

I'm out of gas, Philip. One more song.

. . . lights out . . .

But not yet. Not lights out yet.

Philip. Larry's voice, in Philip's head. *Why didn't you bring us with you? Why'd you leave us?*

NO!!!

Philip is pulling himself up, pulling himself over. His arms feel strong enough to do it, a second, deeper strength well below the discolored surface, the bruises, the breaks that haven't healed, couldn't have healed, not all the way, not yet.

"Duane," Philip says, delirious with it. "One more. Let's play one more."

And the talking, the speaking to nobody, is the final lift he needs.

I wouldn't do that if I were you . . .

He's rolling.

Rolling over the edge of the cot.

Rolling too fast.

The ceiling blurs into the wall; the wall becomes the edge of the door; the door becomes the floor.

Too fast.

The door is open; light from the hall.

Before he hits, Philip sees Nurse Francine in the doorway. Her eyes are buggish, magnified by her huge glasses. She's reaching out, coming toward him.

But the look on her face . . .

Philip has a crazy thought as his nose connects with the solid floor, breaks for a second time:

Another shot, another needle, and you'll be fine, all over again, fine.

Then he connects.

A crash.

The pain that erupts in his nose blinds him, bright white, and he sees, once again, his bandmates, dead, leering, flaking, reaching up and out of the sand, as though having dug themselves out of a hole in the desert . . .

Philip has fallen.

Off the cot.

(off the Path)

Nurse Francine is beside him.

"Look what you've done!" she says, her voice betraying horror. "Oh, *look* what you've done! They'll fire me for this! I'll be fired!"

But Philip is drifting. Hardly hears her. Thinks he hears,

". . . set us back a week!"

Just words, just letters to Philip.

". . . need to heal . . ."

He's bleeding. Feels a needle in his arm.

". . . off schedule . . ."

He has three last thoughts before dissipating into darkness:

That sound in the hall. That was the sound from the desert . . .

and

Why is it here? How is it here?

and

It didn't make me sick this time . . .

Then he's knocked out.

He doesn't hear the sound anymore.

Nor does he see the light.

Lights out.

For how long . . .

. . . he can't know . . .

. . . then . . .

. . . some light. . . .

. . . enough that Philip can see Dr. Szands eyeing him from across the room . . .

. . . a new room . . .

. . . a new cot . . . no cot at all . . . a metal slab . . . like a morgue . . . Szands standing with arms crossed . . . half in shadows . . .

Get up.

Philip attempts to sit up, can't. Attempts to lift his arms, can't.

Straps, Philip thinks.

Szands smiles.

"Welcome," the doctor says. "To rehab."

Philip focuses on the walls. He recognizes the pattern, the look of them.

"Why am I strapped down, doctor?"

Szands laughs; a rich, moneyed laugh; clipped and crisp.

But there is no echo.

Flat sound in here.

The walls are covered with the same stuff the Danes use in Wonderland.

"Convoluted foam," he says. "Soundproof. You've used it before, I'm sure." He stares. Studying. Then, "You heard the sound, no doubt. So . . . that means you know it's here."

Philip doesn't answer. Doesn't ask, what do you mean it's here?

"You should see the orderly who listened to it. Being fired was not the worst that happened to him tonight."

An orderly listened to the sound . . . they have the sound here . . . on tape . . . where?

Szands crosses the padded room; his figure and the color of his pink short-sleeve shirt are cut, strong, in relief against the gray foam behind him.

"This is where little boys go when they can't take care of themselves, Philip."

"What?"

"Do you not remember leaving your bed last night?"

As if cued, the pain in Philip's nose increases. Yes, he took a fall. A bad one.

"I was trying to get up."

"That's right. Trying to get up. And is that what good boys do?"

"What?"

The sky in Szands's eyes is too bright.

"We're more than just a *hospital,* Philip. Certainly, you're aware of how special a place this is. Surely, by now, you're able to recognize how rapidly your body is recovering. One might say . . . you're our creation."

"Come on."

"Oh no, no, no." Szands wags a slim, clean finger. "There will be no *come on* in here. You and I are not compeers, Philip. We are doctor and patient. Specialist and sufferer." Szands lifts a pair of gloves from a tray table. "You broke your nose. The very nose we've spent so much time mending. An eye socket as well. A cheekbone. But let me be clear, Philip. You *rebroke* these bones. And you've set us back quite a spell."

Szands slips a hand into one of the gloves.

"What are you going to do, doctor?"

"What all fathers do to good boys who misbehave. I'm going to teach you a lesson." He slips on the second glove. "We can't have you *hurting* yourself. If you *hurt* yourself then you mock all the work we're doing for *you.* Please, don't pretend you don't understand what I mean."

"Doctor . . . I was just trying to—"

"You're off-center," Szands says.

A rubbered hand upon Philip's mouth.

Without anesthetic, but with a snap, Szands resets Philip's broken nose.

Philip screams.

And the sound does not carry. Not in here.

Szands holds his hands tight to the nose. He twists it again, breaking it once more.

He sets it.

He breaks it.

He sets it.

He breaks it.

And he sets it once more.

By the time he removes his hands from Philip's face, Philip is half under. Through a terrible swirl of bright lights and dark shadows, he sees Szands's face as it must look when nobody is watching.

Then the doctor is leaving his side.

The soft click of a door and he is gone.

Philip fades further.

But a second clicking, the door opening again, and Philip sees a pale face, dark hair, a white uniform.

"Ellen," Philip says. But the word is half dreamed.

And when the face comes closer, into focus, Philip sees the wrinkles, the glasses, Francine.

He feels the point of the needle, too, as it enters his shoulder, as the pain in his face subsides and the dark dreams of the unconscious rush up to greet him.

27

Lovejoy was right.

It's not just a uniform, discarded clothes, unwanted weight in the desert heat.

It's a dead body.

"Jesus Christ," Stein says, the way people say it when they mean to say *this is terrible, this is unexplainable, this is bad.* Hesitating, he lifts the camera to his eye and snaps a quick photo. As if some deeper part of him has taken over, the part that knows he must do his job despite what he's seeing.

It's not Ross. And it's for this reason, and only this, that Philip can maintain a grip on his own reality. But the rest of the facts are mad.

It's a man, they agree on that much; dressed in gray cotton pants, an unbuttoned gray shirt, and tall brown boots. But his chest and bearded face are twice the width they should be; as though flattened, caught in a press. Like putty, like clay, the body looks molded, as though a distracted child left him this way.

His nose lies flat against his cheek like a Picasso.

"Fuck, man," Larry says, crouching by the body. He reaches to touch the face, but Lovejoy grabs his wrist hard and pulls him back to a standing position.

"Careful."

"What? You think it's . . . *contagious?*"

The platoon stands in a line beside what Larry rightfully describes as *a flattened man.* Nearly two dimensional, as though wholly run over by a tank. Even his fingers are unnaturally stretched, a man made of wax, melting under the Namib sun; bent digits, reaching for his ears.

"Crushed," Stein says. He snaps a second photo. The sound of the camera is like a small bone breaking.

Duane holds out one of his own hands, possibly to remind himself of the reality of them, what normal hands look like.

"We need to find Ross," Philip says. Because everyone's thinking it. Thinking about the same fate coming to Ross.

Greer is silently staring, a look of deep concern and wonder on his face.

Despite the grotesquery, the impossible face, it's the ears, and the fingers extended toward them, that each of them comes back to.

Nadoul's wife's ears were found on her mattress in the hut.

"Christ," Larry says, and Philip knows that if they found this body in the street in Detroit, Larry would have already run from it.

The man could be young, could be old. It's difficult to tell. But his uniform speaks of another age, another time, another era.

Now Stein is taking many photos. As if the first couple broke an internal moral seal.

"Look at the holes in his face," Greer says. "The eyes, the nose, the mouth. The ears." Greer bends at the waist for a closer inspection. "Because of how he was . . . *flattened,* whatever's inside of him should've come out. Like roadkill. But . . . there's nothing here. No bloodstains in the sand."

"Scavengers?" Stein suggests.

"No," Greer says. "He hasn't lost a thing. I'd bet he's still got all his parts inside."

Stein photographs.

In the distance, very close to being out of earshot, Philip hears a ripple, a wave.

"Listen," he says, turning to face the desert. Then Philip is on his knees, powering up the Ampex, connecting a single microphone cord. He puts on the headphones and adjusts the input volume.

It makes music, so they're sending musicians.

The others instinctively cover their ears.

Another ripple, faint. With it, Philip feels a trace of illness.

The red light on the Ampex is blinking, the reel is rotating, the machine is recording.

"Be careful—" Larry begins.

Philip holds up an open flat palm.

The sound diminishes. A distant bulge, then gone.

Philip waits forty seconds. Then he immediately rewinds the reel.

"I'm gonna blast it," he says. "I'm gonna get sick."

"Philip," Larry says. "What are you doing?"

Philip presses play.

He heard something. Something inside the sound.

Through the legs of the platoon he sees the body in the sand. He thinks of old photographs, the kind he'd seen on his grandparents' mantel as a kid.

But this body is not old in age. It's old in *time.*

The playback begins. At this volume the static is loud; Philip can hear the platoon breathing, wind across the microphone head, his own movements in the sand.

Then . . . the sound . . . developing . . . like a cry . . . a call . . .

As the sun lowers another notch, Philip gets sick.

He looks to the body, the flattened man, the crooked, long fingers still reaching, the leathery desert skin; an unwrapped mummy in cotton clothes. The elongated chin, distended, the open oblong hole of the mouth.

The scrambled egg eyes.

The sound is loud now. What begins as a headache builds to a rattling. He hears a fluttering, the sound of a ripple, a possible uniform break in the signal; he thinks, *It's a series . . . a series of noises . . . not just one . . .*

Philip reaches for the pitch knob and, with difficulty, slows the tape down, to half speed, then a quarter.

The unnatural distension, the sluggish resolve of changing speeds, brings Philip to gag.

Sonic curtains parting, a fresh sound is revealed.

And Philip recognizes it, *knows* this new sound.

He could end this sickness by removing the headphones. Turning off the machine. For Christ's sake, his finger is on the button.

But he doesn't. He wants to hear more.

This new sound . . . is there a clue to what happened to Ross in there?

He looks to the body as if the body might tell him.

And the body moves.

"Hey!" Philip throws the headphones from his ears and crab-walks backward. He's pointing to the body. "He moved! His fingers *moved!*"

Lovejoy pulls a pistol from his belt. Fires at the body.

But no. Doesn't fire.

The gun only clicks.

The body isn't moving, but Lovejoy fires again.

Nothing.

He looks to Stein.

"Give me your gun."

"What, Sarge?"

Then Lovejoy is reaching for it and Stein hands it over.

Lovejoy fires.

Click. Nothing.

He lets it fall to the sand.

"Private Noles. Give me your gun."

"What's happening here?" Duane says. But he hands Lovejoy the weapon. Lovejoy aims it out into the desert. Fires.

Click.

Nothing.

Larry gives his next.

Click.

Nothing.

"Oh fuck," Duane says. "Oh *fuck.*"

"What's going on here?" Stein asks. He can tell the others are thinking the same thing.

Greer explains it.

"The sound," he says, "rendered a United States nuclear warhead impotent."

"So, are you saying—"

Lovejoy tries Philip's gun.

Nothing.

He drops it onto the pile of others.

"Jesus Christ," Larry whispers. And this time he says it like someone does when they mean to say there is trouble.

The platoon stares out into the desert. As if weighing the risk of facing it unarmed.

"Listen to it at quarter speed," Philip says. He's pointing to the Ampex. "It's footsteps."

Greer turns to him.

"What do you mean, Philip?"

"The tape, slowed down. It's . . . footsteps."

"As if someone's coming," Duane says.

Philip looks to the pile of useless guns.

"As if someone already came."

Again the soldiers look farther out.

But they can't see much of anything now.

The sun is down.

And the desert has gone dark.

"Lights out," Duane whispers.

28

Ellen walks alone. Her small figure, in white, cuts a flickering image, as the edges of the hall, where the floor meets the walls, are dark, and the distance behind her is shadowed. But with each overhead light she is detailed and feels exposed.

Ahead, Nurse Francine is approaching, walking in the opposite direction, emerging then disappearing beneath the overheads, like Ellen does.

"Evening, Ellen."

"Evening, Francine."

They pass this way, white uniformed shoulder to white uniformed shoulder, one on her way to visit Philip in the padded soundproof Rehabilitation Unit, the other on her way to a place she shouldn't be going.

Ellen has no doubt Francine did not notice her left hand stuffed into her left uniform pocket. She also has no doubt it was the right thing to do; keeping the spare keys quiet with her fingers, not letting them clang as Francine, someone who knows the sound of hospital keys, walked by.

At Philip's empty unit, Unit 1, Ellen peers inside, despite knowing that he's not in there.. The cot remains unmade, the sheets rumpled from when Philip rolled himself onto the floor. They say he broke three bones in his face. Rebroke. Ellen cringes at the thought. She scans the room and sees nothing is out of order. She wonders, though, if things have changed in there. Things unseen.

Wearing a mask of professionalism, Ellen leaves the threshold to Philip's unit and continues down the hall, past the office on her left. Inside, Nurse Robin, a regular temp, nods a sweet hello and Ellen delivers one of the finest, most believable colleague-to-colleague smiles that have ever graced her face. But when Robin is out of sight, and Ellen turns left, away from the hospital's front door, no trace of that smile remains.

Ahead, the washroom door is in complete darkness, but Ellen can see a shimmering of the knob. She turns left again, taking the hall without patients, the hall no nurse has any business frequenting unless they're Nurse Francine at night and Nurse Delores during the day: the nurses responsible for the distribution of drugs to the patients.

Ellen keeps her composure, though she is well aware that there exists a door, at the very far end of this hall, the east door to the Rehab Unit where Philip Tonka now lies, three rebroken bones in his face. And presumably beside him is Nurse Francine, who would have entered through the west door, as she injects him with . . .

. . . what?

Ellen grips the keys to keep them soundless and arrives at the unit marked STAFF ONLY: MEDICATION. But the appellation isn't entirely true; the nurses' station also harbors medicine, the kind with names that are already familiar to people like Philip Tonka and the greater part of the United States of America. Ellen wonders if the drugs in *this* room ought not to be called medicine, not until they've been proven to work.

One glance up the hall, one glance back, and Ellen removes the key from her pocket. She's resigned to the fact that if Dr. Szands were to suddenly return from Des Moines early, if he were, say, *inside* the very room she's entering, she would simply laugh, say nothing, and run. There's no excuse she could manufacture that could properly explain her presence in this hall, in this room, and any attempt would be as transparent as Szands's desire for curing Philip quickly has become.

In her six years at Macy Mercy, Ellen has never seen Dr. Szands so focused on the expediency of a patient's recovery.

Why?

Ellen opens the door and, fast, slips inside.

She closes the door behind her, leans against it, and waits.

It's very dark in here.

She's still for a long time, too long to feel comfortable, counterintuitive to how she wants to behave—rapid, efficient, in and out. She waits for her eyes to adjust to the dark; she will not turn on the light in this room, won't have the frosted glass illuminated, worries already that her own shadowed form will somehow stand out from the other dark shapes.

And the white fabric of her uniform might stand out.

So Ellen removes it. Beneath it, she's wearing black nylons, a black long-sleeved shirt, black socks. She folds the white uniform and tucks it onto the bottom shelf of the steel storage rack to her left. From the breast pocket of her black shirt, she removes a box of matches.

One step, two steps, ten steps deep into the room, she strikes the first match.

She's surrounded by bottles, vials, swabs, and gauze.

She blows out the match.

She waits. She listens. She wonders how thick the door is. Would she hear a creaking, a person in the hall? Would she hear someone speaking out there? Would she hear someone being quiet?

She doesn't want to wait, but she waits.

And no sound comes.

She lights a second match.

The bottles are all grouped together; things are not as chaotic as they first appeared. Ellen brings the match head close to the labels, but they don't tell her much.

Zaxan. Midocol. Words and names she doesn't know, doesn't understand, has never had to learn.

She studies, holds the match close to the row of bottles. Nothing but names. Not what they do, not where they come from, not what they're made of. Ellen knows that even if the ingredients were listed, it would be of little help.

She questions why she came in here at all.

What is she hoping to uncover? Hoping to find?

The match is burning too low and Ellen blows it out.

The doorknob turns behind her.

She's stuck, for a moment, in place. Did she lock the door? Is the door about to open? Right now, with her standing in the middle of the room?

The sound of keys in the hall.

Ellen moves fast to the far wall, hoping she doesn't knock something over—a vial, a glass—on her way. The tall steel shelving doesn't quite reach the bricks and certainly won't hide all of her, but Ellen slips into the space there, feels like it's slimmer than she is. Like she's crushing bones, flattening herself, to fit.

The door opens.

The lights come on.

Her face is fully exposed between two steel shelves. But Francine hasn't noticed her. Not yet.

"Sneezin' up a storm," the older woman sniffles. Shakes her head. Talks to herself.

Ellen doesn't move.

Because the space is tight, and the light is bright, Francine looks bigger than she normally does; her body tests the hem of her white uniform; her arms and hands look like wrinkled laundry. Every detail in here is exposed and all Francine has to do is turn her head six, seven inches in Ellen's direction.

Then what?

Run?

"Cold after cold," Francine says to herself. "And that's what you get for working in a hospital."

Ellen looks past her, to where her own uniform is stashed on the lower shelf by the door. It's not hidden well. It shows.

Ellen, needing support, needing *anything,* digs her fingernails into the brick wall at her back.

Francine adjusts her black glasses, eyes the same bottles Ellen was studying. She sniffs the air. Ellen knows it's the match. Knows Francine is about to survey the room, like anybody would, looking for the source of that burning, the unmistakable scent of a recently extinguished match.

Ellen almost says something. She's that sure, that ready, for Francine to spot her.

Instead, Francine wipes her nose with her bare arm. Ellen can see the thin film of snot on the older nurse's wrinkled skin.

Francine removes items from her pocket. A pair of syringes.

"Shoulda been a security guard," Francine says. She's half whispering, still talking to herself.

She takes two bottles from the rack and places them on the table at her waist. She uncaps the first syringe, loads it. Ellen looks at the bottle. She can't read what it says, but she knows which one it is. Francine repeats the action with the second bottle, second syringe.

The belief Ellen has, the absolutely certainty that Francine must notice her before exiting this room, is paralyzing. Any alternative is impossible. Should she do something first? How close *is* Francine to seeing her? And what will follow? Ellen can see it play out; a moment of herself stammering, feigning confusion, perhaps even laughing, desperate to make light, then Francine's slow realization that Ellen is lying; Ellen striking the woman, fleeing; Francine racing from the Medicine Unit, whinnying into a scream, howling for help from the orderlies; *She's getting away! SHE'S GETTING AWAY!*; Ellen rushing from the front doors, scared, out of breath, running to . . .

. . . where?

Francine sneezes.

She breathes deep and shakes her head again. Even this, just this shake, is movement enough to put Ellen in her field of vision.

Ellen holds her breath. Digs her fingernails into the wall.

Makes a scratching sound.

Didn't mean to.

Francine looks up, as if the scratching had come from the ceiling. She stares there, her mouth hanging open, her gray eyes magnified to the size of drink coasters. Ellen listens to her breathe. Inhale. Exhale. Stuffy. A cold.

Now, Ellen thinks. *She will look at you now.*

Francine does. She turns, faces Ellen completely.

Ellen doesn't move.

The overhead lights reflect off Francine's glasses, obscuring her eyes.

Ellen opens her mouth to say something. Francine moves her lips, makes a squishing sound.

Ellen almost speaks; a single guttural syllable, the birth of a moan, rises in her throat.

Francine, I'm sorry. I can explain.

The words are coming, already on the way up, when Francine turns her attention back to the bottles.

She caps both syringes, caps both bottles. She places the syringes in her pocket and puts the bottles back where they belong on the rack.

Sniffling, she turns and exits the Medicine Unit. On the way out, she turns off the light.

In the hall, she locks the door.

Then, silence. No sniffles. No keys. No footsteps.

Ellen doesn't move for another four minutes. She's trembling. She's staring at the door. She's imagining Francine's face, inert, staring back at her, transposed, the immediate indelible memory, as if Francine is looking through the frosted glass now, staring still into the deep shadows of the Medicine Unit, where the shelving doesn't quite reach the brick wall.

But she's not.

Nurse Francine is gone.

Ellen squeezes out from her hiding spot and steps to the table, to the rack holding the bottles Francine used.

She looks to the door, waits. Waits another two minutes.

She lights the third match. Brings it to the bottles.

Even if Ellen hadn't seen the two Francine used, she'd be able to tell what they were; both rest unevenly in the rack.

Ellen pulls them out, sets them on the table.

She reads the labels. Doesn't understand them. Doesn't know what they are. Turns the bottles around. Nothing. Looks underneath them. Reads something.

A-9-A

She blows out the match and waves the smoke away. She looks to the frosted glass, scared to see a shadow pass, or worse, a shadow becoming a solid, against the glass, a face, eyes looking in.

But no face.

She retrieves her uniform. Quickly puts it back on.

She steps to the door and turns the knob and actually pulls the door open a crack before quickly closing it again. She returns to the table and places the bottles back on the rack.

Almost forgot to do that. What else has she almost forgotten to do?

She pauses, forces herself to think. She has the keys. Has the matches. Right? Does she have all the matches? Ellen checks her pockets. One, two, three. Yes, three burnt-out matches. Are the bottles back on the rack? Yes. She did that. Yes. Is her uniform on? Ellen actually looks down to her white uniform, shining even in this darkness. She looks back to the space between the shelf and the wall. Her nails. She dug her nails into the wall. Does she need to check if she's left a mark?

You have to get out of here.

Ellen lights a fourth match. Walks to the shelving, holds the match by the wall. No visible mark. But the flame is flickering, unstable, unreliable.

What is she afraid of? What does she think is happening in this hospital?

Why do they want him to heal so fast, Ellen? What do they need him strong for?

She doesn't know.

Are you afraid?

Yes, Ellen is afraid.

She blows out the fourth match. Turns to face the door. She's ready to leave. Must leave.

She crosses the Medicine Unit once more and places her hand on the knob.

Hesitation. A pause. Listening through the frosted glass. Into the hall.

Anything?

Nothing.

Ellen opens the door.

Enters the hall. Feels exposed by the light though the light is dim. Her hand shakes as she locks the door. Pockets the key. She wonders if it's written all over her face: fear, hiding, confusion. If somebody, anybody, were to turn the corner, walk toward her, would they notice? Would they remark upon it later?

Dr. Szands, I saw Ellen in the second hall tonight. I don't know what she was doing there, but she was doing something.

She was hiding.

She was afraid.

Ellen allows her black hair to hang in front of her eyes. She stares at the ground as she walks. Feels less visible this way. Then she tucks her hair behind her ears and lifts her head up. She's got to look normal. Like she always does. What does she always look like?

She turns the corner, exiting the second hall. The front door is ahead. She could walk right out, never come back. Get in her car and drive home, pack some things, then leave Iowa. Go to California. Find an apartment. She has enough money for gas. She knows how to meet people. She could get a job there, start a new life, exit this place of growing shadows, begin anew.

At the front door, she turns right, heading down the length of the first hall. This is the hall she spends all her time in. And yet, she feels only marginally safer for having entered it. Ahead, only a few feet, typewriter clacking pours out of the open office door. When Ellen steps even with it, she looks inside. She doesn't want to see Francine. Doesn't want the older woman to turn from her seat at the typewriter and look at her with that same open-mouthed expression.

Guess what I'm doing, Ellen? I'm writing a report. Guess who I'm reporting, Ellen? I saw you in the Medicine Unit. Saw you hiding like a scared little girl.

But it's not Francine at the typewriter. It's Robin. The temp. Most likely entering the nurse's notes. Busy work. Making them official. Filing.

"Hello," Robin says, sensing someone in the doorway, turning to see Ellen.

"Hello."

"A lot of work!" Robin says, shaking her head. The age-old exchange between coworkers, the knowing expressions.

"Yes."

"Well, back to it for me."

"Yes."

Ellen continues down the hall, unsure if she should look to the ground, look up, afraid to meet anybody's eyes, afraid she'll suddenly scream out, *Why does he need to heal so fast? WHY?*

She isn't certain exactly where she's going. If Dr. Szands were to exit any door that lined this hall, if he were to ask Ellen what task she was engaged in, she isn't sure she'd have the presence of mind to lie.

Halfway down the hall now. Got here too fast. Retains a blurred, faint memory of Robin in the office. An impossibly fresh face smiling above a new white uniform.

At the end of the hall is the Rehab Unit. And in that unit is Philip.

Is Francine in there? Has she brought the drugs to him? Of course she has. That's what she does. She administers. She drugs.

Ellen reaches the unit too quickly. She stops. The door swings open before she touches it.

Francine's face.

She looks so different, Ellen thinks, out here.

A shriek from behind Ellen. A patient crying out.

"Oh!" Francine shrieks herself, looks past Ellen. Then at her. "Good timing. I need you."

Behind Francine, Philip is sitting up.

"How is he able to do that?" Ellen asks, incapable of keeping the question in. The man broke almost every bone in his body.

"I need to assist that patient," Francine says. "Administer the shots to Mr. Tonka. Can you do that for me?"

Philip raises his fingers to the door. No less bruised, but up. Sitting up. Able to.

Ellen feels a tray at her waist.

"Ellen?"

It all feels half-imagined, half-untrue.

She looks down. Sees the two syringes.

"Administer these shots." This time Francine isn't asking.

From across the unit, Philip is staring into Ellen's eyes.

"Yes," Ellen says.

"And wake up! You're moving like a patient yourself."

Ellen takes the tray from Francine and enters the unit.

Behind her, the door closes.

Just Ellen and Philip now.

Philip smiles. Sadly?

Ellen knows he knows.

This mystery, this healing, is not for his sake.

"Medicine," Philip says.

They share a pause and in that pause a question echoes:

Is it? Is it medicine?

29

Greer says, "In the American Civil War, the Union soldiers wore blue frocks that hung to mid-thigh. Buttons and patches displayed their rank. Brown belts secured water canteens and other necessary items to their persons. Majors wore double-breasted coats, the infantrymen were issued single-breasted. Often the men wore shin-high black leather boots. Their caps were usually bluc wool kepis."

He's looking from face to face around the fire. The Ampex machines hum just outside the circle the platoon makes. So do the hoofprints. Or they seem to make sound, echoing loudly in all of their minds. Greer continues.

"The Confederate soldiers wore gray frock coats that hung to mid-thigh. Bronze buttons and shoulder patches designated rank. They donned gray wool caps. Most of the soldiers wore brown leather boots that went about shin-high."

Duane looks over his shoulder to the tarp, visible in the firelight. Because the body beneath it is so flattened, the tarp looks as if it covers nothing at all.

"So?" Larry asks.

Greer smiles without humor.

"Those boots"—he's pointing to the tarp—"are genuine."

"Genuine what?" Philip asks.

Greer looks him in the eyes. The flames dance in the historian's glasses.

"Genuine past, private."

30

Philip wakes in the frigid desert at night.

He's supposed to be on watch, supposed to be awake, shouldn't have fallen asleep. He shines the flashlight on the actual watch around his wrist, the same one he took from the manager of the Sparklers, never gave back; it's 7:16 P.M. in Detroit. That's 2:16 A.M. here.

Ross.

His friend's name comes to him with a jolt. As if by falling asleep he's missed the answer to what's become of him.

Philip sits up and the tip of his gun digs into his side, through the blankets, through the wool-collared jean jacket he wears. Philip looks down, realizes his gun is pointed at the piano key hanging around his neck, the F. He moves it.

Despite knowing that none of the guns work, Philip had to keep it by his side. The look of it alone could save his life.

Who knows what might have avoided him, seeing the weapon, as he slept?

Standing, he shines the flashlight across camp. None of the remaining Danes wanted to stop. Not even for the night. Ross is out there. Ross is somewhere. The prints that led them to this spot continue beyond it. They have no way of knowing how far they are from whatever made the prints. Philip studies them in the light of his beam right now. Sees where they pass into the darkness ahead.

Philip checks on the others.

It's colder here than it was by the coast. Greer would know why. Greer is buried beneath his unpacked clothes, blankets, and a canvas tarp. Most of the others sleep this way. Only Lovejoy is using the tentpole like it's meant to be used, holding up the tarp like American cowboys once used them, sleeping around fires in vast, open prairies.

Philip rubs his gloved hands together.

He breathes deeply and it hurts, feels like the cold has crawled in, has taken root in his lungs. The exhalation is precise in the flashlight's beam.

He looks out to the desert, to where the hoofprints direct his eyes.

The platoon must sleep. He knows they can't hike twenty-four hours straight and expect to be prepared, both mentally and physically. They're no use to Ross parched, pruned, dried up, and dead on a dune.

Philip thinks of the body they found.

Christ.

He looks over his shoulder to where Lovejoy ordered Greer to put it for the night, two hundred yards from this temporary camp. Philip can't see it. Can't even see the tarp. It's the second time Lovejoy has indicated he doesn't want to be too close to the thing.

But it's Greer's reaction, Greer who dragged the body himself on a plastic makeshift sled, that frightens Philip now.

The historian said the flattened man not only resembles a soldier from the Civil War, but actually is one.

Philip's gotta move a little because it's too cold to sit still. A Michigander, born and raised, Philip knows winter, but this is a different kind of cold.

He takes two steps in the sand and feels something at the tip of his black boot. The light shows him it's one of the cords powering the Ampex machines. Philip and Larry set them up when they arrived here. Duane, anxious even more than they are, paced the entire time. The generator hums quietly; state-of-the-art equipment, every bit of it. Philip follows the length of the cord, walks along it to the first of the two rolling machines. He crouches, turns his flashlight off. The Ampex's red light illuminates his boots and pants; reminds him of the figure he saw on the beach.

Red pants.

Red jacket.

Hooves.

Horns.

But no discernible face. Only the physical rippling of the space between Philip and it.

And now, the memory of it. Coupled with the stories Secretary Mull told on the plane; of Nadoul and Ka, a native of the Namib and his wife who believed something watched her, something attached itself to her, and then left its voice in her ears.

Philip looks over his shoulder. Quiet out here. Only the hum of the gear and the dulcet distant breathing of his platoon.

Bundling up tighter into his jacket, Philip rises and goes to the other machine. Between the red lights and scant illumination of the VU meters he's in total darkness.

The second machine has stopped recording; the reel is full. Before removing it, Philip rewinds it and watches the meters. The headphones are attached, lying in the sand, and Philip neither hears nor sees any spike in volume; no sound he missed while asleep.

No creaking stairs.

The sound Philip heard when he slowed the tape down. The sound, he now recalls, that played through his dreams as he fell asleep on watch.

Philip, dinner's ready!

Memories. The home in which he was raised. Wyoming Street. Detroit. Mom calling down to the cellar. The beat-up piano down there. There was no room for it anywhere else in the duplex the Tonkas shared with the Bermans. He used to get scared in the cellar; his back to the furnace and the shadows the furnace made on the concrete wall, his back to the laundry sink, too, that sink veiled by a dull pink sheet that flapped from the open window, always open in the summer to let the cellar smell out.

Coming, Mom!

Usually by dinnertime he'd already run the scales. So boring, those scales! No matter how many times Mrs. Ruth told him they were necessary, they felt like chains to a very young Philip. Like his fingers were being forced to play melodies he wasn't interested in playing. But Mom's clockwork call would signify liberation; it was time to play *his* way, even if for only a few minutes, his chance to ape the bluesmen he heard through the speakers in Apollo Music.

But the stairs . . .

Always the creaking of that first step and Philip would tilt an ear in that direction, behind him, the stairs between him and the furnace and that fading pink sheet, too.

Coming, Mom!

He'd yell it again but he wasn't going anywhere; wasn't getting up from that piano until he'd reached it, that deep and dangerous place that even kids know about, the inner crawl space where expression can be found, growing dusty, until you decided to take it out.

Creation.

Philip didn't know what to call it back then, but he knew he had to reach it, once, before—

But then, dammit, those creaking steps. Clockwork, too. Philip with his back to the basement, his fingers mad across the keys like he was typing a letter, telling someone who knew how he felt, what it felt like to reach for it . . .

Creation.

Creaking . . . the stairs behind him . . . the shadows and a flapping sheet behind him, too. A monster, perhaps, something terrible behind the sheet, something wakened by the music and the soul and spirit the kid was putting into it. But Philip wouldn't turn around, not yet, not *yet,* not until he got there, touched that place that felt like a joke, a revelation, the future all rolled into one.

Creation.

He played furiously, even then, and the only thing that could rattle him, the only thing on earth that could STOP him, was the hand (clockwork) upon his shoulder, the thing that lived in the shadows, the thing whose breath caused the laundry sheet to ripple, the thing that—

Philip. Mom. Only Mom. Always. *Dinner is ready.*

Now, in the cold and dark, Philip remembers those creaking stairs. And that rippling sheet that might've hidden a Thing in Red, a creature with hooves and horns.

He exhales and his breath is valentine ribbon in the red light.

The reel rewound, Philip removes it from the machine, opens the storage case, and tucks it in beside the others. He gloves a new one, places it opposite the catch reel, and begins to thread the tape through.

Something is moving in the sand behind him.

Philip rises with his flashlight on and gun at the ready.

It's empty desert. Nothing crawls. Nothing emerges from the shadows beyond the light.

But even the desert, with all its open space, has its corners at night.

Philip steps toward that darkness.

"Ross?" It's a crazy thing to say. It's a hopeful thing to say.

Could it be Ross? Returning? Did he escape whatever fate came close enough to touch him?

A second sound. Boots on gravel. Philip turns fast to his right.

To his left.

Only sand. The base of another dune.

He brings the light to its peak.

What if Ross is up there? What if Ross is crawling toward him, near death, unable to speak, unable to stand up?

And what if it's not Ross. What then?

The cold tightens its grip. Holds Philip in place, rooted to the sand.

Seeing nothing upon the dune, he shines the light to the sand at his feet.

Staring up at him is the flattened face of the body they found.

"Jesus!"

Its eyes, both on the same side of its head, are staring into Philip's own.

Philip catches his breath, a swallow of cold, raw air.

The canvas tarp has moved; the night wind has partially uncovered the body.

Philip looks back to camp.

Is he two hundred yards away?

He must be. He is.

Before covering the body again, he studies the distorted features, the oblong bearded mouth, the eyes that appear soupy enough to spoon.

Philip reaches for the canvas tarp.

Hears footsteps in the sand.

He turns. Sees nothing. No one.

Philip brings the light to the top of the dune again.

A man is up there.

"Shit!" Philip says, stumbling back. "Halt!"

But the man is coming. The man is halfway down the dune.

"Halt!"

It's a soldier, Philip can see that immediately. A uniform. A gait. A weapon.

Philip's gun feels like a front, like it's made of plastic, like pretend. But it's the stranger's firearm that chills him. Philip experiences the same cold rush he felt when he saw the Civil War body in the sand. The weapon this second man carries is from another era, another time.

Genuine past, Private.

It's a musket.

The man advances.

"Halt!" Philip repeats.

Philip's first thought is,

This man is . . .

. . . in costume.

A blue coat, yellow scarf, bloodred lapels, yellow buttons that do not reflect the light. Black boots dig into the cold sand until they reach the base of the dune. A tricorn black hat shadows the soldier's face.

Is it the Thing in Red?

Philip looks for horns. Looks for a white beard.

"Come on, man! I'm going to have to shoot you!"

It's a costume. Has to be a costume. Because if it's not *a costume, if it's really what the man wears, then you've lost your mind. You've lost your mind!*

The soldier steps closer yet, into the full sphere of Philip's light.

Since finding the body in the desert, Private Greer has talked endlessly about uniforms. He focuses on the Civil War. But he goes on.

The American Revolutionary War soldier commonly wore a blue frock coat. A tricorn hat. A ruffled shirt tucked into tan breeches, black boots that reached shin-high. A yellow scarf that protected his neck from the cold.

This is not the Thing in Red.

It's a soldier from the American Revolution.

Philip lowers his gun. Useless or not, front or not. This man is beyond *threat.* This is beyond sensible, admonishing words like *threat.*

An American, Philip thinks.

"How—" Philip begins, but the man is lowering his musket. He's pointing to Philip's other hand.

To the light.

He's smaller than Philip. To scale.

"Who are you?" Philip finally asks, his words like the smoke of gunpowder in the air between them.

The man, the soldier, is less than two feet from him. He's reaching.

"Hey, hey," Philip says. "Don't do that! Don't make me—"

But the man grips the flashlight and brings it close to his face. Studies it. Looks Philip in the eye.

"Lantern," the man whispers.

Not just American, Philip thinks. *The first.*

"My God," Philip says.

A savage with an ax would've scared him less than this man has.

This impossibility.

This ghost.

The man releases the light. Takes a step back.

"Hang on," Philip says, lowering his gun. "Wait a second! We lost a friend! Can you help us find him? Can you help us?!"

But the man is backing up, up the side of the dune.

"Wait! Help us! You must know something! Where is he? Where could he be?!" Philip drops his gun, raises his hands. "I'm not going to hurt you! I just need to talk to you!"

But the soldier has backed up out of the range of Philip's light. A silhouette now, at the peak of the dune.

Philip runs toward him.

"WAIT!"

To the top, at the top, shining his light across the breadth of the dune, into the shadowed pits, sand valleys, surrounding.

No man.

No Revolutionary soldier.

No vision.

But a sound, again, behind him, boots again.

Philip spins.

"Lovejoy," he says, breathless, seeing the Mad Blond's face only, revealed in the flashlight's farthest reach.

The former general is waiting at the bottom of the dune.

Philip descends.

When they meet, Lovejoy takes the light from Philip's hand, shines it uphill again.

"Lovejoy," Philip repeats.

Lovejoy turns to face him, his features blackened by shadow.

"I saw him, too," he says.

"A ghost," Philip says.

"Not a ghost," Lovejoy says.

"Then what?"

"Not a ghost. Not a man. A vestige . . ."

Then he scales the dune.

Philip looks to the body at his feet. Thinks of the Revolutionary Soldier touching the flashlight. The physicality of both.

A vestige . . .

But a vestige is only a glimmer, only what remains, and Philip knows that both impossible soldiers are more real than that.

Because of time, because of place, they may not be the source of their own sounds.

But they are echoes.

And echoes are neither alive nor dead . . .

31

Philip wakes in the dark. Bad dreams about Lovejoy lost, starving in a cell made of sand.

Because Ellen didn't give him the medicine she told Francine she would, Philip is in considerable pain. The worst he's known yet.

I don't trust it . . .

She'd whispered this and other concerns, as she drew many pictures for Philip. This time he'd asked for weapons. Descending in chronological order. Beginning with a mushroom cloud (what Philip said looked like a giant's fist, cracking the earth's surface) to a hand cannon, the earliest-known firearm on the planet.

Philip didn't ask for the medicine. And while earlier he could rationalize it as needing to know the parameters of the drug, what it does, what it doesn't do, the bad way has come, and it all sounds like madness to him now.

There are six figures in the unit. Six silhouettes watching him wake.

As he processes this, he understands also that he's back in his original unit, that somebody has wheeled him out of rehab.

But not these men. These men are moneyed. These men are military. And Philip can tell by the privilege in their eyes, the meticulously casual manner of their clothes, and the ice clinking in their drinks that they come from a shadowed height of the military that Philip will never be able to look high enough to see.

But the pain is even more frightening than the visitors.

An Asian American man lowers his face so that it's only inches from Philip's own. His khaki pants and yellow button-down speak more of country clubs than they do of war rooms. But Philip knows better.

"Awake!" the man says. A fluttering, drunk smile appears like fish fins flapping in deep water.

He tilts his drink over the cot, pretends he's going to spill it.

Philip can't move to do anything about it.

Over the Asian's shoulder a silver crew cut appears, then a clean-shaven face beneath. It's a serious countenance and this man also dresses the part; his windbreaker and khaki slacks suggest he's above even the rank of general. *Presidential* is the word Philip thinks. But his thoughts are broken, distorted, by the paralyzing pain.

And it's getting worse.

"Oh yes," a voice says. "Rises and sets like the sun. Like the rest of us."

It's Dr. Szands.

The Asian is very drunk. Philip has seen the same expression in a hundred beer halls, a hundred gigs.

Movement by the window and Philip sees a third man, fair-haired, with angular features. His eyes sparkle with night, as if he's come in through the window.

Philip tries to lift his right hand, can't. Can't even move the fingers.

The syringes look like liquor to him now, the needles left loaded in the Rehab Unit.

The Asian is backing up, toward the unit door, replaced by two men dressed like Scott Malone, the government man who came to question Philip with the sketch artist.

"Careful with your drink, Mr. Serino," one of the men says. He's smiling, but there is no humor. Philip has seen the same expression in used car lots, in department stores, Macy's; the men in this room may be drinking, but they're here on business.

"Progress," Szands says. Concrete pride in his eyes; Philip can imagine the trucks that poured it.

Szands walks to the filing cabinet, folding white cloth. Philip recognizes it as his own hospital gown.

"Naked," Philip says, and his voice is agony.

The room erupts with astonishment.

"He speaks!" the Asian cries.

"Yes," Dr. Szands says. "Just like the rest of us."

Philip is naked.

Exposed.

Displayed.

The Asian claps the man with the windbreaker on the back. He points to Philip's abdomen with a wobbling drink.

"Careful," the second government man says, smiling anxiously, as though, while it may be funny to spill his drink on a patient who can't move, this patient is valuable.

The man in the windbreaker approaches the cot.

He leans in. Examining. Philip smells scotch. But this man isn't sloppy about it.

Music is coming from the office. Lounge music. Island music.

"Amelioration," Szands says, quietly taking center stage. "A man wakes to discover he's suffered a hideous injury, to most of his body. Less than two weeks later, the same man is able to walk out of the hospital that has healed him."

"He's ready then?" the man by the window asks.

Szands shakes his head no.

Philip groans. Because he has to. Because it feels like nails are being pulled from his bones.

Szands looks over his shoulder. Philip recognizes disappointment, and worry, in his eyes.

Philip knows why.

The patient is not supposed to groan. He's supposed to do push-ups, pull-ups, and to outrun his younger self, the man he was before he got hurt.

"Close," Szands says. And his voice is full of uncertainty.

"Show us," the man in the windbreaker says.

Szands wastes no time.

"Sit up, Philip."

And Philip understands, sees clearly that this moment, *now,* is supposed to be the triumph of Dr. Szands.

But Philip can't sit up.

"Philip. Sit up."

Embarrassment. For Dr. Szands. Very close now. Philip can sense it coming.

And what will a man like Szands do? Humiliated before his peers?

The Asian rushes to the cot. With his free hand he reaches a wet finger to Philip's lips, then motorboats them.

He laughs. Heartily. Shrieking like a schoolboy.

He does it again.

Szands grips the man's wrist. When he does, all the humor leaves the Asian's face and Philip is very aware that the other men in this room are more powerful than the doctor.

The Asian yanks his arm free.

But Szands is coming unglued.

His masterpiece is misbehaving.

"Sit *up.*"

But Philip can't sit up. Can't move. Feels the bones of his face tightening.

"Looks like you're further behind than you estimated," the man in the windbreaker says.

"I know *exactly* where we are at, thank you. Sit *up,* Philip!"

No snickers from the others.

Drunk or not.

Szands grips Philip by the shoulders and pulls.

Philip only half screams because the pain of a full one is unfathomable.

"Careful!" the man by the window yells.

"There is no danger," Szands hisses. "The patient is acting up!"

"Doctor, I don't think he can—"

"SHUT UP! *I know what he can and cannot do!*"

Szands tries to position Philip on the cot.

The snap of Philip's bone echoes through the hall.

"That's enough!" the man in the windbreaker yells. But Szands is beyond command.

"Doctor . . ."

It's Francine. She's standing in the doorway. She's holding a tray.

"Bring those to me *now!*"

Francine does.

Dr. Szands administers the medicine.

"Two more," he says.

He's hard with the needles. He stabs.

"More, doctor?"

Francine questions this because Philip has never received more than two shots.

Szands looks at her like he might kill her.

Francine is out of the unit and back in again before Philip can speak. But he's getting closer. The first two are already working.

The others only watch.

Szands grabs the syringes so quick that a needle connects with the band of his watch.

"Two more," he demands, administering the first of the second round.

Philip's bones no longer hurt.

Francine leaves. Returns.

Szands stabs Philip a fourth time.

He drops the syringe to the floor and holds out an open palm for a fresh one.

"Doctor," Francine says, as if she might pull the tray from him. But the power is short-lived.

"GIVE ME THE FUCKING DRUGS, FRANCINE!"

She does.

Szands looks into Philip's eyes. Philip sees no footing in there. No ground. No Path.

"Want to make a fool of me?"

He stabs Philip a fifth time.

By now Philip can speak. But the relief he feels is too big. Too strong to process.

"Help," he half says, looking to the others.

But the adoration in their eyes tells him they are finally seeing what they came to see.

Szands stabs Philip a sixth time.

"More."

Francine does not respond.

"MORE!"

She makes to leave the unit but she pauses at the door. When Szands sees this, he loses what airs remain.

"You are my *nurse*. You will *do as I say*. It's because of *you* that this is happening in the first place."

"Dr. Szands."

Philip is floating, ghostlike, to the ceiling. In his mind he's going to break it, going to leave the hospital at last.

"Why was the patient *not* given his medicine, Francine?! *WHAT DID YOU DO?!"*

"Dr. Szands . . . I had to attend to another patient last night . . . I gave that responsibility to Ellen."

Szands opens his mouth to speak, but stops.

Sweating, mad eyed, he turns to look at Philip.

"Ellen," Szands says.

He smiles. He runs his fingers through his hair and laughs.

"Ellen," he repeats.

"Please," Philip says. "Don't hurt her." But his own voice is a chimera.

The others in the room murmur their approval. The patient has spoken. The patient has turned his head toward them. The patent is reaching out with both arms, as if he might stop the doctor from hurting the nurse in question.

The man in the windbreaker approaches the cot.

Then the Asian.

Then the man by the window.

"Excellent," windbreaker says. "*Excellent.*"

"Yes, well." Dr. Szands is breathing hard. "Forgive me. It *would* have gone much smoother, had . . ."

"No," windbreaker says, extending an open palm. "Truly. This is *excellent.*"

Philip hears the word as if it's looped. As if, like time, it repeats itself, on a wheel, wheeled, until the present is happening long ago, and the things that have passed return to the present. As if, by virtue of being a wheel, it must roll, and by rolling it shakes the earth, the dirt, the dead beneath it, brings them forth, summons them, calls to them, says, *You were once and you are once again.*

To this turning, Philip spins into a relief too big, a darkness with no visible objects to stop him.

32

Greer is talking about ghosts. Old ghosts and newer ghosts and ghosts yet to be, including, Philip thinks, their own platoon: future ghosts; men who could be found in this desert, on these dunes, a hundred years from now, a century ahead; Larry Walker's petrified body in the sand, Philip Tonka descending a dune, archaic weapon in hand, more interested in the modern man's light source than the more advanced weapon he brandishes. And while Greer talks *(Civil War, American Revolutionary War, this is no coincidence, guys, this is the meat of why we're here; this has to do with the SOUND)* Philip is restlessly thinking of home, knowing now that a hundred thousand dollars isn't enough and never was.

Home, Wonderland, the Danes, the Path . . .

"Imprints," Greer says, stuck on this word. "Residual hauntings. The past on a loop. But the thing is, usually imprints don't interact with the present; they're energy, running in place, repeating themselves over and over. That's the loop. But the man Philip saw addressed the flashlight, and that's something there. And the body," Greer thumbs over his shoulder, all the way to the foot of the dune, where the man with the Civil War boots lies still, rewrapped and hidden from the sun. "Another imprint."

"Like echoes," Larry says, tightening the green shirt tied around his head.

"Yes," Greer says, relieved that somebody has made a correlation between sound and spirit.

Philip looks to the sky. Can't picture the plane returning. Can't see it happening.

His pack begins to tremble in the sand.

"Hey," he says. "Guys . . ."

The first thought he has is: *Tanks. Crossing the desert.*

But the sound arrives before the idea takes root.

This time, the sound comes as a beam, a singular force, powerful enough to rattle the reels, shake the boots of the soldiers. Auditory, yes, but there is a flash of something seen; a rippling, ten feet across, passing over their heads, vanishing between dunes in the distance.

As quick as it comes, it is gone.

Not long enough to get sick. Not long enough to study.

"Holy Christ," Duane says. "It's gonna kill us, isn't it."

But Philip's mind is elsewhere.

Looking to the sky, as the others are, bracing himself lest a second, even more forcible example arrives, he crawls beside Greer.

"Could a sound wave shake up an imprint? Bring it back . . . to life?"

Greer smiles as if to dismiss the idea; then the smile falls.

"What do you mean, Tonka?"

"A frequency . . . able to break the pattern, the loop, of a residual haunting. Free the ghosts that enact them."

Greer is quiet for some time.

"If that were possible, why stop with hauntings?"

"Now what do you mean?"

"If a sound were capable of breaking such patterns . . . why not bigger ones?"

Philip makes to ask for more, but Greer is already delivering it.

"Like history. Like history repeating itself. If we're going to be crazy enough to believe a sound can free literal ghosts, Private Tonka, why not figurative ones as well?"

Lovejoy calls from a dune.

"Tell it to me plain, Greer," Philip says.

"If we're comfortable believing that ghosts can step from their loops, why can't man? Why can't this sound put an end to war? You see? Not a weapon after all, Tonka. But . . . the opposite."

It's time to move on. To follow the hoofprints in the sand.

They are unarmed. They are scared.

They are determined to continue.

"Don't let this thread die," Greer says to Philip.

"Do you believe it?"

"Of all the scientific theories that have been warring in my imagination, none *feel* as real as this. And yet . . . the hoofprints . . . the goat . . ."

Philip grabs his pack, stands, and asks himself, *What is the opposite of a weapon?*

He looks to his useless gun in the sand. Picks it up anyway.

It's time to go deeper into the desert.

33

Standing up.

Ellen is repeating these two words as she approaches the office. Dr. Szands is in there, she knows. She saw him minutes before finding Philip standing up *(standing up!)* in his unit. The sight, only ten days into his rehabilitation, has snapped any hesitation.

She is a nurse. Her job is to nurse.

And this *(STANDING UP)* is not healing.

When she reaches the office door, she pauses. She thinks of exactly what she's going to say and how she's going to say it.

This is a military hospital. This is the government. This isn't like the time she complained about the rats outside the Dairy Dame.

Are you sure you have the patient's best interests in mind, doctor? As a nurse, I can't be a part of something that isn't . . . that isn't . . .

But what isn't it?

Ellen will have to tell Dr. Szands that she saw the drugs in the Medicine Unit, A-9-A; tell him about the man in the bar who took the drawing of the goat she did for Philip.

Ellen breathes deep and enters the office.

Szands is standing in the center of the room, arms crossed.

He's been waiting for her.

"Did you refuse to give Philip Tonka his medicine?"

She wasn't expecting this. But shouldn't she have been? What did she think would happen if he didn't get his shots?

"Yes."

"Good. Honesty. Why?"

This is worse. The *why*. 'Cause the *why* can only be answered with *I don't trust you anymore.*

"He's healing too fast."

Szands laughs, and Ellen hears in it a cackle.

"Is there such a thing, Miss Jones? And is it your job to decide?"

On the desk, within reach of his fingers, is a knife.

"Am I being fired, doctor?"

"Yes."

"Very well."

"Nothing to say?" Szands asks.

"No, doctor."

Szands uncrosses his arms. His blue and yellow Hawaiian shirt has never looked as out of place to Ellen as it does right now.

"Most people, when they're let go from their place of employment, express at least some malaise, Miss Jones."

"I didn't administer medicine when I was told to. I understand."

The rancorous look in his eyes . . . the only other time Ellen's seen a look so exaggeratedly fierce was in the comics Jean enjoyed.

"I'll gather my things," she says. "I'll turn my uniform in."

"You will be watched, Miss Jones."

"What did you say?"

Szands doesn't feign innocence.

"This is a matter of national security. Not a love story."

Ellen reddens. She would check her heart for bugs if she could.

She exits the office and takes the hall to the nurses' station. On the way back, on her way out of the hospital, she looks into Unit 1.

Philip's legs are on the cot. He's doing sit-ups.

Ellen walks away.

Leaves through the front door.

She knows, darkly, that this is not the end of it. That this event, this day, is going to stretch out longer in ways she cannot predict right now. But it's not until she gets into her car, turns the key, and rolls her window down that she thinks of how terrible a thing this is.

For Philip.

In Macy Mercy, Ellen is his only friend. Without her, who is going to watch over him? Who is going to say something when they should?

Ellen reverses, shifts, and exits the parking lot. Ahead, the open cornfields of Iowa look like freedom. Like the future.

Go. It's one man. One life. Go.

But in her rearview mirror she sees Macy Mercy, sees it for the first time for what it is: a cold, brick rectangle with only one way in, one way out.

Philip.

As she drives, she turns up the radio, then has to turn it off.

What can she do about this? What can be done?

She thinks. She drives. She feels the false relief of leaving a place she can never really leave, the sense that, with each half mile, each hundred feet, she is safer.

Something keeps her tied. Something tethers her.

"Philip," she says. "I'll be back for you."

But she doesn't know if this is true. Doesn't know how to make this true.

34

Greer drags the body, wrapped like a cigarette in the tarp. Lovejoy points to the prints in the sand.

Faint.

Yet present.

Nobody talks about the "ghost" Philip saw because nobody feels safe. Ross is missing, yes, but the appearance of these impossible soldiers is equally frightening, as if they're beginning to line the path of hoofprints, or as if the prints have intentionally led the platoon into this mad arcade.

A haunted house, Philip thinks. *Or like the house of horrors on Mackinac Island. Only we're out in the open here.*

Even the click of Stein's camera sounds less confident. Like there's less chance of anybody ever seeing the images he captures.

With each minute passing, the other Danes feel more responsible for Ross. And the body Greer drags, the human Picasso, does not bode well for their friend.

Duane hasn't spoken in two miles. And when he did talk, it was only to mutter the word "airplane," as if needing the consistent reminder that there is a planned end point to this experience.

Greer deals with his fear by talking.

"You guys ever hear of Cemetery 117?"

He's got a green shirt tied around his hairline, catching the sweat. Nobody responds; they know Greer will tell them about it either way.

The heat is cruel. *Mean heat,* Larry said.

"They're quantifying it as three cemeteries in one," Greer goes on. "Near the northern border of the Sudan. North of us. But close. Much closer than home."

"How do you know about it?" Larry asks.

"Because I read, Larry. I read the journals. I care about these things. Two of the cemeteries are on one side of the Nile River and the third is on the other, as if the banks were once considered prime real estate for burial." Greer speaks as if he loves the idea of bones and blood, digging for bodies, and . . . "*Prehistoric warfare.* That's what they're calling it. Fifty-nine bodies they found. Most of them around nineteen years old. A lot of women and children, too."

"Sounds like any cemetery," Larry says.

Greer shakes his head no.

"Arrowheads, spears. Listen, *every single* person was wounded the same way. Each and every corpse they unearthed. Still sound like your neighborhood cemetery in Detroit, Larry?"

"What are you saying?" Philip asks. Duane mutters something. Philip can imagine his friend dropping his gear and strangling Greer. But perhaps Duane is beyond being annoyed. Fear is unique that way.

Greer tugs at the rope around his belly; the tarp drags behind him, makes a steady sliding sound.

"These bodies are close to fourteen *thousand* years old, Tonka. Fourteen thousand! You think we might've made peace with one another by now, yeah?"

He bellows a single syllable of real laughter, a cackling punch that echoes ahead.

Sounds a bit like the tape slowed down.

Philip thinks of his and Greer's last conversation. The sound as being able to break the patterns of history. Capable of initiating residual hauntings. The Namib Desert is the perfect host for this. The world's oldest desert. The oldest known people. The first cemetery. The first war.

War and not-war? Is the sound somehow capable of both? Is it able to conjure the soldiers of old wars, all wars, into being, while denouncing them, rendering their weapons unusable?

Why? How? And does any of it matter so long as Ross is missing?

"Lovejoy," Duane says.

Ahead, Lovejoy is crouched in the sand.

Duane runs to him, wild, and Philip understands it's because his drummer believes Lovejoy has found evidence of Ross.

Then they're all running. Larry calls Ross's name. As if the small, dark object at the former general's feet is somehow their friend.

By the time Stein catches up, the Polaroid ready, the others have already seen it.

But it's Greer who can't resist grabbing hold of it and lifting it to his eyes.

"Jesus Christ," he says, the way someone says it with awe.

It's a metal tube, the length of one of Philip's arms.

Greer doesn't untie the rope that holds the body behind him, though it's digging in, irritating his belly. He doesn't wipe the sweat that drips from the shirt tied around his head. But he does wipe his glasses clean.

"This is a hand cannon," Greer says, holding it with all ten fingers. The way he says it, he expects that the others must realize the significance of this discovery. If anybody does, though, it's Lovejoy alone. "This is the first firearm, gentleman. Asian. Quite literally a cannon for the hand. You would put gunpowder in this end and shrapnel here, and when you lit it . . ." his lips curl into an astonished smile.

Stein takes a photo.

"This is absolutely impossible," Greer says.

"A relic," Larry says.

Greer shakes his head vehemently.

"It's mint. As if it were made yesterday. *Today.*" He rubs his hands together. "Absolutely impossible!"

"How old is it?" Stein asks.

Greer laughs.

"How does the thirteenth century sound to you, Private? It's not that there's not a mark on it, that would be the anthropological find of the year. But no . . . it's that it isn't . . . hasn't . . . *aged.*"

"Keep it," Lovejoy says. But he doesn't need to. Greer is already opening his pack, retrieving the necessary cloth to wrap it.

Philip looks to the tarp behind Greer and recalls the historian's excitement with what he called "verified Civil War boots—verified by me." He looks to the hand cannon.

A conclusion comes to him. He feels as assured as when he knows the band got the right take:

The sound is not a weapon. It's the opposite.

But what's the opposite of a weapon?

Lovejoy is already trekking ahead. His blond hair is transparent under the sadistic sun.

Philip sets his own pack in the sand and removes his T-shirt. He wipes his face with it, then wraps it around his head. He drinks from his canteen. When he looks up again, Lovejoy is vanishing over the edge of a dune, descending, as though on an escalator.

Or like he's taking the stairs.

35

Ellen is on the couch in her living room, leafing through the drawings she's done for Philip. Together, they read like a child's science fiction dream. The evolution of weapons, from wooden spears to nuclear bombs. The man in the Revolutionary War uniform. The hand cannon.

The black hole in the desert.

Ellen hasn't had a relaxed minute since leaving Macy Mercy. She's hearing things outside her apartment and in. She lives alone, is used to living alone, is used to the creaks and groans of the building, a neighbor's dog picking through the garbage, the distant sputtering engine of a passing car. But in the two days since she was fired, she's been hearing new sounds.

Footsteps? Outside? The creaking of the glass of her living room window? As if the nose of a stranger is pressed against it?

Ellen brings the drawing of the Revolutionary soldier on a sand dune under the lamplight. She shuffles the papers. To her, the black hole is the most disturbing. It was never dark enough for Philip. Ten layers of pencil deep.

Ellen tucks her hair behind her ears, sets the drawings on the couch, gets up. She takes the carpeted hall to the back bedroom, where her suitcase is already open on the bed, a third full. She quit packing once already today. But she's ready to begin again.

She crosses the room to the nightstand, picks up the phone, and calls her friend Patricia in California.

"Hello?"

"Patty, it's Ellen."

"Oh . . . hi. What time is it there, Ellen?"

"Three in the morning."

"What is it? Are you all right?"

"I need somewhere to stay, Patty. I'm leaving Iowa."

"When?"

"I'm leaving now."

Hesitation. Silence. If Patty could just offer up her place, make it sound normal, like it's okay to leave your life at three in the morning, Ellen might be able to calm down, might begin to see this as the right thing to do. But Patty isn't doing that.

"Ellen. What's wrong? Obviously something's wrong."

Patricia has kids. Ellen knows she's thinking of them now.

"Nothing's *wrong*, exactly," Ellen says. "I just need to . . . leave."

Patricia hesitates. Ellen listens to the static. It sounds like bugs.

"Well, I'm sorry, Ellen, but as you know . . . we only have so much *room* here at the house. But if you're going to be in California—"

Ellen hangs up.

She's heard someone in the hall outside the bedroom.

She steps from the phone, crosses the carpet. The phone doesn't ring, of course it doesn't ring. Patricia is probably happy that she ended the call; she won't be calling back. Ellen reaches the bedroom door and pushes it partway open.

Darkness out there.

Did she turn the lamp off? She doesn't remember.

She turns off the lights in the bedroom.

Now it's dark everywhere.

She listens. Silent. Listens. Doesn't move. Thinks of Philip telling her to add another layer to the black hole, telling her it isn't dark enough yet.

You can't get any darker than black! Ellen had laughed.

Not now. Not laughing now.

Yes you can, Philip had said. *You just gotta see it in a place where it's not supposed to be.*

Ellen stares into the darkness of her apartment. She feels like she's falling, without warning, dizzy, frightened. As if she's tripped into the black hole Philip asked her to draw and there's nothing solid, no support, inside it.

"Hello?" Ellen asks.

The last thing she expects, because it's the worst thing she can think of, happens.

Someone responds.

"Hello, Ellen."

It's a familiar voice, but Ellen still screams, as if somehow her voice might give her that solid surface, that something physical to grip in the darkness.

But it doesn't. And by the time the second voice sounds again, Ellen believes she won't be leaving Iowa after all.

36

The sun is long past its peak, but Philip isn't sure this is a good thing. He's thinking of home, of getting back, of surviving ten more days out here. He's thinking of Mull telling them the plane will be back exactly where it dropped them off, in two weeks on the hour. And with every step the platoon takes deeper into the desert, dragging the rolling reels behind them, Philip grows a little more nervous, a little more afraid.

Are they going too far from shore? Will ten days be enough time to get back?

We've been walking less than a day, he tells himself. *Get ahold of yourself.*

But how? So many overwhelming images out here . . . so many fears.

A nuclear reactor. A toxic reckoning. Dead bodies, sickness, and ghosts. Implausible artifacts in the sand; impossible ideas about men from other eras, other wars; soldiers frozen in time, always imprints, until just the right sound, just the right frequency rattles their dead bones into being.

And who makes this sound? Who calls to them?

Philip looks down to the hoofprints they follow.

"It's back," Duane says, slapping his hands over his ears. It reminds Philip of when Duane plays the drums, rhythm with his hands.

Duane's right. The sound is back.

And yet . . . it's far off. In and out. Like it's been all day. As if they're still the same distance from its source. No closer to discovery.

And yet . . .

Beyond Lovejoy, ahead, Philip sees a series of dunes, a corner of the desert, as if the former general has reached an end point but not an impasse. Counting five of them, Philip thinks the dunes make a hand, rising, as if telling him to stop.

A flash of light and Philip sees Stein is photographing.

"Shadows," Larry says, acknowledging a blackness at Lovejoy and Stein's feet. "Shade."

"Tarp?" Greer asks.

But Philip hardly hears them. Without knowing it, he's stepping with the same stride that made the hoofprints. His boots are carrying him toward the same end.

"Water," Philip says, when he gets there.

Stein snaps another photo and the flash reflects off the dark surface.

"What was that, Tonka?"

Water, deep and blue, so vivid it quenches many thirsts, bodily, emotionally, as the foliage framing the pool wavers from the first cool desert breeze Philip has known.

Behind him, Larry and Greer, Duane and Stein are all talking about mines. Talking about holes in the desert like black holes in space.

But Philip is fixated on the figure swimming toward him.

Curly hair, pale as the old waitress's at Ronnie's on Grand Street. Supple fingers that drag him through the water, across the surface, toward Philip. Fingers capable of such sweet guitar.

"Hi, Philip."

Philip lifts a finger, points, because he doesn't know what else to do.

"Ross?"

Behind him, Larry says something. Asks Philip a question. Tells him to be careful.

"Come on, jump in," Ross says. "The water's fantastic."

Because the sun is partially blocked by the dunes, Ross is partially shadowed. Beneath the surface, his arms and legs dance distorted, rippling with the unseen waves.

"ROSS!"

The exhalation Philip experiences is unprecedented. All the horrible visions of telling Ruth Robinson what had become of her son, all the sadness, madness, and meanness, are gone.

He steps toward his friend.

Pack and gear be damned. Ross is safe.

And swimming.

"Jump in, buddy. You won't regret it."

Smiling, Philip does. As Duane calls out behind him, and as Duane's voice recedes, Philip jumps.

Then it's like Duane's voice is coming from the sky, up high, as Philip understands he himself made no splash, felt no water when he broke the surface.

Diamond mines, Greer had been saying. *Some go miles deep.*

And the world goes dim, too dim, as the words *mirage* and *fantasy* take flight, shot like cannons from Philip's mind, as the rise of his own scream echoes, and the echo lasts so long he can't tell where the bottom is, when he will hit, as he falls into a hole in the desert, a hole as dark as delusion.

37

Delores and Ellen sit facing each other across an orange Formica table in a corner booth. The booth is against the window, and early sunlight comes through the glass, creating shadows on the tabletop of the letters making up the daily specials. Ellen, who is facing the bulk of the all-night restaurant, scans the place, continuously, between every sentence it seems. Delores, facing only a handful of booths lining the adjacent wall, looks less frequently, but still looks.

As of now, they are alone. Or, as Delores says, *without Mercy.*

"You have to be at work soon," Ellen says.

Delores nods. The bags under her eyes don't correlate with the sparkle in them. She came to Ellen's house because she wanted to. And the relief she feels, talking about the hospital, is big. And yet, Delores is conservative, Ellen knows, and watching her tell secrets is like watching a child admit to lying.

"I'll be there," Delores says. She doesn't look at her watch. "I need it understood that I'm here this once. This is my one role in this."

"Are they going to kill him?" Ellen asks it.

"They could," Delores says, lowering her head, acknowledging that she's a part of this, willingly or not, hands in the pot or not; a hospital that could conceivably kill one of its patients.

"They're rushing his healing," Ellen says. "It doesn't take a nurse to notice that."

Delores tells Ellen about the six shots administered by Szands.

Ellen sees red. Sees herself driving to the hospital. Sees herself killing.

"What are they doing, Delores?"

"Well, it's like you said; they're rushing it."

"Why?"

Delores squeezes her hands tight together. This is hard for her.

"Do you know what happened to him in Africa, Ellen?"

"As much as you do."

"Do you?"

"What happened to him in Africa, Delores?"

"Philip was part of a mission sent to—"

"I know that much."

"Yeah, well, they found it."

Ellen leans back against the booth, thinks of the drawings.

"And so?"

"And so Philip must know where it is."

Both look out the window as a truck pulls into the parking lot. They wait to see who exits. An older, sturdy man in overalls gets out on the driver's side, looks up to the restaurant's sign, crosses the lot.

"They think it's a weapon, Ellen. Something worse than a nuclear bomb."

Ellen recalls Philip's six months before waking. The bruises. The bones. How he'll never look the same as he used to.

"What could be worse than a nuclear bomb?"

"I don't know. But I'm sure there was a time when people asked the same question about guns."

A pause. A beat between them.

"Is that what hurt him? Whatever he found?"

"It must be."

"What did he tell the government?"

"They think he's hiding something. They think he's very good at saying just enough."

"What would he be hiding?"

"He says he doesn't remember where it was."

"The weapon?"

"Yes. He also says he doesn't know what it does."

Ellen thinks about this.

"Then how do they know he found it?"

"Because of the way he was hurt. The army doesn't know of a weapon that could hurt you in exactly that way."

At the counter, a man in a suit sips from a coffee mug.

"Why are you telling me this, Delores?"

Delores looks as if, had a dish fallen in the diner, she would shatter along with it.

"I'm too afraid to help him, Ellen. You're not. You're stronger than I am."

How meek she looks, Ellen thinks. *How scared.*

"So what are you going to do? Continue giving him medicine, drugs? Play along?"

"Yes. That's exactly what I'm going to do."

"How can you do that?"

"I'm not *like* you, Ellen! And who knows what they found out there. You want it coming . . . for you?"

"What?"

Delores is crying. But Ellen can't let up.

"And what am I supposed to do about it?" She's almost shouting. "I'm on the outside now!"

Delores looks over her shoulder, passively telling Ellen to keep her voice down.

"You can put a stop to it."

"What? How? I don't even know what the drugs do!"

It's Delores's turn to look surprised.

"Ellen," she says. "Certainly you know *why* they're rushing his rehabilitation?"

Ellen stares. Blank.

"No, Delores. Tell me."

"I thought that was obvious." Delores grips her purse handle, preparing to leave. "They're getting him ready, Ellen."

"Ready for what?"

"To send him back, Ellen. Back to Africa."

For a horrifically plausible second in time, Ellen sees herself reaching across the table and strangling Delores. Because Delores has known these things. Because Delores could've put a stop to them long before now. And now that job is left to Ellen.

When the vision passes, when Ellen is left with the flat reality of her situation, she asks one more question.

"What does A-9-A mean, Delores?"

Her voice is as flat as a body in its casket.

Delores swallows hard.

"It's the only thing they've discovered that's more powerful than the sound."

"What?"

"It *resists* it."

"How do you know? Have you seen them test it on Philip?"

Delores can't even look Ellen in the eye.

"They haven't done that yet," she says. "But they're about to."

38

Philip has badly broken his ankle. He knows that much. It might be many bones. Many things hurt.

He can't stand up. Not yet. The shock of pain was almost as big as the fear was when he fell. So, in the dirt, in the dark, Philip alternately grips the ankle and sweeps his arm across the floor, searching for the flashlight that could be anywhere.

His fingers are bleeding. So is either his forehead or the right half of his face. That side is hot with something.

The gun is lost, too. But the gun doesn't work.

There is no light in here. And without making a sound, he has no sense, no scope of the space.

He doesn't call for help, though he wants to. Doesn't find a place to hide, though he wants to.

Instead, for now, he listens.

Where is he?

The word *mine* makes sense to him. Diamond mines in the Namib. Abandoned in the 1930s. More than twenty years ago. But other words resonate, too.

Cave

Lair

Nest

He can still see Ross swimming, Ross telling him to jump in the lake.

Mirage? But it was so definitive. So . . .

How long has he been out?

He remembers some very scary rumors from World War II. Mental warfare. Gases that made men see werewolves on the battlefield, soldiers whispering that they'd encountered family members in the woods at the bloodied boundaries. Captors removing the hands of American POWs, replacing them with live mines, lowering them into holes, dark ones, places like this.

Climb out, soldier! Use your new hands!

Is this like that? Is he . . . a prisoner?

Maybe. But it feels (cold), smells (damp), and sounds (hollow) more like a grave.

Have you guys ever heard of Cemetery 117?

Greer's story about the fossils of the world's first war; Cemetery 117; unearthed not far from here.

Will they one day excavate here, dig Philip's bones from this buried place?

Greer's words are the easiest to recall in the dark.

Philip closes his eyes. His own dark is mercifully soothing. Better than the impenetrable blackness of the unknown.

He tightens the grips on his ankle, understands that it will need to be set. In his mind's eye he sees his own ghost, a soldier of the Revolutionary War.

Lantern.

Light. Flashlight. VU meters. Stein's camera.

Oh, so many options, but none of them within reach.

Philip holds his breath. He listens.

He waits.

He listens.

He waits.

Quiet as he can, he rolls to his side, then up onto his knees.

He crawls. And every time his right boot touches the ground, his lower leg asks him to stop. His bloodied fingers search the dirt, then gravel, small sharp rocks that indicate an intentional change in flooring.

Philip finds the flashlight.

He turns it on.

For the duration of many breaths, he doesn't feel the pain in his ankle and body.

The awe is overwhelming.

It lasts long enough for him to crawl to the incredibly smooth wooden wall the light has shown him, to use the wall to help him stand. There he looks up to the breathtaking murals.

Adorning the vaulted ceiling, displayed religiously, hundreds of white goats stand in profile; childish renderings; each with their single eye fixed upon Philip below.

And everywhere he limps, dragging his foot across the open space, the eyes from above seem to follow.

The red, blotched background looks less like paint than it does dried blood, and Philip believes there can be no other sufficient explanation for the source of this color.

"My God," Philip whispers.

And his voice is detonation. His voice is cannonade.

The echo is deafening.

Nuclear.

That hideous word. *Nuclear* is a secret whispered behind even the backs of presidents, supposed leaders of the world.

Nuclear.

The word comes to Philip foul-green and oozing, as though the syllables themselves are infected, toxic, and capable of creating the terrifying vision of the mushroom cloud. Philip touches his abdomen with a bloodied hand, mindlessly checking to see that he isn't already experiencing the effects of exposure to radiation. He's seen photos of what nuclear can do. All the Danes have. Philip remembers sipping whiskey with Larry, leafing through an admonishing military brochure, *The Conflicts of Nuclear Weaponry.*

NUCLEAR

It's not hard to trace the chain of thoughts that have led to him thinking the worst. The power inherent in the echo of his voice is astonishing.

IS IT A WEAPON DOWN HERE OR IS IT NOT?!

"GUYS!"

He yells because he's got to. Because if he doesn't call for the others he's going to go crazy here in this chamber of potential nuclear power, unseen radioactive waves that could already be changing him, altering his makeup, weakening his bones.

As the word explodes through the space, as it circles the wooden walls like a marble, proving the laws of diminishing energy, Philip must appreciate it, for he understands, clearly, with an artist's mind, exactly what it could be used for.

It's an echo chamber.

The Danes use an echo chamber of their own at Wonderland. It's a small wooden box into which they play back the song, then record it again, this time with the natural echo off the wood. It's the very box they used on Ross's famous guitar line on "Be Here."

But the sound in this room . . . it's the cleanest, most magnificent echo Philip's ever heard.

Now, he remembers the sound of his fall reverberating. The disorientation of manifold falls, a blind soldier suspended midflight, on his way to a break, then the break, too, the clacking of a bone as big as a tree.

If the thud of him making contact was exaggerated to such a degree, what might the actual source of the sound . . . be? It, too, must be smaller than what escapes this place, must be more manageable, even recognizable.

For Philip has decided that whatever hole he's fallen into, the source of the sound is down here.

He trains the beam across the walls, looking for the way in. From where did he fall? But there is no open top, only the murals. He discovers two archways on either side of the room. Both are framed with the same wood. And between them, beside where he stands, Philip reveals a trail in the dirt, like the trail made by the body Greer dragged across the desert.

Hoofprints, too.

Philip did not fall into this room. He was taken here. And yet, the cacophony of his tumble, the echo . . . there are other rooms down here, other halls, and all of them, Philip believes, must contribute to the force behind the sound and the brilliant echo that accompanies it.

Philip sinks to one knee in the dirt. Grips his bad ankle to ease the screaming pain.

Just as he begins to rise again, he hears something, movement from under the archway ahead.

Philip turns off his flashlight.

The space goes black. And yet, he can still feel the goat eyes above, watching.

He holds his breath. He knows this sound, this coming sound.

Hooves.

Because how could he not, he thinks of the Thing in Red. A fluttering face. Shimmering steel where twin horns meet.

He exhales because he must, and the quiet, strained wisp is a rising wind in this room. And yet, the sound he has made is trumped.

Whatever is coming has arrived.

Philip almost speaks. Almost says *who's there?*

Is it someone who can see in the dark? Someone who knows these halls, these rooms, these dimensions so well that he doesn't need to see anything at all?

Philip thinks of Detroit. He clings to the delusional safety of home. Of the bars and the gigs, the musicians and the women. The way it feels to sit at the piano, his fingers above the keys, as Duane counts into a song.

Even when he hears breathing he does not cry out. Does not try to penetrate the darkness.

Lights out!

Duane's call for the closer, the final song of the set.

Lights out!

Yes, Philip thinks. Lights out. End of the night, end of the road, end of the Path and all it's showed.

An inhale of breath. Something else living, something else breathing.

Philip counts. *1, 2, 3, 4 . . .* as if a song is about to begin, one he needs to know. *1, 2, 3, 4 . . .* like Ross and Larry are holding their instruments, a half breath from striking the strings. *1, 2, 3, 4 . . .* like the night is about to begin, but a new night, a better night, in which people will dance themselves into insanity and the band will play till they bleed.

1, 2, 3, 4 . . .

But it's not a song Philip is counting into, no. It's the rhythmic steps that are coming toward him, then passing, growing distant, going away.

Philip is still.

He counts.

He waits.

He waits.

He waits.

Whatever came has gone.

Philip breathes deep, once, then advances toward the archway through which the thing had arrived. Limping, afraid, Philip crosses the room and enters a hall.

The ground noticeably slopes. To continue would be to travel deeper beneath the desert.

"Ross," he whispers through gritted teeth. "I'm coming."

And the sentiment is spoken close enough to the echo chamber that it repeats, behind him, with iridescent clarity, with increasing volume, as he treads farther into the abyssal tangle of unknowns, touching the piano key, the F, that swings at his chest.

As if something so small, or a key just like it, might bring an end to his time below.

39

Philip is standing. Without the assistance of a walker, without an orderly to lean on.

He's in a room he hasn't seen before. It's colder than the Rehabilitation Unit, which, in turn, was colder than Unit 1. And whereas the Rehab Unit was designed to kill all sound, this room is clearly the opposite; it's a steel cube, walls, floor, and ceiling, all excellent conductors for an echo, all capable of keeping a sound, any sound, alive for an unnaturally long time.

He is free to move about, but the length of the myriad wires attached to his naked body would eventually run out, and Philip understands that whatever happens next is going to be recorded for posterity.

His full form is reflected in the walls. It's the first time he's seen it since waking, and it's a difficult image to accept. The colors are unnerving enough, but it's the bent bones that chill him; the crooked fingers, the uneven face, the ribs without pattern.

Philip reaches to his neck for the F key that no longer hangs there.

From small black speakers embedded in the colorless walls, a voice:

"Private Tonka, hello. My name is General Jack Andrews. How are you feeling today?" Philip doesn't respond. Assessing the timbre of the man's voice as spoken through equipment Philip knows, he imagines Jack Andrews is sitting far from the microphone. Probably because he's not alone. "It's remarkable, truly, what modern medicine has done for you. Astonishing. Now, the room you're standing in is called the Testing Tank and we're going to conduct a test, Philip, and I hope it doesn't frighten you. The United States Army has a responsibility to exhaust all options before concluding . . . anything. It must be obvious to you that we're interested in your body's reaction to certain stimuli."

Philip is thinking of other voices. The voices of ghosts beneath the Namib Desert. The hissing from a prison cell down there.

And the one, so familiar to him, but which he cannot place.

I wouldn't do that if I were you.

A door opens in the steel wall facing him and a red ball emerges, airborne, from the darkness. It bounces once, and, still thinking, still trying to make connections, the Namib and all that happened, Philip reacts in time, catches the ball.

"Great work," General Andrews says.

Beside him is a treadmill. A machine upon which Philip can run in place. But rather than think of how incredible it is that he might be able to run, so soon after waking from a six-month coma, Philip is remembering running through hallways below the sand.

From the darkness of the open door a blue ball comes.

Philip catches it.

"Excellent."

He will go through with their tests, he will perform as they want him to perform. Until he knows where they store the drugs, until he knows he has the means of surviving outside this place, he will behave.

Philip hears a chicken clucking. He understands what's expected of him before the feathered animal emerges from the darkness. It's simple, Philip sees, easy to bend and scoop the thing up. But because of the obvious astonishment in the voice of the general, Philip is very aware how special this is.

"Please," the general says, "the treadmill."

Without responding, Philip climbs up onto the inert track. He doesn't grip the bars that anybody in need of balance would. Instead, when the floor begins moving, he simply runs.

Goats.

Philip recalls the murals below.

"We're going to increase the speed now, Philip. Be advised."

Philip hardly notices. Yes, his legs are moving faster now, but the sensation is of remaining still. As if his mind, his heart, his torso are independent of the physical activity of his lower half. He's running. Faster. Faster, yet.

"Excellent."

Philip absently understands the machine is coming to a stop.

"You just ran a mile in five minutes and fourteen seconds. Magnificent show, Private Tonka."

Philip steps off the treadmill. As he does, a yellow ball comes quick into the room.

He catches it.

"Why did you ask Nurse Jones to draw you a goat, Private Tonka?"

The question, so sudden, is what they're after. Even more so than testing his physical strength.

"I saw paintings of goats below the desert."

"What do they mean?"

"I don't know."

"What do they mean, Private Tonka?"

"I don't know."

"What do they mean?"

Philip is quiet. But the room is not. Not for long.

At first he feels a familiar sickness, a graying of the gut. In the walls he sees himself fall to his knees, feels the cold steel of the floor on his bare flesh.

The sound is playing. The sound is here.

The night Philip rolled from his cot he discovered the sound was somewhere in this hospital, stored no doubt on a reel. And every hour that has passed since then, he has worried that this moment would come.

And yet . . . he is not as sick as before. Not as sick as he got in the control room of Wonderland as Secretary Mull observed. Not as sick as he got while up to his knees in ocean water, the day Ross was taken. And the feeling is nothing like what happened to him below.

Philip stands.

What began as a thudding in his head has mellowed to a distant beat. Duane on drums. His friend practicing in the garage as Philip and Ross pitched beer cans at trees in the yard. Yes, Philip is not only standing again but he is *resisting* the sound. And for the first time since noting his own impossible progress, he understands clearly what the drugs are for.

The United States Army is planning on sending him back to Africa.

But for now, this can wait. These thoughts—Ross, the Danes, the Namib, the Thing in Red, and the red piano, too—the revolutions of these images, the way they orbit his consciousness, the way they turn as though wheeled, on a wheel, close to him then far from him, how they overlap when they come too fast, too many of each, Ross in kaleidoscope, a thousand horns and hooves, Dr. Szands and the drugs, too, ten thousand needles descending upon him, his back to the sand . . . until all of it is the color red, falling from the sky of his own mind, rising from the base, too, to meet in the middle, to connect in a bloodbath explosion of the color red . . . all of this can wait . . . for now . . . NOW . . . Philip is experiencing the sound . . .

. . . and he's not getting sick.

In fact, he can feel the waves washing over his body, gentle fingers, the distant hint of electricity, a rippling, yes, on the surface of his skin. The sound, so feared in the desert, so feared even in here, Macy Mercy, now it makes contact but does not penetrate, does not sink to his soul.

The volume is raised. So is the sensation of triumph. The overcoming of something once thought to be impossible, revealed now as simply unknown.

Philip knows the sound now. Can almost *see* the sound now. Like it's rolling in slow motion, pouring into the Testing Tank through the black speakers: pink and white, purple and blue, swirling, waves, multicolored surf upon him.

He closes his eyes.

He smiles.

The bad thoughts can wait.

For now, he is stronger than the sound.

And when it ends, when two orderlies enter through the open silver door and watch him as though they are nervous now, unsure of what he is physically capable of doing, Philip stares deep into their eyes, then smiles, not wanting to alert them that he *is* planning on doing something.

And that they could get hurt along the way.

"That was a heck of a mile," Jerry, the shorter of the two, says.

Then Francine emerges to remove the wires, the tape, the nodes. As she works, the general himself appears. Thinning black hair. Black mustache. Stout like a bull. Dressed like he's in the war room.

"Private Tonka," he says. Caution and pride mingle in his eyes. "We have one more favor to ask of you . . ."

40

A maze of immaculate wood, dirt floors, and occasional low-hanging bulbs, none of which are on. Philip turns on the flashlight, then turns it off. Stops to listen for hooves, then continues. He's made so many blind decisions, taken so many turns that it would be impossible to trace his way out, but Philip isn't thinking of *out* now. He's thinking of Ross.

Voices ahead?

He stops.

No. But there are whispers down here. Maybe it's wind, trapped in the mad cellar, or maybe it's Philip's mind, hearing things, the echoes of his increasingly vague progress, if the word can be used to describe what he does, his uninformed travels, turns, hopes.

He's thinking of Ross in the pool. Ross in the mirage. He can hear Greer explaining it to him, as if he'd had the chance to:

If we assume we're right that the sound is capable of manifesting the ghosts of soldiers past, and if we assume also that the sound is capable of stopping the wheel of history from rolling, able to end the patterns and circles man makes . . . then why couldn't it rattle our own histories as well? Why couldn't the sound operate on a philosophical plane? You saw Ross swimming, you say? But did you? Or did the sound rattle your own ghosts into being . . .

Dragging his right foot, hunched, sweating, limping, Philip turns on the flashlight, turns it off. More wood ahead, more dirt. A dead end? Maybe. Philip doesn't think so.

Do you get it? Greer might have said. *You got ghosts inside you, too, Tonka. More than just your buddy Ross. You got enough residual hauntings inside you to fill a hotel. And maybe, by bringing forth all these dead soldiers, the sound is showing us, Man, the folly, the cycle, of war. And maybe, by rendering our guns impotent, the sound is showing us that it not only SHOWS, it can take ACTION. In a world with no weapons, are there wars? And maybe, by fooling you into seeing your missing friend, the sound is letting you know that you're not impervious to it either, Tonka. Your cycle may not be on the same loop as war, but you're spinning all the same.*

A gust of (wind? sound?) something behind him freezes Philip momentarily. He flattens himself to the wall.

He holds his breath.

Because the tunnels are purposely built to conduct an echo, Philip can't be sure what any sound is supposed to be. There is no isolation, no singular noise that begins and ends. There are only waves, rising and falling, the ebb and flow of . . . what?

History?

Philip continues. Unarmed. He's vulnerable, he knows, too close to what must be the source of the sound. And at this range, what damage might it to do to his ears, his head, his mind?

Is it playing right now?

Philip stops. Turns the light on.

There's a wooden door twenty feet ahead.

A room?

The source.

The source?

Ross.

This time, Philip leaves the flashlight on as he approaches the door. The splintered wood looks blasphemous compared to the excellent craftsmanship of the walls. There is no knob on the door. No window. No framing. No mat.

If he wasn't already below the desert he'd say it looked like a cellar door.

There is no resistance, either, as he places a flat palm against the old wood and pushes. The slow creaking blends into indistinguishable whispers, the sounds (memories?) of something being dragged, the quiet cacophony surrounding him.

You got ghosts inside you, too, Tonka.

Did Greer say that? Or did Philip imagine that's what he would've said?

The door swings all the way in. And Philip stands at the threshold of a small room. A second door is less than thirty feet away. It's a room, yes, but there isn't much to suggest what it's used for. Dirt floor, dirt ceiling, dirt walls. Philip trains the beam up, trains the beam down, then across the length of one wall, until the light reflects harshly off something steel. He is momentarily blinded, squints, advances, until the details of the costume are revealed.

A red jacket. Red pants. Horns the length of Philip's arms.

And hooves.

All of it hanging from hooks.

Cautious, slow, Philip steps closer yet, close enough to touch the fabric, close enough to see that the steel between the horns is an old coat of arms. And upon it is engraved

ICH DIEN

THE ROYAL WELSH

The hooves, perhaps taken from the same animal as the horns, are high as the heels of cowboy boots. And Philip understands that a man could wear them, could wear all of this, and would look real somehow, could fool someone, anyone who saw him traveling through the world above.

It was a man, Philip now knows. *In a costume.*

The Thing in Red on the beach. The hoofprints in the sand.

"This is no monster," Philip whispers. "This is a madman."

A muffled cry from the other side of the second wooden door. Philip crosses the room and puts his ear to the wood.

"HELP ME!"

Is it Ross? Did that sound like Ross? Is it one of the others?

He waits. He listens. He waits.

Then he turns off his light and exits this room.

In the hall outside, he waits again.

When he turns on the light again he sees a face behind bars.

A subterranean cell.

Philip recoils, steps back against the wooden door.

It's not Ross. It's not the others. It's no face he knows.

But it is a man. Wild eyed. Sweating. Scared.

"Help me!" he pleads. "Help me out of here!"

"Who are you?"

"He's experimenting on me!"

The man brings an arm to the window. Philip recognizes a cast, as immaculately crafted as the wood in the halls.

"Who else is down here?" Philip asks, desperate. "Are there other prisoners?"

But Philip knows there are.

Trembling, the man presses his face to the bars, tries to look farther down the hall. Philip sees scars at his ears, dry blood on his cheeks.

From the direction of where the prisoner looks, Philip hears a sound as recognizable as a fork upon a dinner plate, a car passing Wonderland on Elizabeth Street.

Philip turns off his flashlight.

He hears it again.

The creaking of wooden stairs.

When the prisoner speaks, his voice materializes from darkness between them.

"It's him," the prisoner hisses. "It's *him.*"

41

Delores wheels a television set into Unit 1. Philip, sitting up on the bed, watches her without speaking. He guesses the television is a peace offering, Macy Mercy's or the government's way of saying, *Hey, good work in the Testing Tank, but eventually you're gonna have to tell us what the goat means. And until you do, we'll pretend to be friends.*

"A soccer match," Delores says. "England and Germany."

Her voice is without emotion and Philip wonders if he's detected some shame in there. Perhaps Delores doesn't feel quite right about all of this: the drugs, the way he's healing, the fact that the army, General Andrews, told him he had twenty-four hours to decide whether or not he was willing to return to Africa.

Philip knows there is no deciding here. They're sending him back with or without his word.

Delores plugs the set into the wall and static instantly occupies the screen. She crouches and changes the channel. Her blond hair glistens in the daylight coming through the unit's one window. When she finds the game, she rises and flattens the front of her white uniform.

She looks at Philip.

"It's in color," she says.

To Philip it feels like she's afraid of him. No longer immobile, no longer only able to wiggle a few of his fingers, Philip is sitting up and must look vital to her. He recalls his own image reflected in the Testing Tank walls: the bruises, the asymmetry, the deformity. If Delores ever dreamt of monsters, if she ever woke from a nightmare and raced to her parents' bedroom, the monsters might have looked something like Philip.

"Oh," Delores says, "what timing." Flat. Expressionless. "Looks like the game is about to begin."

On the screen, a band takes the field. Philip doesn't care for soccer any more than he does baseball. But the red uniforms of the English band catch his eye.

He rises from the cot.

Delores inches back, as if she's seen a spider instead of a soldier.

Philip doesn't hear her as she excuses herself and leaves the unit. He's crouched so close to the set now he wouldn't be able to see her if she were standing a foot to his left.

On the screen, the English army marching band plays at midfield. The music is triumphant. The brass. The drums. The strings. Together with the manicured green grass, their red uniforms look like Christmas.

But it's the goat at the head of the band that Philip can't stop watching.

It's a white goat. Long white hair that hangs almost to the field. A trainer crouches beside it, smiling.

"Jesus Christ," Philip says.

The goat wears a metal piece where its horns meet. The sun is reflected there.

ICH DIEN

THE ROYAL WELSH

Philip touches the screen.

The realization is not a small one. In fact, it's overwhelming enough to cause Philip to fall back, to go from crouching to sitting, pointing now at the screen.

"Jesus Christ," Philip repeats. "He was a member of the army band."

The goat that has haunted him, the costume he found in the room beneath the sand . . .

"Their mascot . . ."

"Not coming in well?"

Delores is standing by the door. But Philip doesn't see her. Doesn't even know she's there. The goat is enough to send his mind reeling, but it's the red armbands of the musicians that boils his blood.

The reception isn't great. The camera work is shaky.

But Philip saw one long enough to read it.

EVERY GOOD BOY DOES FINE

"Lovejoy," he whispers, touching the screen with crooked, discolored fingers. "You knew him . . ."

42

Because there exists a sound that can bring forth the dead, dead soldiers, and because that same sound can render the weapons of all eras idle, thus breaking the pattern of history, the repeated wars, the same wheel of death ridden by all the dead soldiers, that sound must also be able to touch the histories of individual men, soldiers who have not yet faced death and who are, here, subjected to hallucinations of the past.

Philip suspected as much when he fell through the mirage of Ross in a pool. But he is experiencing this, confirming this, now.

Alone, limping toward the sound of the creaking stairs, toward the man (not monster!) who dressed as a monster (not man!), who robbed the Danes of Ross and must *(must)* keep him locked up, prisoner, down here, Philip is passing the street corners, movie theaters, concert halls, restaurants, intersections, stray dogs, music stores, bookstores, police, and people who make up, for him, Detroit.

Though the corridor he walks cannot be more than six feet wide, Philip allowed a red Chevy Bel Air convertible to pass only minutes ago. Behind the wheel was nobody, nobody he could see, only the shadows cast from the beam of his own light, the reflection of the smooth wood walls in the windows. In the distance, now, one hundred yards up, Philip spots an aqua Corvette, this one occupied by blond girls, laughing boys, a tray of malts and burgers clipped to the driver's-side window. "Be Here" plays on their radio.

The sights, the lights, the smells, even the sense of a concrete sidewalk beneath his boots; Philip doesn't know if it's night or day, 1957 or '58, '27 or '93.

The sound has not ceased coming in waves, as though, this close, one can hear it breathing.

Sometimes it sounds like voices, whispers, other students in Mrs. Calamut's fifth grade class. Philip passed through that particular room less than an hour ago, as Tommy Morgan talked about the Red Wings and a dark-eyed child in the back row doodled a picture of a man trapped in a sandy cell below an infinite desert of death.

A car horn.

Philip leans up against the wall again, allows a black Cadillac Eldorado and a cherry Ranchero passage. Their wake mingles with the music, the sounds of Detroit midday, Detroit at night, Detroit at first light. But the wall Philip has pressed against is no longer wood. It's orange brick, just like the wall of Perry's Drugs, where the Danes shot the sleeve for their hit 45.

"Look alive, Philip!"

When Philip looks, he sees Private Stein pointing a camera his direction, and beyond him is the city, active, bustling. Dead soldiers pass ghostly through the crowds.

"Come on, Philip," Larry says. "This is for posterity."

Between himself and Larry, Duane stands with his arms crossed, his smile as genuine as Philip's ever seen it.

"We've only got this light for so long now," Stein says. Just behind Stein is a shadowed figure. A near silhouette. But Philip recognizes him as Lovejoy.

"Philip," Ross says. And Philip is almost afraid to look, to see this cherubic facsimile of his friend, still alive, posing for a photo, already a veteran, never to don army green again. "Give them the sly smile. You know the one."

The other Danes are laughing because they know the one. The smile Philip delivers to a girl at the far side of the bar. Half interest, half not. It's enough to drive them crazy.

Philip tries.

But the flash of Stein's camera remains bright long after the photo has been taken, and Philip sees another vehicle is coming. It's the headlights of a military jeep.

Philip recalls the admonishment of the prisoner he found in the cell.

Don't leave me here, he said. *You won't find your way back. He won't let you.*

Who are you? Philip asked.

I came for the sound. Just like you.

Are there other cells?

I hear the moaning of others, yes.

Where?

I don't know.

WHERE?!

I DON'T KNOW!

I'll be back.

No! You won't!

I'll be back.

Don't leave me here! He's testing it on me! HE'S TESTING IT ON US ALL!

The light washes over Philip completely, makes a blindingly bright silhouette of him, then vanishes, rendering the corridor dark as a mean mind once again.

Philip turns the flashlight on, turns it off.

Another decision to make, another turn. Right or left. The sound does not draw him. The sound comes from everywhere and always at once.

And yet, it's so quiet Philip can't be sure it's playing at all.

He continues.

For Ross.

For Detroit.

For the Danes.

The past is present and the present is mad and Philip turns the light on, turns it off, takes a right, makes a left, continues, closes his eyes, opens them, breathes deep, ignores, absorbs, turns the light off.

And when he turns it on again, he screams.

The face of a dead soldier, its wrinkles filled with dirt, is inches from his own.

"Go no further."

Beyond the ghost is a set of stairs. Much like the one Philip took, years ago, to the cellar where he taught himself the unparalleled satisfaction of creation.

Despite the fear, the fatigue, and the fog, Philip grasps, yes, that the source of the sound can be found at the bottom of those stairs.

"Help me," Philip says, fixing the beam to the old soldier's eyes. "Tell me everything you know about him."

43

Ellen sits in her car, a green and dented 1949 New Yorker, the white interior torn in many places. She could sell this thing, make enough money to bus it to California, maybe even fly to Hawaii, begin anew. She could sell everything she owns, leave town with a single suitcase, a single change of clothes. What does she really need? In order to survive, what does she need other than to . . . go?

Her lights are off but the engine idles. It's one thing the New Yorker has going for it: a quiet engine, after all these years. Sometimes it sounds like nothing at all, like Ellen is simply hovering above the road, toward her destination, so often the hospital, so often back home. She's parked far from Macy Mercy now, far from the road, too, having left that behind a half mile ago. The trees act as half her cover, night takes care of the rest. She's sitting with both hands on the wheel, though she doesn't plan on driving any closer. Maybe it's habit, hands upon the steering wheel of a car she's in, or maybe it's because, despite being here, she's still somehow undecided. Inside Macy Mercy is a man who she believes doesn't know the truth about his situation. The doctors are using experimental drugs with a mind to heal him fast, to send him back to the very place he got injured to begin with. The idea of this information being passed to Philip (because eventually it must), without anybody there to support him, is too much for Ellen to bear. She thinks of her ex-husband, Al, and how he fought his personal war demons on his own, often shut up in the bathroom, ignoring, yes, even the calls from their toddler daughter, Jean, who eventually took to the open kitchen window on her own. Ellen can see it, the scene inside the hospital, can see the moment Philip is told he's going back, must face whatever he found, must lead the U.S. government to the source of that sound, so they can use it as a weapon of their own.

She removes her hands from the wheel and exits the car. The way she feels inside, the sky above should be starless, black, but of course it's not. Macy Mercy is situated far from the bright lights of Des Moines and there's little out here to obscure the celestial sheen. It doesn't feel right, though; stars above, Philip below, in there, beyond the one door, in and out, being lied to, tested on, *sent back.*

Ellen takes a few steps across the tall grass, toward the cold building.

Of course, she has a plan. But that doesn't mean she believes entirely in its effectiveness. It doesn't mean she's not afraid, second-guessing every decision she's already made and the horrifying decisions that lie ahead.

Ahead, the hospital lights shine out the windows, distress signals in the dark. She wonders how much Philip knows. How much he's worried about.

The grass brushes Ellen's ankles as she advances, moving closer to the hospital despite her misgivings, her fear. This, too, feels wrong; the supple graze of the grass against her skin. It should hurt. It should scrape. But instead it feels no different from when she walked to the pond in the backyard of her childhood home. The same sweet innocence of nature. Threatless. Safe. When she gets to a tree she hides, flattens herself against the rough bark, then peers around it, to the same front doors she's entered and exited too many times to number.

From here, she can see the windows lining the small front hall connecting the two longer halls beyond. Unit 1 is to the left, the same side of the building the parking lot is on. Ellen doesn't want to go that way. Can't risk someone, even an orderly, fetching something from their car. So she continues, advances, without the cover of the trees, heading directly for the hospital that fired her.

A figure passes the first window and Ellen pauses. She crouches, slowly, into the grass. She waits and watches.

The silhouette passes the second window, then the third; a black shroud splitting the orange light, making inverted cat's-eyes of each window, one at a time.

Ellen rises.

The front door opens.

Ellen freezes.

A man exits. He's dragging two large plastic receptacles on wheels.

Garbage night, Ellen knows.

She waits. The janitor, Gregory, will take the cans to the far side of the parking lot, to the dumpster squared off by wooden walls.

She looks to the windows. Sees no movement.

Because Ellen knows Gregory, and knows that he will be making four or five trips to the dumpster, she decides to get up and go to the hospital now. If someone hears the front door, they might think it's him.

It scares her that she didn't think of this before arriving.

She goes.

Gregory whistles a dark melody and his song travels upon the hollow Iowan night; sparse, devastating, sad. By the time Ellen reaches the front door, he's already rattled open the wooden gate to the dumpster.

Ellen looks through the glass of the front doors.

Sees no movement.

Almost wishes she did. Wishes something would happen to force her to turn back.

Instead, she enters Macy Mercy, making the sign of the cross as she steps over the threshold.

44

The khaki pants and the black shoes, the green cotton coat with four buttons, the matching tie and hat, even the scarf that hides the chin . . . Philip knows this uniform better than he knows any uniform in the history of the armed forces.

World War II. American.

The man's gray eyes are buried deep in the wrinkles of his face. His white mustache shines.

Of the three impossible soldiers Philip has seen in the Namib Desert, none are as ghostly as this one.

"He began as a painter, but became a musician," the soldier says. And his voice reflects isolation. Out of practice. Unused. "He and another played songs for the miners. Two Englishmen strumming guitars for the men who dug for diamonds. They were the entertainment, if such a word could be applied to spending twelve hours a day buried beneath the sun. Even in a desert the sun is more welcome than not."

Dust rises from the folds in his face.

"They were down here six weeks. And by the end of it, the two of them could no longer sing. There was enough dirt down their throats to age them forty years, and by the end of it they sounded more like old seamen than the fresh-faced troubadours they arrived as."

"What do you mean . . . the end of it?"

"Once there weren't any more diamonds, that was the end of it. But not for the two musicians. One afternoon, or night, who could tell, as they were playing their songs, the man who's still down here heard other voices. Someone was singing along to the chords he and his associate were playing. A *phantom harmony,* he called it. Something off key . . . but virile."

Philip almost hears it himself.

"So when the miners deemed the mine barren, the two with the guitars hid below. And when they had the place to themselves, they dug deeper."

"Looking for the sound."

"But they hadn't hid unarmed." His white mustache rolls like surf on the shore. "They had a box of dynamite. Only, when they tried to use it, the stuff was as impotent as their voices."

The nuclear warhead. The guns. The discarded hand cannon.

"But they got to it," Philip says.

The old soldier is quiet a long time.

"They got to it," he finally says. "But they got to fighting first. And the man who is down here now"—he pauses, looks over his shoulder—"strangled the other with rage. He got to it, all right. But he got to it alone."

Philip looks to the stairs.

"Is he down there now?"

The old soldier stares long, does not blink.

"Do you know what more than twenty years with that sound might do to a man? What his mind might look like?"

"Is he armed?"

"He has the sound."

"I have friends—"

"They are down here."

Philip rushes the ghost, almost grips his lapels. Sees a name stitched in white:

ROGER KINGMAN

"Where are they?! WHERE?!"

"I . . . I don't know."

"You saw them?!"

"Yes. But . . ."

"Tell me!"

The old soldier points to the stairs.

"He has them. He—"

Philip passes the ghost of World War II, just as he limped by the ghosts of his home moments ago.

At the top of the stairs, he calls back.

"Thank you." And his voice is determination.

But the old soldier does not respond.

The stairs creak as Philip takes them. The echo is divine.

He holds tight to the vision of an airplane, arriving on time, landing in the desert, as the door opens and fresh-faced military men descend the steps, ready to escort the Danes aboard.

But a madman breathes below.

Philip remembers a slogan from his time in basic training.

A soldier must be prepared for an enemy who is madder than he.

But he isn't prepared. As he continues down the old creaking stairs, as memories of Mom come flooding, he feels as unprepared as the desert at dawn.

As if even the darkness has eyes, as if even the darkness says don't.

45

Inside Macy Mercy, silence. No typing from the office. No chatter from the night nurse, Francine. No footsteps in the hall. Ellen moves fast, toward Unit 1, aware that she's going to have to pass the office on her way.

She's prepared for this. Prepared for a quick glance from one of the hospital employees. She hopes that, in passing, out of the corner of someone's eye, her white dress will look like a nurse's uniform, and not the civilian clothes of an unwelcome threat.

She tries to walk like it's any ordinary shift, a simple action she's carried out a thousand times, walking the hall to Unit 1, here to check on the patient. She tries to bring herself back to the days when Philip was asleep in there, comatose, the days when the nurses guessed at what could've done that to a man: his body hideously disfigured and horribly bruised, most of his face and chest sunken from the broken bones, unable to support the rest of him. She tries to find that resolve, that calm, a nurse carrying out her daily duties, assisting in the healing of a former soldier, a man, here, at Macy Mercy, a military hospital, a man no doubt wounded in the line of duty, whether that line be drawn in a current war or in the name of one not yet come. The door to the office is coming up fast, too fast, but Ellen will not turn to face it, won't give whoever is in there the opportunity to recognize her. A simple flash of white, passing, will only be a nurse to anyone who half notices.

And yet . . . as she comes level with the door, the silence within almost reaches out to her, places a finger and thumb to her chin, turns her face in the direction of the one place she should not look, should not reveal herself to.

The office is empty.

Ellen continues. Unit 1 is only a fifteen-foot walk from here. Once inside, she will tell Philip what she knows, what Delores told her. And Philip, no doubt, will listen to her, will escape with her, will look into her eyes with the expression Ellen wishes her husband and daughter had shown her, the look of the saved beholding the one who saves them.

This time, Ellen thinks. This time she's not letting someone she cares about go unnoticed, locked out, left to wander the kitchen alone, to discover an open window, to decide to climb out of it and onto the dangerous fire escape outside.

Unit 1 comes as quickly as the office did, and Ellen is breathing as fast as she is moving. The door is open, a crack, and she pushes it, bracing herself for a possible interaction with a staff member: Francine, Szands. Or maybe someone else, someone even higher up than the doctor, someone capable of silencing Ellen completely.

Unit 1 is empty.

Ellen steps inside.

She closes the door behind her and uses the flashlight she's brought with her to check the corners, check under the cot, even behind the bookshelf and the piano.

He's not here.

Ellen exits the unit.

The hall is as silent as the office. The whole hospital, it seems, is asleep.

Ellen walks. There are ten doors between herself and the Rehab Unit. So many possible places for someone to emerge from, so much open space in which to be seen, recognized by someone who'd no doubt break all this terrible silence and force the reality upon her: the reality that what she's doing is defying the United States government, blatantly attempting to steal from it.

Ellen begins to remember her dance with Philip, but there's no room for nostalgia inside her mind, her stomach, her heart.

She must be clearheaded. She must be quick. She must be alert.

The silence is almost physical. As if it has followed a noise, so much noise, a thing so loud, so powerful, that only its opposite could remain.

When Ellen reaches the Rehab Unit she finds the door is unlocked and open. Because of the cool air emanating, a sense of nothingness, an absence of life, Ellen knows before she enters that the room is going to be empty.

Empty office. Empty unit. Empty rehab.

But he's here. Somewhere he's here.

Ellen crosses the room, places her palm flat to the second door, discovers it, too, is open, and enters the second hall.

She waits. Still in the hall. To any eye she would no doubt be a woman doing something she shouldn't be doing.

Even when she was employed by Macy Mercy this area was primarily off-limits to her. Ellen doesn't know it like she knows the rest of the building, doesn't know the corners, the shadows, the depths.

She begins walking, cautiously, one hand along the right wall for support, to feel connected, to feel a part of a living world she once trusted.

The first door is marked TESTING. Ellen tries the knob and finds it open. She pushes the door inward, holds her breath, sure that this is the moment the doctor spots her, the moment when gloved hands erupt from the darkness and strangle her, grab her by the neck, drag her into the room, TESTING, where they will do things to her, experiment, drug, change her. Like they've changed Philip.

The room is dark. But it does not feel empty.

She reaches inside, feels along the wall, turns on the lights.

At first, the colors make Ellen think of a painting. Or maybe it's a drawing, yes, something like the very first drawing she did for Philip.

A goat. Backed by infinite red.

These colors . . .

This red . . .

Despite the fact that she shouldn't make a sound, Ellen screams.

46

When the Danes volunteered to be in the army, they did it knowing they were going to be in the marching band. None of them were "army material" in the way that so many others were. They wanted to serve their country, contribute to the fight against Germany and Japan, but by then they'd already dreamt dreams of music, experienced visions of themselves playing in rooms so smoky the audience might not even see the faces of the band.

There wasn't a soldier among them.

And yet . . . twelve years after . . . disoriented by memories and movement, specters and sound, Philip has discovered that material inside himself.

When he reaches the bottom of the stairs, as he spots the thin rectangle of light in the distance, the unmistakable signpost of a door closed on a lit room, as he senses someone in there, *knows* someone is home, Philip understands with majestic clarity that he is capable of doing everything expected of any and all soldiers of the United States Army.

And the fear is no longer overwhelming.

And the urge is as basic as breath.

He limps toward the light.

Armed or not, he is going to kill the man he finds there.

47

Before Ellen arrived at the hospital, Philip was walking the same halls without the assistance of a walker, crutches, or even a cane.

The lock on his unit door was easy to take care of. Philip is stronger than even the doctors and nurses realize. A mirror in the staff bathroom confirmed for him what the distorted reflection in the Testing Tank suggested: he doesn't look any better than he did the day Ellen held a mirror close to his face. But, of course, it's how he's healed on the inside that counts.

It was simple, too, avoiding the night staff, as most of them assumed he was locked safely in his unit, and nobody was looking for a former soldier, wounded musician, to be wandering, searching, vengeful, on his own. Perhaps they fooled themselves: they've successfully healed a broken man, but haven't yet rid themselves of the conventional thinking that says a man who was hurt so badly could possibly be up and moving.

But before Ellen arrived, Philip was certainly up and moving.

The orderlies Carl and Jerry arrived first. They came quickly into the room and stopped, scared, eyeing Philip as if they'd found a vampire in Unit 10.

They tried talking to him, using words intended to calm him down. But Philip hardly heard them. And the orderlies couldn't know the strength their patient had.

Philip tried to maintain an inner peace, a determined decorum, throughout.

Using Carl as leverage (Philip's badly bruised arm secured around the cherubic orderly's neck), rounding up the staff was as easy as he had hoped.

Part of it, Philip understood, was that, to them, the Testing Tank had always been innocuous. But the bigger part was that none of them could see the ideas within him.

There are no X-rays for fury.

Two nurses, two doctors, men in suits, too. Scott Malones. Found in offices lining the second hall, units with titles like MEDICINE and ANALYSIS.

After locking them in the Testing Tank, Philip calmly went to the control room. Because of his knowledge of gear, recording, playback, and how to operate even the most sophisticated sound equipment yet built (some of which he learned in the Namib Desert), it wasn't difficult playing the sound. Wasn't difficult to find either, as Macy Mercy had labeled the reel TONKA.

He left the two-way control room microphone hot for the duration, listening not only to the growing moans of the nurses and doctors, but to the sound itself as well.

His feet on the table, sitting back in the control room chair, Philip experienced only a brief bout of illness. He thought about Ross, Larry, and Duane. He thought about specific gigs in Detroit, and the feeling he once got from making a roomful of people happy.

Soon the small speakers emitted screams. Then the screams became pleading. And the pleading became bleeding.

Philip heard muscles snap. Bones crack. Fists upon the steel walls. Tears, vomit, and defecation.

And when the people went silent at last, Philip let the sound roll another five full minutes. It didn't affect him at all. After a while, he discovered, it started to sound like music. A song. One man's anthem of resistance.

After, Philip rose and left the control room. He unlocked the Testing Tank door and peered inside.

Then he returned to Unit 10, where Doctor Szands was strapped to the cot.

"The only thing I don't know about the drugs," Philip said, "is how much is too much. If I'm going to be taking it on my own, I need to know the signs of an overdose. Call it being thorough, doctor. And I thank you in advance."

But Szands could only take six shots, the same number Philip was given in the doctor's blind rage.

The results were shocking to observe. Szands's body split at the seams.

Philip took the hall to the main office. Inside he found three boxes of files, notes, and photos, all concerning the Danes and the third platoon sent to the Namib. Most of the notes concerned Philip. Ellen had made many of them. But not all.

He shredded the documents with scissors. He carried the boxes of meaningless scraps to the dumpster, whistling a dark tune as he worked.

Then, inspired perhaps by the sound of his own song, its intention, clear to Philip, he did what all musicians do when they feel the need to play.

He went back into the hospital. Found an instrument.

And he played.

48

Microphone cords, unattached, stretched to their length, on the floor of the sloped hall. Like the mouths of baby snakes, all facing Philip, seen in the beam of his light, as if something was recently disconnected here, a machine, a series of microphones, or possibly something Philip has never heard of. The metal heads face him, but the long black cords vanish into the darkness beyond Philip's beam, then reappear at the edges of the rectangle of light, slip under the door there.

Wonderland.

It's the only word he can think of. This hall, this whole place, is like a studio. From the echo chamber to the fine wood walls, the cords in disarray, and, ahead, what Philip thinks must be the control room.

He calls out for his platoon because he doesn't care about being heard, needs to find them, needs to know they're okay, alive, that Duane isn't dead down here, that Philip isn't going to have to face Larry's parents back in Detroit, tell them he lost Larry in a hole in the desert.

Because Philip still believes he's going home.

The thing about the Path is, once you step on it, there's no stepping off. Even if you think you have.

He passes another juvenile drawing of a goat.

How far is the door from where he limps? One hundred, two hundred yards?

Space is just as disorienting as sound down here.

"LOVEJOY!"

Loud. As if, by virtue of volume, he's proving he's unafraid.

"DUANE!"

He expects footsteps behind him, the sound of a man thundering toward him. Maybe a man with an ax, maybe with cuffs, or maybe with a mind to drag Philip screaming to a cell of his own. He expects lights, too, a flash, a beam, not his own, the man who lives down here coming for him, finding him, showing himself.

Peekaboo.

Philip continues. The hall descends, deeper into the earth. It's getting hotter, and Philip can't quit the idea that he's approaching something nuclear, something *terribly* hot, a thing capable of erasing large parts of America, one at a time, all of New York City, all of San Francisco, all of Detroit.

"GUYS!"

Philip is running. Despite the unbelievable pain, the heat, the lack of security, the lack of knowledge of where he's going and what waits for him there.

He searches the walls for more cells.

"LOVEJOY!"

The sergeant. The Mad Blond. The former general who was demoted for defying the army when they said no, but who did not leave the army red with embarrassment; did not take his demotion to mean he had failed, was unneeded, was left to rot in the hierarchy of such an institution. No. Lovejoy goes on.

This means something to Philip. Even now. Running, racing, screaming, scared. It means something.

Lovejoy goes on.

Philip goes on.

Maybe Lovejoy still believes in what the military should and could stand for: a nation's safety and protection; the magic words that help people sleep at night; the things civilians desperately assume the army must hold dear.

EVERY GOOD BOY DOES FINE

Christ, the sergeant's armband is acting as a mantra, propelling Philip closer to that rectangle of light.

Philip passes red pennants nailed to the wall. Flags featuring the same ghostly white creature.

Goats.

But Philip saw the costume.

No.

Not goats.

Rather, a nuclear weapon on the other side of that door.

What do you think the musicians found down here, Philip?

The voice of the ghost of World War II barrels toward him, restrained accent and all.

They were down here six weeks. And by the end of it, the two of them could no longer sing. There was enough dust and dirt down their throats to age them forty years, and by the end of it they sounded more like old seamen than the fresh-faced troubadours they once were.

As they were playing their songs, the man who's still down here heard other voices. Someone was singing along to the chords he and his associate were playing. A phantom harmony, *he called it.*

He races toward it.

Whatever it is (nuclear?), Philip can put a stop to it. He can see it unfolding, can see himself turning off the bomb, the wars, the endless gibbering squawks of Greer's wheel of history repeating itself; the same war over and over, no matter who's fighting it.

Philip trips hard.

He falls to his face, chin first.

When he rolls to his side, as the blood begins to trickle down his neck, when he shines the light back to the ground, to the dirt, to what tripped him, he expects to see a goat.

But it's a body on its side in the center of the hall.

It's a black man. Philip can see that much.

"Duane," he whispers.

Then he scrambles to the body, knowing it's dead before touching it.

49

Ellen screams and knows nobody can hear her because everyone she is worried about is dead.

The color red is so profound in here, so strong, she can't help but remember fastidiously coloring a drawing for Philip, the negative space surrounding a white goat with the same hue she sees.

She wants to look away, she *should* look away, but it's hard. She's never seen anything like this. The crumpled human forms; stretch marks where hidden crushed bones tested the limits of the skin. In fact, the faces are so wide, so *flat,* it's as if they've been run over, and for a count of two Ellen thinks that she's responsible for it, that if she looked closely at each of the heads, she would see the tire tracks of her very own New Yorker.

It's the thought of the New Yorker that snaps her back. Yes, she has a car, yes, waiting outside, yes, to take and her and Philip away from this place.

But where is Philip now?

Just as Ellen turns from the wreckage, can look no longer, stiffens herself against the hall wall, she hears the delicate, sprinkled notes of a song.

Eyes wide, trembling, she looks down the length of the hall.

The truth is, the music matches how she feels. As if she's put on the exact right record for the occasion.

Ellen walks. She does not call his name. She does not say, *we must hurry, we must GO.* Instead, she listens. For the very first time she's hearing the live inner music of the man she nursed for six months, the man who has changed her life in so brief a period of time. It's a chilling, black melody that echoes crisp through the hall like cold, dark wind. Yes, Ellen thinks, whether Philip is writing it now or wrote it long ago, this song is pain, this song is loss, this song is Philip having finally pushed back.

She passes the Medicine Unit and reaches the small hall that connects the two mains. Francine was the worst of it, for Ellen, the way the old nurse seemed to be looking to the ceiling, half the bones of her face unsupportive, her mouth wide open, able to maintain undiluted astonishment to the end.

When she turns right and sees the front door, she does not consider leaving. Does not even imagine herself exiting this place, returning to her car, driving west. Instead, she turns right once more, faces the office, Unit 1, and the music escaping from within.

That wasn't the janitor outside, she knows. It was Philip.

She passes the office. A meaningless square now, a useless room.

She arrives at Unit 1.

She enters.

At first, she can hardly see him, his silhouette, his back to her, sitting at the piano at the far wall. She crosses the unit without speaking and sits on the edge of the cot. She faces him, watches him play.

The music moves her to tears. She cries.

She leans back on the cot and rests her head against the pillow. Swinging her legs over the side of the mattress, she lies in the exact position Philip once lay, for six months, as Ellen herself watched over him, nursed him, and irrationally hoped for a day when he would be able to walk out of here on his own.

That day has come.

But for now, Philip plays.

By turns the music is rage, resolve, acceptance, hate. Some phrases are so dark that Ellen imagines the shadows in here speaking. But there are moments of promise: major chords from the mist, brief melodies that let her know that no matter how dark Philip is feeling, there is more of his story to go.

Ellen closes her eyes but does not sleep.

She hears.

His story. His plans.

His soul.

She listens.

50

Philip doesn't know what the uniform means, when it's from, who wore it, or what side of what war it fought for. In the dark corridor, on his knees, his mind everywhere, his ankle swollen too large for his boot, Philip recalls Greer's words at camp.

In the Hundred Years' War, the uniforms worn by the soldiers changed many times. And yet the English maintained their St. George's Crosses, a red cross upon a white background, woven into flags, painted upon shields.

The man is black, yes. But he's definitely not Duane.

Philip shines his light onto the man's chest; no emblem. Yet, his face. Old. Not old in age, old in *time.*

Routiers were paid soldiers, mercenaries, soldiers of fortune. Rather than siding with fealty or faith, routiers warred for profit alone. They were hired by the English to help terrorize the French, in England's attempt at capturing the French throne. They were nasty, dirty fighters, who didn't wear any crosses at all.

Philip should get up. Should go. Reach the door. Save Detroit from something worse than nuclear.

The Hundred Years' War could, of course, be called the Million Years' War, Greer said. *Because, though they claim it ended in 1453, it's pretty much been going, in one form or another, forever.*

Forever, Philip thinks, getting up at last.

He shines the light ahead.

There are dozens more bodies lining the hall. As though each were clamoring for the same rectangle of light.

Philip counts ten, twelve, twenty different uniforms. Costumes to him, a theater company slaughtered.

In the first Anglo-Dutch war, both sides were dressed like how we might think kings and queens once dressed. Long frock coats ballooned out below the belt; white tights were eventually swallowed by black shoes. Their elaborate hats look regal to us now, but they were killing one another, after all. All wars are fought for the same reason, Greer said, Greer said often. *Because of this, they're all one war.*

Philip sees that now. Greer's Wheel. The repetition of the past. All these dead soldiers of the same living war, stretched over time, pulled like putty by unseen, childish fingers; maybe Fate is a little boy, working with what little knowledge he has of the world. Over time things change, dress and speech, language and weaponry, but not motives or meaning or the music war makes; it's the same argument fought, over and again, until, like Greer said, it rolls like a wheel, Time, a Ferris wheel, every seat occupied by a dead soldier; all together (all in one hall, all on one wheel) the uniforms look festive, so many colors, the carnival come to town, flags attached to the wheel. Only it's no carnival but Man on a loop, over and over again, believing each revolution is wider, covers new ground, means more than the last.

It doesn't. Philip sees that now.

Some of the bodies he comes to are crushed, beer cans by the cots in Wonderland. Others are readable, no different from the faces at funerals, the dead bodies to be viewed.

Limping, dragging, he tries not to look down, but he can't resist. He might see one of the Danes there, dead; Lovejoy with his hands to his chest; a camera still held up to Stein's unseeing eye.

And as he passes each body, steps over some, drags his bad ankle over others, he experiences a three-dimensional history of war's wheel in the thin, meager beam of his army-issued light.

A Roman sandal.

The black-bearded head of a Hun.

Felt hats, blue helmets, crosses, medals, and muskets.

The flashlight flickers, dims, and Philip knocks it against his other, open palm.

Greer once spoke of the "end of nobility in war." When the uniforms went from being opulent declarations of rank to the dull grays and greens of today.

Greer called it "the End of Bright Colors."

By 1914 the world wised up. And you know what we got out of it? Do you know what thousands of years of military uniforms have delivered us? Camouflage. With the advent of camouflage came the inability to distinguish between armies. More soldiers died of friendly fire than at any point in military history. It was like a fun house out there, soldiers facing distorted images of themselves, firing half out of fright. It'd become a matter of hiding, surprise, not unlike using a deer blind to hunt. Surprise was the word of the day. And rightfully so. Everything was an ambush. Can you imagine meeting another army across an open battlefield today? Can you imagine waiting for our generals to formally inaugurate that battle? Shaking hands?! No. Now we hide. We hide because they hide, and they hide because we hide, and everybody's hiding because nobody wants to be out in the open anymore.

The End of Bright Colors.

Philip leans against the right wooden wall to slip past what looks like an Asian man, once a soldier in white, now crushed fruit in the dirt.

Philip told Greer he was wrong. But he sees it now.

You don't agree? Greer retorted, smiling under the desert sun. *There are five thousand species of insect and animal who are hidden, watching us, listening to us right now. And we figured out how to blend in with the trees. Is that our big achievement, Private Tonka? We're finally as smart as the bugs?*

Philip's flashlight flickers again and he cracks it against his thigh. He's shivering but it's not cold.

"DUANE! ROSS! LARRY!"

It's almost as if Philip is afraid to call Greer's name, to make truths of all the theories the historian lives by.

Philip looks down, sees the crushed skull of a man with long hair.

LARRY?

No, not Larry.

But why not Larry, just ahead? Why not the whole platoon?

Philip senses a wave, a tear in the air. He braces himself, expecting the sickening sound.

"Guys," he says, his voice quiet now, as though the exposure to death, with Greer's words in tow, has taken something from him, a vital piece, an inner strength, propulsion, the engine that runs him.

No force comes, no further ripple, no sound.

He advances.

Ahead, the low rectangle of light looks no larger.

How far ahead? Philip doesn't know.

He advances.

He throws up. The sound, then, a little louder now.

It passes.

Philip bends and grips the splintered handle of a heavy club. No gun, but armed again. The sound comes subtle but steady, wave after wave, black surf, like he's approaching the living center of this place.

He opens his mouth to call out and feels once again the glue, his lips like thick honey.

He moves.

He limps.

He grips the club.

Behind him, death.

Ahead, a door.

Because the hall slopes at such an extreme angle now, Philip expects the bodies to tumble with him, to pile up at the foot of that door, to block the thin rectangle of light.

He uses the club as a walking stick, drives the studded head into the gravel and pulls himself forward.

Drives. Drags. Drives. Drags.

When he reaches the door, the light from within shows him a naked form inches from the threshold.

Because the man looks familiar, Philip crouches. But it isn't that Philip might know this man; his features don't spark a memory. It's that Philip recognizes the *time* this soldier comes from.

He looks like every boy did during World War II.

Dog tags are all that remain to cover his body. Philip reads them.

ROGER KINGMAN

Roger Kingman, Roger Kingman, Roger Kingman . . .

Does he know this name?

When Philip rises and touches the door, he finds it is unlocked, open, and the wood under his palm easily falls back, away, illuminated, leaving him standing, exposed, at the threshold of a fully lit room.

The hum persists. But from where?

Philip looks left, looks right, sees red, at the far wall, centered, a red rectangle, no, a shape he recognizes immediately because it has meant so much to him in every phase of his life.

It's a piano.

Painted red.

Philip stares. Wide eyed. Sweating. Injured. Scared. It feels like a nightmare, but warmer than that, deceptively warm.

The piano looks ready for a concert. Surrounded by microphones, it looks ready to record. Or as if the piano might suddenly speak, might explain everything to Philip at last.

He enters the room.

Above the piano, on the wall, a big band bass drum.

Red.

A white long-haired goat is painted on its center. And beneath it, the words:

GOD OF ALL THINGS SMALL

GOATS.

Philip touches the F key around his neck. The F of his own world play.

Every Good Boy Does Fine.

When Philip reaches the piano he leans the club against the bench. He eyes the keys and thinks of Detroit. Being in the cellar himself, just a boy, learning the piano alone. Hears Mom's feet on the stairs. Feels Mom's hand on his shoulder.

Up close, the red paint looks old. Flaked.

His first recital. Meeting Ross. Learning their favorite songs from the radio. Writing songs of their own. The Danes. The Danes in Larry's garage. The Danes playing Martha's Pub the night before heading out to war. The Danes in basic training. The myth of the Mad Blond in camp. The war, and talks during the war, the four of them, the Danes, humming ideas, voicing dreams, saying WHEN WE GET BACK oh WHEN WE GET BACK won't we start something WHEN WE GET BACK TO DETROIT. Then *doing* that. And doing more. Recording a hit, "Be Here," a song that changed Philip's life as it validated the life he was already living.

"Be Here" became Philip's soundtrack on the Path.

And now, the Path has led him to a piano.

Again.

Philip breathes deep and exhales slow.

Then, as any musician would do, having just entered a room with a piano, Philip lifts his right index finger with a mind to absently play a note. He holds it, briefly, above the keys.

Which note?

An F. Of course. Like the key around his neck.

F for the end of EGBDF and the beginning of FACE. For the end of one path and the start of another.

Maybe, he thinks, desperately, as his finger descends toward the piano, *the others will hear me. Maybe they'll know it's me playing.*

But in the half second it takes for his finger to reach the F, a much more troublesome thought occurs.

It's the angle of the microphones. The placement of the stands.

It's the color red, too, in the corner of the room, appearing to Philip suddenly, along with a voice:

"I wouldn't do that if I were you."

But it's too late for that.

Philip is already doing it.

And at the moment his fingertip makes contact with the key, Philip understands wholly and without doubt that this piano is the source of the sound they were sent to find.

But it's too late for that.

He's pressing the key.

One note.

And the sound that erupts breaks almost every bone in his body.

At once.

51

"That was . . . fantastic."

This time Ellen is the one on the bed, looking up into Philip's eyes. The shadows in the unit enhance the unevenness of his face, the incongruent features. But not monstrous now; never again. And despite the reality standing beside her, she sees the face he wore when he graced the cover of the "Be Here" 45.

"Hello, Ellen."

"They wanted to send you back," she says.

Philip's expression doesn't change.

"I know. And they were close to doing it, too. But I stopped that from happening."

He crouches to one knee beside the cot. With fingers bent unnaturally, still healing, and healing in the wrong way, too fast, Philip reaches out and touches her hair. He traces the same fingers down the smooth white of her face. He pauses at her lips.

He kisses her.

Then he tells her almost everything. The mission, Lovejoy. The man in the mine.

"Can you imagine?" Ellen, astonished, asks. "Sending someone *back* to a place that had done that to them? You deserve a medal, Philip."

Again, no change in expression.

"So where *are* we going to go?" Ellen sits up. "I was thinking of California. Hawaii. I don't—"

Philip touches her lips again. The same fingers that just played the most harrowing song she's ever heard.

"Come with me," he says.

"Where?"

"I'm going to the one place they don't think I'll be."

Ellen shakes her head no.

"They'll know you're in Detroit, Philip. You can't go home."

"Not home," he says.

"Where?"

"I'm going back, Ellen."

Ellen lifts a hand to slap him. Stops herself.

"No."

"Yes."

"Why?"

"The Danes."

"How do you know they're there?"

"I learned a lot in the office. The pilot's report, the chopper that picked me up, said I was the only body on the beach. And the fact that I was on the beach means the man carried me there."

"Why?"

"Showing off. I don't know. But I'm gonna ask him. After he shows me where the Danes are."

"The government," she finally says. "They'll know. They'll follow you there."

"They already know where it is."

"What do you mean?"

"Lovejoy knew. He was our sergeant. He knew. And I got hurt nine days before the plane was supposed to arrive. And yet . . . I was picked up. They were watching out there, Ellen. When they ask me where it was, they're not asking for desert coordinates. They want a map of the mine."

Ellen can see in his eyes that his decision has been made. And who is she to stop him from going after his friends?

She sees them again, the four of them on the cover of the 45.

She gets up from the cot, makes to leave the unit.

"Where are you going?"

"The drugs are going to wear off," she says. "And you're going to need a nurse."

"I already got them."

"All of it?"

"All of it. But I used some."

"Philip. How much did you—"

"Not on me."

He doesn't have to say the name for Ellen to know who he used it on. The one face missing from the vault of horrors in the Testing Tank.

She leaves the unit and returns with a number of articles in her hands. A passport. A watch.

"Take this," she says. "It's yours."

She's holding a single piano key, an F, hanging from a string.

"They analyzed this thing for weeks," she says. "They thought it had something to do with how you got hurt."

Philip laughs. But it's not all humor.

"What?" Ellen asks. "Were they right?"

"I'll tell you on the way."

"On the way," Ellen repeats. "Philip, I think it's my job to say one thing, one time. If I don't say it now, I'll feel it crawling to get out of me the whole time. I understand that your friends may be out there, may even be alive, but I gotta say it and I gotta say it once." She breathes deep. "I wouldn't do this if I were you."

She expects him to get angry. She expects him to go without her.

She doesn't expect the epiphany in his eyes.

"Jesus Christ," he says. He looks like he's dreaming, awake, like Ellen just spoke magic words.

"I'm sorry, Philip."

"I know where I know that voice from, Ellen." But Ellen can't know what he means. Can't know that Philip has spent many hours in this very unit trying to recall an accent, a voice, a manner of speaking. "That wasn't a ghost of World War II. That was *him*."

He remembers the name *Roger Kingman* on the dog tags hanging from the naked man's neck. Naked because his clothes had been taken; taken and worn; the old soldier in the hall; his white beard hidden by a yellow scarf; crazy enough to tell Philip his own story: two musicians in a mine; one strangles the other; one stays below.

Philip recalls the costume, horns and hooves, hanging in a room some thousand years behind him.

He imagines a troubled, deceitful man. A man who likes to dress up.

A costumed loon.

And how close was he, then, to having him? To finding his friends? To ending this before it went too far?

"My car is outside," Ellen says. She puts an arm over his shoulders. "Are you sure you can handle this?"

"Yes."

And for the first time in a long time, Philip feels beneath him the strong soil, the abundant, rich dirt, the unmistakable footing of the Path.

PART 2

EVERY GOOD BOY DOES FINE

52

Flashlights, sleeping bags, knives, headphones, earplugs, water, bread, canned goods, boots, blankets, long underwear, socks, tape, hunter earplugs, hunter earmuffs, and guns.

Just in case.

The girl behind the register stares at Philip's face like he's a monster. She smiles nervously. Philip is kind but quiet. Ellen pays for what they've got.

In the parking lot, behind the wheel of the New Yorker, Ellen points to an envelope Philip is opening and asks, "What's that?"

"Government notes," he says. "More information than Secretary Mull gave us about the previous platoons who were sent to the desert. Got 'em in the office. I'm looking for Lovejoy's name."

"What does it say about him?"

"Nothing yet. Still looking."

"But you believe he knew what was down there."

"I believe he knew *who was* down there. But not what. And maybe he was just as curious as anybody would be."

A demoted general. Stays within the military. Why? Was he waiting for, vying for, this very mission?

"Greer's Wheel," Philip says.

Going back.

"Well, let me tell you about Ellen's wheel," Ellen says. "It needs some air."

She exits the lot and crosses the street, pulls into the gas station there. Philip helps her fill the tire, and maybe it's the sound of the air or maybe it's the buzz of traffic passing on the road, but he thinks about the sound. Thinks about it a lot.

Asks himself if he's returning to Africa for the right reasons.

Is it all about the Danes?

Or, like the man who's lived down there for over twenty years, gone mad for it, lost reality for it, lost decades for it . . .

. . . is Philip drawn by the sound?

53

The next flight to Johannesburg isn't until tomorrow morning. Early. 5:10 A.M. Tonight, at 9 P.M., Philip plays the sound for Ellen.

She's lying in the hotel bed, still fully dressed. Arms folded across her belly.

"I think you're gonna need to sit up," he says.

Ellen, some fear in her eyes, sits up.

Using reels taken from the control room of the Testing Tank, Philip threads the handheld tape recorder/player he found in the office. He imagines government men throwing up on each other as they listened.

Now, when it's ready, he crosses the room and kisses Ellen. They've talked about this at length, on the drive to the airport, in line for tickets, on the way to the hotel. If Ellen is going to go with him to the desert, she needs to know what it sounds like.

"Two minutes," he says. "And it's going to hurt."

Ellen nods. She looks exceptionally pretty. Pale and smooth.

"Are you ready?" Philip asks.

"No."

"No?"

"Do it. Press play."

"I love you," Philip says.

"Wait. What?"

"I love you."

"You're saying that now? Right now? Then you're gonna make me throw up?"

Philip smiles. But he's worried about her.

He presses play.

He leaves the hotel room.

Outside, on the balcony, he looks at the plane tickets. Two layovers. It's five hours to Baltimore, with a three-hour stay in the Baltimore airport. From there it's two hours to Atlanta. They won't leave America until close to 7 P.M. tomorrow.

Philip looks out across the parking lot. Studies the cars.

Any of them could be government.

Any of them could be tracking him.

From Atlanta it's fifteen hours to Johannesburg. A commercial flight, it will be different in almost every way from the one he took six and a half months ago.

Philip brings the tickets closer to his eyes and this time studies the fingers that hold them. Badly bruised, dented, forever changed. Below him, in the hotel courtyard, is a newspaper stand. Philip can read the headline from here.

SOUNDS LIKE WAR

He turns to face the hotel room. The drapes are drawn. He studies his reflection in the glass. There's something fitting about the new face that looks back.

Beyond his reflection, Ellen's muffled moan penetrates the closed hotel room door.

He hears her gag, hears her throw up. She's speaking, too; muffled syllables, low pitch, as if she's been slowed down, quarter speed, unnatural.

He recalls the sound of stairs creaking, his mother coming to fetch him for dinner.

Philip, she once said, her hand upon his shoulder. *You're going to be a great musician someday.*

How can you tell? He desperately wanted it to be true.

Because you care about the sound it makes.

Philip pockets the tickets and enters the hotel room.

Ellen is on the carpet, bile and vomit between her hands.

Philip presses stop.

He waits.

When she sits up again, she wipes her mouth with a tissue. It's some minutes before she speaks.

"Can't wait," she says. But the joke is only half funny.

Philip sits beside her, puts his arm around her, tells her he loves her again.

Later, they make love for the first time. Ellen administers the drugs before they do it. Without them, he can't move. Without them, his body is a breathing X-ray.

That night, asleep, Ellen dreams of Philip standing in the hotel room in the dark. She dreams he's ghastly; the bruises are black; the bones have split his skin open. In the dream she gets up and rushes to the bathroom, gets him more of the drugs, injects him. Then, slowly, his body and face return to how she knows him to be. When he's feeling himself again she says,

One day we're going to run out of this.

He nods.

I know.

54

On the flight to Baltimore, everybody smokes. The haze reminds Philip of the fog where the Atlantic Ocean meets the Namib sand. If he squints, he could be there. He can hear Ross talking about a hundred thousand dollars, can hear Duane complaining about the mess of wires and the best way to wrap them. Stein takes a photo of Larry, who holds up the catch reel and says, *We're hunting sound. This is our trap!* Greer studies the landscape, talking about how there's evidence here that the Namib Desert was home to "earliest man," and how a place so empty, so exposed, must keep secrets.

And Lovejoy.

Lovejoy, who was always standing apart from the others, staring off into the distance, but possibly never at random.

Philip has been thinking a lot about Lovejoy.

When they land, and after they've claimed their packs, Philip tells Ellen he'll be right back. He leaves her in the waiting area for their connecting flight and heads toward the bathrooms. Beyond the bathrooms are the pay phones.

Philip calls home.

Mom answers.

"Mom," Philip says. "I'm alive."

55

Because Philip talks a lot about the past, about residual hauntings and the fact that the sound, the frequency, is capable of "rattling ghosts," Ellen is thinking of her daughter.

She can't help it. And she doesn't *want* to help it. The flight from Atlanta to Johannesburg is over fifteen hours and Ellen has consciously chosen to spend her time thinking about Jean. Upon boarding, each passenger was issued a postcard. The stewards suggested everybody write about their experience on the plane. They could easily mail it from the Johannesburg airport. *Make your friends back home jealous,* one of the pilots said, before winking at Ellen.

Now many of the passengers are doing just that; lost in thought, occupied by their own observations, what to say, how to describe the food (lobster), the seats (they don't recline back as far as they used to!), and the other passengers (a lot of smoke! And the man next to me snores!).

Ellen writes her daughter.

> *Jean—*
>
> *On a flight to Africa, if you can believe that. Falling in love. Wish you were here. Wish you were everywhere.*

Philip is asleep in the seat beside her. His fingers are moving silently upon his knee. Like he's playing the piano in his sleep.

Ellen looks up to the other seats, sees a little girl is looking back at her. Smiling.

Ellen waves.

It's silly, but Ellen almost thinks she can hear the song Philip is playing. Outside the window the world is only clouds, then the world is only water. Both proper settings, Ellen thinks, for a ghost.

Maybe Philip plays the music for them.

Jean.

In the hotel room, Ellen experienced the sound. It made her sick and she doesn't want to hear it ever again. And yet, she knows she will.

Maybe it's that moment that Philip plays for, a soundtrack for the day he was changed.

She looks out the window and hears a gorgeously dark melody. It sounds like the clouds. Sounds like the ocean. Sounds like two people traveling toward something terrible, powerful, and true. When she looks ahead again the little girl is no longer looking at her.

Ellen finishes her postcard to Jean.

> *Philip says he saw ghosts in the desert, Jean. To some, that would sound crazy. But for me . . . it's enough. For if Philip saw one ghost, then why wouldn't there be many? And if there are many ghosts, you are definitely one of them. Do you see, Jean? Philip has given me you again.*

Ellen writes, Philip plays, and the world outside becomes night then day again.

By the time they land in Johannesburg, Ellen is no longer scared of Philip's story about disorienting halls in a dark, subterranean lair.

She is ready.

56

By the time they cross the border into the Bechuanaland Protectorate Philip isn't doing well. He's feeling aches everywhere. Something as simple as adjusting his position in the bus seat is enough to make him cry out. Because he's badly bruised and visibly dented, the other passengers, mostly Africans, observe him, then politely avert their eyes.

This is good.

It gives Ellen cover to administer the drugs.

"You know," she says, "I'm pretty sure I was fired for *not* giving you these and now look at me, the first to pull them out of the bag."

"It's bad," Philip says.

"Well, not for long."

Under his coat, Philip unbuttons his pants and slides them down. This action is excruciating.

Ellen injects him.

The effect isn't instant, but it's soon enough that Philip relaxes, inside, and understands once again the strength of the drugs he'd been receiving at Macy Mercy. It's the second longest he's gone without, and he doesn't want to do it again.

But their supply is finite.

"How long of a hike is it?" Ellen asks, obviously concerned.

"The bus is going to drop us off at Walvis Bay. It's on the coast. From there? Three days. We'll buy food and water in Walvis," Philip says.

"You know," Ellen says, "sometimes I feel like I can already hear it."

"The sound," Philip says. This is not a question.

"Yes."

"That's how it works," he says, feeling stronger, sitting up. "I haven't stopped hearing it since it was played for us in the studio."

"Great," Ellen says. "So you're saying you've ruined my life?"

Philip smiles.

"Come here," he says.

Ellen leans toward him.

"Closer."

She does.

Philip kisses her ear.

"It's a good song," he whispers.

"Oh yeah? You've convinced me of many things, Philip Tonka, but you won't convince me of that."

Philip leans back in his seat.

"It's a good song because it sounds exactly how the musician feels."

Ellen shakes her head no.

"If that's how he feels," she says, "we're on our way to meet a madman."

Philip shakes his head no.

"The musician isn't the man in the mine," he says. "It's someone much older than him . . ."

57

The desert is freezing at night. But this time Philip is better prepared. And he has a woman beside him. They keep each other warm.

Huddled beneath the blankets, the bags, and their clothing, they sleep near the fire that illuminates a tiny part of what looks to Ellen like infinite tar, from desert to sky.

They fall asleep and are woken by the sound. Philip, aching again, reaches for the earmuffs beside them and gives one pair to Ellen. They cover their ears, but the sound is strong, still rattles, like fingertips tapping, *let me in, LET ME IN.*

Overhead the sky is a starless midnight, black, obscured by the fog. There are other sounds out here, too. Scratching. Insects. And some of the sounds, Ellen thinks, sound like boots. Army boots. The slow lumbering steps of ancient soldiers, brought to life again.

58

The second night, following a day of exhausting desert hiking, they spend the night in one of the edifices left behind by the miners of the twenties and thirties. It could've been a two-bedroom house, if it had been divided that way. Instead, it's an open space, without interior walls, that probably once contained desks, paperwork, ledgers, and the many tools for cleaning and magnification used to determine the best of a cluster of diamonds.

Now there is only sand.

It's high enough to pour out the windows, connecting the inside of the structure with the desert outside. After leveling a space wide enough for the two of them to sleep, Ellen and Philip lie side by side upon a blanket, looking up to the dark roof. Outside, the moon and stars create enough illumination to give the desert a sense of *whiteness.* As if the sand changes colors as the sun dips below the horizon and the moon reveals the paler grains.

This edifice was not visible from the route the platoon took when tracking the hoofprints to the mine. But Philip knows his landmark.

The five dunes, rising like fingers, like a Polypheme's hand, framing the entrance to the mine, where Philip once saw Ross swimming, inviting him into the cool water.

Will they see something else tomorrow? Or will it appear as what it is . . . an abandoned hole in the sand?

Just before they fall asleep, the sound returns.

While throwing up, Philip tries to trace his path through the halls, the room where the horns and hooves hung, to the cell beyond it.

The Danes must be near there. But locating it will not be easy.

Philip falls asleep envisioning hallways leading right and left, and the uncountable decisions he will have to make below.

When the sun is up, Philip brings Ellen to one of the windows and points to five dunes in the distance.

And the desert, all of it, seems to rumble with terrible, unseen power as they gather their things, leave the small building, and go.

59

At the rim of the hole, they no longer speak.

Their ears are secure beneath plugs, gauze, earmuffs, and helmets. But Philip knows this protection can only do so much.

Ellen's face looks so small to him, wrapped as it is.

The entrance to the mine looks like an earhole of its own; the desert, Philip thinks, must have heard them coming.

And despite having stood at this exact same spot once before, the image is as new to him as it is to Ellen.

He wonders now if, by the beams of their flashlights, the rest of the platoon saw his body dragged away down there at the bottom.

Philip estimates that it's a fifteen-foot drop.

There is a better way down. Ellen is already taking the ladder, the steel rungs embedded into the hard-packed dirt. Some of them are rusted, all of them are old, and when Philip begins his own descent, he imagines two English musicians in red, guitars strapped to their backs, discussing the songs they're going to play for the miners.

At the bottom, the darkness split by their lights, Philip spots a triangle of red on an arch, an entrance, the beginning of the maze.

He points to the white letters stitched into the fading red fabric.

GOATS

So clearly a pennant. The mascot of a child's favorite team.

For Ellen, it's like watching a friend's dream materialize, a wildly unlikely story built up fragment by true fragment, physical evidence, proof of a tale no one should have believed.

They pass under the arch and enter the mine.

Philip looks for tracks, any tracks, possibly even the snakelike groove created by his own body, dragged over six months ago. But there are none. The dirt looks swept beneath them, as though the madman knew they were coming.

They reach a new hall and turn left. The decision is arbitrary, as long as there's a sense of going deeper. Another hall. Another left. Then a right. The ground is sloping. Philip continuously looks to the walls, looks for a cell door, looks for the Danes.

There is no evidence at all of anybody having recently been through here. As if, in the half year since Philip was hurt, the man cleared out, took everything with him, disappeared.

Everything but the sound.

Despite the protection, the earplugs and helmet she wears, Ellen has thrown up twice already. The sound comes in waves, waves Philip remembers, waves he can feel but barely hears.

He does not fear the sound anymore.

Another right. Another left. No cells. No doors. No Danes.

But the sound persists.

Four hours deep, they stop to eat. Crouched in the dark, they do not speak as they exchange bags of dried fruit and bread and drink water from canteens. Philip removes his headgear. Ellen signs for him not to. It's better to be safe than sorry. It's better to be deaf down here than not.

But Philip doesn't fear the sound anymore.

Another hour deep and Ellen administers the drugs again. The needles look like thin fingers in the waning beams and Ellen thinks of the fingers of death she used to swat from the unit doors in Macy Mercy.

Up again, traveling, continuing.

Eight hours deep, Philip points to the splintered wood of a closed, knobless door and Ellen knows that it was behind this door that he found the man's costume. The horns and hooves. The red army marching band jacket and pants. But when they get inside, those items are gone.

Philip hurries across the small room, through the second door, to where Ellen knows he discovered a prisoner in a cell. Philip's already at the barred window, shining his light, when Ellen catches up.

To her, near deaf, it sounds like she gasps when she sees the emaciated body within. But perhaps she screams.

Philip shines his light the length of the hall. Then runs it. Looking for other cells. Other doors.

If this prisoner has been ignored, left for dead . . . why would it be any different for any others?

Reaching a solid dirt dead end, Philip returns and leads Ellen to the series of halls where he saw the streets of Detroit, automobiles, and the faces of friends. This time, he sees only the truth of the place. The present.

But Ellen sees her daughter Jean.

Philip, sensing he's walking alone, turns to see Ellen crouched in the corridor, running her fingers through the empty air before her.

"Ellen!"

She does not look up. And by the time he reaches her, he sees an impassable distance in her eyes.

So he waits.

He watches as she laughs and hugs the empty space, as she cries and says she's sorry. It's only when she begins to remove her own headgear that Philip touches her, stops her from doing it.

When she looks up to him, he sees rage.

He grips her wrist. He tugs lightly.

"This way," he says.

And for a moment he wonders if she isn't capable of trying to kill him. If Ellen might not hurt him in the name of remaining here, right here, with Jean, forever.

But understanding shimmers, and Ellen rises again. She looks back to where Jean was and shakes her head no.

Is the girl gone? Or is Ellen telling Jean that Mommy can't stay?

Philip doesn't ask.

Ellen is the first to continue down the hall, and Philip follows. They turn right, they turn left. They reach dead ends Philip had somehow avoided last time. Often, Ellen stops to speak to someone. Once she grips Philip's arm, terror in her eyes. She pushes herself and him flat to the wall, far from whatever it is she sees.

Philip sees nothing. Immune. And it's not until they reach the top of the wooden staircase that he feels exactly like he did the first time he was here.

It's just a man, he tells himself. He recalls the old eyes, the wrinkles, the dust. How frail the man looked in the World War II costume. So meek that Philip believed him dead.

Just a man. Yes. Just a man down there. And a man can be questioned. A man can be defeated.

They descend the stairs and arrive at what Philip called "the Hall of Death." It was here that Philip saw dozens of old soldiers. All wars at once. As if the Ferris wheel of history came unattached and all the passengers were thrown.

Ghosts.

All of them still here.

Yet, Ellen *can* touch them. And does.

The door that hides the red piano is less than twenty feet away. It was down here that Philip's body was altered, his mind changed, his life begun anew. And yet, he waits for Ellen to study the past soldiers, the impossible men from bygone eras who do not rot, who do not belong here, who were shaken into being by a sound strong enough to immunize weapons, break the patterns of loops, and give her Jean again, if only for a while.

When Ellen rises, Philip is facing the door, only inches from the wood.

He places his palm upon it and pushes.

The door opens easily.

Philip, ready to see the piano, is not prepared for the man who sits at it.

His back to his visitors, his hands raised, about to play.

Philip, predicting Ellen's broken body, imagining her as crushed as the body Lovejoy found in the desert, opens his mouth to scream *STOP!*, but it's too late.

The man in red's fingers are already coming down, toward the keys, the notes . . .

. . . the sound.

60

But the fingers stop above the keys and there they rattle, like the mannequin vampires that sit up in coffins at the haunted house attraction on Mackinac Island.

Philip, breathless, his arm extended uselessly to protect Ellen, waits.

The longer he looks, the clearer it is who sits on the bench.

The figure is emaciated. Wigged. And the red jacket and pants hang loose on the body.

Philip enters the room.

Above the piano is the big bass drum, the white goat. The microphones are arranged just as they were before, all trained on the mallets inside the upright. Before he reaches the figure, Philip sees the mummified face, the vacant eye sockets, the flat dry lips, reflected in the steel metronome that does not stir. Philip leans over the thing's shoulders and briefly observes the ten skeletal fingers suspended midstrike.

This, Philip knows, is the other English musician. Once a friend to the man down here.

Behind Philip, Ellen approaches, and behind her, the door slowly closes.

Then, a crackling. Then, a voice. And the effect is one Philip knows by heart.

The unmistakable static of a control room microphone.

"You," the man says. "I dragged you to the beach. A warning, as they say. *Send no more.*"

Thirty feet to the left of the red piano is a wall of glass, and behind it is a man in costume, false hooves up on the mixing board, horns so big they almost reach the ceiling.

The red of his uniform clashes against the silver spinning behind him.

Philip has never seen so many reels at one time; a hundred, maybe two, rotating in unison, a wall of looping, capable of sustaining a sound forever.

The man's billy goat beard hangs to his thin fingers, tented at his waist. And the fire in his eyes is full.

"Where are they?" Philip asks.

The man brings a finger to his lips. The nail is two inches long, dirty, and sharp.

"I wouldn't do that if I were you," he says. He points to the piano.

"Where are they?"

A flame flickers in the man's eyes, as if reflecting an unseen fire.

"I wonder what it is for you," he says. "I wonder what you *see,* there, in the room."

Philip looks to the red piano. Then to Ellen.

"It's a piano," he says to her. But it's closer to a question.

Ellen shakes her head no. *No, I don't see a piano, Philip.*

"A piano!" the man behind the glass exclaims. "Wonderful! For *you,* Creation started with a piano. Would you believe me if I told you that I set up the bones of my dear friend there in front of a blank canvas, a brush in his fleshless fingers?"

"Where are they?" Philip asks again. Angrier now.

"You never know what you'll find if you keep digging," the man says, and this time his voice is cracked, a static that runs deeper than any faulty gear. "You know, many of the founding fathers were deists. They saw God as a force that had created the universe and then largely withdrew from human affairs." Philip stares at the red paint. Sees a single, subtle wave wash over the instrument. "But did any of them stop to ask themselves . . . where did he *go?*"

For the duration of a breath, it *does* look like the mummified Englishman is sitting before an easel. Then, just as quickly, he's upon a red bench again.

"I discovered Creation," the man says. "Buried in a juggernaut's sandbox. Or who knows, maybe it's just the wind passing over the teeth in the skull of the world's first man." A momentary titter. Then, "Play for me."

Reflected in the metronome, Philip sees Ellen is shaking her head no. No, don't play for him. No, don't answer him. No, we should leave this place we should leave this place *NOW.*

"Philip," she says. And Philip sees she's removed her protection. "It's time to—"

"Play for me," the man repeats. "I'm curious." He smiles and dust rises from his cheeks. "Only a musician would walk into a room as such, under the circumstances you were under, and play a note on the piano. You are a musician, aren't you?"

Philip doesn't respond.

"Aren't you?!"

Ellen shrieks as the voice distorts and rattles the sympathetic strings of the piano.

"Where are my friends?" But this time Philip's voice is weaker.

He sees his own uneven features reflected in the glass, like there's a monster in there, sitting beside the man at the console.

"We must work in concert," the man says, "or we don't work at all. It's magnificent, to me, that what you see is a piano. It's amazing we see anything at all. I wonder, soldier, if it's our mind playing tricks. I wonder if we cannot comprehend a sound with no source and so we invent one. Each our own way to stave off the feelings of futility for having tracked a sourceless sound. Now play for me a song. Any song. And I will tell you what has become of your friends."

"Where are—"

"Do you know how long it's been since I heard any music outside of my own? Do you know what that can do to a man's mind, experiencing the same song, made by the brush of horsehair against a clean canvas? For me, Creation began there. As I child I painted. And as a child, you played. Play for me, musician soldier. And I will give you what you want."

"The song will crush you."

The man laughs. "I've built quite a room in here. I've had a lot of time to get it right."

Philip approaches the piano. The corpse on the bench is slightly slouched and Philip now sees the strings that hold him in place.

"Did you know that Creation trumps Destruction? Simple math." The man is talking fast. "I wonder how long it took you to understand that. I wonder if you do now."

Philip sits down on the bench. Shoulder to shoulder with the dead Englishman.

Will the man tell him where the Danes are if he plays? And if he plays . . . will he survive?

In the metronome, he sees Ellen reflected.

The wall of reels is spinning behind the man in the booth.

The man removes his hooved feet from the console. He leans forward, eyes bright.

In the metronome, Philip sees Ellen's hand vanish into her bag.

"Lovejoy," Philip says, eying the keys. "You knew him."

"Not well," the man says. "But a face to remember. I'll tell you I wasn't surprised to see him down here. We met in World War II. A London pub. It's the one time I left this place, returned to the homeland. Got the equipment I use now. I daresay he was the only one to whom I told what I unearthed down here. The lone soldier to whom I revealed my discovery." He points to the piano. For him, a canvas. Ellen, her back to the wood door, is injecting herself. "I regretted it then, but how could I have known how serious I was about carrying it out? How can any man know how serious he is about something he says he's going to do until he does it?" He delicately taps the head of the control room microphone. "Philosophy doesn't travel at the same speed technology does. It takes a man forty years to realize what it took his father forty years to realize. And what's worse, he resists the truths his father's come to know, until he learns them himself. Meanwhile, technology doesn't wait. All a man has to do is add another piece to his father's technological puzzle and the machines, the weapons, the means, are stronger. In the end you have an army with the same philosophy of the cavemen, but with the weapons of ten billion artless minds. Do you see? What I'm doing is right. I'm pushing back. I've discovered the antidote to war. To history. To the mistakes we repeat as a society and the ones we never learn on our own." He laughs and his laughter is hail. "I told Lovejoy about what I'd found. I told him what lived down here and what I'd done to keep it. And we were drunk. Drunk as a man can handle. And I was empowered by it. My idea. This." He points again. In the metronome, Ellen is using a second needle. "He had strange ideas of his own. More macabre than mine, I'd say. Probably why we got on. Two crackpots of war. I gave him a token, an armband. Our slogan." Tears in his eyes. Ellen is crouching now, sliding down the wood wall. She's using a third needle. *"Every Good Boy Does Fine,"* he says. "A fitting expression, I should say! The next morning I thought I'd lost the thing." He pauses, as though his memory were made of mud. "Have you decided what you're going to play? I daresay, Bach would be a joy. But 'Three Blind Mice' will do."

Ellen is no longer visible in the metronome and Philip understands that she's on the floor behind him, feeling what he felt the day Doctor Szands snapped.

Philip looks to the painted goat upon the drum above him. Up close, the drum itself looks different; a cork in the neck of a bottle.

As if there is more open space behind it.

"What you need," he says, "is a blanket in this bass drum."

He stands up. Does the man see a drum? Does Ellen?

Philip tries to dislodge it, to pull the cork free.

"Sit down."

But what's behind it?

"It dulls the sound, gives it more punch."

"SIT DOWN!"

Philip hears hooves on wood. Then, in the metronome, the color red, a white swaying beard, and watery eyes lost in an aging face.

He feels a thin, strong hand upon his shoulder and thinks of Mom retrieving him, as he searched for the place within himself, the center of things, when the scales had already been played and the practicing was done, that magic minute of creation, the minute when Philip was free.

The man grabs hold of the drum and the drum becomes simply a painting, hanging on the wall, then a drum once again.

Close up, the old man is older. Deader looking than even when he played a ghost.

Philip looks to the piano and the old man's expression changes, as if he's just realizing that he's in the wrong room, too close to the source of the sound.

Creation. Unearthed.

The man turns quickly to leave. Philip grabs his wrist.

With his new strength, his drug strength, he holds tight to the old man.

Then Philip, still standing, still holding tight to the fractured wrist, plays a song of his own.

One handed.

"Be Here."

He hears Ellen moaning. He feels the onslaught wash of sound.

But he does not close his eyes.

Instead, he sees the man in red as he's crushed like a can, so suddenly that it looks like he was taken by a wind, or the wake of a huge rolling wheel.

Ellen is on her side on the floor.

Philip goes to her. She's pointing to the drum.

"Hiding . . . something . . ." she says.

But Philip already knows this.

He returns to the piano bench, climbs upon it, and removes the drum from the wall.

Behind it is a tunnel. And from that tunnel come voices, ensconced in natural flat echo, the voices of men who call to him, who have recognized the song that he played.

61

Wonderland is no more. The Danes have a new studio, far from downtown. It's more of a room, really, what was once used as an office, but now houses Duane's drums, Larry's amp, and Ross's blue guitar. Philip's piano rests against the far wall, so that he has to pass the others as he gets ready to sit down, ready to play. Nobody in Detroit knows about this place. And the Danes look over their shoulders as they arrive, as they enter through the front door, as they wonder, will this be the day the United States government finds us? Will this be the day they take us to similarly nondescript rooms with no instruments to play?

Is this the day they question us until we break?

Philip keeps contact with Stein and Greer, but this, too, is clandestine. Pay phones far from the city. Clipped, brief conversations. And even those don't feel necessary anymore.

Lovejoy was the only one found dead. Not crushed, though. Larry said he died as naturally as a man could, held prisoner in a stuffy, poorly ventilated cell beneath a desert. Philip wears his red armband now, not because he wants to remember the time shared with the Mad Blond but because it reminds him of the terrors that exist in the shadows just to the right and to the left of the Path.

"What key?" Ross asks, whispering, though he's about to play through an amplifier. It's hard not to want to be quiet these days.

And yet, there are precious, magic moments when they get to get loud.

Ellen stands by the door. She always looks concerned these days and Philip knows it's because of the drugs. He's asked her to stop telling him how much they have left. The day is coming when he'll have to face the pain of the injuries he suffered. But when it does, he has a lover, a friend, a nurse to help him.

"F," he says, fingering the key that hangs from his neck. The F from *Every Good Boy Does Fine.* The F from *FACE.* The end of one saying and the start of another.

"All right," Duane whispers, though he is about to play a drum set. "We ready?"

"Ready," Larry says.

"Yeah," Ross says.

"Yes," Philip says.

His dark skin nearly blending in with the shadows, Duane looks something like a ghost himself as he clicks his sticks together.

The Danes should be quiet. The Danes should lay low. They shouldn't draw attention to themselves, give someone a reason to call the police, to wonder about the noise coming from the supposedly unoccupied office on Hilton Road.

But today the Path has led somewhere loud.

And so today . . . they will be loud.

"One, two, three, four—"

~lights out~

ACKNOWLEDGMENTS

In 1985, two years before meeting the guys I'd eventually play 2,000 shows with (touring America as a homeless, crazed band for six years), I was a ten-year-old boy trying to write his first novel. I didn't finish the book. It was too hard.

In those days, the idea of playing music, in any form, was nuts. No different than if someone had said, "Son, you can be a tree if you wanna." It wasn't that I didn't already believe a man might do anything he wanted to with his life (the full scope of that way of thinking was far off, but its crumb trail was in sight), it was that I thought music was made by *someone else*. Somebody born to want to do it, perhaps. Someone taller, too. Better hair. Better jacket.

Someone cooler than me.

Other people.

But then . . . I met a couple of those other people.

At its root, *Black Mad Wheel* is a book about a band. And not a writing session went by without me thinking of the following guys, the guys who not only taught me how to play, to play live, and how to *live* it, but also introduced me to all the sweet songs in the first place:

Derek Berk–drums

Jason Berkowitz–guitar

Jon Gornbein–drums

Adam Mellin–songwriter/singer/guitar

Mark Owen–songwriter/singer/guitar

Stephen Palmer–guitar

Chad Stocker–bass

Thank you, Kristin Nelson, Wayne Alexander, Ryan Lewis, Candace Lake, and Zack Wagman. Thank you, Ecco/HarperCollins. And thank you (on repeat, echoing into forever), Dave Simmer.

Thank you, too, Allison.

And the High Strung. Again.

Now let's go make a freakin' album. How about one in F?